W9-AMB-651

DISCARDED
Valparaiso-Porter County
Library System

Valparaiso Public Library
103 Jefferson St.
Valparaiso, IN 46383

Drowning Ruth

BOOKSPAN LARGE PRINT EDITION

DOUBLEDAY

New York
London
Toronto
Sydney
Auckland

Drowning Ruth

~~~~~

CHRISTINA SCHWARZ

AUG 3 0 2002

PORTER COUNTY PUBLIC LIBRARY SYSTEM

Valparaiso Public Library
103 Jefferson St.
Valparaiso, IN 46383

LP FIC SCH   VAL
Schwarz, Christina.
Drowning Ruth /
33410006851259

This Large Print Edition, prepared especially for Bookspan, contains the complete, unabridged text of the original Publisher's Edition.

Published by Doubleday
a division of Random House, Inc.
1540 Broadway, New York, New York 10036

Doubleday and the portrayal of an anchor with a dolphin are trademarks of Doubleday, a division of Random House, Inc.

ISBN 0-7394-1509-3

Copyright © 2000 by Christina Schwarz

All Rights Reserved

Printed in the United States of America

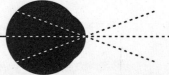

This Large Print Book carries the
Seal of Approval of N.A.V.H.

To Ben

~~~~~

and in memory of
Louise Baecke Claeys
(1902–1999)

~~~~~

and Marfa

Acknowledgments

I am infinitely grateful to Caitlin Flanagan, who has been unstintingly generous with both her trenchant editorial advice and her friendship. Were it not for the reward of reviewing pages with her, I would have quit many times over, and if the plot of this novel is in any way compelling, it is owing to her good sense. I also thank Jennifer Rudolph Walsh, who, with supreme competence and confidence, did for me what I never could have done for myself. She and Deb Futter, whose keen eye spotted the holes I'd missed, utterly changed my life with their commitment to this book. Linda Rudell-Betts helped me to begin and saw me through. Mary Ewens Meyer supplied me with myriad details about life on a

Wisconsin farm and lake in the 1920s and '30s, and Jennifer Stuart Wong shared her psychological insight. Timothy Audley, Kathleen Buster, Anthony Meyer, Nicholas Meyer, Sue Parilla, Ann Schwarz, Carol Waite, and Barbara Wallraff all gave me the benefit of their knowledge in subjects ranging from farming practices to pregnancy. I'm grateful to Alan Buster for telling me to quit my day job, to Thomas Flanagan for his kind encouragement, to Brian Morton for advice on the first chapters, to Barbara and Carol Faculjak for their enthusiastic reading of early drafts, and to Shelley Wall Reback for her decisive response to a crucial plot element. I'm indebted to Mitchell Duneier, Mira Kamdar, Henning Gutmann, Linda Kent, again to Caitlin Flanagan, and especially to Silvana Paternostro and James Chace for helping me find the right agent, to Belinda Cooper for clean copies when my printer rebelled, and to Mona Simpson for vouching for my sanity. Most of all, I thank Benjamin Schwarz, without whom I would neither have begun nor finished, and whose editing made all the difference. He is, among other fine things, the best reader I know.

Drowning Ruth

Part One

Chapter One

Ruth remembered drowning.

"That's impossible," Aunt Amanda said. "It must have been a dream."

But Ruth maintained that she had drowned, insisted on it for years, even after she should have known better.

Amanda

Of course I lied to Ruth. She was only a child. What should I have said? That her mother had been reckless? That I'd had to rescue her, give her new life, bring her up as my own? There are things children are not meant to know.

I suppose people will say it was my fault, that if I'd not gone home that March in 1919, Mathilda, my only sister, would not be dead. But I did go home. The way I saw it, I hadn't any choice.

"March 27, 1919." That's a good place to begin. That's what I wrote in the top right corner of the page. "Dear Mattie." The pen shook as I raised it, splattering ink. "March 27, 1919," I wrote on a fresh sheet. "Dear Mattie."

In the end, I didn't bother to write. I knew I would be welcome. After all, Mattie had been begging me to come home for months. And what could I say? I had no explanation. No explanation but the truth, and I certainly didn't want to tell that.

The truth was that the hospital had asked me to leave. Not permanently, of course.

"Of course, we don't want you to go permanently, Miss Starkey," Dr. Nichols said. It wasn't clear whom he meant by "we," since he and I were the only ones in the office. It made me nervous knowing there were others who had talked about me, perhaps whispering in the hallways, ducking around corners when they saw me coming. They probably gathered in this very office, sipped coffee, shook their heads and tut-tutted me. Who were they?

Dr. Nichols moved some papers around on his desk. He did not look at me. "When this is over . . ." He cleared his throat. "When you're yourself again, then we'll reconsider."

He was referring to my hallucinations, I believe, although it may have been the fainting or even the accidents. He studied the desktop for a moment and then sighed, saying almost kindly, "You'll feel much better away from this stink, believe me."

There *was* a stink in the hospital. A literal stink of gangrenous flesh and vomit, of ammonia and burnt oatmeal and camphor, of urine and feces. But a nurse gets used to the smells and the screams, and the sight of the men missing pieces of themselves.

And I was a brilliant nurse. I had the touch; everybody said so. The men worshiped me. Those with faces lifted them toward me when I bent over their beds. Those with arms held them out.

I loved being an angel. But I had to give it up.

Dr. Nichols had a point. Somehow, I had lost control. One morning I woke up sure, absolutely positive, that my legs had been sawn from my trunk, and although I quickly realized that I had only been dreaming— my legs were right there, two ridges under the blanket—I couldn't move them, couldn't rise no matter how I tried. My roommate, Eliza Fox, had to pull me out of bed. Another time, I'm ashamed to say, I actually fainted across a soldier's chest while giving him a sponge bath.

Several times I had to run from the wards to vomit. My insides spewed out every morning, into bedpans and janitors' buckets and hastily twisted newspaper cones and the snowdrift behind the hydrangea hedge. Twice I lost the hearing in my left ear, and once I spent four hours sitting in the stairwell, waiting for my sight to return. Syringes flew out to stab my arms; glass vials shattered in my hands; file drawers pinched the tips of my fingers.

I forgot soldiers' names and the purpose of errands. Three days in a row I locked myself out of the room I shared with Eliza. And always I was so tired, so very tired, that I simply could not stay awake, no matter how often I splashed water on my face or how much black coffee I drank. Finally, I surrendered and fashioned myself a nest among the towels in the supply room. I slept there every afternoon from one-thirty to two until the day Ward F ran out of soap, and Frances Patterson was sent to get some. Altogether, I had to admit they were right—I was beginning to make a better patient than a nurse. My body had got the better of me and could no longer be trusted. To tell the truth, I didn't know myself anymore.

And so I agreed to go home, not to the Milwaukee boardinghouse full of unmarried nurses where Eliza and I had carefully divided the freezing, mustard-colored room into her side and my side, but back to the farm where I had grown up, where the snowy hills were white as bleached linen and where my sister rocked her little girl to sleep beside the kitchen stove while she waited for her husband to come back from the war. I knew that, at home where I belonged, I could set myself right again.

Outside the train station, I drew the

city's breath, yeasty from the breweries and bittersweet from the chocolate factory, into my lungs and felt better already. My grip on my bag was tight. I wasn't late or excessively early. And now, for the first time in weeks, I was hungry, ravenous, in fact. I went into the station and stopped at a counter to buy myself a bag of peanuts with extra salt and a cup of coffee that didn't burn my tongue. When I'd finished the nuts, I was still hungry.

"Would you wrap half a ham salad?" I said. "No, better make it a whole. And some of that chicken. And maybe a piece of pie. The cherry, please."

Someone down the counter was drinking a chocolate milkshake that looked awfully good, and I was tempted to order one of those.

"That's what I like," the counterman said, punching numbers into the register, "a woman who can eat."

So I changed my mind about the milkshake. As I was paying my bill, they called my train.

"One way, miss? Goin' home?" the conductor asked, steadying himself with his hip along the seat in front of me.

I nearly began to explain that it wasn't right, really, to consider it home any longer, even though legally the farm was half mine. Really it belonged to my sister now, since she lived there, had a family there, and I was just going back for a restorative visit because somehow my body had taken on a life of its own. I wanted to confess that I'd been banished because I had failed as a nurse, because no one, including me, believed that I could coax soldiers back into proper shape when I was such a mess myself. But it isn't in me to say such things out loud.

"That's right," I said.

He winked. "Tickets!" he bawled and lurched away down the swaying car.

Spring meant even less in the country than it did in the city that year, and by the time we pulled up to the icy little platform in Nagawaukee, the sky was heavy with unfallen snow. The wind bit at my face, so that I had to duck my head. I watched the toes of my boots as I stepped down the slick platform stairs and picked my way over the snow that drifted across the street in long pulls like taffy. My steps took me one, two, three buildings down from the platform where I stopped at the door of Heinzelman's Bait and Tackle—"A Dozen Grubs for a Penny." I went in.

The bell over the door jingled, and the coals in the corner stove gave an answering glow to the sudden draft. Then the curtains behind the counter parted, and Mary Louise Lindgren emerged from the back room. She smiled when she saw me, beamed, you could say, and wiped her hands on her apron front in that nervous way she had, as she hurried toward me.

"Mandy! What are you doing home?" She put her hands on my shoulders, pressed her cheek against mine. "Ooh, you're frozen, a block of ice!" She held her warm palms to my face for a moment and then grabbed hold of my wrist and gave it a little tug without pausing to let me answer her question. "Come over near the stove. I can't believe it, just can't believe it's you! I wondered—when I heard the bell—I wondered who would be coming in at this hour, and I thought, It's probably Harry Stoltz, but, of course, it couldn't have been, because he's over in Watertown, and then I thought . . ."

She would have gone on about what she'd supposed and what she'd thought after that and what she'd done next, but I interrupted. "I'm taking a vacation," I said, "a rest." It was true, in a way.

"Mathilda is going to be so happy!" She frowned. "But why didn't she tell me? She was in here only two days ago."

"Mattie doesn't know."

That was all I needed to say, because she broke in immediately. "A surprise! How wonderful! And, Mandy," she leaned toward me and lowered her voice discreetly, though there was no one else in the shop to hear, "I have a surprise too." She waited until she was sure she had my full attention. "George and I may have a little one." She patted her apron front significantly.

I didn't know what to say to this. Mary Louise had been pregnant every one of the five years since she and George Lindgren had been married, and she had lost all five of those babies, each when it was several months along. A person ought to know when to give up, I thought; a person ought not to court disaster. At the very least, she should be wary. She should hold some of her feelings back. But Mary Louise was incapable of reticence, and she didn't have the advantage of scientific training, the way I did. She always acted as if nothing could possibly go wrong, as if this child's birth were written in the stars, and she need only wait for the blessed event. Only her hands hovering protectively over her belly betrayed the worry underneath. What she thought was growing could so easily amount to nothing at all.

"It feels different this time," she said defensively, although I hadn't expressed my concern.

"I hope so." Really, what else could I have said?

We agreed then that I should be on my way while there was still light. A few steps from the store, knowing she would be watching, I turned to look back. She held up her hand and, as I mirrored her, I thought of the time when we were just alike, Mary Louise and I, both happy to be finished with school for the day, running and sliding along this very road, scanning the tower of St. Michael's for the lantern light that we believed signaled the escape of a lunatic, talking about why Netty Klefstaad wasn't speaking to Ramona Mueller, and how we knew Bobby Weiss had cheated at spelling, and what to do with the penny after you'd rubbed it on a wart, and sometimes singing.

Of course, that was before Mattie. By the time Mattie was old enough to go to school, Mary Louise and I walked this same road decorously, with our books squeezed tight against our chests, but Mathilda ran ahead, pitching herself into snowbanks, as we had once done. "Watch me, Amanda! Watch, Mary Louise!" she'd call. Or she would linger behind to study the snowflakes patterning her mitten and summon me back imperiously. "Mandy, look at this one! Hurry up, before it melts!"

I could never make my sister understand that Mary Louise and I had important matters to discuss. For five minutes or so, Mathilda would stay by my side, cocooned with me in a wool shawl, but inevitably she'd pull away and run and slide until she exhausted herself and begged me to carry her. "Piggyback!" she demanded. Yes, demanded, although she was much too heavy. "You're too big now, Mattie," I protested. I sighed. I rolled my eyes at Mary Louise, whose eight brothers and sisters were never so much trouble, even all together. But Mathilda stamped her foot. She wailed and clung to me, so that, eventually, I bent my knees, and she jumped on my back and wrapped her arms around my neck, tight enough to strangle. Mathilda was always interrupting, always demanding, and I always gave in. I always did what she wanted. Always. Except that last time.

When Mathilda was born, I was eight years old and not, in the neighbor ladies' opinion, a promising child.

"What a beautiful baby," Mrs. Jungbluth said as she and Mrs. Tully and Mrs. Manigold crowded around Mathilda's cradle and cooed over her pretty lips, her lovely chin. With seventeen children among them, you'd have thought they'd seen enough babies. But Mathilda, apparently, was special.

"Amanda'll be jealous, won't she," Mrs. Tully said, "to have such a pretty little sister?"

But my mother said, "No, Amanda loves

her sister." She laid the baby in my lap to prove it.

Why would I be jealous? Mathilda was mine. The baby that everyone wanted for herself belonged to me.

A photographer came to the house to take a picture of us on the day of Mattie's christening. They put me in the big green chair—already, my legs were long enough to touch the floor, if I didn't sit back all the way—and I held her, her dress spilling white down my front, one of her tiny wet fingers tangled in the end of my braid, while outside the April clouds chased each other across the sun so that the room was bright one moment and shadowed the next.

"Smile," the photographer pleaded, but I refused. At Mary Louise's house, I had seen a picture of the Madonna cradling her baby and I intended to look like her, solemn and noble.

With the pop and the flash and the smoke, Mathilda began to cry. My mother started to lift her from me, but I was determined to hold on to my baby. I would be the one to comfort her. And Mattie, for her part, wound her fingers more tightly in my hair. She wouldn't let go until my mother opened those tiny hooks one by one.

I turned now onto Glacier Road, which runs up a hill overlooking Nagawaukee Lake. At the top, the wind hit me full force, scouring my cheeks and tearing at my coat. I gasped and struggled forward, my head low, as far as the icehouse. There I rested, stamping my feet in the straw and flexing my fingers, unwinding my scarf and shaking it free of my frozen breath. I left the door partway open for light. Before me now, as I stood looking out, the land fell away down the steep slope, and through the trees the frozen lake lay like a white scar on the earth. I shifted right, adjusting my angle slightly, and the tree trunks parted to reveal the familiar dark stain amid the whiteness, a crescent crowned with the lace of leafless branches in the northeast corner of Taylor's Bay, the island that had once been mine. I shifted again and could make out on the island the green roof of the house where Mattie and Carl had lived until the war.

Once I had thought this place was the

only one like it in all the world, but now I
knew better. Lakes were scattered all over
this part of the country, their outlines different, but their innards just the same. They
were drops and drips and splashes on the
land. They were holes and craters lined
with skin too thin to hold back the springs
that rushed to fill them, and most of them
were dotted here and there with stubborn
little islands, knobs of land that refused to
dip their heads under the water.

To the old farmer who'd sold my parents
their land, my island had been nothing, or
worse than nothing—a useless piece of
soil. He never mentioned it to my parents
when he pushed the deed toward them
across the heavy oak table in what had
only moments before been his kitchen and
was now ours.

They didn't discover they owned the island until several years later. I was twelve
and Mattie four the day my parents spread
the papers out on that same kitchen table
to determine whether a spring to the north
that would have been handy for them really
belonged to our neighbors, as the Jungbluths claimed.

"What's this here?" My mother tapped

her index finger on a blob marked with an X that looked to be in the middle of nowhere.

My father studied the map. "Well, Mother," he said, "it looks like we own the island out in Taylor's Bay."

Mattie was standing close to him, as she always did, one arm crooked around his leg. He scooped her up and tossed her toward the ceiling. "What do you think of an island, missy?"

"Again!" she shrieked. "Again!"

And so he tossed her several more times, while she squealed, until at last he lowered her to the ground, his large hands rucking her dress under her arms.

"Do it again! Please!" she whined, pulling at his trouser. "Again! Please! Again!"

Finally he raised a warning finger, and she started to cry. He turned to me. "Take care of your sister," he said impatiently. "We're busy here." And then he and my mother went back to trying to bend the northern boundary.

After everyone else was in bed that night, I crept down the stairs and unrolled the map to examine the shape for myself.

How oddly small and plain it looked, so different from the rocky, tangled place I knew. I rubbed at it with my finger. On paper, it might have been no more than a smudge of blackberry jam.

Under the rush of the wind now, I became aware of the ching-ching of sleigh bells coming up the road. I wrapped my muffler tight around my throat and lifted my bag. I was about to step outside and hail the driver, when the horse crested the hill and I saw just whose animal it was. I shrank back and pulled the door to. I had done something that I didn't want Joe Tully to know, something worse even than my dismissal, and I couldn't stand for him to see me with that shame in my heart. In the darkness, I pressed against the straw-covered blocks of ice and, my eyes closed, my breathing stilled, waited for the bells to cease, for the sound of footsteps, for the light to flood against my eyelids, because surely he'd seen me, had at least seen something and would wonder. Joe was not the sort who could ignore a glimpse of an intruder, or of someone who might need his help.

The bells came on, nearer, nearer, until I

could hear the horse snort and the hiss of the runners on the snow, and then they passed by and jingled more and more faintly, until at last they were buried beneath the wind. He must not have seen me after all. But if the stranger I had recently become was relieved, some other part of me shuddered with despair, and I found myself weeping, the tears searing my frozen cheeks, at the thought that I'd had to hide myself from a man I'd once loved.

And then, finally, I had to go on. One can only cry so long, and it would be dark soon and colder. Although the wind was fierce, I had only one more hill to climb. At the very last, when I could see the yellow farmhouse and the smoke from the fieldstone chimney, I began to run, taking huge, wild steps, picking my feet up high out of the snow and throwing them down again, swinging my bag, as if I were just a girl, propelled by the excitement of coming home.

I was about to knock at the kitchen door when it flew open. Mathilda stood on tiptoe, her cheeks flushed from sitting near a warm fire.

"Amanda! You've come back!" She had

to lift her arms high to throw them around me, for while I had long ago grown into a tower, she had stayed tiny and delicate, like our mother, a little sprite.

I was pleased by her embrace, but I was less demonstrative than my sister, and I stood rather awkwardly, still holding my bag, until she began to pull me inside.

"Wait, Mattie. You don't want snow all over your clean floor." I stamped and brushed at my shoulders.

She laughed. "Bring it in! Bring it in! Bring all of you in!"

She poked me playfully in the ribs as she took my coat. "Getting a little stout, aren't you? Too much pie?" She giggled.

"I'll be skin and bones again in no time eating your cooking," I said.

"Oh, I'm not going to cook anymore. Not now that you're here."

We laughed at this, knowing how right she was.

"Look at those boots, those gorgeous boots!" she exclaimed, bending over to admire my city footwear, spoiled now with wading through the drifts for which they were perfectly unsuited.

That was my Mattie, thrilled at a pair of

new boots, not even thinking to ask un-comfortable questions about why I'd come or what I intended to do. She was simply pleased to have me there.

"And Ruthie? Where's my baby?" I asked.

"Right here, of course." She swooped down on a pile of rumpled quilts that lay on the rocker near the stove and plucked the little girl out. "Wake up, Ruthie. Your Aunt Mandy's here."

"Oh, don't wake her," I begged, but it was too late. Ruth blinked at me and yawned.

Mathilda thrust her into my arms. "Here, you hold her."

The way things had been with me lately, I was afraid the child might scream, but when I settled into the rocker, she nestled against my shoulder and went back to sleep. It was exactly as I'd hardly dared hope it would be, the three of us warm in that familiar kitchen. I almost forgot to ask after Carl.

"He can see all right again," she said. "But there's some infection in the leg, and he still doesn't know when he'll be coming back." She'd told me in her letters about the gas that had blinded him and the shrapnel that had made a hole in his thigh practically big enough to stick a fist through. I'd assured her that a man was pretty certain to recover from those wounds, but she wanted to worry. *"You're here now, though,"* she said, raising her eyes to mine, and she tossed her head, almost defiantly.

So I would take care of her. That was all right then. That was something I knew how to do. For a moment or two I could almost believe that things were the way they had always been, before Carl or anyone else had come between us.

Chapter Two

Ruth

Aunt Mandy told me to be quiet, but I didn't be quiet. And then my mother went away.

Amanda

"My sister's gone," I told the sheriff.

He yawned and rubbed his face. When there wasn't any lawbreaking, which was most of the time, the sheriff was just Mr. Kuhtz, a farmer. I'd gotten him out of bed. "What's that?"

"I can't find Mathilda." I shifted Ruth,

bundled in a feather quilt against the cruel November night, to my other hip. My arms were nearly limp with weariness, and she was heavy, but I couldn't let her go. I'd been home less than a year, and I had lost my sister.

"Well, how long has she been gone?"

"Hours. I don't know how many. We all went to bed and then something woke Ruth. That's when I saw that Mattie wasn't in her room. Wasn't in the house at all."

"You still out on the island?" He frowned, and I knew Mathilda had been right. People had been wondering about us. "You come over on the ice already?"

Just then Mrs. Kuhtz appeared behind him. "Why are they standing out in the cold, Cyrus?" she scolded. "Come in. Sit down, and I'll get you something hot to drink." She had a very good face for trouble—she looked stricken, full of concern. "Here, give me the little girl. Ain't you just frozen, sweetheart?" She held her arms out for Ruth.

"No!" I said. I pulled Ruth against me so hard that she yelped. "We have to get home. In case Mattie comes back."

"Cy'll find her," Mrs. Kuhtz said soothingly. The sheriff had already gone to put on his clothes. "He'll bring her back."

I turned then, and went off across the frozen grass. When Ruth shivered, I opened my coat so she could share its warmth. Under the quilt she had nothing on.

Where were we going? I wasn't certain, despite what I'd told Mrs. Kuhtz. Not back to the island—that was unthinkable. With no plan, I staggered along the same road I'd traveled eight months before, this time with Ruth, heavy as an anchor, clutched to my chest. Although we were moving away from the water, the lake itself seemed to be beneath my skin, for I leaked and dripped with every painful step. My wet hair had frozen on my head. The front of my dress was sodden under my coat; my vision was blurred. But my feet knew the way, just as they had in March. Back I went to the dark, cold farmhouse, the place we never should have left, where we'd all have been safe, if not for me.

Ruth was asleep by the time we reached home, her head drooping along my arm. Her nightgown was back on the island, so I wrapped her as well as I could in one of my father's old shirts and my mother's shawl. I

lit the stove and rocked her in my lap, while
I waited for water to heat. Then I filled the
hot water bottle and tucked it beside her in
bed under the eiderdown. For a moment,
her deep breaths paused and I held my
own breath, waiting for the worst, but she
only sighed and slept on. Satisfied that she
was warm and safe, I went down to the
kitchen and removed my mittens.

My hand wasn't as bad as I'd feared.
Most of the blood had dried and the punc-
tures were small in circumference. Many of
them were deep, however. There would be
scars, a ring in the meat at the base of my
thumb. Who could have imagined such a
little thing would have such strength? Who
would have thought she would struggle so
fiercely? I found my father's whiskey and
dabbed a little on my wounds. Then I
drank a glass. People said it made you forget.

When Ruth awoke the next morning in a
room she hadn't slept in for months, she
called for her mama. I was sitting in the
kitchen, waiting for the night to be over. My
body had striven against me for sleep, for

escape from the sores and bruises and the paining muscles, but whenever I closed my eyes what I saw behind them was unbearable. In the daylight, I'd promised myself, everything would be different. They would find Mathilda at a neighbor's house, somewhere along the lake, or maybe even in the woods around the bay. She would be wet, maybe, and freezing. She might even have caught a chill. Her dress would certainly be ruined, but that would be the worst of it.

I would heat a bath for her and make a strong soup and bundle her into her bed. We wouldn't talk about what had happened. We'd only be glad that it was over and that we could go on as we had before. I had only to make it through the darkness, and then she would come home. I promised myself that.

Or maybe nothing *had* happened. I hid my hand in my lap and told myself it had all been a nightmare. When the sun rose Mathilda would come down to the kitchen, and we would laugh about the craziness of dreams and how real they can seem so that you wake up hardly able to breathe for the speed of your heart. She would say how silly I'd been not to slide into her bed for comfort and how I would be no good to anyone without a night's sleep. She would tease me about being afraid of my own shadow, and we would make pancakes together for Ruth.

Yes, that was how it would be when the sun came up. As long as I didn't check— that was important—as long as I didn't check to see that Mathilda was in her bed, but simply waited faithfully through the night, in the daylight things would be different.

So in the morning when Ruth called for her mother, I waited, listening for Mathilda's step across the upstairs floor. I listened, and I heard it. Yes, I was quite sure I heard it. But Ruth didn't stop calling. She was crying now, a frustrated cry. Why wasn't Mathilda comforting her?

Finally I went to Ruth. "We'll let Mathilda sleep," I said to myself as I climbed the stairs. "She must be very tired." But the truth pierced me with every step. In between the moments when I was convinced that Mathilda was most definitely in her bed, I knew she was gone.

Deep under my heart, I knew it, but I refused to look at it squarely. My mind slipped off the idea. I focused on the shape of the spaces between the lilies of the valley on the wallpaper; I noticed the twist of red and blue in the rag rug at the top of the stairs; I thought hard about what was in the kitchen that could be cooked for breakfast.

Ruth let me lift her from her crib, but when I set her down, she ran straight to Mattie's room.

"Where's Mama?" she asked, so bewildered, so trusting, it broke my heart.

How could I tell her what I couldn't tell myself? My head would not make the words.

"Shh, sweetheart," I said. It wasn't the right thing to say, I know that. I know that! But it is what I said. "Shh, sweetheart. Let's make some pancakes, shall we? C'mon, let's you and me make some pancakes."

"I want my mama," she said, and when I tried to take her by the hand to lead her down to the kitchen, she wrapped her arms and legs around the bedpost and held on. "I want my mama!" she screamed over and over again.

"Don't," I said. "Don't. It's all right. Really, it's all right. She'll come back soon."

But Ruth would not be fooled. She wailed, and I stood there helplessly, letting her despair for both of us.

When Ruth's cries began to weaken, I felt suddenly tired, so tired that I thought my legs would give way beneath me. I picked her up then—she was too exhausted to protest any longer—and I pulled her onto Mathilda's bed with me. The bed was stripped—we had been away from this house, this life, so long!—so we lay right on the blue-striped ticking, our cheeks pressed against ancient stains. My hand throbbed, and I couldn't stop shivering. I pulled the wool blanket that was folded at the foot of the bed over us and fell asleep.

I dreamed that I was standing at the edge of the lake in summer. Across the dazzling water, I could see Mathilda, sitting on the rocks that rimmed the island and singing, as a mermaid would. So she was all right! Of course she was all right!

"Mattie!" I shouted, relief flooding my voice. "Mattie! Over here!" But she wouldn't look at me.

I waded in, then, toward her. I pushed forward until the water encircled my waist and then cradled my bosom. How easy it would be to disappear beneath that inscrutable surface. There would be no gaping hole to show where I had sunk, no frenzy of turbulent waves to give evidence of my struggle.

"Mathilda!" I called, my chin dipping below the water as I opened my mouth. But she looked away toward the opposite shore, as if she hadn't heard a sound.

I couldn't shout again. The water ran into my mouth, my nose, my ears, my eyes. I was afraid now, and the water was heavier, harder to push. I could barely get a purchase with my feet on the sandy bottom. I clutched at the lake with my hands, but it gave me nothing to hold. Still, I kept going. Mathilda was just ahead. I only had to keep going and I would have her again.

And then I heard her crying. Yes, there you are, I thought, struggling as well as I could toward the noise. She sounded just as she had years and years ago, when she was my baby Mattie and wanted me to comfort her. "I'm coming, Mattie," I called, and water filled my mouth.

I was almost there. The crying was

louder, but my legs wouldn't move. I leaned forward. I stretched my arms out. There was no more breath in me, but I reached; I strained; I *would* have her; she was mine. And then I woke up.

It was Ruth who was crying, Ruth who needed comfort. Drowning in grief, I clung to her for dear life. I had no one but Ruth now, and Ruth had no one but me.

Ruth's mother had drowned. That was a fact. In December they found her body, trapped in the ice of Nagawaukee Lake. The *Sentinel* reported it and Amanda clipped the articles and pasted them to the black pages of a scrapbook, so there could be no question about what had happened.

DECEMBER 4, 1919—
WOMAN MISSING
Mrs. Carl Neumann of Glacier Road, Nagawaukee, has been missing since the night of November 27, according to

her sister, Miss Amanda Starkey, also of Glacier Road. Anyone with knowledge of her whereabouts should contact the Nagawaukee Sheriff's Department.

DECEMBER 6, 1919—MISSING WOMAN FOUND DROWNED

The body of Mrs. Carl Neumann was found yesterday evening trapped in the ice on Nagawaukee Lake by Mr. C. J. Owens of 24 Prospect Avenue, Milwaukee, and his son, Arthur, 5.

Mrs. Neumann had been missing since the night of November 27.

DECEMBER 7, 1919—FUNERAL FOR MRS. CARL NEUMANN

Funeral services for Mrs. Carl Neumann are planned for 6:00 pm tomorrow at Our Savior Lutheran Church in Nagawaukee. Mrs. Neumann is survived by her husband, Carl, recently serving in France with the 32nd Division, a daughter, Ruth, and a sister, Amanda Starkey. Miss Starkey has requested that, instead of flowers, donations be sent to the Precious Blood Children's Home in Oconomowoc.

Carl Neumann had promised to take care of Mathilda and now he would need taking care of. In late December, more than a year after the war had ended, he finally wrote to say that they were sending him home. "I can't believe," the final paragraph began, "that in a month or two, I'll hold your warm, sweet self again, my little Mattie-bird." There was more, but Amanda, blushing, folded the letter hurriedly and stuffed it back into its flimsy envelope. From New York came a final telegram: "HOME FEBRUARY 12 STOP 3:35 TRAIN." Amanda was a little surprised. Surely, the letter she'd sent had reached him by now. Surely, he knew how little was left for him in Nagawaukee. But here he was coming just the same.

"He'll take a train to Paris. And then another train from Paris to the coast. And then he'll get on a ship, a boat bigger than a house." Many times Amanda had traced for Ruthie Carl's route across a world too vast for such a young child's comprehension. She had held Ruth's tiny finger and pulled it around the globe. Ruth only wanted to make the globe spin, but she was interested.

"Where is my daddy now?" she asked every night when Amanda tucked her into the bed they were sharing.

"He's having his breakfast now—a nice soft-boiled egg." Amanda had been surprised at how easily Ruth accepted the notion of the time difference, as if she thought the most outlandish things were likely to be true in a place as far away as France or on a boat big enough to sail the ocean.

"And what else?" Ruth asked.

"And a piece of fish. With bones. You wouldn't like it."

"And then what will he do?"

"I don't know, Ruth. Go to sleep now."

Amanda regretted having told Ruth anything about Carl. With every word he came nearer and grew larger.

Amanda

Who knew what "my daddy" meant to Ruth? There was a father in "Hansel and Gretel" and a Papa Bear in "Goldilocks."

Neither of them was much good. I didn't think Carl was much good, either, I can tell you that.

Carl and Mathilda met on the Fourth of July when Mattie was seventeen. She'd insisted on going to Waukesha for the parade. Margaret Schwann was going. Harriet Lander, Will Audley, Fritz Kienast— all of them were going. It was a party, so she had to go too.

"You'll go, won't you, Mandy?" she begged. She knew my father wouldn't let her go to anything like that without a chaperone.

We were late and the street was crowded, but Mattie pushed to the front of the sidewalk. She was standing on her toes, waving a little flag in each hand, and the red, white, and blue ribbons in her hair were rippling in the breeze, when Carl marched by, beating a drum for the Bayside Meatpackers Band.

He was good-looking, I'll give him that. He had a fine-boned, boyish face, an easy, swinging gait and brown hair that fell into his eyes—the kind of looks a girl can make a lot of, if she's so inclined. He almost lost step trying to keep her in his view, and I knew, as well as she did, that we would have company at our picnic dinner.

Finally we spilled into the street behind the last of the tottering Civil War veterans and picked our way through the horse manure to the park. It was hot, as it always will be in Waukesha in July, so it was no surprise that Mattie loosened her dress at the neck and pushed her sleeves up along her lovely arms. And if this caused her skin to brown, who cared? Not Mattie. To her credit, she didn't look often over her shoulder as we laid our food under an elm, but dished out the bratwurst and potato salad and talked and laughed with Margaret and Harriet and Will and the others as if nothing extraordinary would happen before they cut the cake.

And, in fact, for her, it was not extraordinary that a young man should spot her while marching by and sooner or later would wish to marry her.

On the morning of February 12, Amanda rose in the dark, started a fire in the kitchen stove, and went out to the barn to feed the animals and to milk. She swept the wagon bed and reminded herself to ask Rudy, the hired man, to lay blankets down, in case Carl wasn't able to sit up properly on the seat.

Back inside, as the sun seeped weakly through the skeletal trees, she smoothed the quilt on the daybed in the back room, conveniently off the kitchen. With his bum leg, he wouldn't be able to walk well at first. Certainly, he wouldn't be able to manage the stairs.

Oh, he would be helpless, all right. She plumped the pillows vigorously and then surveyed the room with satisfaction. Would the wound still need dressing? It was possible, depending on how many muscles the shrapnel had torn, how infected it had been, and how well it had been treated— Amanda had no faith in French hospitals. But then Carl was young and strong. He would heal quickly once she got to work on him.

The narrow room was a good place for an invalid, Amanda knew. Her mother had gone there to have her headaches. It was far from the bedrooms upstairs so that a little girl playing as quietly as she could might sometimes be quiet enough.

Amanda

Mama had the apoplexy in August, the year Mathilda met Carl. I'm not blaming them, although I do know Mama disapproved. Her father had been a captain with the Union Army, she reminded us. Any daughter of hers could do much better than a butcher.

"He isn't a butcher, Mama. He's a meat-packer," I said. Under the table Mathilda drove the toe of her boot into my shin. But I was only speaking the truth.

Anyway, as I said, I don't blame them, although their shocking behavior certainly didn't help. I blame the weather.

It had been hot all summer, hot and so humid that just walking, just lifting your arms up over your head to take a plate out of the cupboard could make you so tired you wanted to sit down.

That morning felt as if someone had tucked a wool blanket tight over the world.

Mama woke up delicate, not ill exactly, but not strong either. She hadn't slept well—no one had slept well, for weeks, it seemed—and everything was a trial to her. The coffee tasted bitter; the clatter of the breakfast dishes hurt her ears; the oilcloth was sticky; the sun coming in the kitchen windows stung her eyes; her shoes pinched.

"One of you take the sheep down to the lower meadow this morning," my father said, his head bent over his plate.

"I'll do it," Mattie said quickly.

My father nodded. He sliced his egg and toast in half and then turned the plate to slice them again. "Someone has to stay with Mother," he said, pushing a quarter of toast into his mouth. "She isn't well."

I'd intended to do the shopping. We needed kerosene and brown thread and sugar, although I had hoped to go to town mostly to cool my face in the breeze during the buggy ride and to drink lemonade through a straw at the counter in Baecke's store.

My mother sighed and closed her eyes.

"I'll stay," I said.

After the others had gone, I cleared the

table, while Mama sipped her coffee. I was working the pump to get the water started at the sink when I heard her say, "I think I'll lay down awhile." And then crockery crashed to the floor behind me. I dropped the pump handle and spun around. Mama's cup and saucer were smashed, and coffee speckled the wall. She stood, holding her left hand in her right, and stared at me, bewildered.

"I don't know what happened. I just couldn't hold on to it anymore."

"It's all right. I'll clean it up." Already, I was reaching for the broom.

"But what happened? I don't know what happened." She reached for my arm and leaned heavily on me as I helped her to the daybed.

"I'll just lay down awhile, then I'll feel better, don't you think?" She looked at me trustingly, hopefully, as if I knew something.

"Of course you will. You're just tired," I assured her. And I believed what I said, because I'd had no medical training then.

I went back to work in the kitchen and, by the time I'd finished the dishes and started the bread, she was asleep. The wind was coming up, hot and steady from the west. I decided it was a good day to wash the sheets.

Her voice drifted up the stairs as I was pulling the cases off the pillows.

"I'm cold, Amanda. Amanda, I'm cold."

"Mama, you can't be cold," I called down. "It's a hundred degrees in here."

"But I'm cold." She drew out the last word until her voice quavered.

I took her summer shawl off its hook behind the door and carried it down to her.

"Why'd you take so long?"

"I was upstairs."

She pursed her lips, annoyed. "Put it around me. My arms feel so weak."

I spread the shawl over her, tucking it between her shoulder and the wall so it wouldn't slide off. Then I lifted her head gently and plumped the pillow under it.

"No wonder," she murmured.

"What?"

"Oh, nothing." She closed her eyes.

But then, as I turned to go, she spoke again. "I was just thinking it's no wonder that Joseph decided he didn't want you. You're so rough. Like a man, almost."

Through the long window I could see the

sheep, snatching at what little grass was left in the yard beyond the chicken coop. I stared at them, knowing something was wrong, not knowing what, until I remembered. Mathilda was supposed to have taken the sheep down to the lower meadow. Where was she?

I knew where she was all right. I didn't bother to take off my apron. By the time the screen door slammed behind me, I was already halfway across the yard.

The woods were buzzing and whirring, clicking and cooing with hot summer life. Sweat bees circled my head, and spider webs clung to my neck as I pushed my way down the overgrown path. I could feel the lake before I could see it, the coolness the wind carried off the water, the sense of space beyond the last clutch of honeysuckle and blackberry bramble.

Our boat was gone as I knew it would be, but I knew where the Tullys kept theirs, and I hurried along the shore to find it. It was buried in weeds, hardly touched all summer. I pushed it out into the water and scrambled aboard. And then I rowed, rowed hard toward my island.

I was looking over my shoulder, awk-

wardly, trying to gauge how far I still had to
go when I caught a glimpse of her around
the far side of the island. Just as I thought,
there she was while the rest of us worked,
out to her waist in the lake, the skirt of her
bathing costume floating around her middle like a black wool lily pad.

I was angry, of course. I had half a mind
to drag her into the boat and take her
home dripping to get what was coming to
her. But more than that I wanted to feel the
lovely water around my own ankles. We
could take care of the sheep later. It would
be easy with the two of us working together. I was about to call to her—my lips
were actually coming together to sound
her name—when I heard her squeal.

He shot out of the water like a giant pike
leaping for a dragonfly, spray shimmering
all around. He splashed her as he fell back.
Hooting in triumph, he struck his palm expertly against the water and sent a cas-
cade that hit her full in the face. She shrank
back for a moment, and I was prepared,
old as she was, to hear her wail. But instead she laughed. She dug her hands
deep beneath the water and threw at him
as much as her hands could carry. She

was no match for him—I could see that even as far away as I was. The water she splashed went in all directions at once. It would hardly have wet him if he'd not come closer, if he'd not let her splash him while he splashed her back, more gently now, but still wetting her thoroughly. And so they stood there, splashing each other like children, laughing and shouting, one to the other and back again, as if no one else existed in all the world.

Suddenly, I wanted to be away. I was desperate not to be seen, alone in my boat, watching them together. I struggled to turn around, nearly losing an oar in my confusion, but at last I was rowing. I pushed as quickly and quietly back through the water as I'd come, until the island blocked my view of them and theirs of me, and I was safe.

The moment I stepped back into the house I could tell something awful had happened. The door to the back room was open and from the kitchen I could just see the end of the daybed on which my mother's foot lay oddly twisted. I hurried in and found her, half on the floor, her eyes open wide and her mouth moving, but no words coming out, only sounds, strange, terrible sounds, like the noises a giant baby would make playing with its tongue.

I dragged her back onto the daybed and covered her again with the shawl.

"Quiet," I begged. "Please, please be quiet."

And then I ran to the barn for a horse and rode as fast as I could to the west field to find my father.

———

"Shh," Amanda said toward the ceiling of the room that was ready for Carl. "Quiet."

But she said it so softly, nearly whispering, that Ruth, awake now upstairs, didn't pause in the spirited conversation she was having with herself. Amanda went up to fetch her, wrapped her in a blanket, and carried her down to the warm kitchen. Ruth knew she was plenty old enough to walk, and she kicked her feet a little as they went down the stairs to prove it.

"Shall we have oatmeal?" Amanda measured it out as she asked.

"No!" Ruth said.

"Shall we have gingerbread?" Amanda stirred the oatmeal with a large wooden spoon.

"No!"

"Shall we have parsnips?"

"No!"

"What shall we have, then?"

"Frogs!" Ruth said, and she laughed as if she had said the funniest thing in the world.

"When my daddy comes home," Ruth said, pushing her spoon into her cereal, "will we go to the house with the green rug?"

"What house?"

"The house with the green rug. Where Mama is."

The sudden rush of feeling at the mention of Mathilda nearly choked Amanda, and she gasped, fighting to stay above it. Think of something else, she told herself frantically. Think how clever Ruth is, describing a cemetery plot as a house with a green rug. "Of course you can go there," she said at last. Her voice was calm and steady. "Your daddy will take you. But you understand, sweetheart, that your mama's in heaven, don't you?"

"Yes," Ruth said, and she conveyed a large spoonful of oatmeal into her mouth.

"And if you're very good, someday you'll go to heaven too."

Amanda ate her breakfast standing up, so that she could attend to other chores— shaking out the kitchen rug, washing the glass pane in the front door—as she thought of them. She was rinsing her bowl when Rudy stamped his boots on the porch and came in. He stood in front of the stove, rocking from foot to foot, his fingers tucked in his armpits. "It's a cold one," he said.

"Do you think we should bring more blankets?"

"Wouldn't hurt. Might as well pile on everything we've got."

"We'll leave at two then."

"We'll be early."

"Well, we can't be late."

Rudy saluted. "Two it is."

She frowned. It was easy for him to make fun, but somebody had to take responsibility. Somebody had to see that things went as they ought.

Ruth stirred her oatmeal, picked up a

clump in her spoon, raised it high and spilled it back into the bowl.

"Ruth, don't play with your food." Amanda took the bowl off the table and wiped the child's mouth with the dishrag. Ruth squirmed, pulling her face away from the sour smell.

"Hold still."

Usually Amanda would have urged the girl to eat more, but not today. Today there wasn't time. She went to the back door and called the dogs, who came trotting over the drift that had piled high behind the snow fence. "Come in and get warm," she said to them, setting the bowl on the floor.

Was she going to get started on the dinner or was she going to let the day get away from her? The lining of her coat was cold as she pushed her arms into the sleeves. She put on her mittens, picked up her basket and stepped outside. The air burned her cheeks and instantly froze the inside of her nose, while the sun lay so bright on the snow, she had to squint her eyes nearly shut against the glare. The sky was as blue as heaven as she marched, lifting her feet high and then plunging them knee deep into the snow, making her way to the root cellar.

She banged at the ice around the cellar door with a shovel until she'd chipped away enough to pry the door open. By the time she reached the bottom of the stairs she was blind in the gloom of the cellar, after the bright sun outside. She had to stand still for a moment, one hand pressed against the dank wall, waiting for her eyes to adjust. At last she could make out the vegetables in their barrels and bins.

She would offer to buy his half of the farm, she thought, piling potatoes, apples, carrots, onions and more potatoes in her basket. Not right away, but in time, when he'd healed and was growing restless. He would certainly be restless. He was no farmer, after all, and he was hardly a father. Hadn't he gone off when Ruth was only toddling the minute he'd heard the guns? He would be happy to have some cash, happy to be free to start his life again. And then everything would go back to the way it should be. She and Ruth would go on living on the farm. She would raise Ruth—a girl needed a mother, after all. Isn't that what Mathilda would have wanted? The thought of her sister made Amanda's heart beat hard, and her breath come in shallow gasps. There wasn't enough air in the cold, dark cellar. Abandoning the vegetables that rolled out of her basket and onto the floor, she stumbled up the packed earth stairs and out into the brilliant blue sky.

Amanda

Some weeks later, when Mama was a little better, not talking normally, but no longer making those hideous sounds, I told my father how I had seen Mathilda and Carl together at the island.

I thought he would send her away "to think things over," the way he had sent me to Cousin Trudy when Joe was courting me, but he only sighed as he smoothed my mother's wavy hair with her silver-handled brush.

"A son-in-law would be nice," he said at last. "And now that Mathilda's out of school, she can help with your mother. You could go to nursing school, like you wanted."

What was he thinking? I couldn't go to nursing school now! Not now when Mama needed me more than ever.

One day, Miss Sizer and Mrs. Zinda stopped me on the street. "Isn't it wonderful, all your parents are doing for the young people?" they exclaimed, shaking their heads and clucking their tongues with delight. They said it as if I were one of them and not like my sister, not a young person at all. People like a wedding, it seems. They don't care who is marrying or what it will do to other people's lives.

I was Mathilda's maid of honor. I wished them all the happiness in the world. And then I applied to nursing school. As I had always wanted.

———

Amanda peeled potatoes, dropping the finished ones into a pot of cold water so they wouldn't go gray.

"Hungry," Ruth said, coming to stand at her knee.

"You should have eaten more of your breakfast, then, shouldn't you? I don't have time to be feeding you all day."

But when she'd done the peeling she spread a slice of bread with butter and pressed brown sugar thickly over that.

"You sit right here and eat it, now," she said, holding the sandwich over Ruth's head until the child scrambled onto a chair. "I don't want sugar and crumbs all over my nice clean floor."

"You didn't have to make such a big dinner today," Rudy said as they sat down to pork chops and scalloped potatoes. "Carl's bound to be hungry. I could've waited."

"We have our big meal at noon here," Amanda said. "He knows that."

"Well, for one night, I mean."

"I'm sure Carl wouldn't want us changing everything we do, just to suit him, Rudy." Amanda put a piece of meat into her mouth and chewed it fiercely. "Do you have the wagon ready?"

"Just about," Rudy said, and he dug into his potatoes without further comment.

When they'd finished, Rudy took the extra blankets out to the barn, and Amanda put bricks in the stove to heat. Then she called Ruth in from the yard, where the girl was tumbling in the snow, and half led her, half dragged her up the stairs to dress.

How had the child gotten burrs in her hair in the middle of winter, Amanda marveled, as she gently picked apart Ruth's mats. Every few seconds, she couldn't resist bending close to rub her face against the girl's impossibly soft cheek, fiery red with the cold.

And then she peeled off everything Ruth was wearing and started fresh. Clean underwear first, a cotton shirt with long sleeves, long wool stockings, three little petticoats, her best dress, and then a pinafore over that. Last night, just in time, she'd finished knitting a fancy sweater for Ruth to wear specially that afternoon. It had a cream-colored background and was studded with rosebuds of five different colors, each one a French knot. The whole thing had taken her months. She held it up now for Ruth to see.

"Isn't it just gorgeous, Ruthie?"

Ruth fingered a colored nub. "I like the blue ones," she said.

"See? They're flowers. Roses."

"Roses," Ruth repeated.

"Hold out your arm."

It was difficult to get the sweater on now that Ruth was so fattened with fabrics, but finally Amanda had wormed her in and she buttoned it up to the girl's chin. Ruth looked a little stiff, like a doll. "Oh, you angel!" Amanda exclaimed, giving her a squeeze.

"Itchy." Ruth pulled at the neck.

"No, honey, you'll stretch it."

"No, itchy! It's itchy." Ruth squirmed and stamped her foot. She began undoing the buttons.

"Ruth, it is not itchy." Amanda pulled the girl's fingers away from the buttons and re-did the two Ruth had managed to unfasten. "Wait until you get outside. It'll be nice and warm then. You'll like it."

Ruth threw her head back and screamed to the ceiling. "No! Itchy!" She yanked at the collar, at the arms.

Amanda grabbed hold of her wrist, and Ruth let her knees go limp. She hung from Amanda's hands, shaking her head wildly and kicking her heels against the floor.

"Ruth Sapphira Neumann! Stand up! You mind me now!"

The girl was light and compact, easy to maneuver despite her struggling. With one swift movement, Amanda drew her against her knee. She swung hard, but her hand bounced off the thick material covering Ruth's bottom. Ruth barely felt it, but the shock of being punished made her scream harder.

"Be quiet!" Amanda shouted, louder than Ruth. "Be quiet!" And then, quite suddenly, she burst into tears herself. "Quiet." She was weeping the words now. "Please be quiet." Ruth looked at her with surprise. And then she, too, began to cry.

Amanda sank to the floor beside Ruth and lifted her into her lap. She bent over her, so that Ruth fit like a snug bundle against her body, and tucked her cheek over the girl's head. "Oh, my baby," she crooned, rocking. "My poor baby girl."

After a while she sniffed and sat up. The sweater had twisted. She straightened it and refastened the buttons that had come undone.

"Come on, let's wash our faces." Ruth stood near the basin while Amanda wiped a cold washcloth first over Ruth's face and then over her own.

"And now I'll have to do your hair again." Amanda lifted Ruth so that she stood on the chair in front of the vanity. There they were in the mirror, eyes swollen, hair tangled, not at all the sweet picture Amanda had envisioned earlier. For the second time in twenty minutes, she worked a brush through Ruth's snarls.

"Do you want a bow?" It was taking a chance, asking, because Ruth had to wear one. Really, the whole outfit would be ruined if she didn't wear a bow. The blue one, of course, it would have to be the blue one. But Amanda felt sure Ruth would want it. She held it on top of Ruth's head for the girl to see. Perfect. "Now doesn't that look pretty?"

"No."

Grimly, Amanda slid the pins under the ribbon anyway, securing it to Ruth's fine, dark hair.

"Run in your room now and play while I get ready," she said, lifting her down from the chair. To her great relief, Ruth did.

His leg would heal, and then he would go, Amanda reminded herself, as she pulled the brush through her hair. He might promise to send money. Ruth would probably get a card now and again. And then, after a year or so, the cards would stop coming. He would have a new life somewhere, and she and Ruth would have theirs, right here where they belonged.

Chapter Three

From the train, Carl could see them waiting on the freezing platform, Amanda holding a little girl, his little girl it had to be, on her hip. When he stood in the doorway of the car, Amanda pointed and bent her head to the girl's ear. The girl raised a mittened hand and waved vaguely. Her eyes were on a dog with a red collar far down the platform. She might have been waving at anyone.

He could walk only slowly, using two canes. It took a long time to make his way to them, step after faltering, unsteady step, along the platform that threatened to slide out from under him, against an icy wind that did its best to beat him back. Amanda set Ruth down, but the girl didn't run to meet him. The two of them stood like stones, waiting for him to come to them.

"Say hello to your daddy. Can you give your daddy a kiss?" Amanda gave Ruth a little push with her palm against the back of the child's head, but Ruth shook the hand off and stepped behind her aunt's skirt.

"My daddy is far away."

"Never mind, Carl," Amanda said. "You know how children are."

He didn't though. He had no idea.

In the street, Rudy was holding the horse. He shook Carl's hand and helped him into the wagon. He's relieved, Carl thought, to have another man here, and he closed his eyes for a moment under the weight of that responsibility.

Rudy lifted Ruth and was about to swing her up and over the wagon's side to settle her in beside Carl, when Amanda stopped him with a hand on his arm.

"Ruthie wants to sit up front with me," she said.

She mounted to the seat and turned, holding her arms out for her girl, and then, with a lurch they were off.

The train blew its whistle, as the wagon was turning onto the road out of town. Carl watched the cars heave themselves away from the platform, gather speed, and finally slip smoothly away, carrying men on to St. Paul and Sioux Falls and Pocatello and Spokane. He lay back on his bed of hay and blankets and stared straight up at the dizzying pattern of branches against the darkening sky, so that he wouldn't have to witness the familiar route to the Starkey farm and think how different his home-coming might have been. Rudy looked back at him once or twice.

"The trip's worn him out," he said to Amanda. "Give him a couple of days. He'll be better."

"Up and about in no time," Amanda said.

Amanda

It was obvious right from the start that he wasn't going to be able to take care of Ruth. She didn't take to him, for one thing. I could see that right off. And he made no effort, no effort at all. He was just as I'd expected.

Mathilda and Carl married in December, only six months after they'd met, a strange time for a wedding, people said with knowing smiles, and they were right, although they knew nothing. It never would have happened so fast if our father had been himself, if our mother had not been ill. Rumors sprang up like prairie fires, but I beat them down. People ought to have known by then that Mattie was a good girl, only impatient.

Carl was nothing special, though, as far as I could see. He took Mathilda to all the dances, and I have to admit he was a stylish dancer, but he couldn't say two words unless the subject was horses, and he didn't have a penny saved. "You don't get married for a dance partner," I told Mattie, but my sister was rash and stubborn. She wouldn't take advice from me. What did I know about why people got married?

My mother was too ill to manage the ceremony, so I helped her into her pink bed jacket, and she waited, propped against the pillows, for the newly married couple to come to her.

"Look at these flowers Carl gave me Mama," Mathilda said, pushing the sheaf of forced lilies so close under our mother's nose that she drew her head back in alarm. "Isn't he something to get flowers like these in December?" She held the lilies before her, her elbow crooked gracefully to support their heads, posing as the bride. "Amanda," she said to me, "run down and get a vase."

Mama tried to say something. She clenched and unclenched the fingers of her good hand and worked her mouth around some incoherent syllables. Finally she stretched her hand toward us. I took it.

"What is it, Mama? What do you want?"

But she shook her head and pulled her hand away. She reached for Carl. She meant for *him* to take her hand.

"Run down and get a vase, Amanda," Mathilda said again. "I want to leave the flowers in here for Mama."

On my way out of the room, I paused at the door to look back. What a pretty picture they made. Mathilda had passed the lilies to Carl, and he stood holding them for her, while he told my father how Frenchie had favored her right foreleg on the trip from town. Beside him, Mathilda, with the ringlets I'd spent hours curling with hot irons that morning falling around her face, bent to arrange her own silk scarf around our mother's throat. Apparently I hadn't dressed her warmly enough.

I can't explain what happened next. I'm usually so careful, you see, especially with Mama's crystal. She was enormously proud of those pieces—the eleven goblets, the water pitcher, and the vase with its fluted edge. She very seldom used them. And how I wish I hadn't thought to use the vase that day, but it seemed so perfect for this special occasion.

I planted the feet of the stool firmly, so that all four were steady, and up I climbed, until I stood on the top, and even then I had to stretch, go up on my toes a little, reach with my fingers. I had the vase securely in my hands. I know I did. But then, somehow, it was gone. I was holding nothing and with a crash that makes me sick even to think of it now, the vase hit the floor.

They came running then, Mathilda and Carl and our father down the stairs, Rudy from the kitchen, and I stood above them on the stool and stared at my faithless fingers. I hoped, I think, that there would be blood, that I would have some hurt to excuse what I'd done, but there was none, only the points of glass spread across the floor.

Carl began to pick up the pieces, asking if we had any glue, and Mathilda bent to help him. But I went to get the broom and pushed them aside. It was ruined. And the sooner we all realized that, the better.

————

From his bed, Carl watched through the kitchen doorway as Ruth ate her bacon and turnips. He spoke once, asking her in a false, jovial voice if she liked turnips. He'd never liked them himself, he explained, going on too long, listening to his own voice as if to a stranger's. Ruth didn't answer. Instead, she turned onto her stomach and slithered down from her chair, crossed the room and shut the door between them.

"This house is so noisy," she said.

Amanda scolded Ruth and hurried to

open the door again, but it was funny, hearing her own words in the little girl's mouth like that. She had to smile.

"Say good night to your daddy, Ruth," Amanda said when the table was cleared. And when the child did not, as they both knew she wouldn't, Carl saw Amanda smile again with satisfaction, although she lowered her head to hide it.

He listened to Ruth's steady little footfalls, two to a stair, and then to the creaks of the floorboards, the shrieks of the bureau drawers, and then he heard sobbing, a sound surprisingly different from the thin, penetrating cry he remembered rising from Ruth when she was an infant. Poor thing, with no mother to comfort her, afraid of the dark, he thought at first, but the irritating sound went on, and he pulled the pillow tight around his ears. Why didn't Amanda do something to stop it? And then he realized that Ruth was not crying at all, but laughing.

"Again," she shouted. "Again!"

Amanda was upstairs a long while. He had almost fallen asleep by the time she came down and began to wash the dishes.

"I shouldn't have let her get so wound

up," she said. "She's just like Mathilda that way, never wanting to go to sleep."

Carl didn't remember that about Mathilda. He remembered watching her dream in the early mornings, the way she burrowed into the blankets, so that only the top of her head stuck out, the way she flung her arm around him and held him tight without knowing she did so. But Amanda was probably right. She'd lived with her sister for almost twenty years, whereas he'd only been her husband for three, and for more than one of those they'd not even been in the same country.

Amanda moved expertly about her kitchen, washing her dishes, putting things away, and Carl was reminded that he didn't know where things belonged.

"Maybe Ruth and I should move back out to the island," he suggested.

"That's hardly practical."

"I guess you're right."

Amanda shook out her dishcloth with a snap. "We'll have you on your feet in no time."

"Sure," he said, making an effort to sound hearty, to behave as if everything would be just fine very soon. "I'll be ready to work by planting."

Amanda blew out the lamp and the kitchen went black.

"We'll see," she said from the darkness.

He listened to her steps, heavy on the stairs, and the floor creaking in her room, and finally even the mattress taking her in. And then he could hear only the wind worrying the shingles and the windowpanes.

Amanda

After Mathilda and Carl were married, I had to sleep in the small room off the kitchen. All winter I could hear their whispering and laughing in the night. I could hear their bed moving.

Then they needed a house all to themselves, a house on my island, that's what Mathilda proposed. All spring and summer they worked on it, but every day they rowed back to the farm, Carl to help my father and Mathilda to visit our mother, who was much recovered by then, and to help do the chores around the house. There was no longer any need for me at all. The university had accepted my application to nursing school, and I began to pack my trunk.

I was certainly something the day I waited on the platform in my new hat, the whole family there to see me off. They gave me presents—a silver pen from my parents, a red moroccan leather notebook from Mathilda and a bluebird house from Carl, which surprised me, because I did like birds, but you wouldn't think a boy would notice something like that. I thanked him, of course. I admired the fine workmanship and the cunning shingles set in the roof, the little shutters around the entrance, that made it look like a real house. But how did he think I'd be able to carry such a thing all the way to Madison? Where did he expect me to put it when I got there? I wouldn't have any split-rail fence to hang it on. I'd be lucky if I had a window to call my own.

"I'll keep it for you," Mathilda said.

They stood on the platform as the train pulled away, all of them waving but my sister, whose hands were full.

I'm not blaming them, a married couple needs a place to live, after all. Still, if they'd not built their house on my island, Mathilda would not have drowned. If you look at it one way, it's as simple as that.

———

Carl didn't dream of Mathilda often, although he tried. He thought about her when he lay in bed, trying to make her appear in his sleep. Sometimes he thought about the day they'd met, how he'd taken her on the roller coaster and how she'd loved it. She wanted to ride again and again, and he'd thanked God that he had enough money to treat her over and over. He'd discovered after the first ride that he disliked the roller coaster himself—the sudden drops made him feel sick to his stomach—but it was worth it to have her clinging to his arm, to listen to her happy screams, to feel her smooth hair against his face. He would have ridden with her all afternoon had her sister, waiting grimly at the bottom, their picnic basket over her arm, not finally grown impatient.

"Enough's enough. You always have to go too far," Amanda had said and, wrapping her fingers tightly around Mathilda's wrist, she dragged her off, almost before he was able to say goodbye. When Mathilda turned to wave at him with her free hand before the crowd closed behind them, he congratulated himself for having the foresight an hour earlier to have asked her where she lived.

That was what he thought about before he fell asleep, but his dreams, as usual, wouldn't be steered. They took him far from Mathilda, back to France where the gray smoke mingled with the gray fog, into the foxhole where he had been resting with Sims and McKinley, two fellows from his squad, before a blast tossed him, limbs twisted in every direction, onto the half-frozen mud like a sack of potatoes. He remembered leaving the ground but not returning to it.

He'd opened his eyes at the sound of groaning. It was Pete McKinley, about twenty feet away, struggling to pick himself up. Between them, Henny Sims lay in a heap, unmoving. Carl was about to call to McKinley when he saw the man stiffen, an odd, horrified look on his face. He followed McKinley's gaze to the rim of the foxhole.

Three Huns were staring down at them, bayonets affixed.

His body started involuntarily, but the Germans didn't even glance his way. They must have assumed he was dead, or at least still unconscious. Already they were clambering into the foxhole, moving toward McKinley, who'd managed to get to his knees. One of them stopped where Sims was heaped and used his bayonet to roll him onto his back. There was something wrong with Sims, Carl could see. Something funny about his head. "*Tot*," the Heinie said, and Carl realized that half of Henny's head was missing.

"My gun," Carl thought, and he believed he was reaching for it, believed even that he was standing, ready to fire it into their backs, but it was only an illusion. His body stayed frozen, stuck to the earth.

And then red. That was how this dream that wasn't a dream always ended, with red that washed everything else away.

It was still dark when the door slammed, and Amanda came in, cheeks pink, feet stamping, the milking done.

"Ready for breakfast?" she asked, sticking her head around his door. Cold clouded around her, and she blew on her fingertips.

Ruthie was already at the table by the time he'd made his way into the kitchen and collapsed on a chair. Like a dog guarding its food, she kept her eyes on Carl as she scooped cornflakes into her mouth, her fist clutched awkwardly around her spoon. Amanda cracked eggs smartly against the edge of a blue enamel bowl.

"If you want to visit her grave first thing, Rudy'll take you," she said. "Ruth is all set to go along, aren't you, Ruthie?" She wiped the girl's face with a dishrag and lifted her down from her chair.

The thought startled him. He realized he'd been half imagining Mathilda away somewhere, visiting a cousin, or perhaps living in the island house. He was almost expecting her to return.

"I really don't think I'm up to it."

"Oh, but, Carl," she reproached him, "you really should. What will people think? And here," she added, stepping out to the porch and coming back with a handful of branches studded with red berries. "I thought you might want to take these. I know they aren't really flowers, but you can't be choosy this time of year."

Ruth stood on her tiptoes and reached her arms high. "Pretty," she said, "pretty."

"No, no, honey. These aren't for you. See, they've got thorns." She pricked her finger and a red bead of blood appeared. She held it up for Ruth to see as if it were a prize.

Ruth

"Ho," he said, and Frenchie stopped. I saw over the wall where all the stones were.

"Hup," Rudy said, and I was in the air, and then I was on the snow.

The snow was hard, like crackers. There were no footprints on it. I was careful. I slid my feet. I tried not to let the snow break. The man that was my daddy let me. He didn't make me hurry. He punched the snow with his canes. Punch, step. Punch, step. I wished I had a cane.

We went past the mean gray stones and the stone that was sleeping and the one

with the boat. I knew the way. Aunt Mandy
and I had been here lots of times. We went
up the hill, then down the other side. We
went to the stone that said my mama's
name. It had shiny ice all over it.

He said, "Mathilda," and I knew he
meant my mama.

I looked behind the stone like I always
did. Aunt Mandy said she was there, too,
but I never saw her.

"Where is she?" Aunt Mandy would
never tell me, but maybe he would.

"In heaven," he said, that same old answer that wasn't any good to me. And he
was crying.

I cried then, too, because he was crying.
"Then why don't we go there and get her?"

Heaven was the place where we lived
with Aunt Mandy, before my mama never
came back.

"Someday you will," he said, "but not for
a very long time."

I put my hand on the slippery ice stone. I
slid my mitten over it, back and forth. I
waited for him to say better get home. But
he just stayed kneeling in the snow.

"Why did she go to heaven?"

"She drowned, Ruth. She went under the water and she couldn't get back up."

So then I knew that I was right. Heaven was the place where we had lived, because that was where the water was.

"She drowned me too," I said. "The baby was crying and crying."

"What baby?"

"The ice baby. When Aunt Mandy didn't wait for us."

"What are you talking about? When didn't Amanda wait for you?"

"When I drowned."

He was crying and he was smiling. "Don't worry, Ruth." He wiped the crying off his face and put his hand on my head. "You didn't drown. You're right here with me."

I was here, but he wasn't there. So how did he know?

———

When Carl returned with Ruth from the churchyard, he got back into bed and stayed there. Amanda opened the curtains each morning, registering her disapproval with every yank on the fabric.

"Ready?" she asked, but she didn't mean it as a question.

Surprisingly, after the first few times, he was ready. Twice a day, morning and evening, she unceremoniously threw back the blankets, exposing him to the chilly air, and scrubbed his wounded leg with brisk efficiency. Then she bent the leg, twisted it, pushed and prodded it with her long, thin fingers, until he yelped in pain.

"Oh, for pity's sake," she said, "bite on a pillow if you must make that noise. We can't have you scaring Ruth." And as she wrapped honey-covered cloths around the hole, she warned him, "I'll have to keep this up until you start doing for yourself."

He nodded and promised to try, but he had no interest in making himself better. It was all he could do to sit in a chair and eat the coddled eggs and soup she brought him, while she pounded his pillows into fluffiness and changed his sheets, snapping the clean linen once or twice in the air, before she allowed it to settle around the mattress.

She scared him. He knew she disapproved of him, that she hadn't thought him good enough for her sister. He'd tried to woo her with the birdhouse, but it hadn't worked, and Mattie had cried the day she'd had to carry it back home from the train. He knew she didn't want to talk about how Mathilda had died, but the pain in his leg made him angry and bold.

"Amanda," he said one night when she came in with his medicine, "why were you living on the island?"

She looked straight at him with her hard, blue eyes. "Why, Carl, that was your home. Of course, that was where Mattie wanted to be. Did you take your medicine?"

"Yes. But why did she leave it, then? Where did she go?" Carl pushed himself up, so he was sitting tall against the pillows. "You know what I don't understand," he continued, without pausing to let Amanda answer, "why she would've left Ruth. Why would she have left Ruth in the house at night alone?"

"Ruth wasn't alone, Carl. She was with me." Amanda went to the window and stood with her back to him, her form reflected in the dark glass. "Besides, you know how reckless she was, Carl. Mattie was always taking chances, always doing things she shouldn't have done, things I told her not to do. She probably thought it was a fine night for skating and didn't think to test the ice. That would be just like her." She pulled the curtains closed and turned to face him.

"Was she wearing her skates, then? When they found her?"

An exasperated sound escaped Amanda's lips and she swept her hand through the air. "She's dead, Carl. What does it matter?"

"But . . . I loved her," was all he could think to say. "Why can't I know?" He knew he sounded like a little boy, but he couldn't help himself.

"If you loved her, you should understand. Love makes you do things and afterward you wish . . ." Her face was so hard and bitter, it scared Carl and made him clench the blanket to his chest. "But then it's too late. You can only be sorry." Her mood changed, and she patted his feet, briskly, while he forced himself to hold them steady under her hand. "I've got something I'll bet you'd like to see."

She went out of the room, but before he

could relax, she was back. "Here," she said, opening a scrapbook on his lap, where it pressed against his sore leg. "Look. It was in the newspaper. This should tell you what you want to know."

She stopped at the door on her way out. "Carl," she said, "I know you're sorry you left her." And then she left him alone.

The clippings seemed to Carl to have nothing to do with his Mathilda. They told him nothing that mattered, nothing that explained. Mathilda disappearing in the night—it didn't make sense to him. And what did Amanda mean about his being sorry and people doing things for love? Had Mathilda done something desperate because he'd gone? She'd begged him to stay, but wasn't that what every wife would do, and they didn't all drown. Near what he now knew was the end of her life, he hadn't gotten the letters from her he'd expected, but that was the Army's fault, wasn't it? No, he couldn't imagine Mathilda drowning herself for love of him. He'd have to ask Amanda more questions, someday when she was in a better mood and when he felt stronger. Perhaps, he mused sleepily, it had been some other woman they'd found frozen. And maybe tomorrow or the next day or the day after that Mathilda would come back.

She would stand right there in the doorway, looking . . . how would she look? He'd been away from her so long, already his memory had lost the range of her expressions. He could summon her only in a few guises—glimpses of her face that for no particular reason had stuck in his mind. He flipped backward through the album— Mathilda bent over baby Ruth with an adoring smile; Mathilda both proud and amused, posing with her ankles neatly crossed for their wedding portrait; Mattie, her lank hair escaping her braids, third from the left in a grade school photograph; baby Mattie on her father's lap. He looked through a clutch of pictures no one had bothered to mount that had been pinched between the pages and the back cover. In one, Mattie and Amanda sat on the edge of the porch. Mattie was looking away from the camera, her eyes narrowed like a cat's, as if she were trying to make out some form in the distance. Carl pretended she was gazing beyond the border of the photograph at him.

He wouldn't have called her reckless. Impulsive, maybe. Willful, certainly. And decisive. He remembered her haste to marry, once she'd accepted his proposal. But she was never crazy. He couldn't imagine her wandering onto thin ice in the middle of the night. But as he closed the book, Carl reminded himself that in the last couple years he'd seen people do many things he could never have imagined. Sometimes there was no knowing what people would do. She was gone anyway. He wouldn't see her again. Burying his head in his pillow, Carl waited for his dream.

Carl's wound interested Amanda. It was the kind she hadn't seen often at the hospital, the kind that would get better despite the infections that had slowed its healing. She hadn't expected that he wouldn't want to improve, but it didn't matter much. His body went on about its business all the same, oozing its cleansing pus and growing its scars. He didn't have any say in the matter.

During the day Ruth nosed around the door of Carl's room, curious as a cat. Often, when he opened his eyes, he would see her face pressed to the crack between the door and the doorframe, staring at him. When she was sure he'd seen her, she scurried away.

She began to bring him bits from outside. She set them on the end of the bed when she thought he was sleeping: an oak gall, three pine cones, a railroad spike, a cardinal's feather. She lured him out.

"Where did you find this?" he asked.

At first she said nothing. And then she said, "Outside." And at last she said, "Do you want to go outside?"

"No."

But finally, on one of those days when spring blusters its way through a chink in winter, when the sky was a soft blue and water rushed through the ditches, he changed his mind. He'd been watching Ruth from his bed as she ran and slid through the slush and soggy grass in the backyard, chasing the ducks and geese with her arms spread wide. Impulsively, he reached for one of his canes and tapped on the glass. Startled, she turned toward the window. He waved, and she, still running, raised a hand to wave back. And somehow, well, it was no great surprise, the ground being slippery and uneven, her coordination still not fully formed, she lost her balance and went down hard.

He was up and out of bed before he thought, and then, when the black dizziness swarmed over his eyes, he was just as quickly down again. It passed, and he struggled to his feet. Staggering and swaying, leaning heavily on both canes, Carl made his way out the door to rescue his little girl. But if he expected to find her sobbing on the ground, he didn't know Ruth. Long before he was back on his feet, she was darting at the duck who had waddled close to see what sort of creature had made such a splat. Her grin, her baby teeth shockingly white in the midst of her muddy face, was the last thing Carl saw before one cane slid right, the other left, and he found himself sprawling and crawling through the slush in his nightshirt, with Ruth standing over him, delighted with his clever trick.

"What you do, Daddy? What you do?"

Amanda laughed when she met them, soaked and filthy, struggling in the back door, but she soon set her mouth in a firm line. After all, Carl had to be made to real-

ize the extra work he'd created, gallivant-
ing around with Ruth. It wasn't bath day,
but she'd have to heat water now, and the
state of their clothes meant a morning's
struggle over the washtub, and she
doubted if even that would be enough to
get Ruth's coat clean.

Every day, from then on, Carl and Ruth
went out to play together, and Amanda,
going about her tasks, found herself half
irritated and half charmed when she came
upon them making snow angels or racing
sticks in the freezing ditch water. She had
to admit that it wasn't altogether unpleasant to have Carl around, even though he
wasn't much help with the chores. If he
were to stay through the fall, she could get
the farm working well again, and then she
could always hire another man next spring.

"I'll take Ruth into town with me today,"
she announced at breakfast one day in
early April, "unless you two have other
plans."

"Well, we *were* going to start building
our playhouse, but that can wait until this
afternoon," Carl said, pouring himself a
second cup of coffee.

"You could help Rudy fix that wagon."

"I could," Carl agreed. "Will you pick up the mail?"

"I always do."

In the post office, Ruth waited patiently for the cocoa Amanda had promised her, amusing herself by passing her hand back and forth through the dust motes in a shaft of sunlight. The air inside was chilly and dank and smelled of wood and glue.

"Spring's coming," Ramona Mueller, the postmistress, said brightly. She'd said that to everyone who'd come in that day. It was a nice, safe thing to say.

"I hope so," Amanda said.

Ramona was satisfied. Most people said something along those lines.

Amanda picked up a page from an old circular and accordion-pleated it while she waited for Ramona to sort through the pile of mail behind the counter.

"I hear Carl is better."

"Oh, yes, much better, thank you."

"He's lucky he's got you to help out with Ruth."

Amanda flushed. Helping Carl with Ruth? Was that how they saw it? That wasn't how it was at all. "Well, a girl needs a mother," she said finally.

While the women talked, Ruth, placing her feet precisely heel to toe, so as to follow the path of a single floorboard, made her way to the low-hung window at the front of the post office. An automobile was rolling slowly up the street. Ruth's experience with motorcars was limited, and she'd never seen one like this, with a special seat in the rear for riding backward. When the car stopped, the boy in this seat stood up, bent his knees, and jumped to the ground, his unbuttoned coat flying out behind him like a cape. He waited beside the car then, polishing its bright black flank with his sleeve, until the man who'd been driving came around. Together they started up the steps of the post office, and Ruth hurried back to stand beside Amanda.

"I guess this is it," Ramona said as she laid a small pile of catalogs and bills on the counter. "No letters today."

Amanda put the mail in her basket and turned to go, taking Ruth by the hand. Just then the door flew open, admitting a rush of fresh April air. Amanda's heart seized as if it might stop beating right there in the middle of the United States post office.

The man in the doorway smiled at her slightly, the corners of his mouth twitching and his eyes crinkling fondly, as if they shared a private joke. "Amy," he said.

Amanda looked at the floor for a moment in confusion. Finally, relying on convention, she gave Ruth a little tug, so that the child stood between her and the man.

"Say how do you do to Mr. Owens, Ruthie."

"Hajya do," Ruth said obediently, but she meant it for the boy. He was older than she, which would have been enough to make him interesting, but something else about him fascinated her. He was wearing a pair of glasses, very small to fit his face and very round. Ruth hadn't thought that children could wear glasses. She wanted to try them on. Did things look different from behind them?

The boy looked down at her through his two windows rimmed in gold. "Hi," he said, sticking his hand out importantly, "I'm Arthur."

"Clement Owens," the postmistress sang out from behind her counter. "You've got so much mail, I hardly know where to put it all."

"Well, here I am to pick it up," he said, but he continued to stand just inside the door. "I'd been hoping to run into you sometime, Amy. I have to thank you."

Amanda stared at him.

"You told me such wonderful things about this place I figured I had to come out and take a look for myself. And now I'm building my own summer house on the north side. You see, I'm already using the post office. I've got a gorgeous lot—southern exposure, nice view of the whole west end of the lake. You ought to come see it sometime. I think you'd like it. Wait till we get the walls up, though. That's when you'll really be able to get a sense of it."

There was a buzzing in Amanda's ears, the force of her own blood pumping in her head, she thought clinically. What could he be talking about? Suddenly, she realized it made no difference what he said, she only wanted to get away, to be away, never to have seen him, never to see him again. She took a small step forward and sideways, almost as if to suggest that she might push past him to escape.

Her behavior puzzled Clement. They hadn't parted on such bad terms, had they? And even if they had, didn't what had come before make up for that? They'd been so delighted with each other—he remembered that vividly. He remembered her quick, bright smile and with what shy pleasure she'd allowed him to tuck her hand under his arm. She couldn't have changed that much, could she? What was the matter with her that she couldn't treat him with friendliness in a public place? And then he remembered. "Amy," he said, laying a hand on her shoulder, "I'm very sorry about your sister."

She jerked her shoulder abruptly, throwing his hand off. Ducking her head, she brushed past him and almost ran out the door he still held open. She hurried down the steps with Ruth in tow, so fast that the girl's feet missed almost every stair. They flew down the street, past the parked car in which sat a woman in a peacock-green coat. They turned the corner and still raced on, did not slow, did not stop, until they reached the stables where she'd left the buggy.

"We forgot the cocoa," Ruth said anxiously, as Amanda plunked her onto the buggy seat. Amanda didn't answer.

When he heard the screams coming from the house, Carl was coming up the path that ran through the woods to the lake. He broke into the best limping run he could manage up the final hill. Despite the chilly air, he was slick with sweat, and his legs were shaking and his breathing ragged by the time he burst into the house.

In the kitchen, Ruth was wailing through chattering teeth as she struggled to climb out of her bath. Her little hands gripped the rim of the metal tub, and she pushed herself up on her toes, trying to lift her leg over the edge. It was a pitiful sight. He grabbed her up and wrapped her as well as he could in a dishtowel that hung near the sink. He held her close until she stopped crying, and then he shifted her to his hip and went to his sister-in-law, who all the time had been looking out the window, rocking slightly, holding one hand by the wrist with the other.

"Amanda, what's going on here?"

She turned toward him and smiled. "You see? I told you. She isn't drowned." She reached to take Ruth from his arms, but he hesitated, held her back. "Give her to me!" she demanded, and then repeated, her voice frantic and shrill, "Give her to me!"

And when he still wouldn't relinquish the child, she tore at his arm and pummeled the shoulder he turned toward her, howling, "Mattie is mine! Mattie is mine! Give Mattie back! Mattie is mine!"

"Stop it! Damn it! Stop acting crazy!" He pulled Ruth away and ran up the stairs with her, slowing at the top, when it was clear Amanda wasn't following. When he came back down half an hour later, having soothed Ruth to sleep, she was no longer in the kitchen.

He moved through the house, opening doors and quietly calling her name. "Amanda," he whispered outside her room. When he got no answer, he hesitated, and then, tentatively, pushed the door further open and looked inside. The room was empty. Half guilty and half curious, he stepped in.

Amanda had taken for herself the room

her parents had used when they were alive. It was large enough for three windows, two on the wall that overlooked the flower garden, now just a wide strip of black mud—he'd need to cultivate that soon—and one that caught the afternoon light. All three windows were tall and so deep that the glass started below Carl's knees. It was dizzying to stand too near them. He looked at the ground below, with a sudden, terrible thought, but no, the windows were closed.

The dresser top was prettied with a runner on which lay a silver grooming set, the back of the hairbrush monogrammed with initials he knew to be her mother's. Beside that an oval frame held a photograph of a solemn, straight-backed girl, her lap buried in a froth of christening lace from which peeked an infant's face.

Carl wanted to slide one of the dresser drawers open, but he didn't dare. She'd know if he'd touched anything; he was sure of it. He looked quickly over his shoulder toward the door, but the house was quiet.

At first, thinking she'd gone off to calm

herself, he didn't worry much and tried to go on with the afternoon. He cleaned the tub and mopped the water off the floor. He played with Ruth when she woke up. He did the evening milking. It was hard, though, to keep his mind on these things when she still didn't come back. Where was she? Finally, at dusk, he asked Rudy to watch Ruth and went to look for her.

He searched the barn, the chicken coop, and the root cellar hurriedly, holding his lantern high in the corners. He knocked on the door of the outhouse. He hoped but didn't truly expect to find her in any of these reasonable places, but he needed to feel he was looking thoroughly, systematically, and it made sense to start with the nearest, sanest possibilities. At last, with expectant dread, he started for the lake.

It was cold, cold enough to make Carl wish he'd worn gloves, and he passed the lantern from hand to hand often as he walked, pressing the free one into his pocket. Halfway, he began to run as well as he could over the dark and knotted ground, groping his way down the same path he'd hurried up that afternoon.

Finally he broke from the trees, and the lake, which had only days before shed the last ragged scraps of the winter's ice, rippled wide and black before him. And yes, unbelievable though it seemed, there Amanda was, almost as he'd imagined her as he rushed through the woods. She wasn't floating, though, but standing up to her shoulders in the water, her head a silhouette in the white spill of moonlight. He splashed in without stopping to lay down the lantern, so that when he reached her he had to fling it into the water to grab hold of her with both hands. He dragged her back toward the land, maintaining his own footing on the bottom with difficulty, especially since in the numbingly cold water he couldn't feel his feet and could barely sense his legs. How long had she been standing there? What had she meant to do?

"Amanda! What're you doing? What're you doing?" he repeated over and over idiotically.

She gave no answer, but neither did she resist him. By the time they reached shallow water, he realized he'd been carrying her and would have to continue. She either couldn't or wouldn't support her own weight.

"She's obviously hypothermic," the doctor said, "and I'm sure there's frostbite in the feet and fingers, but I think she'll be all right that way." He looked significantly at Carl. "It's her mind that worries me."

"Yes," Carl said, nodding energetically, relieved the doctor had noticed. "There's something wrong with her, isn't there?"

The doctor recommended St. Michael's. "A little rest," he assured Carl, "will do her good."

Chapter Four

In April 1920, when Ruth was four, her Aunt Mandy went away.

"It doesn't surprise me one bit," they said. On Cottonwood Drive and Maple Avenue, in the dry goods store and at the butcher, in the bank, in the tavern turned tearoom and in the post office they all agreed that there had always been something a little funny about Amanda, even as a girl.

"That time I brought that great big dish of potato salad over," Mrs. Alberti said to Mrs. Zinda over coffee. "This was years ago, of course, back when Lucy was getting ready to have that darling Mattie. Well, Amanda came to the door—she must have been only seven or eight, just a little bit of a thing then. I was going to take my potato salad to the kitchen, look in on Lucy, you know, but that girl took my dish right out of my hands. It was so heavy the bones in her spindly wrists were standing out, and 'Thank you very much,' she says, and with one foot pushes the door closed, right in my face. Isn't that the limit? I don't know that I ever did get my dish back. It was the nice square one. You know, with the lid. I think you've got one like it."

"You remember the way she was when Lucy and Henry got sick the other year," Trina Eschinger said. "Throwing her own sister out with that tiny baby. And then running off like that when the old folks died."

Yes, Amanda had always been funny. This didn't surprise them one bit.

Amanda

If only I could have kept her small and close, but no, she wouldn't stay in that dark, secret place. She forced her way out, for all the world to see, and then look what happened.

It is you and then it isn't you—that's the trouble with a baby. And it keeps on and keeps on, growing and growing, monstrous. There's nothing you can do. You are no match for it. But that comes later.

I was so happy those months with Mama on the davenport, all mine, waiting for Mathilda to come. Tucked under her arm, I listened to her read and waited for the tap tap tap of Blind Pew and the light fairy laughter of Cowslip and Parsley. She could do all the voices. We dressed my doll Suzanna for the ball in a fold of Mama's shawl—Mama knew all the most interesting places a doll could go and what she would say when she got there. Sometimes we studied the photograph of my brother Randolph, who'd died of diphtheria just after I was born and would never be more than three years old. The picture was taken before he was buried and Mama had hired an artist to paint open eyes over his closed ones, but they didn't look the same as his real ones, she told me. Other times she played the piano and we sang as loud as we could, so Rudy and Papa could hear us down in the meadow.

Every day then, when I left for school,

Mama was on the davenport in the front
room. I knelt beside her so she could fix
my unruly hair in its tight braids. When I
came home again, she was there still, just
as I knew she'd be. Her arms would be
open, and she would be waiting for me to
bend close, to brush her hair, to draw a tiny
heart with ink on her arm, to bet with her
which marble I would hit. She would be
waiting for me to draw the paper clothes
that she would then cut out for my paper
dolls, waiting for me to get us milk and
brown sugar sandwiches from the kitchen.
Every bit of her was there, just waiting for
me.

They tried to come in, those women with
their rhubarb and their kuchens and their
potato salads. They wanted her too. But I
wouldn't let them. She was mine, all mine.

———

"Did you hear Amanda Starkey's in the
bin?" Ramona Mueller asked, the next time
Clement Owens stopped in.

"The bin?"

"You know, St. Michael's Sanatorium.

You seemed to be acquainted, so I thought you'd want to know." She looked at him expectantly, ready for questions, but he disappointed her.

"That's too bad," was all he said as he took his pile of envelopes from her hands.

The news troubled Clement. He wished the postmistress had kept it to herself. Although, why should he care, after all? He had nothing to do with Amanda now. He stood near his car, slitting the envelopes open with a pocketknife—an inferior one, since he'd lost the good one with the silver monogrammed case.

Had the craziness been there, underneath the neat nurse's uniform, all along? She'd seemed so transparent, with her heart on her sleeve, with her quick blush and easy laugh. She'd been amazed by the simplest things: a glass of champagne, a bunch of violets. And all the while she'd been hiding craziness. She had shown herself to him as one thing, and now she turned out to be another. He cranked the car and got in, slamming the door hard behind him. Well, she wasn't going to get him to feel sorry for her this way.

He sat for a moment, listening to the

soothing rumble of the engine. After all, it must have been hard for her. All those deaths, the parents, then the sister. Anyone might crack.

Amanda

I see I haven't said enough. I thought I might omit this part, let it settle silently into the muck where it belongs, but it seems that isn't possible. People want to hear everything, don't they? Spy every strap and pin and hem. It's not enough for them to run a finger along the scar or even to see the knife slice the skin, they must hear the blade purring against the whetstone. All right, then, if that's the way it has to be.

We met because Private Buckle was delirious. Poor Private Buckle—he'd not even got over there yet, had only reached Camp Grant when the Army discovered a limp and shipped him home. But a fever had stopped him before he'd gone a hundred miles. So here he was at the hospital, delirious, thrashing his arms and kicking his legs, whipping his head back and forth against the pillow and saying terrible things.

I was having an awful time with him. I'd get a compress on his forehead and he'd tear it off. I'd get his arms settled, and his legs would start up.

Obviously, I was busy, so I didn't see the man until he was standing on the other side of Private Buckle's bed, holding the patient's feet quiet, while I struggled with his head. The man's skin had a red cast to it, almost as if he had more blood than his body could hold, and his hands around Private Buckle's ankles were very large and steady. He smiled at me reassuringly and somehow, working his way slowly up from the feet, moving his hands in little circles and talking softly, he managed to soothe Private Buckle, almost to hypnotize him.

"There we go," he said when the private lay barely twitching beneath the sheet, the compress firmly on his forehead, his breathing calm and his heart rate steady.

"Are you a new doctor?" I asked.

"A doctor? Oh, no." He laughed. Just then Dr. Nichols came onto the ward.

Seeing the director made me nervous.

We'd never explicitly been told not to let strangers handle patients, but I was pretty sure the hospital wouldn't encourage it. Dr. Nichols was smiling, however. He clapped the man on the back.

"What brings you here today, Owens?" he asked, and they shook hands and went off together.

Later that afternoon, while I was drinking my coffee and eating an anise cookie in the cafeteria, the man appeared again.

"This," he announced, setting a brown box on my table, "will revolutionize medicine." He pulled a chair out and swung it around, so he could sit on it backward, resting his elbows on the cane back.

"What is it?" Clearly I was supposed to ask.

"It's a vacuum box. You put your instruments in here, your scalpels and scissors and needles and what have you." He dropped my spoon into the box. "Then seal it up like this." He worked a lever that looked like the latch on a pickle jar. "And then activate the vacuum for thirty seconds." He flipped a switch and a tiny red light on the top lit up. "That's how you know it's on. And then, when you take your instruments out again, they're perfectly sterilized."

"Wouldn't a good scrub or some alcohol work just as well?" I took my spoon back and wiped it with my napkin.

"You have to understand the science. You see, when the air molecules are removed, the germs just can't stick to the metal. The effect lasts much longer than if they'd been wiped off with alcohol—we've proven it—and there's no danger of recontamination with a dirty cloth." He was so certain, so enthusiastic, he seemed almost like a child.

"So are we going to start using those here?"

"Oh, you know, they have to do all sorts of tests, but I'm sure it's only a matter of time." He stroked the top of the box fondly.

"I'm afraid I didn't get your name this morning," I said finally. "Is it Owen?"

"It's Owens, the last name is. Clement is my given name."

I gave my own name then and held out my hand, which he shook rather too vigorously.

He offered to get me a second cup of coffee, but while he was at the counter, I realized my break had ended five minutes before. No time to make apologies, I told myself. As I hurried out the door, I saw him arranging a whole plateful of cookies, ladies' fingers and lemon icebox and more anise. It seemed that we would probably never meet again.

We met because of Private Buckle and then I killed my parents. Had I mentioned that? No, I thought I hadn't. Of course, I didn't mean to kill them, but in a case of death, how much does intent really matter?

I killed them because I felt a little fatigued and suffered from a slight, persistent cough. Thinking I was overworked and hadn't been getting enough sleep, I went home for a short visit, just a few days to relax in the country while the sweet corn and the raspberries were ripe. From the city I brought fancy ribbon, two boxes of chocolate, and a deadly gift from Private Buckle. I gave the influenza to my mother, who gave it to my father, or maybe it was the other way around.

When I saw the fever on my mother's

cheeks, I made Mathilda take Ruthie to the island, although for all I knew it was already too late.

"But it's so lonely there," she said.

"Better lonely than dead," I told her. It was important to be efficient, to be blunt. "Think of Ruthie."

I was a good nurse, as I've said, and I brought all of my training to bear. I followed the doctor's orders to the letter, even though I needed no instructions; I knew the course. I forced spoonfuls of honeyed tea and chicken broth between their lips to give them strength. I dosed them with quinine at eight, at twelve, at four, at eight again, day and night. I opened the windows in their room for fresh air. I tucked the quilts tightly around them to make them sweat. I changed the linens twice a day, more often when the blood from their noses began to stain the pillow slips.

"Mathilda?" my mother said as I bathed her face with a warm cloth.

I assured her she would see Mathilda later, when she was better.

"Where's Mattie?" my father demanded, throwing the blankets to the floor.

I tried to explain about contagion, about

how she was safe with Ruth, about how they would see her once they recovered. But they were delirious with fever. They refused to understand. "Mathilda," they called. "Mattie!" Finally, when their skins had turned pale blue for lack of air, I pretended.

"Yes, Mama. Yes, Papa," I said. "I'm here."

My mother smiled then. My father sighed and relaxed. They were comforted.

I wonder now if, in some way, I thought I could be Mathilda after that. I wonder if I thought I could act like her at least, with her charm and her daring. If so, I should have known better. Of course, I didn't think about any of that then. I only thought to ease their suffering, to help them heal, to be a good nurse.

I did everything right. Everything. But it meant nothing. They got away from me. Their lungs full of fluid, they drowned in their bed, first my mother, then my father. I was helpless to hold them back.

Mathilda and I buried our parents on an Indian summer day in Nagawaukee's graveyard, under the lurid, mocking sugar maples. Neighbors and friends had been with us all morning, but now, on the way home, their buggies turned off one by one onto other roads, until there was no one else, either before or behind, and we were alone. At the gate, I jumped down and fumbled with the new latch.

"Here, like this," Mathilda said, coming up beside me. Her eyes were so red and swollen that she could barely see, but the gate opened easily under her fingers. In all those months I'd been away, the house and the farm had become hers.

I knew exactly what was in the kitchen, since I'd taken each dish at the door. There was white bread, brown bread and pumpernickel. There was hot potato salad, cold potato salad, scalloped potatoes and sweet potatoes. There was venison, corned beef, a ham, a turkey, two chickens and a duck. There was tongue, pork sausage, white sausage, blood sausage and braunschweiger. There were hard rolls and sweet rolls, cherry preserves, cauliflower in cream, leeks in cream, creamed corn, sugared carrots, sauerkraut, pickled beets, apple pie, pumpkin pie and tapioca pudding. The door of the icebox would hardly close and bowls and plates hung precariously over the edges of the kitchen table and covered the counter and the seat of every chair. A dozen pears, a rhubarb pie and a jar of tomatoes had found their way into the front room and three cheeses and a tin of molasses cookies congregated on my mother's daybed in the back.

"Can I make anyone a sandwich?" I asked.

"Oh, throw it all away!" Mathilda cried. "How can you stand to look at it?"

She ran upstairs, sobbing, and Rudy and Ruth and I stood not looking at each other.

"I bet Ruth is hungry, aren't you, honey?"

But Mathilda's behavior had upset her. She burst into tears and followed her mother.

"Eat something, Rudy," I said. "No point in letting it go to waste."

My father disapproved of wasting food. He sucked marrow from bones. He ate skin and tendons and gristle, and he expected us to do the same. We were not allowed to "spoil our supper" by eating between meals but once, when I was seven, I was so hungry I opened the icebox. Just looking at some food, I thought, might ease my stomach. In a back corner, behind the meat and the butter, there was a little cup of something thick, rich and white. A week or two before, my mother had made a vanilla custard that was so sweet and creamy I had licked my spoon until all I could taste was the silver. Could this portion have been forgotten? And if it had been forgotten, who would notice if I took just one little bite?

I reached deep into the cool interior, slid my finger gently along the smooth surface and carried a tiny ridge of the whiteness back to my mouth. But as soon as my tongue touched my finger I knew it wasn't custard. It was something terrible—slimy and disgusting. I wiped my tongue on my sleeve and turned to go out to the pump to wash my hands. My father was standing in the doorway.

"What are you doing in the icebox?"

It was impossible to lie to my father. "I thought it was some custard, but it's gone bad or something."

"Your mother wouldn't keep bad food in the icebox," he said, reaching around me to pull the cup of white stuff out.

I had nothing to say to this. It was true that she was very careful, but it was also true that custard tasted awful.

"What have I told you about eating between meals?"

"It's wrong."

"How do you know your mother isn't planning to use this custard?" He frowned at the gully my finger had made.

"She forgot about it."

He looked at me sharply. He hated lying. Maybe she hadn't forgotten it. How did I know?

"You thought you'd just take it. Is that right? Steal it and spoil your supper. Stick your finger in it so it's no good to anyone else."

It was difficult to tell which of these he thought the worst offense. He was shaking the cup under my nose now. I turned my face away.

"No, I . . ." But what he said was true. I tried a different tack. "I was hungry."

He sighed. "You have to learn to control yourself, Amanda. Do you see me stealing food out of the icebox, spoiling my appetite so I can't eat my good supper?"

"No, Papa."

He slammed the cup down at my place at the table. Then he crossed to the drawer and took out a spoon and banged that down beside the cup. "You want this? You eat it. Now."

Even had it tasted good, I wouldn't have wanted it any longer. The idea of doing so blatantly what he had forbidden repelled me. My stomach tightened. My throat constricted. I felt sick.

"I can't."

"You should have thought of that before you stuck your grubby finger in it, shouldn't you? Now eat it." He took hold of my shoulders and pushed me down into my chair.

Slowly, I pushed the spoon into the white mass. It felt almost like ice cream, only not so cold and much more slippery. I lifted the spoon, tried not to breathe through my nose and stuck the stuff into my mouth. I swallowed as quickly as I could, but it stuck on my tongue. I forced it down in large spoonfuls, trying not to taste it, not to feel it in my mouth, not to think about what I was doing. My father watched, his arms crossed, waiting.

The tip of my spoon scraped the bottom of the cup when my mother walked in.

"Amanda! What are you doing? Henry? What is she doing?" She grabbed the cup away from me and stared at us.

"She started that custard. She's got to finish it," he said.

"Custard!" She thrust the cup in front of him. "This isn't custard, Henry! This is suet!" Now she banged the cup down on the table. "Didn't it taste awful?" she asked me. "What did you want to eat that for?"

"I didn't. I . . ." But I couldn't explain. I didn't want to put my father in the wrong. And really, he hadn't been wrong. I had disobeyed. I'd been stealing food out of the icebox. If it had really been custard, I probably would have eaten it. Probably I would have spoiled my supper, whatever that meant. My father was sniffing what remained in the cup now, frowning, as if he still didn't quite believe us.

Suddenly, my stomach gave a horrible turn. I ran out the kitchen door and into the woods behind the house. I was still retching under a honeysuckle bush when my father came up behind me. He handed me his handkerchief.

"I'm sorry, Amanda. I should have listened to you," he said. He tucked the damp strings of my hair behind my ears.

It made me want to squirm, his saying that. I tried to push the words away. "I shouldn't have been in the icebox," I said.

"Well, you won't do it again, will you?"

"Never ever!"

"That's my good girl."

I would have eaten that suet a hundred times over to hear those words.

———

I stepped into the hall now, took my father's jacket from its hook and slipped my arms into its sleeves. The cuffs dangled far below my hands. The jacket smelled of pipe tobacco and hay, molasses and grease, as all of his barn jackets had, ever since I could remember. I stuck my hands in the pockets—shreds of loose tobacco, two washers, a pencil stub, a list for the lumberyard—"eight 2x4s, four 4x6s, ten

2x8s," each number formed precisely, just the way he entered them in his ledger. He made his eights by drawing two balls, one on top of the other. "Like a snowman," he'd said to me as I sat on his lap, the pencil he'd just sharpened in my hand. I suppose he taught me to write, although I'd never given that a thought, believing it no more than my due as his child. I remembered his huge fingers wrapped around my tiny ones as he guided my hand—a hand I wouldn't even recognize as my own now—over the page, until we'd made all the numbers up to ten.

"Look at how she's going to town, Mother," he'd said.

Later, when he discovered I had his knack for figures, he showed me off every chance we got. "Mandy'll tote up the bill," he'd say. "Watch this." He'd hand me a slip with a column of numbers and in a second or two I'd announce the total. What I liked best, though, were the early mornings when we quizzed each other while we milked, just us and the cows in that big warm barn.

I took the jacket off, folded it, and set it

near the front door. Maybe Rudy could use it, or one of the Manigolds. I went upstairs to my parents' bedroom.

Mathilda refused to answer me when I knocked on her door. I could hear her singing "Lavender's Blue" to Ruth, her voice unconvincing, quavery, broken by sobs, while I sorted through the drawers, separating things to give away from things we ought to keep. My mother's dresses smelled of lavender water. She kept them perfectly, the sleeves and bodices stuffed with paper to hold their shape, old shawls draped over their shoulders to keep the dust off. It looked as if there were six copies of my mother in the wardrobe, each without a head. I was far too tall to wear those dresses, but perhaps Mattie would want one or two. I carried them to the attic and closed them in a trunk.

That night I woke up sweating, my heart racing.

"Good," I thought.

I hoped I, too, would be ill. I hoped I would die. How could I have brought such disaster on them and yet suffer hardly a cough myself? I writhed in my bed, desperate for the fever and delirium, the heavy

limbs and cloudy head that would over-
whelm the sharp, clear picture of what had
happened, the irrevocable fact that they
were no more, not one, not the other, both
gone forever from the earth. But it was only
fear that made my heart beat faster. There
was no escape for me. I could not even
cry.

"I can't stay any longer," I told Mathilda
the next morning. "I have obligations."

I was ready. I had repacked my little bag
even before the funeral. No sense waiting
until the last minute, my mother always
said.

"You'll be fine," I told Mathilda. "Rudy
will help you."

Rudy drove me to the station and I
didn't look back, not once, although I
could feel Mathilda staring after me with
those red, swollen eyes, all the way to Nagawaukee.

Back in our mustard-colored room, Eliza
was kind. She brought me coffee while I
unpacked.

"I did the best I could for them," I told
her, and tried to tell myself. "Now I have to
get back to work. My sister doesn't understand how busy we are here."

Under the tissue in the top drawer of my dresser, I slipped my father's list of lumber and my mother's hairbrush in which a few strands of her hair were tangled. Again, I woke at night in a panic. I was going to have to start my life all over again from scratch, I thought. There was nothing behind me now, nothing to stand on. And then I thought of Mathilda, and I clung to her image to right myself, to pull myself back to the surface.

In the daylight, it was better. I worked a day shift and, at the hospital, wounded men clamored for my attention. I had to remember dosages and schedules. I had to bandage and massage and produce soothing words. As if those things mattered! As if they would make any difference! I knew better now, but I did what I was supposed to do just the same. Were there others like me, who knew that all of our efforts were only a way to pass the time, to distract and comfort ourselves? I studied the faces of the doctors and nurses, even of the orderlies. Was I the only one who understood? "I don't care if you don't like it," my mother used to say when I complained about church or school. "You can act right." And that was true too. I could act right, and I did.

And so, although I was no longer so confident, no longer so sure of my every move as I had once been, I kept busy. I volunteered to take the worst patients, the most contagious, the most pitiable injuries, the men who threw their bedpans across the room in a fury. None of it bothered me.

I had been back only a few days and was running up the stairs from the dispensary when somewhere between the second and third floors I heard a familiar voice.

"Damn," he was saying. "Damn. Damn. Damn."

"What's the matter?" I hurried to turn the next landing. There I saw what the trouble was—papers everywhere, in ragged heaps and shingling the steps nearly to the top of the flight where Clement stood.

"Oh, dear," I said, or something sympathetic like that, but I couldn't help smiling a little as I bent to gather the pages that lay near me.

Clement stood still, looking down at me glumly. "One of the nurses asked me to take these to the basement on my way out."

"I don't think she meant for you to throw them."

"You don't say." He laughed. "And it seemed like such a good idea at the time."

He came several steps closer to me and began to collect the pages from the stairs. "This is going to take me hours to sort out! Do you see a folder for Zimmerman? Stuart? *O'Toole?*" He held up papers and dropped them again, one by one, to the floor.

"Well, you're not going to do it that way, are you?" I said. "Here. This won't be so bad." I cleared a few steps and began sorting the loose pages alphabetically, making neat piles. "Join in any time."

If not for me, I'm sure he would have buried Charles Bogusewski's ulcerated stomach in Peter Halliday's chart, and Peter's gassed lungs in Ronald Faculjak's chart. "No one's going to look at these things again, anyway," he said.

But I wouldn't permit such a thing. "Accurate record-keeping is essential," I told him, "even when the files are going to the basement. You'd be surprised how often doctors need to revisit the course of an illness."

I hadn't meant to be funny, but he laughed, and very soon we were talking and laughing more than filing. The things we said were too vacuous and nonsensical to bear repeating, even if I could remember them, but we put a great deal of effort into amusing each other. Certainly it was the most pleasant half hour I'd ever spent sorting papers. When we'd finished, I helped him carry the folders down to the records room, and there we spent another ten minutes, talking steadily, but not saying very much, until he asked, "Would you like to have dinner with me on Thursday?"

Eliza lent me her rabbit-fur stole. I wasn't ready at seven, what with the number of times we had to rearrange my unmanageable hair, but luckily he was late and we were watching out the window by the time he came down the street. Eliza assured me that the two-seater he was driving was a very good kind of car to have.

We drove all the way up to Appleton to eat at a supper club.

"This place has the best steak," he said. "You have to try it." He told the waiters how long a steak should be cooked and how much ice to put in a glass.

"I guess I'll have a cup of coffee," I said.

"Coffee! You don't want to ruin a meal like this with coffee! The lady'll have champagne."

"Clement, I couldn't!"

"Why not? You don't like it?"

"I've never had it, of course."

"Well, you've got to try champagne." And the waiter had already gone, so what could I do?

He was right. Now I knew why people liked a drink. My champagne was fizzy and almost sweet. Nothing like the whiskey my father used to swallow on cold winter nights.

After supper we went dancing. "Amy," he said, as the band played "The Blue Danube," and he waltzed me smoothly around the floor. "I'm going to call you Amy."

Such a light, pretty name. No one, not even Joe, had ever called me Amy before.

"It suits you," he went on. "It means love, you know, in French."

My face got hot, and I had to look at the floor, but I stored the moment up, so that later I could examine again and again just the way he said it, and recall the scent of starch on his shirt collar and the warm press of his hand against my back.

It turned out that we always drove far away when we went out. We went to Madison and Fish Creek and Racine and several times to Chicago. It was romantic, thrilling, to drive so fast along those long dark roads, to find out what lay behind those doors he ushered me through, his hand hovering a whisper from my waist, to dance in those dark places to colored music, to eat steaks and snails. I would get so tired that I would fall asleep on the way home.

Some evenings I said, "Why don't we just be cozy tonight, get a hamburger someplace close?"

And he'd say, "You want a hamburger, I know the best hamburger place in the country." And we'd wind up all the way in Fort Atkinson or Sheboygan or Fond du Lac.

It was just like with Joe, except better, since this time no one was saying "Hadn't you better think about this?" or "You're young, what's your hurry?" When my mother said those things, what she really meant was, it's all very well to be friends with Catholics, but you don't want to marry them. And what Joe's mother meant when she said, "Of course, she's a sweet girl, but sweet isn't everything," was that Lutherans make excellent neighbors but aren't fit to be wives. Clement, as far as I could tell, had no religion, and that suited me. When I thought of God, now, He was hovering somewhere over France, not paying any attention to me at all.

Generally, I wouldn't let a man put a hand on me if we weren't dancing, unless maybe he wanted a good-night kiss, but the first time Clement touched me, we were parked somewhere along the edge of Lake Michigan, water so vast, you couldn't see to the other side. That night he only ran his fingertips over my face—my eyelids, my cheeks, the outline of my lips— carefully, gently, yet firmly, as if he were painting my features on my face. Nobody ever did anything like that to me before. I wasn't sure how I was supposed to respond, so I waited to see what would happen next.

Nothing else did happen, for weeks it

seemed, until I was used to his fingers on my skin and, for all my shyness, I couldn't help tilting my chin up, ready for more, and then he put his fingertip just along my collarbone, just inside the edge of my dress, and then he kissed me, as light and melting and unsatisfying as spun sugar.

When he told me he loved me, I laughed. Not in a mean way, but lightly, warning myself really, more than him, not to take it too seriously. You have to be careful with your feelings, I think. It's a mistake to let them go just because they're summoned. But, like Mathilda, Clement was very good at getting his way. It wasn't too long before I gave in and let myself believe him, let myself love him back. It seemed like a sure thing. It felt just like it was supposed to. I began to think about what would happen sooner or later; I imagined the house with the spreading elm in the front yard, the sunny kitchen and the clean, white linens, the children, four or five, at least, with his rosy cheeks and my almond eyes. Of course, I would miss my work, but I was secretly a little pleased to see my proper course lay elsewhere.

I told him about the farm and the lake. I

told him how fresh and cool it all was in the summer, how clear and sparkling in the winter. I might have given the impression that every day there was a picnic, because I wanted to please him. And I suppose I wanted to please myself. It was a relief to pretend that everything was just as it should be, picture perfect, waiting for me to come home. I dreamed of the summer afternoon when we would row out to my island together. I imagined him leaping from the water like a pike, and how I would splash him and how he would splash me, and then how he would wrap his arms around me and pull me under the waves with him.

But I should have known better, for there were clues, if I'd cared to see them. One night we planned to go to Chicago, which usually meant dancing. I waited on the glider on the front porch, my hands in a sealskin muff.

"Where're you off to, all dolled up?" Thea Martins asked, passing me on her way out. She had a boyfriend who lived on the next block, and he was always asking her to meet him somewhere or other instead of picking her up like a proper date.

"Oh, wherever he takes me, I guess." Whenever you told Thea where you were going, she claimed to have been somewhere better the week before.

"Well, have a good time." She waved her hand behind her head as she hurried down the stairs.

Two men went in to pick up their dates, and then five girls came out together, all laughing, their breath making little clouds. My new cloth dancing slippers were pretty, but hardly appropriate for waiting outdoors in late October. I paced the porch a few times and then walked a few yards down the street in the direction from which Clement always came.

He lived on the east side, I knew that, although I realized I didn't know where exactly.

I told myself that if I went inside for a few moments, maybe ran upstairs to change my hankie, he would have come.

Eliza was lying on her bed, rereading *Jennie Gerhardt.* "Call his office," she said. "He's probably doing a deal." She said the words "doing a deal" disparagingly. She didn't like Clement's approach to business, the way he threw himself behind every new idea. She thought he ought to stick to one thing, tried and true. She also disapproved of the champagne.

We found the number he'd given me, and I went downstairs to use the telephone. I let it ring twenty times. Then I called again and let it ring twenty more. He's probably just down the hall, I thought. What if he answered just as I hung up? I called again and let it ring thirty times.

Eliza shut her book. "Get something to eat with me."

But I couldn't. How awful it would be when he showed up, if I wasn't there.

"Oh, you poor thing," Eliza said when she got back from her supper and found me still sitting by the window in our room. "You must be starving."

"No, I had a sandwich," I lied. I took off my new shoes and put them away in the closet.

"Well, I'm going to bed," she said. "There's no sense sitting up like this."

Before she turned out the light, Eliza said kindly, "You probably got the date wrong." But we both knew I hadn't. When I heard her breathing deeply, I couldn't help myself. I got out of bed and went back to my chair by the window, and that's where I finally fell asleep.

All that worry, wasted. The next afternoon Thea knocked on the door to our room.

"Visitor for you downstairs," she said and winked. "Looks to me like someone's sorry."

My cheeks went hot, and I stepped in front of the mirror for a moment.

"You look fine," Eliza said without glancing up from her book.

He was standing in the parlor, holding a large bunch of lavender tulips in front of his face. Those were expensive flowers in October. "I'm sorry, Amy," he said, peeking around them, pretending to be afraid of how I might look or what I might say.

"It's only that I thought you might have been hurt," I said, taking the flowers from him, "or worse." Although those were not, in truth, the only possibilities I had feared.

"It was an emergency," he said. "I'm an investor in a lead mine in Hazel Green, you know, and I had to go out there to look things over. The country needs lead now. I was doing my patriotic duty."

"But couldn't you have called?"

"And waked the whole house? You wouldn't want that."

"Next time," I said, "I'll sit right by the phone and pick it up, first ring. Then I won't worry you've been in an accident."

"No," he said, "I don't like the idea of your having to wait up. It isn't healthy. And you know, sometimes these meetings go so late, you can't imagine. And there isn't always a phone, Amy. That's the way my business is. I've got to go where the opportunity is. You understand that, don't you? You'll forgive me, won't you? That's a good girl."

With a war on, you see, people had to do things they wouldn't otherwise. That's what I told Eliza.

"Why isn't he in France," she asked, "if he's so crazy about patriotic duty?"

I knew how to answer that. One of those nights as we drove and drove, he'd told me how he'd tried to join more than a year before, that very first summer. Although he was nearly forty, he'd stood in line with the young fellows who could imagine nothing better to do with their youth, and the doctor had turned him away.

"I guess my heart's not what it should

be," he said. "They said it's because I had rheumatic fever once."

He looked away from me, out over the dark fields, as he told me this, as though it were a difficult thing to admit. It made me love him more to think that, while he knew so much and could do so much, he was fragile inside.

The war ended, but Clement was still busy. The next time he stood me up, he'd been doing a real estate deal in Oshkosh. "You've got to stay and have a drink, or they'll think you've cheated them," he said, and he lay a dozen apricot-colored roses in my arms. What he said seemed likely enough. What did I know about business?

"Roses should be red," Eliza said, but what did she know about roses?

"Anyone can find a red rose," I said, arranging them as well as I could in my tooth cup. "These are special. They bring them by train all the way from New York." I had to prop them against the wall to keep the cup from tipping over, but they made the mustard of our room seem a rich, warm gold and they lasted almost a week.

The time after that I left the porch when an hour had passed and had a bowl of soup in the drugstore and then took myself to a movie. It was so difficult, always having to explain to Eliza.

What was a night waiting here or there? It wasn't as if I had anything better to do. And he did. He had important things to do, and if, now and again, he couldn't leave them just to have a good time with me, well, how could I complain? I knew he would rather have been with me. He loved me so much, you see. That's what he said, and it made me so happy to believe it was true.

And then the United States Army decided it wanted to see the vacuum box. He ran from his car up the walk that evening and bounded up the stairs. "I'm in, Amy! In!"

He wrapped me in his arms and swung me around. The cloud of breath that issued from his mouth smelled faintly of gin.

I tipped my head back and laughed. He was so excited, he'd forgotten to give me the pink carnations he held. I tugged at them playfully, and he laughed, too, and released them.

"In where?" I asked it so casually, expecting to hear about another partnership I wouldn't understand, another investment with the "smartest fellows" he'd ever met, an invention that did something I didn't know needed doing. I buried my nose in the flowers, such a sweet scent.

"In the Army!" he said. "They're going to use me, send me to Washington, maybe to France! Say, I bet you can't guess why."

"But the war's over," I said. I sat down again on the glider, and he sat beside me.

"I know, it's funny, isn't it? The war's over, and now the Army wants me. But you haven't guessed why," he said, and he put his arms around me and began to nuzzle my ear.

"Clement!" I pushed him away, embarrassed.

"Well, aren't you going to guess?" He looked hurt.

I tried to make it up to him, tried to come up with some reasonable or at least amusing answer, but my head was buzzing. My fingers picked absently at the string around the flower stems. I couldn't think.

"I can't guess," I said finally. "Tell me."

"They want the vacuum box! Isn't that amazing? They want to test it in Washington and then, if they like it, I'll help 'em.

We'll take it everywhere, all over the country and to Europe too! I can't believe it." He
was pacing back and forth on the porch
now, his shoes squeaking against patches
of hard-packed snow. "Here, let me help
you with that," he said, producing a silver
pocketknife and opening the blade. But he
could not hold still long enough to cut the
string. He gave the knife to me and began
to pace again. "But I *can* believe it," he
said, hammering the words down with
conviction. "I can believe it. Because I
know that this is a great thing, an important thing." He turned to me again, put his
hands on my shoulders and kissed me.

"When?"

"When what?"

"When do you go?"

"In a week. There's hardly time to get
everything together." He stopped, then,
and seemed finally to sense my mood. "So
tonight," he said, "you'll celebrate with me,
won't you?" He took my hand and pulled
me gently to my feet and drew me against
his coat. He pressed his mouth to my ear.
"It may be our last night for a long, long
time."

A light layer of snow made the tires hiss

against the road as we drove and drove
that night. When he tucked his arm around
my waist, I couldn't remember why I'd
never before slid tight against him. All
along I should have been holding on to him
as tightly as if there were no tomorrow.

We stopped at a roadhouse in Racine,
where I tried my first martini, and a tavern
in Kenosha, where I enjoyed my second,
and another place in Winnetka, where I
drank, but hardly tasted, my third.

As he steered me toward the door of a
plush Chicago hotel, a tall woman with almond eyes and a long, graceful neck,
smiled dreamily at me in the glass. "Look,"
I said, pointing at her, "so pretty."

In the room, while he rang for champagne, I thought the strangest thing. This
will show them, I thought. This is what
happens when they leave me all alone. It
almost made me cry, thinking that. But
then he hung up the phone and drew me to
the window to look at all the lights, and I
forgot that I was alone. Forgot entirely.

When it was over, I was frightened,
sorry. I couldn't look at him, knowing what
we'd done. I couldn't look at myself. I kept
my eyes on the whorls of a cabbage rose

patterned in the carpet. "We shouldn't have," I told the cabbage rose. I kept saying it over and over, sitting there on the side of the bed, bent over a pillow clutched tight over my lap. "We shouldn't have."

But he draped the sheet gently over my shoulder. He was so dear. He took all the blame on himself. He loved me so, he said. He couldn't help himself, he said, couldn't I understand that? He begged me to forgive him, and of course I did. I understood.

"It's all right," I said at last. "Of course it's all right. We'll get married now. Tomorrow morning. Or tonight, maybe even tonight, there might be someone . . ."

"You know it's impossible," he said, shaking his head sadly as he stroked my hair.

"Well, tomorrow morning, then. Tomorrow will certainly be all right."

"I thought you understood," Clement said. "I thought you knew. I'm married already."

Chapter Five

———

Clement and Theresa Owens lived with their three children in a brick house on Prospect Avenue with high ceilings and pink globes around the new electric lights and a door knocker shaped like an angel.

Very early Sunday morning, Clement felt the smooth skin of Amanda's thigh press against his own. He awoke suddenly and threw the blanket back.

"What is it?" Theresa mumbled.

"Must be those stuffed peppers you made me eat last night. I told you peppers don't sit well with me."

Clement took himself downstairs to recover.

Dawn found him in the kitchen, sipping coffee and staring out at the ripening day.

A light was on in the big house next door, and occasionally Clement's glance would be drawn across the strip of side lawn and through the hedge that separated his house from his neighbors'. He watched the neighbors' cook bend over to pull something from the oven and felt suddenly hungry.

Amy had been a mistake in the end, he thought, lighting the oven. Of course, none of them were ever pleased when he broke it off. One had laughed unpleasantly, he remembered that. A couple had railed, but most cried. He was good with tears. He wasn't hardhearted. He felt bad for them. But they all knew as well as he did that the fun had to end sometime. Sometimes he wasn't even the one to call it off. He didn't like when that happened, but he never made a fuss—a lady had to consider her own situation. But poor Amy. Thinking he would marry her! Where had she got that idea? Hadn't he been perfectly clear all along? Well, if not perfectly clear, clear enough for any reasonable person to see what was what. He sighed, feeling vaguely that she had wronged him with her expectations, and slid two thick slices of bread into the oven to toast.

He'd been hoping to see her again, obviously. How else explain what he'd done, convincing Theresa that this particular lake near this particular town was the only possible place to build a summer house? Why a summer house at all, for that matter? He swallowed some coffee and winced at the bitterness.

Of course, it hadn't been like that exactly, he reminded himself, spooning sugar into his cup. He wasn't such a fool as that. He had simply gone to Nagawaukee one day out of idle curiosity, or so he told himself, thinking he would take a look at the place she'd told him so much about. Nothing wrong with looking, was there? And then, well, anyone with imagination could see the possibilities. Advertising copy had run through his head—the pretty lakes strung together like sapphires, or nestled like robin's eggs among the green hills. In a nearby town there was even a spa.

Clement checked his toast, toffee-colored on one side, perfect. He turned the slices over and shut the oven door, careful

not to make noise. The Schumachers had
bought a place out there and so had the
Koches and the Steinmans. Brewers and
bankers and lumber barons were buying
and building all over the area. Once he'd
shown Theresa the fieldstone mansion the
Schumachers had built on Lake La Belle,
she was willing to let him have the money
for several choice plots, long stretches of
lakefront property that up until now had
been wasted on cows. Reselling this land
to people who liked the idea of owning an
"estate," a place where they could be connected to the salt of the earth, the fresh,
open air, and an aquatic playground, would
be simple. He would keep some of it, some
to develop, some to rent—there was no
reason why only those who could afford to
buy should have access to such a para-
dise—and he had chosen one twelve-acre
plot for his family.

He'd got a deal on that particular site,
since the slope on the property that bordered the lake was alarmingly steep and
the only spot for a house was a little too
close to the water. And then, too, there
were more fashionable lakes and more de-
sirable locations even on Nagawaukee it-

self. But those drawbacks pleased him—it never made sense to buy at the top. You made money only when you could see what others couldn't. And he could see that spread. He would put the land to work—which was another reason not to pick the sort of neighborhood where enterprise was frowned upon. He planned to do some farming, maybe produce cheese— some people in Janesville were having excellent luck with a white cheddar—or raise angora goats. And he planned to build an impressive house.

His idea was a sort of Greek temple, with white pillars rising from the wide front porch to the roof. Because of the hill, the house would have to be narrow, but that was no matter since no one would see it from the side anyway. It was the facade that counted, and the facade would be grand. He would put a white lattice gazebo on the front lawn, and friends would gather there—men in cream-colored suits and women with parasols, their gauzy summer dresses rippling in the breeze off the lake.

The architect had tried to talk him into something more modest, something retiring in browns and greens, a Swiss chalet set back in the woods, furnished in rustic pine. "Perhaps," the architect had suggested, "you might make some of the furniture yourself." Clement was not one to scoff at a suggestion. He liked the notion of himself sawing through the sweet-smelling wood, building fine, sturdy pieces his family would wear smooth for generations. He even went so far as to consult a man at the lumberyard, who sketched a small chest and made him a list of wood and tools. And then one afternoon he took his youngest son, Arthur, into the backyard for company, and managed to cut the bottom of the chest and two sides, before ruining three boards and gashing his index finger.

He told the architect he would not be making his own furniture and insisted on his original plan. What good was a house people couldn't see? Theresa agreed. In fact, she'd had ideas far better than the architect's to Clement's mind. She understood the purpose of the house, the way the wind had to sing through it from end to end, the way the porch had to invite picnickers in off the lake at noon and command the sunset at the cocktail hour.

She'd suggested the house be three stories, with spacious attics, as well. She sketched the kitchen in a separate building, connected to the dining room by a breezeway to keep the main house cool. She insisted they also buy two lots to the east, so as to have plenty of space for a boathouse and land for Maynard or Avis or Arthur, maybe all three, to build houses for themselves. That was the way people did it, she said. He knew what she meant by "people"—the kind of people who would be putting him up for their clubs.

Well, all's well that ends well, Clement assured himself, spreading a thick layer of butter on his toast. If he'd never known Amanda, he'd never have found this place, this new setting that had invigorated him, made him feel like a young man, full of promise all over again.

The cook came into the kitchen, tying her apron around her waist. "Up early again, Mr. Owens?"

"The early bird gets the worm, Trudy." Clement took a large bite from his buttered toast, as if to prove his point. Then he poured her a cup of coffee from the pot and added some to his own.

"Well, if it's worms you want, you'd better get out in the yard," Trudy said, pulling out the flour bin. "I'm making popovers."

"One of these days I just might do that," Clement said. Carrying his coffee with him, he went upstairs to bathe.

It was that damn vacuum box, he thought, while the water rushed into the tub. If that had been a success, his thoughts would never have gone back to Amanda. You'd think he'd never failed before, the way that disaster had got under his skin. And Theresa—he frowned at himself in the mirror, was his hair getting thin at the temples?—a wife was supposed to support you, not continually remind you with patronizing sighs that it was her money you were spending and that she'd always said this or that was a foolish risk. Amanda had not thought the vacuum box was foolish. She understood its potential, and she was a nurse, which ought to count for something. She appreciated his other projects, too. He remembered her asking about the lead mines. Did they use canaries there? she wanted to know. That was the night she squealed when the waiter brought the caviar to the table. But she'd tried it when he urged her, and she'd liked it when he said she should. He eased himself into the hot water, thinking what a pleasant thing it was to spend an evening with a woman like that, a woman who really believed in you.

But in that dim post office, she was not at all as he'd remembered her. He would never have imagined she'd still be angry, not after more than a year, but there wasn't an ounce of friendship in the way she looked at him. She'd looked older, too, and thin in the cheeks, which was not, as he considered it now, unattractive on her. If he could've touched her face, he thought, or even her hand, it would have been better, it would have brought her back to him, but that was impossible with Theresa in the car just outside and that woman watching from behind the counter.

And what was Amy doing with that little girl? In his mind, Amanda still wore her tidy nurse's apron all day and sat demurely on the glider of the nurses' residence at night.

Through the door, Clement could hear his wife, sliding the chair back from her dressing table, opening the drawer in which she kept her combs and her hatpins, preparing for morning Mass. He knew just how Theresa looked, holding her back very straight as she sat before the mirror, brushing her hair deliberately.

"Theresa! I'm out of soap!" he called, wrapping the bar he'd been about to use in the washcloth and pushing it under his knee.

"In the little table," she said, and he heard the dressing-room door close behind her. Did she expect him to stand shivering and dripping in the middle of the bathroom, searching through drawers? What if he really had been out of soap?

But it would serve him right if she never wanted to do anything for him again, wouldn't it? Clement began to scrub himself. The idea that he'd been chasing a woman who turned out to be a lunatic scared him a little. Well, it was over now, all of that. Theresa would see that from now on things would again be the way they'd once been between them.

This is a lesson for me, he told himself, a warning. From now on I'm faithful to my wife.

Saying that always made him feel optimistic. He sighed and lay back in the soothing warm water. He closed his eyes and draped a wet washcloth over his face to soften his beard. He began to think about that camera that took pictures of bones right through the skin. Couldn't that be used somehow in mining?

Avis Owens, sixteen years old, padded down the hall wearing the robe and slippers in which Clement had, on one recent uncomfortable morning, mistaken her for a woman. Maynard, eighteen, groaned, stuffed his face in his pillow and then, in one dramatic desperate movement, threw off his blankets and swung his bare feet onto the floor.

Arthur, six, came to full wakefulness as the water splashed into the washstand that stood against one wall of the room he shared with his brother. He stayed still with his eyes closed, listening to the hangers scraping along the rod and the dresser drawers sliding open and not being banged shut. When Maynard left the room, Arthur got out of bed and went in his pajamas to squat beside his city of blocks. He did his best work in the morning, while the bolt on the bathroom door slid open and shut, open and shut, the water rushed through the pipes, feet galloped down and up and down the stairs, china clinked in the kitchen, and finally the front door slammed and slammed and slammed.

And then, for a time, the morning's noises lulled and the only sound in the house, as the shaft of sunlight across the bedroom floor headed steadily toward the closet, was Arthur's faintly adenoidal breathing and the dense click of the wooden blocks. Just after eight chimes on the front-room clock, his mother's slippers shuffled along the hallway floor, and then she would be standing over him, stretching her arms like a cat and afterward retying the belt on her housecoat. Hiking the housecoat up, she'd sit on her heels beside Arthur on the floor and move blocks purposefully about, as if she knew where they were supposed to go. He let her put them wherever she wished, although of course he had to move them later. Finally, when she was bored with her efforts at play, she swooped over him with a kiss. He smelled her coffee-laced breath and her sweetly lotioned hands. At last, their day would truly begin.

Theresa had left the raising of Maynard

and Avis when they were young and uninteresting to nursemaids, but Arthur was different, or perhaps she was, and she dreaded September when he would start school, and she would no longer be able to have him with her all day.

This morning, after church, they were going to pay a call on a Mrs. Herman Kessler, who'd promised to make a contribution toward the new public library. Theresa knew that people who gave money liked to see a thankful recipient rather than send their check through the anonymous post. At 62 Newberry Street, they were shown into a bright parlor where Mrs. Kessler and her friend Mrs. Jones were leafing through a sheaf of watercolors.

"Look at this one!" Mrs. Kessler commanded, holding for Theresa to admire a roiling seascape, in which blues, greens and grays had been mingled to form a sort of mud. "I don't know where my Charlotte gets her talent. I can't draw worth a stick and Herman can hardly sign his name."

"It's lovely," Theresa said.

"Remarkable," Mrs. Jones concurred.

"The way she's captured the feeling!"

Mrs. Kessler said, holding the painting at arm's length and squinting in an attempt to bring some aspect, any aspect, of the picture into focus. "That's the mark of a true artist."

Theresa politely agreed. And then, since she'd met Mrs. Kessler and Mrs. Jones when they were serving on several Red Cross committees during the war, they discussed when they'd last seen and what they'd last heard about this woman and that, and laughed about the day they'd shoveled three hundred pounds of peach pits for the gas masks, while Arthur had nothing to do but take a cookie whenever it was offered and turn the pages of a picture book he'd brought along.

"You know, I think we saw your daughter last week at the Milwaukee Turners," Mrs. Jones said finally to Theresa. "Do I remember rightly that her name is Avis?"

Arthur began to listen then. It always seemed strange to him that people he'd never seen before should know his sister and brother.

"How good of you to remember," Theresa said.

"She was with another young lady," Mrs.

Kessler said. "A girl with an unfortunate nose."

"Meta Kunkel. Yes, it's really too bad about her nose."

"I'm sure she's a lovely girl," Mrs. Kessler said, with the complacency of one whose daughter's nose was straight and neat.

"She's not a girl I would choose as a friend for Avis, but one's children don't always do just what one would like, do they?"

Theresa thought Meta was awkward, loud and humorless, and unlikely to attract the sort of people she wished Avis would associate with. In particular, she wanted Avis to show more interest in the young men of her social circle. It upset her to see her daughter—with so many opportunities and so much talent (although Avis had never seen a body of water larger than Lake Michigan, *her* seascapes really did capture the sense of the ocean)—squander her chances for happiness. Still, Theresa comforted herself, Avis could be quite pretty when she got herself up. Surely she would grow into a more appropriate attitude.

Mrs. Kessler sipped her tea and didn't answer, but her look above her teacup was pitying and smug.

"Maynard," Theresa said, "my older son, has got a very good position. He's with the First Bank, you know. And the things they have him do! Really, it makes me nervous sometimes to think of all that money."

Of course, Maynard did not yet have any real responsibility. He mostly carried papers from one office to another for bank officers to sign. But they were very important papers. And the vice-president was always assuring him that he would go far.

"So he's not going to college?" Mrs. Kessler said, biting a lady's finger carefully so the powdered sugar wouldn't fly.

"Well, no. He didn't see the point. You see, he worked at the bank as an errand boy in the summers, and when he graduated from St. John's, they offered him this job right away."

"I'm not saying he needs the education. Goodness knows, my Freddy came out of Yale as stupid as he went in, but it's the friends you make, the society. You can't expect him to get ahead unless he knows the right people."

"Probably he'll go to college in a year or two," Theresa said rashly. "I wouldn't be surprised."

A significant look passed between Mrs. Kessler and Mrs. Jones, whose son would be a junior at the U. of C. that fall, and Theresa could see that she had somehow shown herself to a disadvantage.

Mrs. Jones opened a fresh subject. "I understand you're building a summer place."

"Yes," Theresa answered warily. What would they make of a too narrow house on a too steep slope on the wrong side of the wrong lake?

"Oh, I wish I could convince Herman to do that," Mrs. Kessler said. "You can't get away from the smell of the river here in the summertime. It's simply unbearable. But he won't leave the city. You miss too many opportunities, he says, when you're away. That's all very well for him, but what opportunities would I miss? He doesn't give a thought to Charlotte. She doesn't see why we should have to stay in town—especially when all of her friends go. 'If we must stay, we have to have a place on Lake Michigan,' I tell Herman. But he won't do that either. 'This house was good enough for my father,' he says, 'and it's good enough for me.' So here we are, completely dependent on the good graces of relatives and friends who have summer places." She smiled at Theresa.

"We would love to have you stay with us as soon as the house is ready," Theresa said. "We'll be joining the yacht club and the tennis club, and I know Avis and Maynard would be delighted to take Charlotte with them to the various functions." In fact, Avis was dead set against joining any clubs she judged "hoity-toity," and Maynard had never managed to get the knack of tennis, but Theresa trusted that these minor hitches would solve themselves, once she got her family into a new setting, where their true personalities had room to flower. She was counting on this house also to rectify one major problem—the waywardness of her husband. Already she could see a change in Clement. He arrived home promptly every evening so that they could pore over the blueprints together. He described his plans to her with the same excitement he'd shown when they were first courting, and he was eager to hear how she'd receive them. And he knocked on her bedroom door frequently. Yes, he'd certainly come back to her, and she was convinced that this new project, for which he welcomed her ideas as well as her money, just as he'd done in the early days, would keep him close.

Later, when Theresa paused on the steps of the Kesslers' house and released Arthur's hand so that she could fold the check and slip it into her purse, she decided that the visit had been satisfactory overall. That the house was all right was a particular relief. She hadn't been sure before this. Clement had been sure, but then he was positive about every one of his schemes—his enthusiasm meant nothing. But Florence Kessler wouldn't approve just anything nor would Alice Jones.

Now Theresa felt free to imagine her family there—Arthur pushing a toy sailboat along the shore with a stick, his knees grass-stained, and his hair grown sweetly shaggy; Maynard, at the tiller of a real sailboat, squinting up at the bright white canvas, maybe even winning a regatta and then presenting her with the silver cup; Avis sitting with a nice boy, a friend of

Maynard, perhaps, in the gazebo the final hour of Sunday evening, enjoying the agony of the thought that they wouldn't see each other again for at least a week.

And she and Clement? Too soon, too soon, she thought. She didn't dare count on it. But she kept the notion warm, like a seed beneath the frost line.

At four o'clock each day Theresa and Arthur took a nap together on the cool satin comforter that covered her bed. Before they fell asleep, each would lie listening to the quiet, steady breathing of the other, watching the afternoon shadows slowly stain the ceiling. Sometimes Arthur would rest his head on Theresa's stomach and wonder at the continuous gurgle that no one but he could hear.

At five-thirty Arthur went out to sit on the stone front steps to wait for Clement to come home. He couldn't be dissuaded from this duty, even in the worst weather. When it rained or hailed, he stood close to the house, under the overhang that protected the front door. When it was sunny or snowy, he amused himself while he waited by jumping from step to step. Sometimes he ranged over the entire yard, using the steps only as a base. Always, though, he kept the street strictly in sight, for he worried that, if he did not, his father might not come safely home, and he knew his father ought to come home, even though he sometimes wished he wouldn't.

Chapter Six

On the advice of Pastor Jensen, Carl had arranged for Hilda Grossman, a second cousin once removed on his father's side, to come from Tomahawk to do the house-work and keep an eye on Ruth while Amanda was at St. Michael's. Hilda had made clear that she was not entirely pleased with the arrangement.

"I'll say it straight out, Carl," she'd said, dropping her carpetbag so that it fell at her feet with a thump. "I know there was something funny going on in this house. You might think we're ignorant up in Toma-hawk, but we hear things. Another one mightn't have come, but you're in a fix and family's family, so here I am." She crossed

her arms over the hills of her bosom and
waited for him to answer.

"What do you mean, something funny?"

"I don't know, but I do know that a decent woman doesn't hide on an island for
months, not speaking to another soul, and
I also know that a decent woman drowns
in broad daylight, when everyone can see
what's what, not in secret in the middle of
the night. That's what I know."

Carl narrowed his eyes, as if trying to
sharpen his vision. "I don't understand.
What are you driving at?"

"I'm not saying anything more. Gossip is
wicked. That's how I was taught. I just
wanted to make my position clear."

But she'd only made things more murky
for Carl. What had happened while he'd
been away? He should have pressed
Amanda when he'd had the chance; asking
her now was out of the question. That night,
in his room, Carl searched the photograph
of Mathilda that stood on his nightstand. He
picked it up by the frame and shook it, trying . . . what? . . . to make her speak, to
change her expression? She smiled on,
looking as if she meant to live forever.

For the first week or two after Amanda went away, Ruth was restless. She wandered from room to room, stopping to stare out of every low-silled window. She picked up objects as she went, light, little things—her blanket, her bear, a spoon, a stocking from Amanda's drawer—and she dropped them absently along her way, so that by the end of the day the house was strewn with litter. And she cried, although really the sound was more of a whimper, a weak keening that seemed to hover at the base of her throat, spilling out at the least provocation and often with no provocation at all and was unstanchable once begun.

Once or twice Hilda patted her lap and held out her arms to the little girl. "Come to Hilda, now," she said, smiling reassuringly at Carl. But Ruth turned away, would not even come close. Hilda, embarrassed, seemed to close her heart against Ruth then. "There's no pleasing some people," she said, standing abruptly and brushing her lap away.

Carl held Ruth and rocked her, but never for long. She slipped from his arms and out of his lap like quicksilver, and he was unable to arrest her drift until she fell asleep in some corner, exhausted.

And then one day at breakfast she held out her glass in both hands.

"What do you say?" he prompted, lifting the milk pitcher.

When she said nothing, only thrust her glass forward again, he realized that he hadn't heard her speak a word in days.

"Ruthie, what do you say?" he repeated, more sternly this time.

Still she said nothing.

"I'd like some milk, please," he said.

Ruth gave the table one smart rap with the bottom of her glass.

"That's enough, Ruthie." He set the pitcher back on the table and reached to take the glass out of her hands. It was impossible to say, really, what happened next. Did she drop it deliberately or only release her hold before his grip was firm? In any case, the glass hit the floor with a crash.

Hilda came down to breakfast as he was sweeping up.

"Ruth doesn't get anything today unless she asks for it properly, Hilda," he said, dumping the shards into the wastebasket. "She knows how to talk."

"I understand," Hilda answered, pouring coffee into her cup as if the kitchen were her own. She seemed almost pleased, Carl thought, at the chance to punish Ruth, and it made him think better of his words.

"I don't mean you should starve her."

Hilda looked at him thoughtfully and took a sip of her coffee. "You let females walk all over you, Carl, you know that? Even this little thing here. You don't do her no favors, letting her have her way."

Her talking like that made him angry, but maybe she was right, about Ruth anyway. What did he know about raising a little girl? He worried about her, losing two mamas, no wonder she wasn't acting right, but what could he do about it? Hilda knew best, he thought, he hoped, as he hurried out to the barn.

At noon Hilda made a cheese sandwich and held it out to Ruth on a plate. When the little girl reached for it, Hilda lifted it high. "What do we say?"

Ruth began to whimper.

"Crocodile tears won't get you nowhere with me, young lady." Hilda took a bite out of the sandwich and chewed it deliberately as Ruth began to shriek.

Hilda set the sandwich down and rummaged through a drawer. When she turned to face Ruth again, she was holding a wooden spoon. "I'll give you something to cry about." She grabbed Ruth by the arm and landed three or four good smacks on Ruth's bottom.

"That'll learn you." She picked Ruth up around the waist, carried her upstairs, deposited her in her room and shut the door.

Hilda made supper for them every night, usually boiled potatoes and some piece of meat, cooked until it had relinquished the very last of its juices.

"She isn't even properly trained," she complained, spreading mustard onto her potato with her knife.

"What do you mean? Trained in what?" Carl usually kept his head down as they ate, so as not to have to watch her chew, but he looked up now, puzzled.

"You know. Trained."

When Carl, still uncomprehending, shook his head, Hilda blushed and lowered her eyes. "You know. She wets herself."

It was such a relief to see Hilda looking

that way, disconcerted, unformidable, that Carl laughed. And amazingly Hilda laughed too.

"It's nothing to laugh at," she protested, but she was still smiling. For a few brief moments they looked at each other, struck by the difference, but neither knew how to go on.

"Well, what do we do about it?" Carl asked finally.

"I guess I know how to train a child."

Hilda's training method consisted of not allowing Ruth to change her panties when she wet them. And, of course, that meant she wasn't allowed to sit down anywhere in the house.

"You have to learn to live with your mistakes," Hilda said.

Ruth took to hiding her wet underthings and wearing nothing under her skirt for the rest of the day.

"I'm sorry to have to tell you this, Carl," Hilda said, meeting him at the back door the day she discovered Ruth's trick, "but a normal child, a decent child, doesn't run around naked. You can see she wasn't brung up right. It's no wonder the sister's in the nuthouse. And it makes you wonder about the mother, too. I'm sorry to say it, but it does."

She did not seem sorry to say it. She seemed pleased, triumphant. Carl was outraged. "You have no right to say such things about my wife or my wife's family. If that's the way you feel, you can go back to Tomahawk. I'll give you the money for your ticket."

Hilda seemed surprised by his anger. "And leave you alone with a child like this? I think I know my duty better than that."

She turned, then, abruptly, and went into the kitchen and busied herself among the pans. Carl put his jacket back on and took himself back out to the barn, although he had already decided he was through for the day, and began to soap Frenchie's bridle.

How dare she, he thought, say such things about Mathilda, about her family? She was only a jealous spinster, trying to cause trouble for another woman, a happy woman, a woman who'd had a husband who loved her. He rubbed the bridle hard, until the rag he was using slipped and the friction of his fingers against the leather burned his skin. Why couldn't a woman

just drown? People drowned all the time,
that's what Amanda had said. Amanda,
who couldn't tie her own shoes now. But
that had nothing to do with it, he assured
himself. Of course people drowned. It
didn't mean there was something wrong,
something to be wondered about.

The doubt gnawed at him, though.
Doubt about what, exactly, he couldn't say.
If only he could speak to Mathilda, just for
a few minutes. If only he could see her,
then, he thought, he would know; he would
be reassured. But his memory of her had
continued to soften around the edges.
Sometimes he was disturbed to realize
that he was remembering not her but the
way she'd posed for a photograph he'd
studied the day before. And so . . . and
so . . . perhaps Hilda, while not knowing
anything for certain—how could she know
anything for certain?—sensed something
that he was too dull to perceive.

Ruth began to smash things. She poked at
the flowerpots on the porch railing with a
stick until they crashed on the slates below. She pushed the milk pitcher off the

table. She dropped her Grandmother Starkey's collection of Mexican glass animals one by one onto the hearthstone. She tore pages out of books and ripped the stereograph pictures in two. She sawed the edge of the kitchen table with a butter knife.

"Horrible, horrible child!" Although Hilda came as fast as she could the moment she heard a bang or a crash, she was seldom quick enough to get a good grip on Ruth, who scuttled away, half running, half sliding down the stairs into the cellar, where she crouched in the space under the laundry sink, pressed tightly against the wall, next to the bleach and the lye. The fingers flailed before her, clawing for a hold on her scalp and then slapping about wildly in frustration. Hilda did not go easily to her knees. She bent before the cupboard, one hand clutching the sink for support, the other groping blindly in the dark recesses. Her breasts and her legs, planted wide, blocked escape with a wall of flowered yellow. Finally she rearranged her weight and shoved her shoulder in more deeply to extend her reach, until she could grab a bit of Ruth's skirt or a handful of her hair. Then she'd drag her, howling, out and up the stairs to the drawer with the wooden spoon.

When Carl came in, Hilda met him at the door with a paper sack of broken pieces so often that he began to wonder what fragile thing could possibly be left in the house to destroy. The only variation to this pattern came on a wet afternoon, when for a moment Hilda's hand, groping for Ruth beneath the sink, paused in mid-air. That day Ruth bit, relishing the living flesh between her teeth, the slightly salty tang of the skin. For a shimmering half moment the house was silent. Hilda stared at her hand in surprise, and then she screamed like a peacock. She held out her bandaged hand as soon as Carl reached the porch.

"You better know," she said, "you're raising a wild animal."

Carl felt guilty. He tried to make it up to Hilda by being extra polite himself, by not interfering in the way she treated Ruth, by moving her things into the best bedroom. What would they do if she left them?

Carl stood just inside the door of the common room at St. Michael's, wishing his sister-in-law would pull herself together. Amanda had moved her chair, turning her back on the room, so that she could stare into the woods where the snow clung stubbornly, refusing to give way to the spring. She had been in the sanatorium for nearly a year.

Her hands were busy, the fingers of one working at the thumb of the other, a habit he'd noticed lately. He could see that someone had encouraged her to dress herself—the policy when a patient was well enough—for her skirt was twisted and her blouse misbuttoned. Her hair, curly, and inclined to wildness, a quality he had once thought rather nice, looked, well, like a lunatic's. "Amanda?" he said, and she jumped, separating her hands and letting her arms hang limply at her sides.

She turned to him and nodded gravely. "Hello, Carl. And how've you been keeping yourself?"

"Oh, fine, fine," he said, seating himself on the neighboring chair and reaching over to squeeze her hand. She allowed him to do this but did not return his gentle pressure.

"Don't you want to fix yourself up a little?" he asked.

Amanda touched her bodice and her hair as if surprised to learn that she was not completely presentable.

"Well . . . I suppose," she faltered. "I . . . well, I have no mirror, you know," she said accusingly.

"I can be a help to you, then," Carl said softly. "The buttons aren't right," he began, reaching a hesitant finger toward her, first at a place toward the middle of her stomach where the fabric was skewed, and then, thinking better of that, touching the stray corner of cloth that jutted too high around her neck.

"They've hidden my slippers again, as you can see," she said, holding her stocking feet out to prove it.

Seeing her long, thin feet and skinny ankles stuck out like that seemed almost worse, more embarrassingly intimate, than seeing the sliver of camisole through her misbuttoned blouse. While Carl cast his eyes down and searched under the chairs for her slippers, Amanda discreetly redid her buttons.

"That's better," he said, settling her cardigan over her shoulders. He wished he could smooth her hair a little while he stood there behind her, but he wasn't brave enough to touch it. And anyway, what would he do? He had no idea how women did what they did to their hair.

"Well, I don't want to keep you now," she said when he'd finished.

"Oh, you're not keeping me at all." He leaned back in his chair and crossed his legs comfortably. It was nice to be there, away from Ruth not talking and Hilda talking so much. He could see why she wanted to stay.

"I know you've got to be getting home," she said, more firmly this time.

So he sighed and rose from his chair. He told her that he would be back the next day, unless he had to wait for the farrier, in which case he would come the next. When he was gone, she tipped her head back against the chair, so that the tears that filled her eyes would not spill over.

Amanda

I told you to go back, Mattie. I told you that. I told you. Why won't you ever mind me?

You were trouble from the day you were born. You don't remember it, but I do. All that crying and crying in the night, so much crying that Mama and Papa couldn't stand it—they put your cradle in with me. You don't remember, but I sang to you. I rubbed your back. I lifted you up and bounced you on my lap. I brought you into my bed and tucked your head under my chin, but still you couldn't rest. I fell asleep to your wailing, and it raged like a storm through my dreams. You wouldn't remember that.

And then that first summer you got quiet, so quiet, like a doll lying there in your crib, and fierce red spots bloomed all over your body. Papa made up the daybed for me in the back room downstairs. He forbade me to go upstairs where you and Mama were for fear of contagion, I know now, although I didn't then.

I tried to keep to a regular schedule, tried to wash my face and my teeth when I got up in the morning and before I went to bed at night. I wandered around the yard and the barn all day or laid my paper dolls out on the floor. Sometimes the hired girl remembered to make me a sandwich. Otherwise, at dinnertime I stood on a stool to reach the crackers down from the cupboard. I dipped the broken ones, the ones nobody would miss, in a jar of blackberry jam. Morning, noon, and night, I could hear Mama crooning beside your cradle.

One afternoon I must have fallen asleep because the hot sun slanting across my face woke me. My hair stuck in the jam smeared across my cheek. I felt exhausted, hot and hungry. And something was wrong. I could hear nothing, no sound at all from the room overhead.

I made my way up the stairs, one silent step at a time, ready to run down the moment I heard Mama's shoes on the landing or Papa's hand at the door. At the top of the stairs, I could see into the bedroom where you lay, all alone and still. I went in. I laid my hand on your tiny brow. It was as hot as a loaf right out of the oven.

And then Mama came at me. "Don't touch her! Don't you touch her! Get out of here this instant!"

I hardly recognized her, her hair flying every way, her shirtwaist stained, not the neat, pretty Mama I knew. I snatched my hand away and ran out of the room, down the stairs, out the back door. I ran across the yard and into the woods. The brambles clawed my skin, but I clamped my teeth together and did not cry. The slim branches slapped against my cheeks, but I ran on. I ran until I came to the edge of the lake. The water was flat and green. It lay like a smooth path from where I stood to a burst of trees and rocks at its middle, the island. Out there, the sun fell full on lush leaves, so that the place glowed.

I wandered along the shore, catching my breath, keeping my eye on the island. Had I known how, I would have thrown myself into the water and swum to it. And then I came upon a boat, a small wooden rowboat, its robin's-egg blue paint nearly rubbed away. Its bow rested in the mud. Its stern floated free, so that even I, with my puny strength, could pry it loose from the shore.

I climbed in, picked up one of the oars, and used it as a pole to push myself into the deep water. And then I paddled away, away, to my island.

That was the first time I escaped to that place. I believed everything would be all right there, you see. I thought so then. I thought so later. But later I was wrong.

———

"Well, Carl, how was she?" Hilda asked, passing him a bowl of pickled beets.

Carl shook his head. "Not so good, I think."

Hilda nodded. She took a large bite from her buttered bread and then, with exaggerated daintiness, dabbed the crumbs from her lips with a corner of her napkin and smoothed some stray hairs behind her ear. Carl noticed for the first time a coquettish tilt to her head, and he cleared his throat nervously.

"Ruthie's behaving better, I noticed," he said.

"Oh, Ruth and I get along good nowadays, don't we, Ruth?" Hilda reached to pat Ruth's head with a stiff hand, but Ruth ducked her touch. "She's a good little helper," Hilda went on, pretending she'd only meant to retrieve a few peas that had rolled from the girl's plate onto the oilcloth. "I wouldn't be surprised if she's beginning to think I'm her mama."

She gave Carl a sort of dreamy smile that made him push his chair from the table and gulp the remainder of his coffee standing up. "Gotta take a ride into town. Running out of . . ." but he was out the door before he'd finished the sentence.

———

Ruth had stopped breaking things after the night she dropped a pocket watch over the railing at the top of the stairs.

"This was my papa's," her father had said to her, stroking the shattered face with his thumb, and then he covered his own face with his hands until Ruth was frightened and climbed onto his knee to pull those hands away.

She watched Hilda often now, quietly shadowing her at a distance of about five feet and copying her walk, the angle of her head, the weary gesture she used to push the hair off her forehead with the back of her hand. That afternoon she sat on the rug in Hilda's room, observing Hilda at her simple toilet.

"A little attention to appearance can make a big difference," Hilda said, eying Ruth's reflection in her mirror, while she patted cream on her flat cheeks with her fingertips. "Here," she said, taking from a drawer the corset she wore only on Sundays under her church clothes, "are your hands clean? Feel this."

Ruth ran one careful finger along the edge.

"Real Belgian lace," Hilda said. "See how fine it is? That's the highest quality you can buy.

"And this here is to make your face nice," she explained, taking a tiny pot of rouge and a red lipstick from the back of a drawer.

Once she'd shown the effect to Ruth and examined it herself in the mirror, she carefully wiped all traces of paint away before leaving the room.

"I invited some ladies," Carl said that evening as he stomped his feet on the back porch.

Hilda, standing guard to be sure he shed his muddy boots, narrowed her eyes and tried to peer behind him, as if she expected half a dozen women to be clustered on the lawn. "What are you talking about?"

"I thought you might be lonely way out here, so I invited some ladies over to the house next week," he said, as casually as he could manage. Avoiding her look, he turned to hang his jacket neatly on its hook. "Kind of a party, I guess."

"Carl, you didn't!" She blocked his way into the kitchen, her hands on her hips.

"What? Did I do something wrong? Wouldn't you like to have a little company?"

"I run all over kingdom come after that child. I break my back over the housework every day. And now you want me to have a party!"

"I just thought you'd like, you know, to see some people. Your mother had the ladies over every Thursday, I remember."

"Wednesday. And what do you expect me to do with these people I hardly know?"

"I don't know what ladies do." Carl shrugged. "Play cards, I guess. Drink coffee. Eat cake."

"Cake! You want me to bake? And there ain't hardly three matching cups in this house."

"Well," Carl said, slipping past her, "all right. I'll tell them tomorrow never mind coming."

"And then they'll think I can't manage company. No, the damage is done." She sighed heavily and returned to the stove where she vigorously stirred with a wooden spoon a substance that had begun to explode in angry bubbles.

Throughout that week she sent Carl on at least one trip to town a day to buy special items like fresh playing cards and cute little pads of paper and quarter length pencils from Baecke's, and nuts and dried fruit and sugar in cubes from Mr. Pucci. She hired Thekla Manigold, one of Mary Louise's younger sisters, to help out for the afternoon and directed Rudy to burrow through the attic for card tables. For three evenings in a row, supper conversation consisted primarily of Hilda's debate with herself over buying a fancy layer cake with pink and yellow roses from Klein's or baking her own much-admired-in-Tomahawk stollen. She even sewed one of her best handkerchiefs to a ribbon to make Ruth a tiny apron and made her practice walking extra carefully around the room, stopping before each chair to offer the cream pitcher and sugar bowl on a silver tray.

"If this is a nice party," she told Ruth, "I wouldn't be surprised if we wanted to start a club. My mother and I belonged to three card clubs in Tomahawk, you know."

"Carl," Hilda said, the evening before the event, "you'll come in, won't you?" She kept her eyes on the applesauce she was spooning onto her plate. "Just for a half hour or so, twenty minutes. I know everyone'd want to see you. And Ruth's been working so hard on the serving," she added.

Carl looked at his daughter. She hadn't caused any trouble for weeks, months even, but still she wouldn't speak. He wished she *would* cause trouble—there was at least some noise, some expression in that—but what could he do? You couldn't make a child talk. You couldn't even make her break things.

He made a show of chewing his meat, stalling for time. He knew Hilda wanted

him for her own sake, not for Ruth's, but
what was half an hour? Surely he could be
gallant for that little time to please her. She
was taking care of his daughter, after all, as
well as she knew how. And if that wasn't
very well, he realized it wasn't altogether
her fault. He'd known his cousin as a child
in Tomahawk, and he reminded himself
that she could hardly have helped growing
into the hard and unpleasant woman she'd
become—she'd almost been born that
way. "All right, I'll come in," he said to
Hilda. "What time?"

"Oh, let's say four o'clock." Hilda
beamed. "Give people time to settle
down."

The next morning Hilda hurried everyone through breakfast. By dinnertime the
stollen was frosted, the cushions plumped,
the clean antimacassars smoothed, and
the teaspoons polished and examined for
fingerprints. To save time and to keep the
kitchen clean, she'd made only cold sandwiches for the noon meal.

"I know you have better things to do
than sit around here waiting for a bunch of
hens," she said when Carl and Rudy

seemed inclined to linger over their coffee. They drained their cups dutifully and pushed their chairs back.

"You're not forgetting?" Hilda said to Carl at the door. "And you'll put on a clean shirt?"

"I'm not forgetting," he assured her, while he swung Ruth into the air once or twice. He gave the girl a little push between the shoulders to send her on her way. "You be good, now."

Hilda went into the bathroom in her slip, and Ruth watched her sponge soap and water under her arms and around her neck. She watched Hilda's hair, charged with one hundred strokes, rise into the air as it reached for the brush and then, under Hilda's artful fingers, coil like a sweet roll behind the woman's head. Wedged between the wardrobe and the wall, Ruth watched Hilda take her corset from the wardrobe, slide her arms through the straps, pucker her lips and blow, until she'd squeezed all the air from her lungs. Her fingers strained to pull the sides together over her waist and ribs. One, two,

three hooks done. She took a small, shallow breath and pushed even that air out
again. Four. And then they heard a ripping
sound. Hilda stopped breathing. The
sound ceased. She breathed again, and
there it was. One of the seams was giving
way.

Quickly, Hilda loosened the hooks to
ease the strain. "No, no, no, don't let this
happen," she whispered.

But it had happened. The damage was
done. Up one side was a long tear and
there was no time to repair it. She sank to
the bed and sat for a moment or two, her
head bowed. Then she straightened her
shoulders, slipped the corset off her arms
and dropped it on the bed.

"It's a lucky thing," she said to Ruth, "I
listened to my mama and spent my money
on quality when I bought this dress. It fits
fine even without a foundation, don't you
think?" She turned sideways in front of the
mirror, sucked her stomach in and
smoothed the fabric over it. "It'll have to
do," she said. "No one's wearing those
bulky things anyway nowadays. I heard
Mrs. Lindgren saying so just the other
week."

Hilda leaned close to the mirror and examined her face. "Just the teeniest dot of color," she declared, pressing her finger into the rouge pot and then massaging the paint in a little circle into each pasty cheek.

"Well?" she said, turning toward Ruth, her cheeks a dramatic scarlet from the rough rubbing. "How do I look?"

Ruth pressed her palms to her own rosy face.

Hilda frowned. "I bet you think you're something," she said. "What's that on your dress? Mustard? Well, you can't wear that now. Hurry up. I don't have all day."

But there was still plenty of time, and when Thekla arrived, half an hour before the guests were due, Hilda and Ruth were ready and waiting, sitting at the kitchen table, so as not to muss the cushions in the front room.

At three-twenty Clara Gutenkunst and Ida Brummer knocked at the door, and soon after that the rest of the ladies appeared, so that by three-thirty, the appointed hour, the entire party was assembled. Thekla, carrying coats, ran lightly up and down the stairs, and Hilda ushered the ladies in and sat them down

around the room. There was to be some
general conversation before they got down
to the cards, and then, after the first hand,
refreshments.

It was a little awkward at the very first,
as such things are, with the women uncer-
tain about whether they ought to be ad-
dressing every comment to the room at
large or only to the one or two seated
nearby. Still, this quickly sorted itself out,
and as they were all well acquainted, they
didn't lack for conversation, especially
since one particular topic held great interest for nearly all of them. Although some
asked quite forward questions and craned
their necks to take in as much of the house
as possible, and others only waited, smiling politely, to hear Hilda's answers, there
was hardly a one who was not morbidly
curious to see what had become of the
place "after all the tragedy this house has
seen," and to hear about Amanda. Of
course, one had to be delicate. This was,
after all, her own house. And then there
was Mary Louise to consider—since "they
were such friends." Nevertheless pockets
of gossip buzzed here and there, all around
the room: "I understand she cut off all her

hair." "They needed five men to drag her out of the house." "Tried to drown the little girl, that's what I heard." "Oh, that poor motherless child!"

Abruptly and rather loudly Hilda said, "Shall we play cards?" She was already snapping the legs of one of the folding tables into place.

"Oh, yes. Let's play," Mary Louise seconded.

"How would you like us to sit?" asked Leota Prunerstorfen, and those who had been about to pull chairs to the tables any old way hesitated.

"Oh," said Hilda, and looked blankly around the expectant group. "I hadn't really thought."

"I think Hattie might head up the first table, don't you, Hilda?" Mary Louise said, and Hattie Jensen, one of the eldest women there and wife of the pastor, nodded and graciously stepped to her accustomed place. "And then Dolly, the second. And Albertina over here, I think." And she went on, as she knew Amanda would have liked, ably sorting the women into two congenial groups, as if she were arranging flowers.

Hilda withheld the stiff packs of new cards until everyone was seated and then ceremoniously handed one to Hattie Jensen and brought the other to her own table. They were well into their first hand when, above the noise, the kitchen door opened and closed.

"Just a moment," Hilda said, her cheeks suddenly flushed, and she left her place at the table and hurried into the kitchen.

Rudy had come in with Carl and stood awkwardly in the doorway, holding his hat. Softly, shyly, when Hilda was close, he said, "You look very pretty."

Hilda looked at him severely and then turned away to take Carl's arm and draw him with her into the front room. "You all know Carl, of course," she sang out with unnatural gaiety that made the other women glance at one another over their cards. A murmur of "how d'ye dos" rose from the two tables. With his diffident manner, Carl was charming, they all agreed, and they knew he'd been bravely wounded in the war, although Clara and Ida remembered that he'd only been a meatpacker when poor Mathilda married him.

"You'll stay for refreshments, won't you,

Carl? Why don't we have them now?" Hilda suggested, which made Hattie Jensen raise her eyebrows, for they were in the middle of a hand, and she seemed likely to win.

Hilda went to the kitchen door. "Thekla, we're ready for our coffee."

"Sure," the girl said, "I'll bring it right in." She closed her magazine and went to the icebox for the cream.

"Where's Ruth?" Hilda looked around the kitchen and leaned down to peer under the sink. "I thought she was in here with you."

"Now that you say it," Thekla said, turning in an ineffectual circle to scan the room, "I haven't seen her for quite a while."

"Well, you oughta been watching her. Find her when you've got the coffee out and make sure her apron's on straight. She's probably filthy dirty by now."

When Hilda rejoined her guests, she was smiling, but she darted anxious glances toward the door until Thekla had safely deposited all the coffee cups and the two coffeepots on the side table.

"Stollen in just a minute," Hilda announced and began pouring out. "Cream and sugar, Mrs. Jensen?"

Leota Prunerstorfen, who didn't care for coffee and was hoping a pot of tea might also appear from the kitchen, saw Ruth first. "Ruth Neumann, what the dickens have you got on?"

Then everyone had to look at the little girl standing in the doorway, proudly holding the tray of sugar and cream before her. Pins stuck in all directions out of her hair; her cheeks were smeared a brilliant red, and her little arms were stuck through the straps of some large, lace-trimmed pink garment that hung down to her ankles.

"Why, she's wearing a corset!" Leota exclaimed, and then clapped her hand over her mouth, shocked at her own words.

Best, Carl thought, to act as if this were a joke, and he began to smile, looking at Ruth. Now that she did not quite look like the little girl he knew, he suddenly recognized Mathilda's playfulness in her, and the idea made him sad, but also comforted, in fact, almost happy. It was the first time since her death that he'd thought of his wife and felt happy.

Carefully, Hilda set the cup she was holding down on the tray. And then, looking neither right nor left, not stopping for a coat, she walked through the room and out the front door into the chilly April afternoon.

Mary Louise had lifted Ruth under the arms. "Let's get you cleaned up," she said, and carried her upstairs.

"We ought to be going," Hattie Jensen said, pushing her chair away from the table decisively, and that galvanized the group. They got up and someone thought to send Thekla for the coats, and to everyone's relief there was much noise and confusion in sorting out whose was whose.

"She'll get over it," Ida Brummer said to Carl.

"Yes," Dolly Brennan said, giving him a motherly pat on the shoulder, "by suppertime she'll be right as rain again, you'll see."

But they didn't know Hilda. At dawn the next morning she was waiting in the kitchen with her bags packed. "My train leaves at five past seven."

"But who'll take care of Ruth?" Carl asked helplessly.

Hilda looked at him scornfully. "She's the Devil's child," she said. "Let him take care of her."

The sun was warm by the time Carl returned from the station, though the air still whispered of winter. While he collected the eggs and slopped the pigs, Ruth drew patterns with a stick in the mud outside the pigpen. When the animals were fed, Carl lifted Ruth out of the dirt, intending to carry her in. She shrieked and clutched the fencepost, straining away from him with all of her strength. Her boots left muddy streaks on his trousers and she'd soiled herself; he could smell it. Five years old and no better than an animal! He kicked the fence in frustration.

"Then stay there!" He let her slither down his leg and drop back in the muck. He stalked off, walking as fast as his bad leg would allow, and didn't look back until he was inside the house. Then, from the kitchen window, he watched her as he made his coffee. She had thrown away her stick and was using the heel of her hand now to push ditches in the dirt and then the flat of her palm to wipe them smooth again.

The sun beat through the glass, and the yellow kitchen clock ticked thickly over his head. He opened the window, and Ruth glanced up for a moment, startled. She seemed surprised to see the house, to see the window with him in it. She frowned and lowered her eyes again quickly as if she hadn't meant to look.

What the hell was he supposed to do with her? The cat jumped up on the counter and rubbed its back against his elbow. He lifted his coffee cup and swallowed the dregs, rinsed it and left it on the drainboard. He moved toward the door but turned back again. He wiped the cup with one of his shirttails and placed it gently upside down in the cupboard.

When he picked her up, she screamed again, but this time he held on. He bathed her, dressed her in her best dress. He combed her fine, straight hair and fixed a huge blue bow to the top of her head. Then he put a fresh shirt on himself and hitched the horse to the buggy and they set off for St. Michael's.

The wheels of the buggy jounced recklessly over the rutted road, and Carl de-
voted all of his attention to the driving.
When they reached the well-groomed
track that led up the hill to the sanatorium, he glanced at Ruth on the seat beside him. The bow was half undone and
had slipped down her head and her hair
looked as if it had never been brushed.
What was that clump in the back? Burrs?
One stocking had slipped to her ankle,
the shoe on the other foot had come untied. Her dress had bunched strangely
over her sash. She was disintegrating before his eyes. He clucked Frenchie on and
drove faster.

The track was carved through a thick
wood and branches sliced the sunlight into
a thousand pieces. At the top of the hill the
trees thinned, and the building emerged,
cream-colored brick, five stories high and
square. A smaller building on the right of
Lannon stone and newer construction
housed the director and his family, consist-
ing of a wife, two roly-poly boys and an
Irish setter. The children and the dog were
chasing each other about the green lawn

and paid no attention to Carl and Ruth as they went inside.

The place had once been a monastery and the monks' former cells were now private or semiprivate rooms, but except that the windows and heavy doors could be locked only from the outside, the atmosphere was one of a spa, or so Carl imagined. Cream and maroon tiles formed the floor of the vestibule and of the lobby, easy to care for yet attractive. The stairway was made of a dark, highly polished wood. Occasionally a cacophony would echo through the halls, a sudden scream, a laugh that continued too long, or a spitting stream of imprecations, but most of the patients, at least those in Amanda's wing, kept their troubles to themselves.

He was familiar to the receptionist, and she looked up from the letter she was writing just long enough to smile and wave them on. "She's upstairs this morning," she said.

He removed his hat and climbed the uncarpeted stairs, pausing on the second-floor landing to smooth back his hair and straighten his tie and to gaze out the win-

dow down at the boys, who were now doing their best to ride the dog. Ruth's little
hand worked its way into his.

Outside the door of Room 312, he
stopped. He knelt in front of Ruth and tried
to put her costume back together.
"Ruthie," he said, "you behave now. If
you're good, she might come home. All
right? You be good." She stared at
Amanda's door and said nothing. He
sighed, straightened and knocked.

Like Ruth, Amanda gave no answer, but
then she never did. His knock was a warning, rather than a request.

He opened the door, and gently pushed
Ruth ahead of himself into the room. "Look
who I've brought to see you today,
Amanda."

Tentatively, as if she thought Ruth might
only be an illusion, Amanda rose from her
chair and reached to touch the girl's face
with her fingertips.

Ruth jumped back. "I hate you!" she
shouted. "I hate you!" Carl stared at her,
more shocked by the fact that she was
speaking than by what she said. Amanda
stared at her too. Horrified at her own

words, Ruth backed away, back and back, until—"Ruthie, be careful!"—but it was too late, she'd lost her balance on the stairs and fell, bumping and sliding to the landing.

Amanda reached her first, gathered her in her arms, rocked her as she screamed, her lip bloody from banging against her teeth. "It's all right, Ruthie. It's all right," she said. "For a moment there, you were flying. I saw it. You were really flying."

At last Ruth's sobs became quiet tears, and she snuggled her face into Amanda's shoulder. "Aunt Mandy," she whispered.

"What, Ruthie?"

"You can come home now. I made her go away."

Amanda

She was reckless just like you, Mattie.

After you learned to walk, you ran from room to room, shrieking and laughing. I told you to be careful, but you wouldn't stop. You would never stop until you

tripped and fell or pinched your finger in a
door, and then how you would scream and
cry, as if you were the only one who had
ever gotten hurt.

You were only four the first time you followed me through the winter woods. I was
already halfway across the ice when I
heard your voice.

"Wait, Mandy! Wait!"

I turned and saw you, so ungainly in
your layers of wool, the peak on your
brown velvet cap drooping as you struggled toward me over the ice.

"Go away!" I shouted, my voice boom-
ing across the glassy lake. "Leave me
alone!"

But you never cared what I said, did
you? Not when you wanted your way. You
scuffled on, your boots scratching along
the snowy ice. I started back, all set to
drag you home. Why should I share my island with you? But you reached me before
I'd gone ten steps, and you grabbed my
leg with your mittened hands to steady
yourself.

"Please take me with you, Mandy."

I couldn't refuse you.

The island was better, so much better, with two. Remember the little leanto we built out there? Remember our garden, our "crops"? You wanted radishes and I thought we should have nasturtiums. We planted them both, remember?

And remember when you were a queen? You made a crown out of honeysuckle. You painted your face with bloodroot. "Go to Suscatoon," you said to the dragonflies, "and bring me back some salt. . . . What's a queen name?" you asked me, your hair all draggled, your face dirty. "What should my name be, if I'm the queen?" "Imogene," I said. I only thought of it because it rhymed, but you decided it was the prettiest name you'd ever heard. From then on, whenever we were on the island, you wanted me to call you Imogene, remember that? Queen Imogene. Do you remember?

We would wade out into the water and splash, and when it got too deep for you, you would cling to me, your little arms around my neck, your skinny legs hooked around my middle, weightless in the buoying water. I loved that, your holding tight that way, your needing me to hold you up.

You felt safe with me. You knew I would take care of you.

But then, somehow, you began to drift away. Just a few inches at first—you would let go with your legs but keep your arms tight, or loosen your arms but keep your legs locked around me. I told you "no." I told you to hold on tight. But you wouldn't. You began to let go altogether, a moment here, a moment there, ducking underwater and then grabbing hold of me again, dashing the water from your eyes with one hand and coughing. But I scolded you. I held tight to your smooth, slippery skin. "It's not safe," I told you. "You stay with me." I wouldn't let you swim away. I wouldn't let you go.

You should've listened to me, Mattie, when I told you to go back. You should've let me alone. You and Ruth with your wailing and your crying—letting the whole world know my business—why couldn't you let me go?

Why did you let me go, Mattie? I told you to hold on. I would never have let you go, but you made me. It was you. You made me do it. I'll never forgive you. Never!

Wait, Mattie—I'm not angry. Don't be scared—I won't scold you. I'm laughing, see? It's all right. I didn't mean it. You can come back now, Mattie. You hear me? Come back.

Chapter Seven

Amanda

All of that with Clement Owens was water under the bridge, a month gone at least, by March 1919, when I went home to start over, to start fresh with Mattie and her baby Ruth.

The trouble was I didn't feel much better at home than I'd felt working at the hospital, and after what had happened the last time I'd come home ill, I was cautious.

"Better not get too close," I warned Mattie the next morning, when I staggered in from the milking after losing my breakfast behind the barn.

Still, there was no fever and now that I

was away from the hospital I was sure I'd be able to shake it.

"It's nothing," I snapped, when on the third or fourth day Mattie suggested I call Dr. Karbler. "I'm a nurse, aren't I? Don't you think I know?"

I'd bowed out of kitchen duty and stuck to outdoor chores, despite my promises that first night, because the thought of food made me queasy and the fresh air seemed to help. On Friday, Mattie announced that she'd made me a treat.

"This'll bring your appetite back," she said, dramatically sweeping the platter of perch from the oven where she'd been keeping it warm.

Perch had always been one of my favorite dishes, but that evening I broke into a sweat and could barely make it outside in time.

"Too bad," Mattie said later, feeding me crackers and cheese. "But Pickles was pleased. She ate a whole fish." Then she giggled.

"What?"

"Oh, I was just thinking of the last time perch made me sick, back when I was car-

rying Ruth. Poor Carl. He swore he'd never
go fishing again." She smiled.

But I couldn't smile, for Mathilda's
words had caught me. After she'd gone to
her room, I struggled to fling them off. I got
up and paced. I threw open the window
and thrust my head into the cold air, but
the harder I tried to escape the more firmly
the idea set in my brain. It was true, all
right.

I'd tried to pretend otherwise. I'd told
myself it was only worry or grief or loneli-
ness that was making me dizzy and tired
and sick. But I hardly needed to be a nurse
to realize that something more solid than
unhappiness was growing inside of me.

I'd tried to return to the way things were,
but it was no use. Coming home couldn't
change me back into the girl I'd once
been.

All I could think to do was run away
again. When I was certain that Mattie and
Ruth were asleep, I packed my bag and
sat on the edge of my bed, one hand
pressed against my abdomen, and thought
about where I could go to get away from
this thing.

There were places, I knew, where the sisters took you in until it was over, even if you weren't Catholic. I'd heard about another nurse going to one of those places and now I shuddered at the shame and scorn I'd felt for her. Frieda, her name was. Maybe that's what I'd call myself.

I'd go there. The sisters would teach me how to pray. Maybe I'd stay on afterward, become a nun. But they probably didn't let you do that. Thinking that I could never become a nun, I started to cry. It was a silly thing to cry about—I didn't even want to be a nun. Still, I burrowed my head into the pillow and sobbed. Then I lay for a long time with my face on the wet pillowcase. At least Mama and Papa wouldn't know, I thought. At least they were safe from my shame.

I drew my feet up on the bed without taking off my shoes. Downstairs, Mathilda was playing the piano and singing "Hello, my baby. Hello, my honey. Hello, my ragtime girl." Now and then a discordant note rang out and I knew Ruth was on her lap, her little palms patting the keys, because once I had sat on my mother's lap in just that way. I was so tired suddenly, so tired I decided that I could spend one more night at home. No one knew the truth. No one was likely to know it for months. I could afford a little sleep.

Mama always went into the back room when she felt one of her spells coming on. She drew the curtains and lay on the daybed, turning her face to the wall and squeezing a pillow over her ears to keep the cicadas' hum and the birds' songs out. My father would close her door.

"You see how it hurts her when you don't act right," he would say to me. "Now be good and quiet." And then he would leave the house.

I tried to be good and quiet. I went up to my room and played with my doll or looked at my picture book, but after a while I always got scared, thinking of my mother in that dark room, all by herself, thinking she might be crying, thinking she might be dead, thinking she might have gone away. So I crept downstairs and carefully, silently turned the knob and pushed open the door a crack, just to see, just to make sure.

And, of course, she was always there,

her back to the room, her head buried. Except the one time she wasn't.

The daybed was empty. The blanket that usually covered her shoulders was crumpled on the floor. The room was small, but I ran across it and dropped to the floor to look under the furniture. No, she was gone.

I searched then, the bedrooms, the kitchen cupboards, the wardrobe, the pantry. I asked the hired girl who was wringing out clothes on the back porch. "Where's my mama, Gert?"

"She's gotta be somewheres. Maybe she went to town."

Gert didn't know Mama the way I did. Mama wouldn't go to town sick. She wouldn't go without telling me.

I tried to open the trapdoor that led to the attic. I thought of how goblins and witches might have snatched her away. I thought of how she would be calling to me, frightened, her arms stretching for me from a place I couldn't see. I thought finally of a likely place—the outhouse—but she wasn't there either. I walked through the barn, calling her, checking all the stalls.

Finally, running back to the house, I noticed that the cellar door was open. I

stepped slowly down into the damp darkness, keeping my shoulder tight against
the wall so I wouldn't pitch off the open
side of the stairs. At the bottom, I found
her, sitting on the dirt floor, her forehead
pressed against the sweating stone.

She turned to me then, her face
strangely white in the dimness. But she
wasn't my mother. She mocked me.
"Mama! Mama!" she said, making fun of
the way I'd been calling her. Then she
rolled her eyes to the ceiling. "Please.
Keep that intolerable child quiet," she said.

I didn't know what child she meant. It
wasn't until years later that I realized she
meant me.

———

When I woke the next morning, I knew
where I wanted to run to, a place where no
one need ever know, no one except Mattie.

I was still dressed from the night before,
still wearing my shoes, in fact, and I
clomped downstairs and built a fire in the
stove. I began to make French toast, turning my face away when it came time to
crack the sickening egg. Mattie loved
French toast.

"Better?" she yawned, sinking into her chair at the table. Mattie was always slow to wake.

"Much." I flipped the toast. I did feel better and for a moment I allowed myself to hope that I might have been wrong in my thinking the night before. But then I saw the remains of the perch in the cat's bowl and gagged.

"Listen, Mattie," I said, sitting beside her and pushing the sugar bowl away, so that I could lean close. "I was thinking we might want to move to the island for the summer, you and me and Ruthie. The fields are rented anyway. Rudy can take care of the animals. Why should we stay?" When she didn't answer, I pressed on. "It'll be fun. Like taking a trip. Just you and me and Ruthie."

"Oh, no, Amanda. It's too cold." She cut the corner off of her toast.

"No, it's not. Or at least it'll only be cold for a few more weeks. It's already April. And think how easy it'll be to move things over on the ice."

"On the ice! Amanda, what are you thinking? The ice must be rotten now. We'll go through."

"No, we won't. The spring's been so cold. I'm sure it's good. I'd check it first, of course. I'd make sure." And if I went through, well, so much the better, I thought bitterly.

"Mandy, you have no idea how bleak and cold that island is this time of year. It's all right for an hour in the afternoon, when you want a place to skate to, but not to live on day after day, night after night. You forget, I've done it. I know what it's like. I thought I'd go crazy some of those days."

"That's right, you have done it, haven't you? You've had a chance. Where's my chance, I'd like to know? Who was it that found that island, after all? You and Carl would never have had such a cozy little spot if it hadn't been for me."

I worked every angle, while Mattie chewed nervously on the ends of her hair. It was difficult to change her mind, but I knew I could do it if I tried hard enough. I was the elder, after all. I knew better.

Rudy didn't like it either.

"You two girls out there alone," he clucked, shaking his head. "No good."

"But there'll be three of us," I teased. I knew how to handle Rudy. "We'll have

Ruthie." I chose not to remind him that I, for one, could hardly be called a girl anymore.

This time, though, he frowned. "You know what I mean, Manda. You could freeze—it's not all that warm yet. You could burn the house down."

"We could do those things here too, Rudy," Mathilda said. Although I'd barely convinced her to go along with my plan, this new attitude didn't surprise me. Mathilda was always more inclined to do something when you argued for the opposite.

I reminded him that one of us would check in every few days, and if he was worried, all he needed to do was come out for a visit. I was pretty sure he'd never do this. Rudy was the wait-and-see type. Flames would have to be shooting from the island before he'd decide he'd better have a look. Oh, I knew everyone so well. Everyone except myself and now this other one I carried in me.

"We'll wave every day at noon," Mathilda said.

It took us only two days to organize ourselves, to pack and arrange with the grocer and the butcher to deliver food to the locker on our tiny beach as soon as the ice was out. We'd go to the farm, at least Mattie would, for butter and eggs and milk. And soon we'd plant our own vegetables.

Rudy kept bringing more things in from the barn and adding them to the pile—lanterns and wrenches and oil. "This'll come in handy. You'll see."

And Mathilda kept piling on the books. "Just three more," she pleaded when I claimed the sled was getting too heavy.

We were forgetting essential items, but we were only going a mile—it would always be easy to come back. At least it would be easy for Mathilda.

And so it was easy for her to go. It was a game to her, hardly different from when we were young and went to the island for relief from our real lives at home. But for me it was serious. I would be different when I came back. If I ever did come back.

We set off in the morning, so as to take as much advantage of the light as we could. The sky was gray, the snow old and frozen hard. It was the kind of day that makes you fear that God, distracted by finer things, has forgotten you. But Ruth had no such worry. She went before the sled, carrying an icicle like a torch, pushing her feet purposefully into the crunching snow, and announcing herself to the world in high-pitched, dissonant notes.

"Wait a minute," I said when we got to the edge of the lake. "I have to test the ice." I put my hand on Mathilda's sleeve to hold her back.

It had been a cold March, but still it was late in the season, and there had been days of thaw—Mattie had been right to worry about the state of the ice. I scanned the center of the lake for the telltale dark streaks of open water. All was flat and white. I climbed over the heave at the shoreline and shuffled forward slowly, barely lifting my feet. The surface was ugly, grainy, made of snow that had melted to slush and then refrozen in the recent snap.

I raised one foot high and stamped. The lake didn't protest. No groans or squeaks, no terrifying crack. I made my way forward over deeper water, walking heavily now, bouncing to bring the full force of my weight down on the ice. I imagined falling through, me and the other one, sinking through that cold water to the bottom.

"Wait, Aunt Mandy! Wait for us!" Ruth's voice piped from the shore.

I turned and waved to them. Mathilda stood small and still, wrapped in a hooded maroon cloak that had belonged to our mother. It made me shiver to think how loyal she was, ready to do what I asked, trusting it would be all right as long as I said so. Ruth, brilliant in her bright red coat, was pulling hard on her mother's mittened hand, letting her head and shoulders hang precariously over the ground. She knew her mother would never let her go.

I didn't think, then, that my baby could be like that someday. I didn't think, really, about my baby at all. I concentrated solely on getting us to the island. It seemed the only thing that I could do.

We set Ruth on the sled, and Mathilda balanced her and the load while I pulled. The closer we got to the island, the smoother the ice became, until finally the sled began to overtake me. I stopped pulling and grabbed onto the side opposite Mattie, and we let it drag us both forward almost more quickly than we could find our footing. I nearly fell, and then Mattie almost went down and then I again, while we whizzed along, slipping and laughing, all three just children out for an afternoon's slide.

The island was ringed with a jagged collar the ice had pushed up in its aggressive expansion, as if it were trying to climb onto the land. We had to circle twice before finding a spot low and gently pitched enough for Mattie to scramble over and help Ruth and me after her. We left our sled of supplies on the ice and went to see how the house had fared closed up for so long.

The house, painted a soft gray with green trim, looked in the summer as if it had grown there, but in winter it stood out among the bare black trees. We opened the door to musty wood and chilly motionless air. Maybe Rudy was right, I thought. Maybe we couldn't live here, two women all alone.

"We'll have to get this going first thing," Mattie said, opening the door of the wood stove.

Mattie and Carl had lived just fine on the island in the cold, I reminded myself. Mattie knew what she was doing. We would get through this last little bit of wintry weather, and then it would be spring.

"I'll get some wood," I said.

Crossing my arms over my tender breasts, I stood for a moment on the porch steps, surveying the vast, flat whiteness that was the lake and the crosshatched black that marked the shoreline. Through the trees, I could see the roof of the Tullys' barn. In an hour or two people would be lighting their lamps and their windows would shine among the trees like eyes, staring at us, exposed here on the ice. Maybe there was no hiding here. Maybe this place was a mistake.

But by summer, I assured myself, piling wood into the curve of my arm, it would be different. By summer the island would be shrouded in leaves, and I could keep my business to myself with no one the wiser.

Ruth

Aunt Mandy had a mouth at the bottom of her thumb.

"What's this?" I asked her. My finger petted the white circle on her tan skin.

We were sitting in the big green chair,

me squeezed between the arm and her, because that is how we liked to sit.

"This is from your mama," Aunt Mandy said. "She gave this to me, so I would remember to listen to her."

"What does she say?"

" 'Never leave Ruthie.' That's what she says. 'Never leave Ruth.' "

Aunt Mandy didn't mind my mama. She did leave me. But then she came back.

———

One morning in May, when Amanda had been home from St. Michael's for about a month, and the sun was dewing the grass outside in a way that promised summer, Carl and Ruth sat at the kitchen table waiting for their breakfasts.

"One of these nice days, Ruth," Carl said, "I'll take you out to the island, where you and I lived with your mama. How would you like that?"

"No," Amanda said. She slapped the pan of eggs she'd been about to bring to the table back on the stove. "This darn hotpad. Burned right through it."

Carl looked at her, surprised. "What?"

"She wouldn't like it. Ruth doesn't like the water."

"Yes, she does. You like the water, don't you, Ruth?"

Ruth looked from her father to her aunt and wasn't sure what would be right to say, so she said nothing.

"I want you to close that place," Amanda said, her hands on her hips. "Board it up. Nail it shut and forget about it. I can't believe you'd want to take Ruth there, after . . . well, after everything. What's the matter with you?"

Carl looked at his empty plate. Maybe there was something the matter with him, for he wanted Ruth to see the place where she'd begun. It bothered him that Amanda had managed to wipe Mathilda from Ruth's life. As far as he knew, she told the child nothing about what had happened before his return, nor would she let him speak of the time before he'd left.

"It'll only make her sad," she'd told him. "She's lucky she was too young to remember."

He agreed with Amanda in principle. What good would it do Ruth to know that her mother could swim like a sunfish and liked her bacon crisp? What difference would it make to her to hear about the day Mattie had braided her a crown of black-eyed Susans and chicory? But still, he wanted her to know, for Mattie's sake. Maybe Amanda could let Mathilda disappear, as if she'd never been, but he couldn't.

He waited for a Tuesday, Amanda's day to go to town, and he told himself he was only doing what she'd asked. He was boarding the place up, wasn't he? And he couldn't leave Ruth at home all by herself.

He found her under the lilacs, the cat's tail slipping through her hands, and he scooped her up from behind and hoisted her into the air.

"You're coming with me today, young lady." He kissed her neck, smelling her young skin smell. She, suddenly tall enough to be among the flowers, lifted her face to the fragrant purple.

"Where?"

"You'll see."

He set her down, picked up his toolbox and led her along the lilac hedge to the back of the yard, where he held the leafy branches open and motioned for her to step first onto the path into the woods.

"For a walk?" she asked, used to traveling this path with Amanda.

"You'll see."

The trail was narrow, and she scampered ahead like a rabbit, squatting before a lavender hepatica on the right, scaring a scarlet tanager from its perch on the left, drifting back to the right to peel off a white curl of birch bark. Carl limped, tried to stretch and flex his bad leg. He passed her, as she knelt before a patch of moss and stroked its spores with her palms. He rounded a bend, and she ran to overtake him. At the giant oak where she and Amanda always turned back, she stopped and waited. He took her hand, and they proceeded, she more circumspect, somewhat awed, although there was little difference between the part of the woods they now walked in and the part through which they'd just passed.

He sensed her holding back, her strides shortening and slowing until, finally, her shoulder was skewed, and he was nearly dragging her forward.

"What's the matter, Ruthie?" They

stopped, still several yards from the shore, and he squatted to look into her face. "It's all right. It's just water. Like a bath. A giant bathtub." He looked across the calm sur- face, swollen with mild waves, and was pleased with the comparison. "Just like a bathtub."

But she squeezed her eyes shut and turned her head away, as if he were trying to force her to swallow medicine.

Helplessly, Carl looked east along the shoreline. "We need to wait for Mr. Tully, anyway." When he released her hand, she stood firm and even looked up, studying the water, a good sign. Encouraged, he sat on the ground, pulled off his boots and rolled up his pants legs.

"Well, I'm going in." He picked his way gingerly forward, the sharp stones and the cool water shocking his soft white feet. When the water reached to his rolled cuff, he turned carefully, grappling for footing on the bruising rocks. He looked back at her across that narrow span of water. She stood small and scared, the weeds nearly up to her waist. Looking at her that way, he saw for the first time, in her wide mouth, in the hint of the plane that would be her finished cheek, in the angle of her ears, not Mathilda's face, as before, but his own. It was a shock, that recognition. How could he not have seen it earlier? He felt a surge of connection with Ruth that could have been nothing other than love, and he wanted to pick her up and lock her fiercely against his chest. But at the same time, seeing how small she was, and how scared, how utterly helpless and alone, he also felt something else, something that made him dip his hand into the water—the water that was after all not like a bath, but cold and vast, uncontainable—dip his hand deep, nearly up to the elbow, and then raise his arm and flick the water from his fingertips toward her. Toughen up, he thought. The spray was gentle, so light really and at such a distance that it couldn't possibly have hit her, not a single drop, and he smiled quickly, as if it had all been a joke.

Still she began to cry. He hurried toward her, wincing at the stones and the noise both. "It's all right." He knelt beside her, wrapping his arms around her. "I'm sorry. It's all right."

Joe Tully's boat scraped against the

rocks, and he climbed out, plopping his heavy shoes into the water, but then hung back, awkwardly. "Did she fall? Did she hurt herself?"

"No, no, she's fine. She's just a little scared."

"Maybe you'd better take her home?"

"No, she'll be all right. You'll be fine, won't you, Ruthie? Sure you will."

Ruth had stopped crying, and though she seemed to be looking at Tully, she was, in fact, looking beyond him, at his boat. Carl got to his feet, and the men shook hands.

"Thanks for coming out, Joe."

Joe nodded. He never knew how to respond to the thanks people were always pressing on him. He winked at Ruth.

"She's growing like a weed," he said, knowing that was what he was supposed to say about little children. "And Amanda?" he added, looking back at Carl. "She's all right now, is she? I've heard . . ." He glanced down at his feet for a moment, started afresh, "Well, she's doing fine, is she?"

"She's doing fine, Joe. Come by for dinner this noon and see for yourself."

"I might do that. If you think it's all right. I mean, if you think she wouldn't mind."

"I'm sure she'd be happy to see you, Joe," Carl said absently, brushing the mud from his knees.

Ruth sat in the very center of the boat and kept her face toward the land.

"I saved Amanda's hat right about here once," Joe said as he pulled on the oars. "A straw one with a blue ribbon. Does she still have that, I wonder?" But he looked over his shoulder then at the island, not wanting Carl to answer, embarrassed that he even remembered such a thing. Carl, staring out across the water, thinking private thoughts, said nothing.

Long before there was a house on the island, Mathilda had brought Carl there.

"This is it," she'd announced. He held one oar clumsily out of the water and puzzled over how he was supposed to get both unwieldy things into the boat. He had insisted on being the one to row, though she was an expert and he could hardly keep the boat from spinning. He glanced at her, not sure whether he hoped she would offer advice or pay no attention. She was perched on the gunwale, a precarious place. He was just about to say, "Look out, be careful," when she threw her head back, and before he could shout, almost before he could open his mouth, she lost her balance, fell backward into the water, and was gone.

He scrambled forward to the spot where she'd gone in. The water showed no sign of her. That was what made him hesitate, not knowing where she might be, not having any clue at all, not a ripple, not a bubble. Otherwise, he would have leaped in after her, although he couldn't swim. Later, he told himself that over and over. If he'd known where to jump, he'd have gone right in.

And then he heard her voice. "Carl!"

He heard her voice, but she wasn't there. "Carl! Over here!"

It was coming from behind him. Somehow she'd got all the way to the other side of the boat without his knowing. Her head, with her hair pushed down around it, was sleek as a muskrat's. The water rippled around her shoulders, but she was clearly standing on the bottom. She laughed at him, laughed at the fear on his face.

"Here I am, Carl. Did you think I'd drowned?"

All Carl could think, once he knew she was safe, once it was clear that it had been just a joke, was that he hadn't gone in after her. He told himself later that he'd known she was all right, but it wasn't true. He told himself that he would have jumped once he was sure, in another second, maybe two. Who knew what he would have done, given just a little more time? But secretly, he knew he'd been tested and had failed.

To make up for it, he swung his legs over the side and slipped in, gasping as the cold water reached the sensitive skin of his stomach. She laughed and started away from him toward the shore. He pushed after her.

"I'll get you! I'll get you!"

It was an awkward chase. Their feet slipped on the rocks. The water held them back. Still, he was stronger, faster. He did catch her, first a bit of her sleeve, then her whole arm. She spun around to face him and for one confused instant he had no

idea what to do with her now that he had
her. But she knew. She tilted her face invitingly, and he kissed her.

She'd led him on a merry chase, Carl
thought fondly. She'd gone out for an
evening with him and then danced too often with other fellows; she'd broken dates
at the last minute with no excuse; she'd
provoked arguments, and cried, and declared she never wanted to see him again.
But he'd caught her at last. One fall night
when the air was cold and sharp, the
words just slipped out of him, as if they'd
been summoned by something beyond his
will: "Marry me."

And what had she said? He couldn't remember, but it must have been yes or sure
or all right, because soon enough they
were married.

Joe feathered the oars when they reached
the island so that the boat bumped very
gently against the rocks, and then Ruth
was lifted again, swung through the air,
and set on her feet on the dry land, a different land entirely. At a little distance, among

the thick trees and weeds, stood a gray and green house.

"There should be some lumber back behind the outhouse," Carl said, taking Ruth's hand and leading the way up the overgrown path. He stopped, though, a few feet back from the front steps. "Should we take a quick look inside?" He seemed to be asking the house itself.

Joe yawned. What Carl ought to do was sell that place and concentrate on what he had that was good. But everyone was a fool about something. "Sure, whatever you want."

Carl flexed his knees and stomped once or twice on each of the steps up to the porch. The house's solidness pleased him, since he'd built most of it himself. But then, he thought, why shouldn't the place be in good shape? It was only five years old.

He'd thought he and Mathilda would go to Chicago, or maybe even Toronto, and as long as his plans were vague, she'd been enthusiastic. When he realized that, in fact, she couldn't stand the idea of moving away, they were already married, and he accepted her father's offer to pay for the materials for a cabin on the island. He was surprised now at how small the place seemed, almost as if it were a scaled-down model of the house he'd known so intimately.

In the kitchen Carl peered into the cupboards at the familiar china—white with green ships painted on the rims, another gift from her parents. They'd moved in as soon as one room was habitable and there'd been so much happy momentum at first. He'd worked for her father on the farm, rowing over every morning at dawn. For a while Mathilda went with him to help her mother, but then she began to stay on the island to work on the house alone, accomplishing much more than he expected, even during the month or so when she always seemed to be sick. She cleared brush, drew plans for more rooms, painted the porch ceiling pale blue. In the evenings he brought George or Wally and Rudy or a couple of the other hired men, and they floated the lumber along behind them on a raft and added the bedrooms and a real kitchen. Just as it was growing too dark to see, they would hear a shout from the pier

and would drop their tools and hurry down
to help Amanda with her baskets of cold
chicken and potato salad and pickles and
rhubarb pie. Often, Mary Louise, George's
wife, would come along and it was like a
party, every night a party with Carl and
Mathilda and their house and their island
right in the middle of it all.

But in September the life of the place
drifted away. Amanda went off to Madison
to go to nursing school. The fishermen and
boaters dwindled, too, when the temperature dropped and the lake lay quiet under
the brittle autumn air. The leaves fell, and in
every direction the water and the land beyond seemed more vast, and Carl and
Mathilda, left to themselves in the center of
it, more tiny and alone.

The warped drawer Joe had been pulling
on came open with a crack.

"Hey, pencils," he said. "We could use a
couple of these if we need to cut down
some of that wood."

"Sure, take 'em."

Joe left the drawer open and Carl
glanced into it. Among the pencil stubs

and paper scraps and the odd springs and screws and spools, he saw a slim silver penknife. Where had Mathilda gotten that? He plucked it out, slipped it into his pocket, and followed Joe outside.

Carl hadn't built shutters, so he and Joe had to improvise with the lumber stacked behind the outhouse. It was simple work really. They measured a window, cut pieces to fit against the sill and the top of the windowframe, then more pieces to span the height of the window, and nailed them together.

"Must have been cozy living here," Joe said, holding a finished cover over one of the row of windows that ran the length of the enclosed porch, so that Carl could nail it in place.

"Cozy? Sure, I guess." Carl swung his hammer steadily. Thinking back, he supposed it had been cozy. On the island, he and Mathilda had had a sort of honeymoon that went on and on for months. That was what Carl remembered—how happily they'd clung to one another, before the war. That was the story he told himself now on the nights when he couldn't sleep.

At the time, though, he'd felt a little

afraid when he and Mathilda were there all alone. He loved her, of course, he never doubted that, but nevertheless he felt almost as if—well, this was strange—but almost as if he'd been taken prisoner. He knew it didn't make sense, especially since he actually left the island every day. It was Mathilda who was trapped if anyone was, but she didn't seem to mind. The canoe was always there for her, but she seldom used it.

Most evenings she was waiting for him on the little pier when he rowed home and wrapped herself around him almost before he was completely out of the boat. More than once she nearly pulled both of them into the water with her exuberant embrace. She told him in exhaustive detail about every moment of her day, every shrub she'd cleared, every rooster she'd stenciled on the kitchen wall, every stray thought that had occurred to her throughout the day. She sang and danced. One day she decided yellow would be best for the baby's room, the next day she decided blue, the next week it was yellow again, definitely yellow. She told him that the lake wasn't as cold as one might think and wasn't it funny how she'd hated school as a child and why shouldn't a woman vote if she wanted to, but she would never bother personally, and hadn't the sunset been gorgeous, just gorgeous? And she would laugh at herself and at his confusion and at her own complete happiness, and he would laugh too, uneasily, glad that she was happy, but not at all sure of it, not at all certain that they were on firm ground.

Because at other times the house was dark and still, the curtains drawn, when he docked the rowboat. He found her sitting on the porch in the darkness, sucking on a strand of hair, or curled in the bed, her eyes swollen with crying. Sometimes she was terrified about the baby. What if it died? What if it came out wrong? What if it was a monster? Or she was convinced the water was rising, the wind would carry her away, the lightning would strike him down in the fields. Or she had merely burned the supper. She was no good as a wife. She would be no good as a mother. He never should have married her. These were the things she said.

"My pretty bird," he said, sitting beside

her on the bed. "Don't worry. Everything will be all right."

"You don't know that," she said scornfully.

And, of course, she was right. But in Carl's experience, it was what people said when they didn't know what else to do.

But while he was frying potatoes and eggs she would appear at the kitchen table, her bathrobe fastened with a bow around her thickening waist, and gradually her euphoria would return, until once again she was regaling him with stories of the spelling bees she'd won and the boys who'd kissed her behind the school and the afternoons she and Amanda had stolen away from their chores to this very island together. She laid his hand against her swelling stomach, so he could feel how tight her skin was growing, how well the baby was developing. She talked on and on about her plans, about all the children they would have, how the farm would prosper with his help, how they would buy more land and more cows, how they would build a second story onto their island house.

Increasingly, though, he found it difficult to listen to her describe the myriad ways in which she was nailing them to this spot, to this course of life. He had become convinced that he didn't like farming much, and he wasn't good at it. At least that was what his father-in-law made clear every time he turned away in disgust or stepped in with a sigh to take over a job that he thought Carl was performing awkwardly or not quickly enough.

One night Carl told Mathilda how her father had shoved him so hard when he was filing one of Frenchie's hoofs that he'd sprawled on the barn floor under the horse.

"You've got to be gentle with her," Mr. Starkey had grunted, easing his hand along the horse's foreleg until she lifted her foot again. He gripped the hoof between his knees. "She's not a slab of beef, you know."

Mathilda turned away from him, reaching for one of the books she kept piled near their bed. "You have to understand," she said. "He's had Frenchie all her life. He knows what's best for her." The hand she put on his shoulder then to comfort him stung. "There's a lot you can learn from him, you know, if you give him a chance."

But Carl knew Mr. Starkey wasn't trying to teach him about horses.

Carl and Joe finished covering the porch windows and started down the south side of the house. Joe talked off and on about the Almanac's predictions for that summer's weather, about the new variety of cow corn he'd planted, about the way the fish seemed to have moved from the west side of Taylor's Bay to the east that spring.

By February, the tiny girl Carl had married was transformed into a woman whose every footfall pounded through the house. She bossed him, demanding that he rearrange the furniture, repair a windowframe that allowed a draft, sand a rough spot on the floorboards. Every morning she gave him a list of things to bring back from the farmhouse or from town: blankets and pillows, soap and crackers, knitting needles of various sizes, rugs and books and bottles and wood and wood and wood, always more wood for the stove, until she'd built a stockpile big enough to last three years. He pulled the stuff in a sled over the ice, which looked, under a glaze of snow, as soft and black as the skin of a plum.

There was very little work to do on the farm. In the mornings Carl cut ice on Taylor's Bay and dragged it up Glacier Road to the icehouse. On clear afternoons Mathilda wanted to skate.

"It won't be perfect again for years," she'd said. "I can't let a chance like this go by."

And when he'd protested that she couldn't risk falling because of the baby, she'd scoffed. "I'm not going to fall, Carl. I know what I'm doing."

He hadn't known how to stop her and, after all, she turned out to be right. She skated carefully, easing her ungainly weight from one leg to the other. He could see why she liked it—on the ice, she could move as gracefully as ever. And if, occasionally, she needed to grip his arm to steady herself, well, he was there, wasn't he? He'd make sure nothing happened to her.

But later, he hadn't been there. Carl remembered Amanda's impatient words: "She probably thought it was a fine night for skating and fell through. That would be just like her." Maybe it was true. Maybe Mathilda had been reckless, had gone out skating late in the night because she couldn't sleep and the ice seemed perfect. Maybe that was the end of the story and there was nothing to blame but the treacherous ice.

Ruth had arrived with the slush of spring. She was light, buoyant even, and yet when the midwife first shifted the tiny bundle into his arms he felt as if he might drop her, so heavy was she with helplessness, with the need to be protected at all costs. He knew he could not let her fall, ever, in any way. He braced himself proudly to bear that enormous weight, but the moment she opened her blue-gray eyes he felt the first gentle bite of doubt. He was overcome with weakness in his arms, and such a weakness in his legs that he had to sit down.

Mathilda was always asking him to feed the stove. The windows must not be opened. The door must be shut promptly.

The house was stifling. He felt sorry for the baby, swaddled so tightly in all those blankets, only her pink face showing. What if she was frightened? What if she was too hot? How would they know?

One night in the third week of Ruth's life, Mathilda didn't awaken when the baby began to cry. Carl edged out of the bed, happy to let his exhausted wife sleep. He lifted his daughter from her bed and for a minute or so she quietly gummed his shoulder. When she began to whimper, he carried her out of the bedroom and into the front room, his feet freezing on the cold floorboards. He sat and rocked her as her whimpers turned to cries, stood and swayed with her as her cries became howls. He swooped her up and down, his hand firmly cradling her soft skull and weak neck. He jiggled her very gently and danced with her and held her tight against his neck and still she cried, screamed to the limit of every breath as if there were nothing in her but anguish.

"Stop that! What are you doing to her?" Mathilda set her candle on the table, plucked Ruth from his arms and put her on her breast. The baby didn't stop crying in-

stantly, but soon enough, and Carl was relieved, although also a little angry with her.
Was that all Ruth cared about? Something
he couldn't give her? Disgusted then with
himself for resenting an infant, he solici-
tously wrapped a blanket around his wife's
shoulders and settled a pillow under her elbow.

"You were just hungry, weren't you?"
Mathilda crooned to her baby's feathery
scalp. "Daddy didn't understand."

She seemed pleased, he thought, to be
able to do what he could not.

"Put more wood in the stove, Carl,"
Mathilda said. "It's freezing in here." He
filled the stove, and then he left them,
mother and daughter, together and went
alone to bed.

Carl drove more nails in, sealed the top of
the shutter, then the bottom. Shadows of
round young leaves splattered against the
sunny wall. Three sides of the house were
closed. The job was nearly finished.

Here, now, with the cozy house before
him, the memory of his wife and baby girl
snug inside, he was ashamed of his once

fierce desperation to show Mathilda he did
not belong to her, not the way she thought.
She might have her island, her house, her
father's farm, her child, but she didn't have
him. Even so, he would never have thought
of really leaving her, but going to war wasn't
leaving. A man was supposed to be a soldier. A man was supposed to do his duty.
And then when he returned, her father
would have to stop shaking his head, and
things would be different. She would . . . she
would what? What did he want from her?

She had screamed and fallen to the
ground when he told her he'd not taken his
exemption for dependents.

"You've denied Ruth?" she said. "You've
denied me?"

No, he hadn't done that, had he? That
wasn't what he'd meant. He'd only meant
not to make excuses, not to weasel out like
a coward. It wasn't as if Mattie and Ruth
truly depended on him.

She'd ordered him to go back, to tell
them it had been a mistake. She had
pounded the floor with her fist in an agony
of emotion; she had sworn that he would
die, that she would die without him. Then
she'd told him coldly that he would be

sorry. Then she'd announced that she and Ruth would go along, would stay outside his camp, would take a steamer all the way to France. And then she had simply cried.

He was sorry, but also relieved. He wanted to take it back and tell her that she had no reason to cry, but he also felt calm in the knowledge that it was too late. There was nothing he could do. All he could offer her was: "I'll be back. You'll see. I'll be back before you know it." He tried to raise her face to kiss her.

"I may not be here then," she said, looking at him with hatred.

Carl's hammer slipped from his fingers and fell to the ground. Until this very moment, he'd forgotten those words. But she hadn't meant them. He knew that. She'd only said them in anger. He bent to retrieve the hammer and wiped the dirt out of the claw. He pounded five nails into the cover Joe was holding over the last window in the final wall.

"Mama!" The scream was coming from inside the house, now completely boarded shut.

"Ruth!" How had he forgotten her? Carl thought, running for the door. Joe began to pry open the cover they had just nailed in place.

"Here I am, Ruth!" Carl threw the door open and a swatch of sunlight ran down the middle of the dark house. "Here I am!"

He found her, finally, under the bed in the back room that had been his and Mathilda's. "It's all right, sweetheart. Everything's all right," he said. "We didn't know you were still in here. That's all. Don't worry. Everything will be all right."

Unlike Mathilda, Ruth believed those words. She let him comfort her, as he walked through the dim house, checking window locks and closing doors. Back outside, he gently pried her arms loose and lowered her to the ground. In one hand she clutched a green sack, cinched with a leather thong. "Where'd you get this?"

Mathilda had snatched the bag when he'd brought it home for Ruth. "Marbles for a baby? Are you crazy? She'll choke." The thought horrified him, and she softened when she saw the look on his face. "It's all right, Carl. We'll save them for her. She'll

love them when she gets older." And she
added—he remembered this now with a
pang for her kindness—"I always loved
marbles. Ruth is a lucky girl." Then she tied
the thong extra tight and deposited the
sack in the bottom of the toy chest.

Joe, Carl and Ruth came quietly up the
path to the farmhouse, but before they
reached the door the screen snapped
open and smacked against the wall.
Amanda stalked across the porch,
grabbed Ruth by the shoulders and drew
her against her skirts.

"Hello, Joseph," she said, nodding
curtly at him. "You'll stay to dinner, won't
you?" Without waiting for his answer, she
looked down at Ruth and shook her lightly.
"Where have you been? You're a mess."
She did not look at Carl. She slid the ribbons from the ends of the child's braids,
raked her fingers through her hair and then
began to rebraid tightly.

"We went to the water—ouch, it hurts—
and it got dark."

"Run along and show Mr. Tully where to

wash up for dinner," Amanda said, giving her a little push between the shoulder blades toward the house.

The voices rose over the squeaking of the pump handle and the rush of water in the sink.

". . . the lake! To the lake! How could you do such a thing?"

"What's wrong with taking her there? That's what I'd like to know. For crying out loud, she was born there."

"You have no right to go there now."

"What do you mean I have no right? It's my house, isn't it?"

"You wouldn't know anything about it, Carl. You weren't there. You left her."

"Oh, that again . . ."

"Yes, that again. If you hadn't left your wife and child, Mattie never . . ."

Ruth stood in one corner of the doorway, pressed against the screen.

"Hey, Ruthie, where'd this come from?" Joe lifted the sack Ruth had dropped in the toolbox. "Do you know what I think is in here, Ruthie?" He tossed the sack up and down, catching it in one hand. "I think these are marbles. How about you and me play a game of marbles before dinner,

Ruthie? C'mon." When she didn't move, he went to her, peeled her gently off the screen and drew her into the room. "Do you know how to play marbles, Ruthie? Here, I'll show you."

She was interested in the colors of the little clay and glass balls and in their cool smoothness. She wanted to study them, to line them up, maybe to watch them roll, to rub them between her palms, but she tried to hold her fingers the way he showed her, tried to bend her thumb right. Finally he let her just roll them, aim and roll them, so that sometimes they knocked against each other with a satisfying click.

Ruth

We walked where Aunt Mandy and I always walk, and then when it came time for let's turn around, better get home, got to get the supper on the table, we didn't stop. We kept going where I didn't know the path went and then there were blue spaces between the trunks and under the branches, and then the water. I remembered the water, a sky on the ground, where you fall and fall and fall and fall. We were at heaven and I was afraid, because that's where you go when you die.

The water was lumpy, with ripply skin. We went on it in a boat and the shore didn't look anything like the place where we had been standing, even though I knew we had been standing right there.

And then the boat bumped on another shore.

"Do you remember this, Ruth?" he asked. "We lived here when you were a tiny baby, Mama and you and I."

"I can't remember when I was a baby," I told him. "I think I was a good baby. I think I didn't cry."

"All babies cry, Ruth."

"No, I didn't."

I knew the smell inside the house: wet wood and mittens and the green smell of the water. It was the smell where my mama was.

I looked for her. I looked in the secret spaces, under the red blanket, under the beds and in drawers, where her smell was so strong, I thought she must be standing behind me, but she wasn't. I found a mouse house made of scarf and paper, but I didn't find her. Still, I knew Aunt Mandy was wrong. Here was where we should be waiting. Here was where she would come back.

In the kitchen, I looked in the cupboards. I found a bowl, a cup, and a frying pan, with cottony nests of spider's eggs in the bottom. I stood on a chair to look where the pencils were. I remembered her sharpening with the knife—"There you go, Ruthie. Keep it on the paper. That's a girl."

Then half the sun that lay on the kitchen floor disappeared. That was when the pounding started. Pound, pound, pound. Quiet. Pound, pound, pound. The other half of the sun was gone then too.

In the other rooms there still was light, so I went to the room with the chest where my toys lived.

There were leaves in the chest and sticks and snail shells and rocks that had been green and red and blue and yellow under the water, but they'd all turned brown in the chest. "Look, here's a pretty one," she said. She was good at finding the pretty ones and she gave them all to me.

The pounding came again. Pound, pound, pound. Quiet. Pound, pound, pound. Quiet.

Mama's skates were in the chest. I felt the soft inside where her feet went in, but I remembered about the shiny part. "Never touch," she said. She put wooden sticks over the silver.

The little green sack was in the chest. "For when you're older," she said. Five is older.

There were stones in the sack. You could tell by how heavy it was, by how it clicked and clacked when you moved it. They were pretty ones, I bet. The string was tight. She could have got it undone or even Aunt Mandy, but I couldn't.

I took the sack to Mama's room and sat on the green rug beside the bed where we said, "Now I lay me down to sleep." I used my teeth. I have good teeth. One of them is gray from when I fell down the stairs, but it works just like the white ones. The string was leather. It tasted nice and felt good in my mouth. I worked on it. I'm a good worker, that's what Aunt Mandy says. I worked on it until I got it loose.

The stones inside were pretty. Some of

them were soft red-brown, like flowerpots, but the best ones were jewels, colors like stick candy. All of them were perfectly round. They rolled when I set them on the floor. They rolled into the grooves of the braid on the rug and two of them, a lemon and a cinnamon, rolled under the bed.

Under the bed was where to go the day the noises were scary. "Go to your room," Mama said, but I didn't want to go. They were angry. They scolded me. "Go away now, Ruthie," they said. But I went under the bed in the dark and low. Aunt Mandy bent down. "Here, now. See? Shush, now, Aunt Mandy's got candy." I didn't want candy. I wanted to stay, but Mama said no. "Go to your room. There's nothing to be scared of." But I could see that wasn't true.

Under the bed is a good place to hide when you hear the screaming, when you hear the breathing, when you hear the "God, oh, God, oh, God."

In the dark and low, on the now-I-lay-me-down-to-sleep, I shush and suck and suck. I suck my candy sharp as a needle. I lay me down to sleep and then I wake. Still there are the noises. They won't stop mak-

ing the noises. I hold my hands over my
ears, but still they won't stop. Back and
forth go Mama's shoes. Back and forth,
until I'm tired, until the baby cries, and then
it's quiet.

I put the stones in the bag and then
there was the pounding, right over my
head. And then all the light went away. It
was dark as night, dark as the water when
I couldn't get up.

"Mama!" I screamed. "Mama!" I found
where she was. But she wasn't there.

And then he came. He lifted me up and
carried me into the sun and back to the
water where I didn't cry. I'm sure I didn't
cry.

Amanda

Once Mattie and Ruth and I had settled on
the island, whenever I wasn't sleeping like
a dead woman, I was a virtual whirlwind, I'll
say that for myself. All through that April
and May and into June, I pushed my trouble out of my mind and put the island in order. I tilled the garden and planted the

seeds along the rows Ruth and I lined up with string. I made out the grocery lists and collected the deliveries from the locker, even the chunks of ice for the icebox. They were heavy, but I dragged them up the hill on a blanket. I washed Ruth's pinafores and combed her hair and taught her how to count to twenty and saw that she kept her shoes on and stayed well back from the water. Mostly, I watched while she played her endless games to make sure that the stones and twigs stayed out of her eyes, her dolls stayed decently dressed and her face stayed reasonably clean.

Mathilda did all these things, too, of course, but she did them less seriously and with less zeal. She was always wandering off to write a letter to Carl or to stick her nose in one of the books with which she'd weighted our sled. Now that the weather was warm, often she'd let Ruthie play right at the edge of the water while she read, and I worried that she wouldn't notice the difference between the plop of Ruth's pebbles and the splash of the child herself falling in.

One night, when the moon was so bright that it made a ghostly day, I awoke to the sound of splashing and Ruth's squeals. Terrified, I rushed down to the shore. Mathilda was holding Ruth by the arms and spinning her around as fast as she could, dragging the little girl through the water, while the moonlight licked the waves around them like a flame.

"Stop that! Stop that right now!" I stamped my foot.

Mathilda stopped spinning and turned to face me, drawing Ruth against her body as she did so, her arms wrapped around the child's middle, so that Ruth's feet dangled, dripping over the water. Ruth wasn't big enough, though, to cover Mathilda's nakedness. I was shocked—the two of them there like that, without a stitch on, where anyone could see. I couldn't think where to put my eyes. I turned and hurried back to the house and felt my way down the dark hall to my room.

I lay on my bed, my hands pressed one over the other on my chest to calm my racing heart. Then I let my hands slide down. I let myself feel through the thin cotton of my nightgown the part that had begun to swell like bread dough. I tried, as I had for weeks now, to push it down, but it was solid—it would not budge.

And then, inside of me, it fluttered.

———

"Stand still. These are sticking together." Amanda was trying to rat Ruth's hair around a handful of burrs. "Good. Just like a witch." She cackled to make it a game, and Ruth giggled. "And now a little of this on your cheeks." Gently, she smeared rouge on Ruth's soft skin. "Not too much. Now you remember what we practiced?"

Ruth nodded.

"All right, under the covers and close your eyes, and remember, not a word, no matter what he asks you."

Amanda was keeping Ruth out of school as long as possible. No one had argued with her that first year after she'd been released from St. Michael's. Ruth was only five, after all, and what with the months of not speaking and the toilet accidents, she hardly seemed ready for kindergarten. The next year, though, had been more difficult.

She'd had to remind Carl that he knew nothing about children, that he could not imagine the trauma Ruth had suffered at losing her mother, that she was teaching the child more than any school would have. The last part, at least, was true. Ruth, although she wasn't a wizard with arithmetic as Amanda had been, could already add and subtract, and although she hated the cruel Struwwelpeter, she could read every word about him. She could identify trees by their leaves, and birds by their calls, and could point out at least four constellations. She understood that blue and yellow made green, knew how to differentiate a Guernsey from a Jersey and had raised a lamb whose mother had died of distemper.

Carl was fairly easy to persuade, but Amanda knew Ruth's precocity wouldn't impress the school board. When that body sent someone to the house to investigate, she pretended that Ruth was ill, and even staged a convincing epilectic fit.

"Perhaps you'd better wait in the front room, Mr. Schmidt," Amanda said calmly, as Ruth, her tongue lolling from her lips, began to jerk and then to bark.

It'd worked wonderfully the first time, but this year Carl, who'd left a pair of pliers in his room, came home to find the school board member on the davenport.

"It's very sad about your daughter," Mr. Schmidt said. "I'd hoped she'd be better this year."

When she heard Carl running up the stairs, Amanda realized there was nothing more that she could do. Ruth would have to go to school.

Part Two

Chapter Eight

It was a morning ripe with the smell of manure, an odor acrid when it first penetrated the nostrils, but compelling and pleasant like a good cheese the longer it clung to the air. The school and its playground were bordered by fields, all freshly spread and drying in the warm September wind. On a hillock at the west end of the playground twelve girls had settled, most with their legs crossed Indian style, skirts pushed to the ground in the space between their thighs, cradling their dinner pails. In the cluster was the entire female enrollment of Lakeridge School with the exception of Ruth Neumann, who always ate her lunch alone.

A few who had finished eating leaned

back on locked elbows, tilting their chins to catch the last of the year's sun. At the crown of the hill sat Imogene Lindgren, her knees crooked together, legs angling off to one side in imitation of older girls. At eight and three quarters, Imogene already gave clear indications that she was to become a woman, and although none of her girl-friends, nor even Imogene herself, could have defined this quality, they all studied her carefully, as if she were one step ahead in the game.

For the boys, too, Imogene was mes-merizing and, almost without knowing they did so, two or three would always be cir-cling and circling, making tentative forays toward her and then drawing quickly back or veering off toward one of her retinue, a safer target.

"Watch this, watch this," one de-manded, darting up and poking her in the shoulder with the tip of his finger. Then he rolled his eyelid until it was inside out and glistening red above the eyeball, turning his head this way and that to give the widest audience a chance to admire.

Delighted shrieks and groans rose up. Several girls, giggling, threw their hands over their faces and one, who had been seated on the slope of the hill, tumbled over sideways. Imogene was not beyond this sort of pleasure, but she knew better than to express it and instead rolled her own eyes in disgust and put the last bite of her ham sandwich into her mouth.

A small knot of boys, seeing that an emissary had paved their way, then approached. Imogene watched them out of the corner of her eye as she finished her pickles, neatly folded the waxed paper that had kept the sandwich from soaking in brine and wiped her fingers on the clean white handkerchief that her mother had edged in lace. Among the younger children, the popular game of the last few weeks had been a version of hide-and-go-seek and tag, boys against the girls. It was understood that whoever was caught might have to submit to a kiss or reveal a glimpse of underpants, although the unwilling on either side could, without too much difficulty, delay this prize until the bell rang to rescue them.

Leaving their pails in a row by the school wall, the girls went off to find hiding places in the count of one hundred. By forty, Imogene had observed with increasing dissatisfaction that each bush and corner on the playground had been inhabited so often that it was marked by a telltale path of trampled dust. By fifty, she gave up looking for a place where she couldn't be found, and instead ran to the three concrete culverts that had been left over from a drainage project and were now abandoned in one corner of the playground like a ruined shrine to some forgotten god. This sort of hiding place was more to her liking anyway, since from one of the tunnels she could leap out easily and turn the tables, becoming the aggressor.

On sixty, she crawled into the first tunnel and immediately scrambled out, horrified by the crooked, unbroken trails of ants that covered its floor. The second tunnel, as it turned out, was already inhabited, but Imogene crouched at the entrance for a moment, peering in.

Ruth Neumann was a mess, as usual. Her fine hair had pulled halfway out of her braid on one side, so that it bulged in a snarled mass over her ear, and the hem of her skirt was coming down. She was so blatantly odd that she'd been a scapegoat almost from the first week she appeared in school four years before. Even Imogene had occasionally joined her schoolmates when they felt particularly mean in taunting Ruth, usually about her upper right incisor, which was dead at the root and rotted to the gray of pencil lead, a baby tooth that clung to her gum although the girl was eleven. Many a dull lesson had been whiled away by sketching a face with a wide grin, shading in the appropriate tooth, labeling the modified drawing "Ruth" and, when the teacher's back was turned, holding up the ingenious creation for general viewing.

Ruth rarely seemed even to notice or would quietly look at the perpetrators and those who laughed, not with reproach, but with curiosity, as if she saw something unnatural in their faces. This experience was at first disturbing but ultimately boring and eventually only those who could find no other means of maintaining their status punctured her solitude.

In the culvert, Ruth was simply sitting, examining the pocked surface of the concrete and enjoying its coolness through the thin cotton of her skirt. Whenever her body warmed an area, she shifted to another cool spot. A few lines of ants marched around her, but she didn't seem to mind. From time to time she shot a clay marble from the small handful in her pocket through the tunnel with just enough force so that it rolled to the edge but did not fall over.

Imogene was not only queen of the second and third grades but also marble champion of the entire school, or at least she and everyone else believed she was. But here is what she saw when she looked into the tunnel: a blue mib, very slightly lopsided, rolling slowly, slowly, slowly to the edge of the tunnel where it gently nicked a brown mib and then lay still. In other words, she saw a marble shooter who could beat her.

This didn't upset her. Imogene appreciated skill, especially if she could make use of it. She duck-walked into the culvert's entrance, blocking most of the light. Ruth glanced up at her but didn't move.

"What are you doing there?" Imogene asked.

Ruth didn't answer, but she looked down at her hand and rolled another mar-

ble, slowly, slowly, slowly, to the edge of
the concrete tunnel.

Offended, Imogene forgot her attempt at
condescension. "Look, you're shooting
marbles," she said, slapping one palm
against the tunnel floor. "I can see you're
shooting marbles. Why don't you just say
so?"

"If you can see I'm shooting marbles,
why do you want me to say so?" Ruth said
to the cool concrete beside her hand. And
then she squinted up at Imogene, dark
against the hard, bright blue of the sky and
smiled, showing her black tooth full to the
world.

Imogene's fingers stung where they'd hit
the concrete. She narrowed her eyes for a
moment, hesitating, and then she let her
anger evaporate. Forgetting about her hiding place, oblivious to the ants, Imogene
crawled into the tunnel beside Ruth and
explained her excellent plan.

Imogene coveted an aggie as blue as
the sky at noon. This marble had somehow
come to be in the clutches of Bert Weiss,
at eight already a swaggering, self-satis-
fied boy, who picked his nose often and in
public. Imogene wanted that marble for

herself, but she'd also become convinced that she had a duty to free it from the fat, greasy sack of marbles that Bert kept in his desk.

So far she'd gone about her quest in the wrong way, as it turned out. She'd practiced for months and pumped an older boy she knew, already in seventh grade and tired of marbles, for his secrets: a lick of saliva on the finger for certain shots, shoulders positioned a particular way for others. Her skirts had become permanently brownish at the hems and across the front from squatting and kneeling in the dirt to shoot. She had become good, then better and better, collecting many other children's prize marbles along the way, until her own supple cowhide marble bag was stuffed nearly full. In these early games, the blue marble had appeared often among the brown mibs and the green and red and yellow crystals and the rainbow swirlies and the cat's-eyes, but Bert, ever vigilant for opportunities to thwart another's pleasure, began to notice Imogene's interest in that particular sphere, and when her aim improved he pulled it out of the game.

Pulled it out of the game. Just like that. Just like that it was gone, dropped into the limp gray bag, and he tugged the draw-string tight, squeezing out the fresh air, as she watched. He would not take it out again.

But now she had a plan.

"Hey, Bert," she whispered to the greased hair in front of her the next day, as Miss Crawley began her scratchy litany about the letters that go above the line and the letters that go below the line in cursive script, "marbles today at recess, got it?"

"Nah, marbles is for kids," Bert said into his shoulder.

"No, I've got a good idea. We'll play teams."

Miss Crawley turned from the series of *l*'s she'd been admiring on the board. "Who is talking? I will have no talking while I am talking. Do you understand that, pupils?" She turned back to the board. "Now the *l* should not be confused with the *i*, which comes only to the halfway point and, of course, has the dot. Now I do not want to see any more of those large, scrib-bled dots above your *i*'s. There is no need to make a rat's nest. What is called for here is simply the touching of pencil to paper. Like this." She made a series of small taps with the chalk across the top of her row of letters. Some of them did not show up. "You see?" she said. Ahead of Imogene, Bert shrugged his acquiescence to her suggestion, just as Miss Crawley turned, smiling, to the class. Her smile dropped from her face. "Bert, you are driving me pret' near to the end of my rope. Do you have something to share with the rest of the class?"

The plan played out just as Imogene had intended. She let Bert choose his own partner, Otto Schmidt, and then told him to pick a partner for her as well. He scanned the group of onlookers, rapidly dividing the good players from those who could hardly balance a marble between finger and thumb. And then he saw Ruth, standing perhaps just a little bit closer than she ordinarily would, chewing a hangnail and looking down at her shoes, apparently hoping to be part of the group without being noticed. Imogene's heart jumped a little as she saw his eyes squint with triumphant glee.

"There, she's your partner. Ruth the Tooth. Let's play."

The blue aggie lay trapped in the bag at first, and Imogene had trouble concentrating on the game because of it. Even without meaning to, she made several poor shots right at the start and sacrificed an apricot cat's-eye, one of her favorites, to the greasy pouch. Ruth bungled every shot admirably, just as Imogene had instructed. She seemed unable to keep the shooter from slipping out of her hand and kept catching her heel in the hem of her skirt when she tried to kneel. At last their performance encouraged Bert's maliciousness to get the better of his caution and he produced the blue marble. "Ain't she pretty?" he observed, shining the orb on his yellowed shirtfront. "What will you give me to put this one in the game?"

"A nickel," Imogene said promptly.

"You ain't got a nickel."

"I have, too."

"Show me then."

"I can get one."

"Ha! Fifty years from now! No, I'm thinking I should get something better than that to risk this beauty."

Imogene seethed. The marble meant nothing to him. This was pure meanness. "Well, what do you want then?"

"I want"—he looked around and licked his narrow lips—"I want the black tooth." He stared at Ruth.

Somebody snorted a laugh. Somebody else made a retching sound and was rewarded with a wash of giggles. Imogene looked at Ruth. For a minute she hesitated, seeing out of the corner of her eye the blue marble glowing with hope in Bert's hand.

Then she said, "Forget it. That's ridiculous." She reached to pick up her remaining marbles from the circle.

"Wait," Ruth said, "I'll do it. See, it's ready for pulling anyway." She parted her lips to move the tooth back and forth with her tongue.

"You shouldn't," Imogene said. "It's not right."

"It's my tooth," Ruth said, "I can do what I want with it." And then she smiled at Imogene, as broadly and brilliantly as she had smiled from the culvert. "Let's play."

"Tooth first," Bert said. But just then Miss Crawley came into the yard, ringing the bell. "After school," Bert said and dropped the blue marble into his bag and drew the drawstring tight.

When they were finally released into the September afternoon, a gray layer of cloud had thickened the smell of manure to a pungent miasma. Ruth was among the last out of the building and the children who had gathered several yards from the door had begun to punch each other lightly about the arms and kick each other a little about the ankles by the time she appeared. They quieted immediately and watched as she drew from her dress pocket a piece of string she had stolen from the supply cabinet while Miss Crawley's attention was focused on the third grade's times tables. Tying it on the little tooth was difficult; it slipped off several times before she was satisfied that it was secure, but at last she declared herself ready and walked over to the school's toolshed, the string dangling from her mouth.

"Ain't you afraid it's going to hurt?" a small girl asked at her elbow.

"Not too much. I worked it during arithmetic," Ruth answered as she opened the shed door. She had to kneel to tie the string around the handle. "Now who's going to slam this?" she asked, looking at Imogene.

Imogene hesitated. The thought of yanking that tooth out of Ruth's gum made her feel sick. But Ruth continued to look at her steadily. Finally Imogene took a deep breath and grabbed the door. "You ready?"

"Ready."

Imogene inhaled again and held her breath. Ruth's eyes were still wide upon her, but Imogene squinted her own eyes until they were nearly closed. Then she slammed the door as hard as she could into its frame.

The blood was everywhere. It seemed to be spurting in all directions, running out of Ruth's mouth and all over her dress. Without thinking, Imogene produced her handkerchief and pushed it into Ruth's right hand. As Ruth looked blankly down at it, a few drops of blood seeped from between the fingers of the hand that she was holding to her lips and stained the white cloth red. She glanced in alarm at Imogene, who looked slightly disgusted.

"Use it," Imogene said impatiently, and

Ruth stuffed the handkerchief into the raw space.

The tooth dangled from the door handle, pearly gray and red where it had yanked free. Ruth untied it and then polished it with a clean corner of the hanky. "Here," she said, handing it to Bert, "let's play."

Winning the marble was easy. One quick flick of Ruth's shooter and it was out of the circle, out of the game, and no one was much interested after that.

Imogene felt in her chest an overwhelming desire to run home as quickly as she could and sit beside her mother on the long, low sofa in the front room. But she gritted her teeth and walked beside Ruth, for their way lay in the same direction. As they walked, Ruth pressed her tongue into the newly empty space and Imogene rolled and rolled the blue marble between her fingers in her pocket.It felt heavy and tainted. She drew it out, half expecting its color to be blotted, but the blue glowed on, indifferent to the blood that had been spilled in its winning.

"Here, let's see once." Ruth held out her hand.

Imogene hesitated a moment and then

put the aggie in the center of Ruth's palm. Ruth plucked it out between the thumb and index finger of her left hand and turned toward the sun. She held the marble in front of one eye while she shut the other. "Look, you can see right in there."

"Give it here," Imogene said, and Ruth passed the globe back to her.

Ruth was right; you could see into it. Imogene studied the layers of deeper blue that ran through it and a small cloud of lighter color that drifted near one edge.

"I'm going to keep this forever," Imogene said. "Feel how smooth." She held it against Ruth's cheek and rolled it slowly upward with her palm.

They walked on, stopping now and again to look into the marble from a new angle, handing it back and forth, blinking as the sun filled their eyes.

"My mother says your mother is dead," Imogene said. She glanced at Ruth out of the corner of her eye, not knowing how the other girl would respond. Did you cry when someone mentioned your dead mother?

But Ruth was busy polishing the marble on the hem of her dress and hardly seemed to care. "Yes."

Emboldened, Imogene pursued the is-
sue. It was interesting, after all. She
couldn't think of anyone else she knew
who didn't have a mother. "How did she
die?"

"She drowned."

"In the lake?"

"Of course. Where else would a person
drown?"

"There's other water than Nagawaukee
Lake, you know."

"Well, that's where she drowned, anyway. In Nagawaukee Lake."

Imogene had the marble back again and
she rubbed it between her palms before
asking an even more daring question. "Did
you see when it happened?"

Ruth thought about this for a moment. "I
guess so," she said finally. "I drowned
too."

"That's stupid. If you drowned, you'd be
dead."

"Sometimes you die, sometimes you
don't. That must be how it is with drowning."

Ruth said this with such authority that
Imogene felt her own position as the one
who knew the most, who was most inter-

esting, who would clearly be the one to say which answer was right and which game was played and for how long, slipping. "My mother found me in the garden, like in the Green Fairy book," she countered.

"Really?" Ruth seemed suitably impressed, and Imogene felt generous again.

"You sure are going to look better when that tooth comes in," she said.

Not knowing what to say to this, Ruth threw the marble up and caught it.

Imogene gasped. "Don't lose it."

"Don't worry," Ruth said, tossing it up once more to prove she could. When she caught it, she handed it back to Imogene, who slipped it into her pocket.

They had reached Imogene's turnoff. "Well," she said, "I guess I'll be seeing you tomorrow."

"Wait a minute." Ruth reached into her pocket. "Here." She held out the gory handkerchief.

"How about washing it?" Imogene said, leaning a little away from the thing. Ruth looked at the handkerchief and nodded, as if noticing for the first time that it was soiled, and then began to fold it carefully.

Imogene, watching, amended her words.
"You can keep it."

"Are you sure?"

"Of course, I've got plenty. So long,
then."

Imogene walked on a few steps toward
her house and then turned back. Ruth was
still standing in the road, watching her.
"Ruth!" Imogene called. "You want this?"
She drew the marble out of her pocket and
held it up.

"No. It's yours. See you tomorrow."

Imogene waved and half ran, half
skipped with her delight in her treasure all
the way home. Ruth, on the other hand,
was in no hurry. Had Imogene looked
again, she would have seen Ruth turn and
start back toward the school. She walked
with her chin very high, placing one foot
carefully in front of the other, as if she were
balancing something on her head. By the
time she reached the playground the sun
had begun to set in crimson streaks and
the manure had mellowed in the cool of the
evening so that it now just seasoned the
air with a hint of organic richness.

She returned to the culverts and chose

again the one in which Imogene had found her that morning. This time, however, she took a running start and tried to hurl herself on top of the concrete cylinder. On the first try, she didn't jump high enough to reach the summit and slipped back to earth, grazing her elbow slightly on the way down. On the second try, her footing was off and she veered away at the last moment. On the third try, she ran so fast that she could not keep track of her steps, planted her feet hard in the dust about a foot from the tunnel and flew into the air, spinning her body as she went so that she landed smack, sitting nearly at the top. She had only to grip hard with her thighs and wriggle her way upward and she was there.

Inching up as she pressed against the concrete had pulled her dress tight across her throat and she leaned first to the left and then to the right to loosen it. Then she crossed her ankles, one over the other. Despite the overcast afternoon, the concrete had soaked in enough sunlight to warm the backs of her legs. For a moment she leaned back until her body draped over the curving tunnel and looked at the playground upside down. If she concentrated very hard, she could almost believe that the trees and honeysuckle hung from a green sky and that the orange and red rivers of the sunset flooded over a periwinkle ground, but soon the blood throbbed in her head and her skinned elbow began to sting. She sat up, spit a little on her fingers, and rubbed the sore spot with the pink saliva.

Ruth smoothed her skirt neatly over her knees and then drew the lace-trimmed handkerchief from her pocket and smoothed it over the skirt. It was a little stiff where the blood had dried, but she was able to press it fairly flat. Delicately, she pinched the lace edges between her first two fingers and thumbs and set the crown on her head. Sitting tall upon her throne, she gazed at the empty playground rolling out before her.

Chapter Nine

———

It had worked out all right. They had made do. That was what Amanda could hardly get over every morning when she woke to the sound of Carl's chair scraping on the wooden floor as he got dressed to go out to the milking. He never could keep from moving that chair, she thought fondly. It was almost as if he wanted her to know he was up and their day was beginning.

There had been that year or two of wondering who would stay and how exactly things would be arranged, but somehow they'd settled into a family at last, the various tasks of life divided comfortably among them, and the days now turned like a wheel with three spokes. So that even though Carl had been distracted lately, Amanda and Ruth simply shifted themselves to accommodate his moods.

Joe had begun to visit regularly, ever since the day Carl invited him to dinner, and on Friday nights he escorted Amanda to the pictures and a fish fry. They felt an affection for one another based on their old love and sustained by avoiding personal conversation. If he'd hoped for something more, he never hinted at it, except to ask occasionally if Amanda would go out on a Saturday. She never would. Saturday was the night she and Carl listened to their programs on the radio.

All this would have been enough, really, more than enough, but then Ruth had found Imogene too.

The first time Ruth mentioned Imogene, the night she'd come home with blood smeared on her cheeks, Amanda had felt her own blood drain away. She was tempted. She could feel the retort coming to her tongue—"There's no Imogene. You can't know an Imogene." But, of course, there was and Ruth did.

"You've ruined this dress," Amanda had

said instead, pulling the garment a little too roughly over the girl's head. "I doubt I'll be able to get this out."

"Imogene says the fairies brought her." Ruth's voice was muffled by the fabric over her mouth.

Amanda bent over the pump to hide her face. "That's just a story, Ruth," she said.

Carl wasn't interested in fairies either. He put one hand on Ruth's forehead, the other on her chin, and tilted her head back to study her gums.

"Here," he said, wetting his handkerchief with the contents of a bottle he kept behind the flour bin. "This'll make it better."

Ruth frowned at the taste, but she held her jaw steady and let her father minister to her.

It wasn't accurate, of course, to say that Ruth had found Imogene. Imogene had been there all along, as Amanda well knew, for after she was released from St. Michael's she often went into the bait shop to assure herself that the child was showing no signs of the inauspicious way she'd come into the world. Although she understood the safety of her secret depended upon holding herself as far as possible from the girl, she couldn't seem to help drawing near.

Mary Louise would push Imogene forward for Amanda to admire, but at the same time would hold tight to her shoulder. "Hasn't she grown? Genie, you know Miss Starkey. Say how do you do."

But Imogene would hang back, as if in obedience to a message she felt through her mother's fingers.

When Ruth started school, Amanda found herself in town more often. She was in the shop one day in March when Imogene was feeling weak and dizzy, and she was the first to realize that the girl had scarlet fever. She insisted that she be quarantined along with the Lindgrens, although the doctor might have been persuaded to let her go home.

"We can't risk infecting Ruth," she declared, brushing aside Mary Louise's protestations. "Besides, Imogene needs me. I haven't forgotten my training."

Imogene's illness scared Amanda so much that she could hardly catch her breath when she thought of what might happen, but once the real danger had passed, she wished her recovery would go on forever. She cut paper dolls for the little girl, not just the kind that stood stiff and simple, joined at the hands like a fence, but also shapes that resembled real women, who could model clothes Amanda cut from the catalogs. Ruth had never been interested in the just-looking, the just-laying-out of paper dolls, but Imogene loved it.

"Look!" Imogene announced to her mother one evening, swatting aside the pillow slip Mary Louise was mending and climbing onto her lap with a sheet of paper in her hands. Amanda had drawn whiskers on the girl's face and colored the tip of her nose black. "Miss Starkey taught me to write my numbers."

"Those are beautiful, darling," Mary Louise said, but that night she had a talk with Amanda. "I'm taking Genie back to the shop with me tomorrow. It isn't fair, our keeping you from Ruth and Carl like this, and I think she's well enough now. I mean, thanks to you, she's completely recovered. I don't know what we would've done without you, Mandy. I was so worried. But everything's all right now, isn't it?"

So Imogene went off the next morning

with her hand in her mother's, and Amanda went back to the farm. She didn't stop visiting, though, and Mary Louise was always pleased to show her daughter off. "Amanda, you should hear the way Imogene can do her sums. What's five plus seven, Genie?" And later, "What's five times seven, Genie?" And later still, "What's five times seven plus seventy-five minus fifty-seven," until the numbers were so quick and complicated that only Amanda and Imogene knew the answers.

As Imogene got older, it would have been natural for Amanda to encourage a friendship between the girls, but she did not. Something alarmed her about Imogene, something that made her feel it was too risky to bring them together. She'd noticed it one Sunday morning, when she'd stood across the street, watching the family emerge from church, Imogene riding on her father's shoulders. The girl looked exactly like Mathilda.

"That'll be fifteen cents, please," Imogene said in her most grown-up voice. She'd hoisted herself onto a stool behind the counter in her mother's bait shop, so that she could reach the register.

"Arthur, have you got a nickel?" the man asked the boy who stood beside him. "I'll pay you back when we get home."

"That's all right," the boy said. "You gave it to me in the first place." His hair fell forward over his glasses as he reached into his pocket.

"My son and I are thinking of starting a tour boat company at Nagawaukee Beach," the man said. "If there was a boat that drove around the lake, would you girls ride on it?"

"Dad," Arthur said. He shuffled his feet in embarrassment and looked at the floor.

"Nagawaukee Beach is too far," Ruth said.

"But it would stop for you anywhere around the lake and bring you back again."

"Just going around in a circle?" Imogene said.

"A big circle, all the way around the lake. And it would be a nice boat, two decks and a mahogany rail. Red velvet seat cushions. Or maybe a nautical stripe."

"I like the red," Imogene said. "Would there be food?"

"There could be. That's a good idea. Don't you think that's a good idea, Arthur?"

"Yes," the boy said politely. "Shouldn't we be getting home, though?"

After the door had closed behind them, Imogene said, "You know the big white house with the pillars? Down the road from the Franciscans? That's theirs."

Everyone who'd ever been on the lake knew the house with the pillars. "The White House," certain people said, smiling snidely behind their martinis, as they cruised by, but it drew them nevertheless. "Who'd have thought there'd be so much money in swamps?" they said, referring to the Florida land boom, which had made the Owenses' fortune secure, not so much because Clement Owens, like every man and his brother, had known when to get in, but because he'd known when to get out.

Imogene propped her head on one hand, sighed, and sifted aimlessly with the other through a box of lead sinkers. Ruth kept an eye on her as she drifted around the shop, examining the merchandise— tubs of night crawlers and leeches, tanks of minnows, coils of line, baskets of red and white cork bobbers. She clasped her hands behind her back. "Look, but don't touch," Aunt Mandy always said.

Ruth wanted her own store when she grew up. Only it didn't have to be a bait shop. In fact, she thought she might prefer a dry goods store or a grocery or maybe a penny candy store—a place where the goods weren't alive and didn't make such a mess. What she wanted was a stock of items, all on their own special shelves, and a big case on the counter with lots of tiny drawers. She would know without looking what was in each one, the way Mrs. Lindgren did.

Ruth liked the way you just had to wait, when you had a store, for people to come in and tell you what they'd been up to since the last time. She liked the account books, with their special columns for credits and debits, and the neat way Mrs. Lindgren made her numbers.

Mrs. Lindgren was only good at writing the numbers, not at the adding and subtracting, so sometimes Imogene had to go over the figures for her. Imogene could do sums in her head faster than other people could write them down. Most of her other chores, she hated. She only pretended to dust when she went around with the cloth, and whenever Mrs. Lindgren asked her and Ruth to clean out some of the tubs, she mainly just pumped the water and talked while Ruth did all the scrubbing. Ruth didn't mind. It was fun working as long as Imogene was in a good mood, telling about the people they knew or what she'd done with her cousins up north. Ruth hoped she would get to work the register sometime, but Imogene said better not, her mother wouldn't like it.

After their bloody afternoon two years before, Imogene had sought Ruth out, as was her right by virtue of her popularity, mostly because she was curious. She craved drama and expected Ruth to do and say unusual things. For the sake of the company, Ruth was clever enough to oblige. Even now, when curiosity had long since given way to familiarity and familiarity had ripened into affection, Ruth still felt she'd better get Imogene interested or soon enough she'd be saying Ruth might as well go home. Ruth picked up a knife with a flat, curved blade. "What's this for?"

she asked, just to say something. It took a lot of effort, sometimes, to have Imogene for a friend.

"Ugh. To take the scales off. I hate fish." Imogene said the last part quietly, so her mother, who was doing the bookkeeping in the back room, wouldn't hear her. Mrs. Lindgren always told Imogene that she should be grateful—fish bought her dresses and hair ribbons, chicken dinners, train trips to Milwaukee, a warm house. It was a funny idea, Ruth thought—a perch standing on its tail with a shopping basket over one fin, choosing a nice piece of cal-ico and seven mother-of-pearl buttons at the dry goods store.

Imogene went on lifting handfuls of sinkers and letting them fall back into their box through her fingers.

And then Ruth thought of something to offer, something so big and important, she couldn't believe she hadn't already used it up. "Want to see where my mother is buried?"

Imogene sat up straight. "Really?" She slid off the stool.

"Sure. If you want to." Ruth said it like it was nothing, like she could show her a hundred things just as interesting if she was in the mood.

"We're going out, Mother," Imogene called toward the curtained doorway behind her.

"Have a good time, girls. Don't be late," Mrs. Lindgren's voice came back.

Ruth liked the way Mrs. Lindgren treated them as if they were old enough to know what they were doing, so different from Aunt Mandy, who'd never stop fussing, even now that she was fourteen and Imogene was nearly eleven.

Ruth didn't bother to walk all the way to the cemetery gate, instead, when they reached the rock wall, she boosted herself onto it and swung her legs over.

Imogene balked. "Ruth, anyone could see right up your dress!"

"So? Everyone here is dead." Ruth stood on the wall, then, and grabbed the branch of a pear tree that hung over her head. She walked up the trunk, until she could hook her knees over the branch, and hung there. "Don't worry. No one can tell it's me." Her voice was muffled by her skirt, which hung upside down over her face.

"Ruth, please!" Imogene said, but she

giggled and scrambled onto the wall herself. "Help me up." Too short to reach the
branch on which Ruth was now sitting, she
held her arms as high as she could over
her head and scratched the air with her fingertips, waiting.

Ruth leaned precariously toward her,
supporting first herself and then both of
them by hooking her instep under another
branch. She wasn't strong enough, however, to pull Imogene up. "I have to let go,"
she said and dropped her onto the soft
cemetery grass.

"Come down, then," Imogene demanded. "Let's go."

Usually Ruth didn't like visiting the
graveyard. Walking up the gravelly path
with Amanda, her feet always slipping a little back for every step forward, it had always seemed too hot or too cold. She'd
felt sorry for her mother and her grandpar-
ents, too, stuck there, twelve back, six,
seven, and eight in, baking or freezing,
nothing to see—even though she knew
dead people, being in heaven, didn't care
about those things. Today, though, scuffing
through the grass with Imogene, the place
felt different, like a playground.

"Look at this one," Imogene said, stopping in front of the stone with the ship carved on it.

"He was a sea captain," Ruth said importantly. "He drowned like my mother." In fact, she had no idea why Albert Morgan had a ship on his stone, but she didn't think he'd mind her making up a story about him. "And here are the ones from the war." That part was true—Aunt Mandy had told her.

"This is a baby." Imogene read the dates on the stone in front of her, and they looked for more children, thinking what it would be like to be already under the ground forever, eaten by worms.

"But their souls go to heaven," Ruth said. "Aunt Mandy told me all children's souls go to heaven."

"Everyone knows that."

Ruth

When we found my mother's stone with the thick green honeysuckle growing behind it, I was almost sorry I'd brought Imogene there. You shouldn't visit your dead mother just to impress your bored friend. I traced the letters in my mother's name, hoping she'd believe I'd come just to see her, hoping she'd forgive me.

"That's funny," Imogene said.

"What is?"

"She died on my birthday. November 27th. Same year, too."

We looked at each other. It was a strange idea, frightening somehow, as if for a moment the door between the world of the living and the world of the dead had blown open.

"Maybe you're her, reincarnated," I said for a joke to push the scariness away.

"What's reincarnated?"

I explained what Rudy had told me about a soul getting a new body when it died, about how you could have another life as a completely different person or even as a cat or a goldfinch, and about how a person living a long time ago could be born again as you. Not that Rudy and I really believed it, although after Rudy told me, I looked for my mother whenever an animal was born on the farm. None of them seemed to know me as I knew my

mother would, and obviously neither did
Imogene.

As we walked back into town, we talked
about what we'd be in later lives and what
we might have been before.

"I'm sure I must have been someone famous," Imogene said. "At least once or
twice. Maybe Pocahontas. Everyone says I
must have Indian blood in me. My hair is
so dark and both my parents are blond."

"That's not how it works. When you
come back, you don't look anything like
the person you were. It's not like you're related." And then because I wished I hadn't
shared my mother with her, I said, "What
makes you think you were someone special, anyway? It's much more likely you
were just ordinary. There are a lot more ordinary people than famous ones, you
know."

I said it mean and I meant it mean and I
waited for her to be angry, but Imogene
was too sure of herself to let anything I
said upset her.

"Oh, I'm positive we were both famous,"
she said. She stopped, grabbed my arm,
turned me toward her, and stared at my
face without blinking. "I know what you

were," she said finally. "You were a Chinese spy. Your eyes have that little slant and you're always so quiet, watching people. You know things, but you don't tell." She smiled, pleased with her story.

I didn't know anything, though. I only thought it seemed very strange that, while my mother and I were drowning, Imogene was being born.

———

When Ruth opened the kitchen door, Amanda looked up from the brilliant red rhubarb stems she was dicing. "Where have you been all day? You knew the beans needed weeding and the potato plants are full of bugs and I bet you the birds ate a good dozen tomatoes."

Ruth sighed. She wished things would stop growing. That was another good thing about a store. Everything stayed steady, just as it was. "I'll do it now," she said, turning to go back out.

"You'll be eaten alive out there at this hour. There's a proper time for things." In one hand Amanda held five rhubarb stalks together on the table; with the other, she wielded a long knife. "Anyway," she said, slicing quickly through the crisp stalks, while she slid her fingers along just fast enough to escape the knife, "I already did it for you."

Ruth, ashamed of herself, looked at the floor. "Dad said I could go."

"Well, no use crying over spilt milk. Wash up and I'll give you a ruby."

Ruth worked the pump handle and began to wash her hands.

"Maybe," Amanda said quietly, "you'd like to bring Imogene over here."

"What?" Ruth pretended she couldn't make out the words over the squeak of the pump and the rush of water.

Amanda dipped a piece of the rhubarb in sugar. "I said, why don't you bring Imogene over here?"

Ruth held out the back of her hand so Amanda could balance the rhubarb on her finger, like the jewel in a ring. It was their joke from some long-ago time of childish misunderstandings.

"Wouldn't it be fun, all three of us here together? Don't you like being here with me?"

"Yes," Ruth said, but the truth was she did and she didn't. As she chewed her rhubarb, she felt Amanda's love, insidious and irresistible, press around her in the hot kitchen, and she pursed her lips and squinted her eyes at the mix of sour and sweet. For the first time, she realized that she liked Imogene partly because her friend had nothing to do with Amanda.

Carl sat on the floor in one of the bedrooms of the island house, drawers pulled from the dresser spread out around him. An oblong of light fell across the floor from between the boards he'd pried off the window. He'd been through all of these drawers and the cupboards and the interstices between the walls and under the floorboards many times before. For months now he'd been rowing out to the island—sometimes once a week, sometimes every day, to look.

It was like riding a ferris wheel. One day he would be relaxed, untroubled, sure that Amanda's story was true—she and Mathilda had lived on the island because they loved it there, because Mathilda wanted to be in the house she'd shared with him. And then the doubts would begin and the uncertainties would build, until at last he would have to drop whatever he was doing and hurry singlemindedly to the house to search for clues of something else.

He tried to stay away. What if you find something, he said to himself, then what? Nothing good can come of it. Concentrate on your work. But he neglected the farm, thinking of one more spot he hadn't checked, vividly imagining the white edge of a folded love letter or the golden glint of a keepsake ring. Some man had seduced his wife. Carl had suspected it now for more than six months. He had merely to find the evidence.

He'd discovered only one clue. He pulled the silver knife out of his pocket, as he did several times a day now, and examined it. It was a good knife, expensive, not something casually left behind by someone building the house. Besides, he knew everyone who had worked on the house and none of their initials matched these: C.J.O. This had belonged to some other man.

So what if it had, he told himself and told himself and told himself. It might mean nothing. It probably meant nothing. But then how to explain Amanda's reaction when he showed the knife to her?

He played over and over in his mind the morning he'd run across in his sock drawer the knife he'd picked up years before when he and Joe and Ruth had been to the island together. He'd laid it on the table at breakfast, asking Amanda if she knew who owned it, thinking he ought to return a valuable object like that. She'd grabbed it up, turned it over, and then immediately pushed it back at him.

"I don't know. How should I know? The junk that collects! You should see the stuff I found behind the icebox last week." She'd picked up his plate before he'd finished his breakfast and scraped the last few bites of egg into the slop bucket, muttering, "I can't be held responsible for every odd pocketknife that turns up in a drawer."

At the time, it didn't even occur to Carl that Amanda's behavior might have anything to do with Mathilda. In the first place, his sister-in-law was always high strung

and quick to take offense, so her reaction
hardly seemed unusual. And in the second
place, he'd nearly forgotten about his wife.
At least, he'd packed her away somehow.
He was ashamed to admit it, but when he
thought of her lately, it seemed almost as if
she'd been married to some other man, a
friend he'd once known well but had long
since lost track of. He missed her with a
sense of nostalgia, in much the same way
he missed his own youth, and even when
he tried, he couldn't find a trace of the unbearable agony and black despair that had
once overwhelmed him. He was sorry for
Mathilda because she'd lost so much of
life, and he was sorry for Ruth that she
couldn't know her mother. But for a long
time now he'd forgotten to feel sorry for
himself.

But then he'd heard Mathilda's voice. He
heard it first in the barn, just a snatch, a
word or two, or maybe not even an entire
word but a piece of a word and an inflection, a note that was so unmistakably familiar that he said "Mathilda" aloud without
thinking and looked toward the hayloft,
certain she must be sitting there, yellow
straw tangled in her dark hair, her feet

swinging as she smiled down at him. Of course, she wasn't. Of course, she'd not come back to life. Still, he knew she was there somewhere. He strained to hear more, but the voice was gone, drowned out by Ruth calling the geese to their supper.

The second time Carl heard Mathilda's voice he was placing a salt lick near the spring. This time it was much more distinct. It was singing "Lavender's Blue" and seemed to be coming from among a clump of cattails. Although he knew it was only a memory, somehow released with intense clarity within his head, although he knew there would be nothing to see but air, he couldn't help but follow the sound, his feet sinking with every step into the rich, inky, marsh soil. Gingerly, he parted the stiff stalks of the cattails and their sharp leaves to find the singer looking at him.

"Hello, Daddy. Look at all the mallow I've got for Aunt Amanda."

Carl lost his footing and slipped to his knees. After that, it seemed that almost everything Ruth did reminded him of Mathilda—the way she raised her eyebrows when she talked, the way she held her head as she studied her lessons, the way she sat with her legs tucked underneath her, the way she splayed her fingers wide when making an emphatic point. He wanted to grab her hands and squeeze those fingers together. Instead, he frowned and looked away.

That was when he took the knife back out of his sock drawer again. Turning the silver over and over in his hands, trying the blade against the ball of his thumb for sharpness, he found himself puzzling over Hilda's implications years before. Why would two young women choose to live alone on an island? Why did they stay on through the fall?

Rudy was no help. Carl cornered him one evening in the tack room.

"I tried to get them girls to come home, Carl," Rudy said, rubbing hard on the bridle he was oiling. "I rowed out there. I told her, 'You girls better come on back now. It's gettin' cold.' "

"What do you mean, you told her? Who did you tell?"

"Well . . ." Rudy stared at the bit as if trying to see an image of the past in the shiny metal. "It was Mattie I guess I told. I never saw Amanda much, or just to wave to, up on the porch. I don't see what's the difference. What one did the other did, this kind of thing."

"This kind of thing? You mean they'd done this before?"

"Not like this, not living there. But when they were younger, that's where they'd go—a beeline for that island whenever Mrs. Starkey got on them about something at the house. We had one helluva time finding 'em, me and Mr. Starkey, before we caught on. Of course, he'd give 'em hell for runnin' away, especially Manda. You know, she was older, she shoulda known better, that kinda thing. But he liked it, too, the way they stuck together. 'I never had a brother,' he said to me, and I knew what he meant."

Carl was impatient with this sort of reminiscence. "But this time, Rudy, when they were living there, what did Mattie say when you told her it was time to move back to the farm?"

"Och, you know how Mattie was, Carl. Not even Mr. Starkey could get her to do anything she didn't want to do. 'No, Rudy, we like it here,' that's what she said. And she and the little one did look good and healthy. In fact, I'd say she'd gained a little, rounded out some, so I knew nothing was wrong. Now if I'd of talked to Amanda, it might have been different. She's a good girl. She'll do what you say. But you know how Mattie was. She went and put her hands on her hips and shook that pretty head. She wouldn't hardly let me get out of the boat." Rudy clucked his tongue and turned at last to hang the bridle on its hook.

Weak old man, Carl thought, letting a couple of girls tell him what to do. But he knew, in Rudy's place, he would have done the same.

When Rudy turned back to face him, there were tears in his eyes. "I know what I shoulda done, Carl—I've thought of it plenty of times before—I should of grabbed Ruthie. If I'da took Ruthie back before the ice come in, then they'd of come after her and none a this would of happened. I shoulda thought of that, I tell myself. Every day, I tell myself."

"It's all right, Rudy," Carl said, putting a

comforting hand on the old man's shoulder. Amanda was right. No use crying over
what couldn't be changed.

She wouldn't let him get out of the boat.
That's what stood out to Carl when he
thought about this conversation later. Why
not? Why not give him a cup of coffee, a
piece of kuchen? What were they doing on
that island, Carl wondered, that they didn't
want Rudy to see?

For a week or so it baffled him. He
couldn't think of any explanation that
made sense. And then he remembered
Madame Poker.

It had hardly been a village, that place he'd
stumbled on with McKinley and Sims one
gray afternoon. A few dirty huts. An empty
pigsty. A church without a steeple, one wall
blown in. It couldn't have been much to
look at before the war and now it was just
a jumble of abandoned stone.

Or not quite abandoned. Henny Sims
came running from behind one of the
houses, buttoning his pants.

"There's a man in there! Jesus, at least I
think it's a man."

Just then an old woman appeared at the door, her back bent so far she had to crane her neck to look up at them, her gray hair standing around her head like a halo. She spoke French and McKinley translated.

"He's mine," she said. "You can't have him. I'm keeping him. He's mine." And then she lifted what Carl had taken to be a cane but was in fact a poker, and held it in both hands, point toward them, as if it could keep the three armed men at bay.

The Americans looked at each other and Sims shrugged. "He's not much anyway," he said, "from what I could see. I think he's missing an ear, at least."

"Let's let the fellow be," Carl said, eager to get away from the place.

"All right by me," McKinley agreed. "Anybody desperate enough to live with that oughta be allowed to desert."

No one could be more unlike the crone than Mathilda, but Carl suddenly realized that she and Amanda and that old woman had all been up to the same thing. Although while poor Madame Poker was hiding a Frenchman, pushed by years of war to the brink of insanity and perhaps beyond, Mathilda and Amanda were harboring a plain old American shirker, a man who would let others, like Carl himself, go off and do the dirty work for him, risk their lives while he lazed about letting two women take care of him.

Carl made a fist around the silver pocketknife and slammed it hard against the table. They'd been hiding a shirker. A shirker whose initials were C.J.O.

It was an impossible leap and at the same time a simple step from the notion of a strange man hidden in the island house to the certainty that that shirker had loved Mathilda. Had she loved him back? Of course not. She had been kind to him, misguidedly thinking she was doing right, perhaps even hoping that someone would do the same for Carl if necessary. Of course she hadn't loved him.

But the thought itched and stung. Love made you do things, Amanda had said, and then you were sorry. What did she mean? He worried the idea, tugging at it like a hangnail little by little, until he drew blood, until he had to find out one way or another, until he found himself again in the island house, prying up the floorboards, opening the windowframes, rummaging through every drawer, searching for the evidence.

Finally, the force that had propelled Carl all afternoon began at last to ebb, and he fitted the drawers he'd spread around the bedroom back into the dresser. He felt spent, suddenly calm, knowing that he was wasting his time, that all had been innocent on the island, that there had only been an accident, an unlucky accident, one cold November night. He felt foolish now, as he always did after one of these episodes, and he glanced over his shoulder, superstitiously sensing that someone might be watching—Mathilda, maybe— and laughing at his frenzy. He left the house and rowed slowly back across the water, resting on his oars from time to time to let the fresh afternoon wind dry his skin. Poor Mattie, to have lost all these years and years of glorious summer days.

"Elbows off the table, Ruth," Amanda said, passing a plate of white bread to the girl. "How many times do I need to tell you?"

Carl kept his eyes on his plate. He knew that he ought to correct Ruth more often, not leave it all to Amanda, but he hadn't even noticed the girl's elbows. "This ham is excellent," he said.

"I'm glad you like it. I knew you'd need a good meal after those ditches."

Carl shifted in his seat. "As a matter of fact, I didn't do the digging. Pass the potatoes, Ruth. We watered the new trees in the orchard today."

Amanda's knife made a sharp click as she set it on the edge of her plate. "I thought I explained the importance of those ditches, Carl." She tapped her index finger on the table top. "My father always made sure the ditches were clean the first week of June, and we're already into the third week now. What if we get a big rain? That field will be standing in water."

"But what if we don't? Those saplings are just drying up out there."

"Carl, you have to think ahead on a farm. You can't just be running from one emergency to another. You'll never get anywhere that way."

"What happened to that baby?" Ruth said suddenly. She held her fork in the air, a beet slice skewered on the tines.

No one responded for a moment, as Amanda and Carl decided whether they were relieved or annoyed to be distracted from their argument.

"What baby?" Rudy asked finally.

"More tomatoes, Rudy?" Amanda held out the plate.

"The baby we took to its mother," Ruth said. "How did it get lost?"

"A lost baby?" Carl said. "Who loses a baby?"

"She must be talking about a lamb," Amanda said.

"I'm not talking about a lamb. It was a baby and it was crying, so we brought it to its mother."

"The stork brings the baby to the mother," Rudy said.

"No," Ruth said, "we did. Aunt Amanda and me."

"Aunt Amanda and I," Amanda corrected.

"Maybe you read it," Carl said, "in a book."

"That girl, always the book," Rudy said.

"This wasn't in a book," Ruth said. She pushed her beets around her plate, painting with their pink juice.

"Are you sure?" Amanda said. "Because I know sometimes when I read a story and then I dream about it, when I wake up, I'm not sure what I've read and what I've dreamed and what really happened."

Ruth put her elbow on the table, her chin in her hand. She looked over her shoulder at the floor, away from the rest of them. "It was a real baby," she said sullenly.

"I remember walking with you when you were just a bitty baby. You must have had colic something terrible, because you cried and cried," Rudy said.

Ruth frowned at Rudy. "No, I didn't! I did not cry!"

Amanda's chair scraped back from the table. She grabbed Ruth by the back of the collar and stood her on her feet. "You apologize to Rudy this instant, Ruth Sapphira Neumann!"

Ruth hid her face in her hands. "I'm sorry, Rudy. I'm sorry I shouted at you."

"That's all right, sweetheart." He winked at her.

"Now you go to your room," Amanda

said. She followed Ruth out of the kitchen and watched her climb the stairs. "Ruth," she said, when the girl reached the top.

Ruth stopped but didn't look back.

"I'll save you some pie."

Chapter Ten

Amanda

"Swim!" the little voice piped just beside my ear. "Swim! Swim!"

I opened my eyes to see Ruthie standing beside my bed, just as she had every morning for the past two weeks. "Let's go swimming," she announced and clapped her hands.

"All right, sweetie. Shh, shh, yes, we'll swim."

I pulled her into the bed with me. It was the middle of July now and so hot that even the sheet over my shoulder made me sweat and kept me from falling asleep at night. It seemed I'd closed my eyes only an hour before. "Let's sleep another minute."

But Ruthie wouldn't stay still. She bounced on the mattress and wriggled in my arms and the word "swim" burst from her in a whisper every few seconds. Finally I gave up. At least the water would cool us.

"Be quiet, Ruthie. You'll wake your mother," I said, struggling to pin up my braid.

"Shh, shh!" she said, jumping up and down on the bed and clapping her hands again.

I went to her and held out my arms, and she leaped into them with a final tremendous squeal. I carried her out of the house and down to the water.

We swam, although you could hardly call what I did in the water swimming, in our nightclothes, since Ruth had no bathing costume and mine wouldn't have fit me even if I'd thought to pack it along.

We played awhile in the shallows, me sitting on the lake bottom, letting the cool water lap over the tops of my thighs and around my waist, Ruth, squatting, getting her bottom wet but keeping her knees dry. I trailed my arms through the water and patted cool handfuls around my neck. Ruth splashed, wetting us both, thrilled with the sensation of flinging something her fingers couldn't hold and with the sight of the scattering droplets. Then she laid her palms gently on the water, testing the surface tension, before plunging her hands under, where she studied her fingers, which no longer seemed related to the ones she knew in dry air. She grabbed for pretty rocks and laughed when she came up with only a fistful of water, because the stones were so much deeper than they appeared.

Soon she would wander farther out, and I would have to scramble after her. By the time the water was above my knees, she would almost be swimming. I would support her tight little tummy with my palm, but she hardly needed my help. She kept herself afloat, paddling like a turtle, her neck straining to hold her chin above the water, her feet pumping wildly behind.

Always at some point she'd scoot away from me. She'd move a little distance and then stop, checking to see if I'd noticed. I'd look away, pretending I didn't see, until she made her way under the willow whose vines hung down to the water.

"Where's Ruth?" I called. And her laugh

would come from the tree. "I wonder where Ruthie could be." Finally I'd pull back the drapery of leaves and grab her up and we'd struggle through the water to the shore.

This morning Mathilda was standing in the doorway. I set Ruthie down on the beach, and she went running toward her mother. Mathilda didn't look at her, though. She stared at me as I stood there, my nightgown plastered against my middle.

When I was fourteen and Mathilda was six, she burst into our room one morning as I was dressing. I had been careful around that time to be sure she was safely downstairs or fast asleep before I changed my clothes, but on that day she caught me. My nightgown was already over my head and my dress was all the way across the room. She stopped in the doorway, her eyes wide.

"Shut the door!" I said.

But she just stood there, staring. Slowly, she brought both her hands up to her chest and inscribed two little arcs in the air. She had no words to describe this impossible thing. I was no longer the sister she knew.

"Amanda," Mathilda whispered now. That was all.

It was my turn to catch Ruthie up and hold her tight against me. I needed her to cover my bulging secret.

————

The maple leaves were only the size of a child's palm, but the afternoon sun was hot as July. It had been a whole week of the calendar lagging behind the weather, when anyone could tell it was summertime but still school went on interminably, refusing to give up and be done with it.

Imogene and Ruth, Ray and Louis walked along the sidewalk, not quite together.

"Step on a crack, break your mother's back," Louis said.

Ruth worried. Did it count if your mother was really your aunt? She placed her feet cautiously and was relieved when the sidewalk ended and she could move freely along the edge of the road. Ray and Louis kicked a stone as they went, raising dust.

"Ach, so much dust," Imogene said, turning her face away.

Ray kicked harder then to produce a bigger cloud.

"We oughta do something," he said.

"Yeah," Louis said. "Let's do something."

"We oughta go somewhere."

"Yeah, let's go somewhere." Louis stopped and turned, waiting for Imogene and Ruth to catch up. "Do you wanna go somewheres?"

"Where?" Imogene asked.

"I don't know. Somewhere different."

Imogene looked at Ruth. "We know a place."

Ruth frowned. "No, we can't, Imogene," she whispered. "My aunt won't like it."

"We'll go without you then." Imogene skipped ahead to join the boys.

Ruth watched them start down the road together. She was sorry, but she couldn't move from where she stood. She knew she was right.

Ten steps, eleven, twelve, and then Imogene ran back and grabbed her hand, pulling her forward.

"Please come, Ruth. I don't want to go without you. Please don't spoil it."

And so reluctantly, when they reached the path, Ruth followed them into the woods. The woods were green, but a tender green, and the leaves were not yet massed into dense, impenetrable walls, but barely overlapped each other at the edges to make a lacy, scalloped screen. The stiff branches were sending out new, flexible green shoots, and the dirt path was carpeted with bright little nettles and young poison ivy plants, easily crushed under the children's heavy shoes.

"We have to take the boat," Imogene said self-importantly, resting a hand on the gunwale. "We'll get in, and then you boys push it in the water," she directed.

They did, and then scrambled aboard, wetting their feet, but it was Ruth who fitted the oars into their locks and began to row. It was her family's boat, after all.

Then Louis slid onto the seat beside her. "Here, let me do that," he said. And she let him.

Zigzagging slightly, they made their way toward the island.

Imogene had the front seat. "I'll test the

water," she announced, dangling her fingers over the side. "Perfect!

"You know this island is where Ruth was born," she said a minute later. "And where her mother drowned. That's why Ruth isn't allowed to go swimming."

Ruth scowled. Imogene shouldn't be telling these things. "She didn't drown on the island."

Imogene went on, imperturbable. "Well, of course, I didn't mean on the island, but somewhere out here. She might have gone down right here, right in this very spot." She leaned over the side and stabbed one finger into the water.

Ruth studied the place. You could stare and stare at the water, but you could never see down more than a few feet. A whole other world could be going on under there and you'd never know it.

For a time, when Ruth was young, she'd believed that her mother was a sort of mermaid who lived in a house at the bottom of the lake. She liked this idea in the daytime and expanded on it endlessly, giving the Mathilda she knew from photographs a seaweed garden and neighbors, imagining an underwater post office where Mathilda would pick up the stones on which Ruth had scratched messages before she knew how to write. In her sleep, however, this benign vision became a nightmare. She dreamed of hands reaching out of the waves to grab her, pulling her down by the feet, by the arms, by the hair, holding her under until at last she awoke, gasping for breath.

Ruth blinked now and looked up at Imogene. "No," she said. "I don't think it was here."

"Say," Louis said, resting on the oars, "where do I go?"

They were nearly to the island.

"Go around to the right," Ruth said. "There's a beach."

They pulled the boat up as far as they could on the little spit of sand and wrapped the painter around a sapling for good measure.

"Hey, let's see the house," Ray said.

"It's all boarded up," Ruth told him.

Ray ran ahead anyway and pushed on the door. "It's open," he yelled.

"You go ahead," Ruth said from the bottom of the steps. "I'll be down by the

water." And while the other three went inside, she turned and went back to the lake.

A willow grew so close to the shore
there that its tendrils hung over the shallow
water, making a sort of house. Ruth, while
she wrapped a vine around her hand and
hung for a moment or two to see if it would
bear her weight, peered beneath the
canopy. The water seemed more still and a
deeper green under there. The sound the
waves made bouncing against the rocks
seemed louder, while the noise outside—
the other children laughing and talking—
was muffled. This was where a mermaid
would live, if there were such a thing. Now
Ruth knew there wasn't, of course.

And then, suddenly, the others were
back.

"There's nothing in there," Ray said.
"Just a bunch of furniture and stuff."

"I thought it was pretty," Imogene said
loyally. "How come it's open, Ruth? Are
you going to move back here?"

"No, not that I know."

"Maybe some tramp's got in there,"
Louis suggested.

"I bet it's a gangster hideout," Ray said.

"It is not," Imogene said. "Don't worry, Ruth."

But Ruth, still thinking about the cave beneath the willow, wasn't listening.

Louis was taking his shoes off. "I'm going in."

"Me, too," Ray said, unbuttoning his shirt.

The boys stripped down to their short pants and raced each other in, shouting when their feet slipped on the rocks.

"It ain't cold!" Ray called. "Come on in!"

Imogene was already wading gingerly, holding the hem of her skirt high. "It is, too, cold, Ray Johnson." She looked back at Ruth. "My mother says the water's not really warm enough for swimming until July. She'd throw a fit if she knew I even got my toes wet this early." But she kept on wading, deeper and deeper, until she lost her footing and sat down with a splash. The boys laughed and she laughed with them, pushing her wet hair back from her face. "Well, I'm in now. I guess I might as well swim. Come on, Ruth. Come in with me. It's nice. Really, it is."

Louis shot a spray of water from between his teeth. "Yeah, come on, Ruth! Come on in!"

The others splashed Ruth and shouted, getting louder and louder as they tried to outdo each other, but when she still hung back, shaking her head, they lost interest.

"Look, I found the dropoff," Ray said and disappeared.

"Let me try," Louis said when Ray's head bobbed up again.

"Let's see who can swim the farthest underwater," Imogene said. "I'll judge."

Ruth watched them, the willow fronds draped over her shoulders like a cape. "You always liked to hide in the shallow water under the willow tree," Aunt Mandy had said, night after night, when Ruth was tucked in bed with her eyes closed. She was telling Ruth one of her stories about "the olden days" to put her to sleep. "And your mama and I would call—'Where's Ruthie? Where's our girl?' And then finally you couldn't stand it anymore. You would laugh and we would find you. We would always find you." Ruth bent to untie her shoes.

Slowly, with her eyes on the other three

to distract herself and with her hands
wrapped tight in willow vines, Ruth inched
her feet into the chilly water. Imogene was
demonstrating her strokes now, dipping in
and out of the blue-green water like a frog.

Ruth waded tentatively into the lake, re-
viving the forgotten sensation of cool water
on her skin, of rocks slimy with algae beneath her feet, of the sun glinting through
droplets on her lashes. Deeper and deeper
she went, pushing against the gently re-
sisting waves, ruffling the surface with her
palm, bending her knees to feel the water
rising tingly and soft around her thighs.

"Hey, Ruth's coming in!" Louis yelled.

Ray had been showing Imogene how to
hold her nose and turn a somersault. "Hey,
Ruth," he said, "you wanna swim? We'll
teach ya. C'mon, it's the easiest thing there
is." All three of them came toward her,
pushing steadily forward so that the water
made V shapes behind them.

Where was she? Amanda pulled the edge
of the curtain back as if that single inch of
fabric could be concealing Ruth as she
came up the drive. She should have been

home an hour ago, and there were the sheep, practically in the backyard when she'd told Ruth they needed to be herded to the lower meadow that afternoon. Suddenly an idea struck her so hard she nearly staggered. She knew where Ruth was.

Sure enough, when she reached the lake, the boat was gone. So she would have to use Joe Tully's boat again, she thought grimly, marching along the shoreline around the bend in the bay.

The Tullys' rowboat was grimy from lack of use and slugs were stuck to the seats, but Amanda wiped it down with a couple handfuls of grass and then launched it with one mighty shove. She stepped in so smoothly at the last possible moment that her feet stayed perfectly dry. She rowed hard, until she heard their voices, squawking like gulls fighting over a fish. And then, on the far side of the island, she looked over her shoulder and saw them, one small, dark head sliding along the top of the water, two boys cheering the swimmer on, and Ruth in the lake beside them.

How many times had she warned Ruth to stay away from the water? At one time or another Carl and Mary Louise and even

Joe all had begged her to let them teach
Ruth to swim. Then she would be safe,
they claimed. Then no one need worry. But
that was a foolish hope, as Amanda well
knew. Mathilda could swim like a duck and
still she'd drowned. Ruth would only be
safe from the water if she stayed far from
it. And now she was in it, up to her waist,
with two boys, their narrow white chests
defiantly naked, beside her.

Ruth heard Amanda's voice before she
saw her bearing down on them. "What are
you doing?" came the shout, so fierce that
Imogene heard, though her ears were half
under water, stopped swimming, and let
her feet touch the bottom. All of them
stared at Amanda, too surprised to answer.
"What are you doing here?" she yelled
again, clearly aiming the question directly
at Ruth.

"I'm . . . I'm swimming," Ruth said.

Amanda heard Mathilda's voice coming
from the water beside the girl.

Imogene laughed. "Well, she's not really
swimming yet. But we're teaching her."

Amanda heard Mathilda's laugh from the

water beside Imogene. She looked from one girl to the other. She looked at the grinning boys. Amanda felt rage, like a wave, begin deep within her gut, and then grow until it filled every artery and vein, until her very eyeballs and fingertips swelled with it. She heard her own voice, as if from a distance, mimicking Ruth's.

"Swimming," she said. "I'll teach you to swim!"

The children stared at her as she began to row stern first toward them. Nearer and nearer she came, with long, powerful strokes that made the water bank along the transom and spill into the boat. First the boys, then Imogene, stepped back and back, and finally turned and ran for the shore. Ruth, though, stood still, waiting.

Amanda brought the boat right up to the girl in the shallow water, so close that their faces were even, and Ruth could see how tightly her aunt was holding her jaw. She could see the sweat wetting the roots of her hair. She could see the tiny lines, like little cuts, along the top of Amanda's lip.

"What . . . ?" was all she managed to say, before Amanda leaned toward her, holding out one hand. Ruth took it.

"Get in here," Amanda said, pulling her hard, and Ruth fell forward into the boat, face first onto the seat. "Get up."

Ruth was frightened—the voice didn't sound like Amanda's. She obeyed, though, smoothing her sodden skirt over her knees, keeping her eyes on the water streaming from the hem of her dress around her feet.

Amanda began to row. She didn't look at Ruth but kept her gaze on the island over the girl's shoulder. She clenched her teeth and pulled hard on the oars until the veins in her arms stood out like wires. They went farther and farther out into the lake, but Ruth did not look back.

Finally Amanda stopped rowing. She lifted her oars to let them drip for a moment before tucking them inside the boat. Then she stood and took a step toward Ruth. The boat pitched wildly and she gripped the gunwales to steady herself. She stood still until the boat stopped rocking and then came toward Ruth again. "Stand up," she said when she was close. "Up on the seat."

"No. What are you doing? I don't want to."

"On the seat, I said."

Slowly, Ruth pulled her feet onto the seat under her, and slowly, she straightened her knees. The boat rocked and she crouched, grabbing the gunwales.

"Stand up, Ruth."

"But, Aunt Mandy!"

"I have to teach you, Ruth!" Her voice was shrill, frantic. "Stand up!"

Even more slowly than the first time, Ruth stood.

"Turn around."

Ruth turned. Amanda stood behind her so close Ruth could feel her there without a touch. "I told you not to go to the water, Ruth."

"I'm sorry."

"I told you, and you did it anyway. Can't I trust you, Ruth?"

Ruth stood defiant. The sun glinted and sparked on the green water in diamonds and stars, flashes that dazzled her eyes. Do it, she thought. Go ahead. Do it.

"If you come to the water, you have to learn to swim."

Amanda's push was hard, but not so hard that Ruth could not have kept her balance if she'd tried. But Ruth did not try.

She flew out over the water, her shadow dark on the waves beneath her, and then at last she dropped.

With a rush the water filled her ears and her eyes as it closed over her. It wrapped itself around her legs, around her arms, around her neck. It pulled her deeper and tried to hug her to its bosom. For an instant, she let it. For an instant, she sank.

And then, with a jolt, she panicked. She thrashed, struggling against the softness that would not push back. She kicked and kicked and beat her arms, and finally she rose.

Her head broke into the thin air and she gulped, swallowing a mouthful of water. She saw with relief that Amanda was right there, standing in the boat, looking down at the water, watching her.

"I'm doing this for you, Ruth. I have to teach you to swim," Amanda said again. Then she sat down and started to row toward the shore.

Ruth's panic this time was mixed with confusion. "Stop!" she gasped, and water ran into her mouth again. She whipped her arms and legs in every direction. Her feet tangled in her dress. Her hands pounded against the water. But she knew it was all right. She could tell now that she'd be able to stay afloat for a moment or two, the time it would take for her aunt to fish her out.

But Amanda didn't fish her out.

"Come on, swim," she yelled, holding the oars out of the water.

The boat was only a few yards away. Ruth kicked and thrashed. She threw her arms in front of her, one and then the other, reaching for the boat. Somehow she began to move forward. The space of water between her and the boat got narrower and narrower until she could almost touch the stern. She held out her hand. She reached, waiting for Amanda to grab her, to rescue her, to pull her in, but Amanda dipped the oars back into the water, and the boat slid away.

Amanda did this over and over again, allowing Ruth to get almost close enough to save herself and then rowing away. Ruth screamed and gulped the green-tasting water; she begged Amanda to stop, to save her, but Amanda only turned her head to get her bearings and to wipe her tears on the shoulder of her dress, and rowed on.

When they were nearly to the shore, Ruth stopped screaming. She was too tired then, too cold. At last Amanda lifted the oars into the boat. She sat still until Ruth came alongside and then she smiled and held out her hand. Amanda reached down for Ruth but Ruth swam on.

Somewhere on the other side of the boat a fish jumped. Ruth heard its body fall into the water with a heavy splash. Amanda heard it, too, and, startled, instinctively turned toward the sound. When Ruth saw Amanda turn away, she held her breath and went down. She ducked under water and came up behind the curtain of the willow.

The waves sucked loud against the rocks and bits of sun fell between the leaves and squiggled on the water in bright splinters and specks. She sat on the lake bottom, her knees drawn up to her chin. Through the vines, she could see Amanda staring at the spot where she had been. She saw her face as if magnified, all disbelief and fear.

Then Amanda lunged and threw herself sideways off the boat. One of the oars slipped in behind her. She was flailing then, diving, clawing the water, slapping the air. "Ruth!" she screamed. "Ruth, come back!" But Ruth gave no answer. She wished she could let Amanda save her, but it was too late. She was no longer drowning. At last she parted the willow vines and moved through the water, not gracefully like Imogene, but in a fury of splashing that nevertheless propelled her steadily forward. She kicked up a froth behind her, so all of them would see that she could swim.

Chapter Eleven

——

Amanda

Mattie didn't say, "How could you?" as I would have. It wasn't her nature to do so, and I was almost sorry for that. It was hard having to shoulder the whole of it myself, the recriminations and the guilt. Sometimes I felt I could barely crawl forward under the weight of it.

"Who is he?" Mattie dared to ask instead.

The thought of him and what we'd done made the bile rise in my throat. "Never mind," I told her. "I'll never see him again, if I can help it."

And if perhaps I'd hoped otherwise, if

once or twice I'd longed for him to appear
and pull me into his arms with a story that
would somehow make everything all right,
I knew as I said those words that it would
never be so.

Mathilda said very little to me for two
days after that, but on the third night she
stood in the doorway of my room, crying.
"Poor Amanda. It must be so awful for
you."

"It's my own fault. If I'd done right, this
never would've happened." But I cried
then too. What were we going to do, this
other one and I?

Mattie got into the bed with me, and we
slept together as we used to, when she
was a baby and needed comforting.

The next morning she told me that she
had a plan. "We'll say we found it."

"Found it where?"

"Oh, anywhere, it doesn't matter. Say
some girl came to us. Yes, she knew you
were a nurse, so she came to us for help. A
poor hired girl. But it was a terrible birth.
Yes, the worst you'd ever seen in all your
years of nursing."

"Only three."

She shook her head impatiently. "It doesn't matter. It was a terrible birth and she bled and bled. And you did your best. You did everything mortally possible, but still, it was no use." Her head drooped dramatically and tears caught on her lashes. "And there was no one else, no one at all to raise this poor little thing, so you brought it to me. Because you knew I would be good to it and raise it with my daughter just as if it were my own."

For a while I protested that I couldn't ask such a thing of her. I would find some other way, I insisted; I couldn't drag her into this. But hadn't I done so already? When I made her come to the island with me, hadn't I been hoping that somehow she would take care of me, the way I'd always taken care of her?

The heaviness seemed to lift when I heard Mathilda's plan. Perhaps I hadn't spoiled our lives after all. I would be Aunt Mandy to this baby, as well as to Ruth. I would hold it on my lap and rock it to sleep. I would kiss its soft head and teach it to count and keep it safe from all the world. And I would be safe too. No one would ever know what I had done.

That night for the first time since we'd been on the island, I knelt with Ruthie and Mattie on the green rug beside Mathilda's bed and whispered along as they recited, "now I lay me down to sleep." I couldn't sleep, however. I was too relieved. For the first time I felt excited at the prospect of this little one, who was rolling and kicking now inside me, as if he or she were excited too.

"Mathilda will be your mama," I whispered, stroking my firm, round belly, "but I will always love you." And I did feel that now I would be able to love this restless being. "Go ahead," I said. "Dance."

When I'd lain awake an hour or more, I woke Mathilda. "Let's take Ruthie for a swim."

While Mattie and Ruth splashed in the shallows, I swam far out into the lake. I floated on my back to let my baby rise like a pale little island out of the black water, and I smiled up at the milky white moon.

Afterward I made us a feast—mashed potatoes and bacon and raspberries drenched in cream. Ruth fell asleep over her berries, but the eastern sky was pearly

gray by the time Mattie and I crawled, exhausted, back into our beds.

———

It had been a mistake, what she'd done
with Ruth, pushing her in the water that
way. Amanda tried to tell herself that at
least the girl could swim, but she knew underneath that teaching Ruth to float hadn't
been her purpose. What that purpose had
been, she wasn't sure, which frightened
her. She found herself glancing upward at
odd moments. What would Mathilda think?

She'd wanted to pull Ruth back to her;
she knew that much. Ruth belonged to her,
not to those boys, not even to Imogene.
Amanda felt indignant even now, remembering the scene, the children's silly paddling, their shrill voices. She had to shake
herself even now, three years later, to
throw off the bitterness she'd felt. How
could Ruth betray her for those others?
She and Ruth were meant to brave the water together and emerge triumphant from
the element that had taken everything from
them. Instead, with a creeping sense of

disquiet, Amanda felt that the lake might have stolen from her again. Since that afternoon Ruth, whom she'd once brought back to life, whom she'd lifted bleeding from the bottom of the stairs, whom the school had had to pry from her side, had been slipping through her fingers.

Ruth was subtle about her escape mostly, only spending more time than she used to in the barn with her chores, taking longer to walk home from school, asking her father for advice when before it would have been Amanda, always Amanda. Someone else mightn't even have noticed the change, but Amanda did. She knew she oughtn't to respond, knew she should let the girl withdraw—eventually, she would turn back—but it was impossible. Almost against her will, Amanda found herself grasping for Ruth again and again, but every time her fingers closed they seemed to scratch, and the girl who'd once clung to her as if she were life itself shrank away.

But it wouldn't go on forever, Amanda thought; it couldn't. And in the meantime Ruth had brought her Imogene.

"Girls!" Amanda called from the bottom of the stairs, as she mopped her face with her sleeve. They'd promised to help her can tomatoes, and the water was boiling, the kitchen already hot.

She liked calling them, liked the idea of the two of them asleep in her house together, as they should have been from the first. "Girls," she called again, pushing a note of impatience into her voice. "You don't want to sleep the day away."

Still there was no answer. Amanda climbed the stairs and opened the door to Ruth's room. When Ruth was awake, her sixteen-year-old face, its baby roundness disappearing as its adult bones emerged, seemed almost an affront to Amanda, as if this development, too, were part of Ruth's efforts to transform herself into someone her aunt wouldn't recognize. Unconscious, however, curled tight, as she was now, she was still the little girl Amanda knew intimately. And here was precious Imogene, also looking younger than her years as she lay sprawled across the bed, one perfect foot hanging off the edge. Amanda cupped her hand around it.

Who knows how odd her Ruth might have become if she'd been left to herself, shunned by those horrible children at the school? Instead, Imogene's approval had made her, if not popular, at least accept-able, and consequently she'd learned to care what others, besides Amanda, thought of her. She'd begun to curl her hair and smile just like any other girl. She even wanted a bob. Although Amanda missed the child, at once frightened and fierce, who'd seemed attached only to her, she knew this change was for the best, and she was grateful to the girl whose foot lay in her palm.

"Wake up, Imogene," Ruth said sud-denly, lifting her head from her pillow and startling the girl so that she gasped and yanked her foot out of Amanda's fingers. "We're up," Ruth said to Amanda. "You can go back downstairs."

But Amanda went into Carl's room and made the bed and then tidied her own room, listening to the girls chatter as they dressed. She was plumping pillows when she noticed Imogene standing in the door-way.

"My mother usually does my hair for me," the girl said. "Will you do it, please?" She held the brush out.

Amanda sat on the bed and patted the

space next to her. Her hand trembled as she took the brush, but steadied as she stroked Imogene's hair, lifted it in her fingers, smoothed it with her palm. She held a piece to her cheek and lowered her nose to the crown of the girl's head. But Imogene was getting restless. Too polite to say anything, she squirmed in her seat.

"Shall I do it in braids," Amanda said, "the way I used to do Ruth's mother's?"

"Like in the picture?"

"Yes."

"Good." Imogene nodded, satisfied.

They'd been examining the picture on Ruth's dresser last night, asking Amanda to repeat the stories she'd told Ruth about Mathilda. It was a casual picture of the two sisters, sitting on the edge of the porch. Amanda remembered how her mother had stood in the yard with her head bowed over her new Brownie camera.

"Look at me," she'd said, and Amanda had obeyed, but Mattie had been distracted by something at the last second—a dog barking or a chicken fluttering its wings or just a flicker of light in the lilacs—who could know now? Their mother had thought the photo a failure because of

Mathilda's inattention and had dropped it
in the back of a scrapbook, not even both-
ering to mount the corners with black paper triangles.

Carl had liked that picture, though.
"That's just like her," he'd said. "And a
good likeness of you, Amanda," he'd
added kindly. He'd had the photo enlarged
and gave it to Ruth in a pretty wooden
frame for her twelfth birthday, the age
Mathilda had been when the picture was
taken, as near as Amanda could remember.

"Where's Dad?" Ruth said when they
were finally all in the kitchen. Carl was seldom where he was supposed to be lately,
and his absences troubled her.

Jealousy pricked Amanda and at the
same moment she burned her fingers
pulling a freshly sterilized jar from its boiling bath. "If you'd gotten up earlier to help,
you would know," she said crossly. "He
went up to Slinger with Rudy to see about
a new tractor."

Carl was irritable too. "Wasted a whole
morning," he complained when he and

Rudy were driving home. He hadn't been sleeping at all lately, since closing his eyes only opened the curtain on a scene once dreamed, now unforgettable—Mathilda sinking through a dark abyss, her arms and legs twisting, a loop of hair drifting away from her face to reveal her mouth, either screaming or laughing, it was impossible to tell.

"Well, what can you do?" Rudy agreed that the tractor hadn't been worth the price.

"I just don't like to waste time is all. And we need a tractor."

But they couldn't afford a tractor, even if the farmer had accepted a reasonable offer. It'd been stupid to use the gas to drive up and see it. Weiss and some of the others had been talking about dumping milk right onto the Watertown Plank Road, not that Carl believed they'd actually do it, but they all might as well—prices were so low, it was costing more just to keep the cows fed than the milk brought in. Amanda had, in fact, suggested he look for some work for the winter, when the farm, as she said, would pretty much run itself. She liked, Carl thought, to point out how little he mattered.

But no—he shook his head, trying to make himself see the situation clearly—that wasn't fair anymore. After all, she was asking for his help. She'd started nursing again, assisting Dr. Karbler with deliveries and helping Hattie Jensen recover from her fall, and even Ruth had set up a stand at the intersection to sell vegetables and pies, minding her "store" after school. He ought to do his part, at least for Ruth's sake. But he couldn't. Not if it meant leaving, even for a few months. Not with Mathilda behind every tree and door teasing him to find her.

He was thinking about the island house. About an hour ago, while frowning at the tractor's gunked-up engine, he'd remembered a space, a little pocket under a loose kitchen floor-board, where a teething ring of Ruth's had once hidden. It was a place he'd checked, but now he realized that he hadn't examined it carefully, at least he could picture without any effort at all a photograph or a letter slid in there on one edge, so that only if you knew at just what angle to look could you find it. When they got home, he would row out there, look from every angle.

Rudy rested his elbow on the windowframe and gazed at the passing fields. When had Carl gotten like this, so impatient, so easily thrown off course? It was no use talking to him when he was acting like a horse with a burr under its saddle.

The girls were sitting on the porch shucking corn when the men drove up. She was a nice friend for Ruth, that Imogene. Carl worried about Ruth being lonely, the only child on the farm. It would have been nice if he and Mattie had had another. He slammed the door of the truck behind him and went to the pump in the yard to wash up. The cool water made him feel better, and he threw some over his head, raking his fingers through his hair.

"You girls having a good time?" he called across the yard. He went on without giving them a chance to answer, "Aunt Mandy inside?"

"In the kitchen," Ruth said. "Where's the tractor?"

"No good," Carl said, shaking his head and frowning. He started toward the porch.

In the distance a dog barked, and Imogene turned her head toward the sound.

Halfway across the yard, Carl stopped. Something indefinite brushed against the edge of his memory.

"What's the matter, Dad?"

Carl didn't answer. He stared at Imogene, her profile and her braids. There was something strange about her—no, it was something strangely familiar. She turned her gaze on him then, across the yard, and his mind caught a notion and held it fast. He'd never have seen it if she'd been closer, if her hair had not been braided, if she hadn't been sitting precisely there, where Mattie had sat the day that picture was taken. He'd never have realized that Imogene was Mattie, a young Mattie, younger than he'd ever known. She was the Mattie in the photograph.

Without a word, Carl turned and went back to the truck. He got in and backed onto the grass as he turned around. Then he drove back up the road, dust clouding thickly behind him.

The bell jingled over the bait shop door, and Carl stood for a moment just inside, letting his eyes adjust to the dimness.

"Carl!" Mary Louise exclaimed, coming out from the back room. "It's good to see you." She leaned against the counter smiling. And then, when he continued to stand without speaking, she asked, "Did you come in just to say hello?"

"No." Carl, recollecting himself, crossed to the buckets and tanks of bait along the wall and peered into them, distractedly.

"So you've finally taken up fishing?"

"No," he said again. But he continued to drift around the room, idly fingering various items, keeping his eyes from Mary Louise. He paused at the counter to her left and began sliding open the tiny drawers in the chest.

"Can I help you find something?"

"Yes. No. I'll take this," he said, lifting from a drawer a hook whose barb had caught in his flesh.

Mary Louise held out her hand for it. "I hope my daughter's been behaving," she said in a way that implied no doubt. "I think it's wonderful the way those two are such friends. Just like Mandy and me. I wish we had the time we used to."

Carl interrupted before Mary Louise

could go on. "It's Imogene I wanted to talk to you about."

Mary Louise stiffened and closed her palm around his change. "There isn't anything wrong, is there?"

"No, no, not that. No, I'm sorry." Carl held both hands up, shaking his head. "I think . . ." he began, and then stopped. He started again. "There's something about her. I mean, have other people noticed it? Her hair. Her nose."

Carl thought he'd spoken so clearly that, when Mary Louise looked merely puzzled, he felt immediately light, even merry. He smiled. "Oh, I'm crazy. I must be crazy," he insisted with relief. "How could I have thought such a crazy thing? And then"—he pulled his hand over his face, all the way from his forehead to his chin—"to come right in here and shoot my mouth off. Of course you're her mother. Well," he shrugged, "I wouldn't blame you one bit if you just threw me out." He shook his head, astounded at his tactlessness, but more than anything pleased, so very pleased to find that he'd been wrong. "It's just," he tried to explain, "Amanda has this picture . . ." He broke off and looked down at the counter, still shaking his head at his mistake, not knowing what to say next until he discovered whether she was angry with him or would laugh or would ask, as so many had lately, what had gotten into him. And really, it was a question that bore thinking about. Look how he'd been living, letting these ideas yank him this way and that.

Carl was so preoccupied, he hardly noticed that Mary Louise had been standing motionless, her eyes wide and fearful. Finally she seemed almost to fall forward and clutched the counter with both hands to keep herself upright. "You won't tell Imogene. Carl, promise me you won't tell Imogene."

Carl's skin began to tingle. He tried to speak but couldn't find his voice. He managed to raise his eyes to hers, to shake his head slightly.

Mary Louise came around the counter and put her hand on Carl's arm. "You have to understand, Carl. She's ours. She never had anyone else, right from the start. It was a terrible birth, Amanda said, the worst she'd ever seen, in all her years of nursing.

You know, the poor thing barely lived an hour afterward."

"Who?" Carl managed to ask.

"That poor hired girl." She spoke as if he knew exactly to whom she referred, as if he were privy to the whole story and they were only reminiscing. "The one who had her. I don't remember whose farm she was on—some place way over by Nashotah, I think. It must have been a long buggy ride, because Ruth was practically frozen when they got here. It must have been awful. The birth, I mean. You should have seen the blood on Amanda's hands. But, you know," she said, lowering her voice to a whisper, "she couldn't have kept the baby anyway. No husband."

"No husband," Carl repeated.

They both stood silent for a moment, and then Mary Louise spoke again. She seemed relieved to have unburdened herself. "I'm surprised Amanda told you about that girl and all. She was so definite about keeping the mother a secret. To save the family's feelings, you know. And that was fine by us. To us, it was a miracle to have that baby. That was all we cared about. And I thank God for it every day."

"Was Mattie with her?"

"What?"

"Was Mattie with Amanda when she brought you the baby?"

"No, Carl. That was the night . . . Amanda had Ruth with her. I told you, that poor little girl was ice cold. We had to heat a bath for her, feed her some broth. By the time Amanda got back to the island . . . Mattie was gone."

"Why wasn't Ruth with her mother?"

"I don't know. Maybe Mattie didn't feel well? Or maybe Amanda and Ruth had been over in Oconomowoc together that day. That makes sense if she ended up helping with a baby way over in Nashotah. Anyway, Amanda explained, I think, but I don't remember now. It didn't seem important after what happened."

Carl felt his legs begin to move him toward the door, but Mary Louise stepped from behind the counter into his way, her face anxious again. "You won't tell Genie. You did promise."

"No, I won't. I promise I won't." He practically pushed her out of the way in his hurry to get out the door.

He drove while his thoughts flipped and

darted, like a fish on a line. That ridiculous story about Mathilda disappearing, falling through the ice. It hadn't been a poor hired girl who died in childbirth without a husband—it had been Mathilda. And Mathilda had had a husband, oh, yes, but he wasn't the father of that child. Carl saw it clearly now. This baby had killed her, this Imogene, the child of this other man. C.J.O.

He slammed his palms against the steering wheel, once for each initial, letting the truck careen until one tire caught the ditch, and he had to work to keep himself upright and out of a field. Breathing hard, he pressed on the accelerator, forcing the truck up the first steep hill of the Hog's Back. Liar! Amanda was such a liar! Did she take him for a fool? But he had been a fool. Despite his doubts, despite his checking, he'd believed her story. He'd trusted he'd never find the evidence he'd felt compelled to search for.

Cresting another hill, he covered his face with both hands, trying to hide from the humiliation. For thirteen years he'd worked Mathilda's farm, raised her daughter, lived for her the life she'd chosen, when she deserved none of his love. And

Ruth, what did she know? Had she sat on this man's lap, some greasy shirker she'd been told to call "uncle," while her mother, full and round as a melon, perched on the arm of his chair?

The truck stopped at the base of Holy Hill. He got out and climbed the stairs to the cathedral. Carl wasn't a religious man. He'd not been in a church since he'd been in France, where he'd wandered inside a few, mainly out of curiosity. Still, the atmosphere affected him. The air, cool and still, seemed to belong to a world separate from his turmoil. It slowed him, and he moved to a pew, where he genuflected, a habit he'd learned as a child, and then sank immediately to his knees. Behind him, an old woman murmured in a steady, soothing drone.

Carl rested his forehead on his folded hands and felt suddenly tired. The sad fact was, he didn't remember Mathilda vividly enough even to hate her. He thought how young she'd been, how naive and eager to please. She'd been all alone for months, for more than a year. After her parents died, she must have been frightened, not knowing if he'd ever come back. How could he hate her for needing someone to care for her? He knew she would have been sorry for what she'd done. How could he hate her, when she'd been so horribly punished?

And C.J.O., had he been punished for what he had done to her?

Carl closed his eyes. There in the dank church, he felt the cold ground that had chilled him through his woolen jacket, saw the pitiless silver bayonets, and heard Pete McKinley's frantic screams cut off by the sound of steel thrust through cloth and flesh, like a knife pushed into a pumpkin, and the gurgle of blood in the windpipe. Through all of this, Carl had lain still, craven as a possum, but his cowardice hadn't saved him. They weren't fooled. They turned toward him, first one, then another, at last the third. They began to make their way across the foxhole. He saw the snaggled yellow teeth of the one who was nearest, the one who was raising his bayonet, ready to drive it home. And then the shell began to whine. He watched the fear bloom in their faces, as it must have done in McKinley's a few moments before. And then the red.

Carl's head jerked. He had fallen asleep on his knees. Get up, get up, get going, he thought, but he wasn't sure where he ought to go. Slowly, he slid back onto the pew. The muttering woman had gone. He studied the wall lined with crutches left behind by those whom Christ had healed. He stood and rubbed his knees. At the door he lit a candle for Mathilda, feeling guilty, knowing he should have been doing this all along. He should never have left her alone.

———

It was dark by the time Carl's truck rolled into the drive. Imogene had gone home and supper was long since over. He made some vague excuse about having helped Joe with his corn.

"Next time you ought to let me know, Carl. We waited dinner for you and then supper, nearly an hour."

"It won't happen again," he said.

The night air was pleasant, still warm enough to sit outside, and Amanda had settled herself on the dark porch in one of the rockers with a bowl of late beans to snap. She could hear Carl behind her in the front room, opening drawers. He would leave them open, too—she would have to remember to close them on her way to bed.

"Looking for something, Carl?"

But he'd gone into the kitchen and didn't answer.

Carl sat at the kitchen table, going through the scrapbook Amanda had shown him when he first returned from France. He examined the pictures of Mathilda minutely. He wished he had a photograph of that girl, Imogene, although he'd recognized her relation to Mathilda more by general impression than by an actual matching of features. It was hard to tell exactly how they were similar when you looked closely at Mattie. Still, he was certain that the noses were the same shape and the width of the forehead, the set of the mouth. Yes, he was sure of that.

But if having that baby had killed Mathilda, how had she ended up in the lake? Who'd said that she drowned? Amanda. Who had lied.

Carl closed his eyes, trying to clear the confusion. Could Amanda . . . ? But to imagine her pulling Mathilda's dead body onto the ice, cutting a hole to push her through, revolted him. Maybe she did fall in and drown. Who said the baby's mother had died in childbirth? Amanda. Who had lied.

It was hard to think. Mathilda *was* dead. She *was* Imogene's mother. She *had* been in the lake. He pressed his palm on the table top as he articulated each fact he felt sure of.

Yes, she'd definitely been in the lake. Someone had found her there. Carl paged back through the yellowed articles Amanda had pasted into the book. The paste released its hold as he touched them and the one he was searching for fell like a leaf into his lap.

DECEMBER 6, 1919—MISSING WOMAN FOUND DROWNED

The body of Mrs. Carl Neumann was found yesterday evening trapped in the ice on Nagawaukee Lake by Mr. C. J. Owens of 24 Prospect Avenue, Milwaukee, and his son, Arthur, 5.

Mrs. Neumann had been missing since the night of November 27.

Carl started back from the table, his breathing quick, his fingers trembling. He was out of the kitchen and through the front room before he could think, before he could stop himself.

She sat in the dark, her rocker creaking, her fingers steadily snapping the beans.

"Amanda," he said. He was surprised to hear how calm his voice sounded.

She looked up at him, and though he couldn't make out her features, the expectant tilt of her head was just like Mathilda's. Seeing that steeled him. The sisters were in on this together. He demanded an answer as if he were asking his straying wife herself. "Tell me who Imogene's father is."

"Why, George Lindgren. You know that."

"No. And Mary Louise is not her mother. I know about the baby, Amanda. Tell me who the father is."

"How . . . ?" she began.

"Who is he?" He said it gently but firmly, as if speaking to a child.

Amanda stopped rocking. The crickets and the cicadas were deafening, their insistent chirping pounded like her own pulse. She'd dreaded this moment for so long that she'd almost felt safe, almost felt sure it would never come. She looked at Carl standing in the doorway; the light was behind his head, so his face was only a blank shadow. She knew that face so well now.

Amanda leaned forward in her chair. He, who had also lost Mattie, would help her. He, who had suffered, would forgive her. She would tell him, and he would know what she had to do, how she could make it better.

"Is he the one?" Carl reached forward then, the yellow newspaper clipping in his hand. He pointed to the name. He would not be too afraid this time.

It was so easy. All she had to do was nod. When she looked up, the doorway was empty, as if he'd never been there at all.

Ruth

I was just at the part where Maggie Tulliver, carried away by the flood, was trying to steer her boat into the current of the Floss, when he spoke to me from the doorway of my room.

"Ruthie."

"Hmmm?" I could hardly bear to tear myself from the page, so perilous was Maggie's situation, but I glanced at him and took the strand of hair I'd been chewing out of my mouth.

He came in, the tails of his green and black checked shirt hanging loose, as if he'd already begun to get ready for bed. He sat on the ladder-back chair where I hung my skirt and blouse at night. I kept the book open, propped on my knees, my finger on the line. I leaned back against the pillows, waiting to hear what he wanted, but he just looked at me, not saying anything. Then he got up again and went to the window. I stole a look back at Maggie. Would she be able to rescue Tom?

"Ruth," he said, turning back to me, "how well do you remember your mother?"

"I don't know. I remember her, I guess."

"You remember living on the island with your mother and Aunt Mandy?"

"A little." I was still thinking about Maggie. My neck ached with the tension of the flood—I had to get back to it.

"Why did your mother go on the ice, Ruth? Do you remember that?"

I did remember that. I remembered the ice, so shiny, so black, like running on the sky. "Ruth, come back!" my mother called. "Mandy, bring her back!" She howled like the wind. I stopped, but I didn't go back. And then she was around me, her heart in my ear. She was around me so tight I could hardly breathe. And then we drowned.

"No," I said to my father. "I don't remember. I don't remember anything."

Chapter Twelve

At 6:30 A.M. on September 10, 1931, Clement Owens was checking the hybrid alfalfa plants that had germinated at the lake but were now maturing in his little greenhouse in the city. Too bad he'd had to transplant them, but it was well into September, time the family moved back to town. Anyway, here he could continue his work after the frost.

"Mrs. Owens says to say your breakfast is ready." Mimi, a new girl Theresa had hired as general help, stood outside the greenhouse.

"Look at this, Mimi. Five new leaves since Tuesday. Seven, if you count these buds. I think I should count the buds, don't you?"

Mimi hung back. "I don't know, sir." Mr. Owens's projects had always made her uncomfortable, and she'd been particularly wary since the distillery in the cellar blew up in August.

"All right. Tell Mrs. Owens I'll be right in, would you?"

She nodded and hurried back to the safety of the house.

On the roof of the carriage house, Carl lay on his stomach, sighting down his rifle. His lips twitched in a sort of giddy giggle. Looking through the glass at this man in his bathrobe, it was hard not to think of fish in a barrel. Although he'd actually never shot a fish. Such a slippery target. Would it be easy? A small stone was boring into his chest, and Carl shifted his weight. There was something to remember about glass houses. Throw stones at people in glass houses?

All it would take would be one shot to the brain, and then Carl would be off, down the tree into his truck and back home. Where everything would be different. So different once he'd shot Mathilda's . . . this man in the blue and gold paisley bathrobe.

Of course, he ought to make sure—shout out the name, make him look up, maybe tell him why he deserved to die and watch the fear spread over his face. No sense shooting the wrong man.

But this had to be C.J.O. Who else would move with such assurance in a bathrobe, as if he owned the place? Owens bent over a plant and seemed to stroke its leaves. Carl thought of those fingers on her skin. What had she said to him? What had she done? Had she worn that light pink nightgown with the tiny silk bows? Had she been shy when he untied them one by one? Had she smiled at him that way? He shifted again uncomfortably. Had she held her hands over her breasts, so that the nipples peeked between her fingers? Or had she been different with him, a woman Carl hadn't even known?

Carl closed his eyes. He could feel the pinch of the cold metal as he squeezed the trigger, the noise exploding in his head, the recoil punching his shoulder. The blood would spread, red soaking through the blue and gold. Dark, wet red. He opened his eyes and aimed carefully. One shot, clean and quickly over. One shot to the head.

But he did not pull the trigger. There, with the man in his sight, the compelling fury that had driven Carl out to the island so often, the fury that had taken him to Mary Louise, that had pushed him through the scrapbook, that had shoved him onto this roof, dissipated like gas. He struggled to retrieve it. He reminded himself of what this man had done, of where it had led, of Mathilda spent and bloody. But these ideas had no connection to the red-faced man in the greenhouse. Maybe, Carl thought, if he'd seen them together, seen this man's thick fingers on the translucent skin of Mattie's breast, he could have shot him. But it was too late. Now Mathilda and Clement Owens came together only in his mind, and his mind wasn't nearly strong enough to make him kill a man.

He lowered his head and lay his cheek against the slate shingles. A moment before, he'd felt no fear, but now his heart began to flutter wildly, as if it had suddenly escaped confinement and was desperate to be away. He could sense the blood rushing through every passage in his body, making his ankles and his fingertips jump, and he pressed himself against the roof, willing himself still. For a few seconds, like a very young child, he even shut his eyes to make himself vanish.

At last he heard the greenhouse door close with the brittle snap of glass, and then the door of the house open and shut. He raised his head and in less than a minute scrambled down the tree, stole across the yard and hurried back to his truck.

From the cab, Carl watched the quiet facade of the Owenses' house and tried to stop shaking. Except that the brick looked warm and bright in the morning sun, it was no different from the way it had been three hours ago when he'd first seen it in the furry light of dawn, the lives inside undisturbed.

Carl knew he'd done the right thing. He'd almost killed a man, almost changed everything, but then he hadn't. At this moment, life was as promising as it had been yesterday. Yesterday he hadn't seen that promise, but this morning he did. He'd teetered on the edge of disaster, but he hadn't fallen.

Light-headed with relief, he started the truck and drove west on Wisconsin Avenue, where the sun flashed against a hundred windows and clanging streetcars and honking automobiles hurried him forward in an exhilarating rush over the river and into the solid, quiet residential neighborhood beyond. And then these houses, too, began to thin, and in scant minutes he was leaving it all behind, that city in which lives went hurtling on, and his rifle lay stiff and silent on a carriage house roof.

On Blue Mound Road he had to stop. The tank was half full—he didn't really need gas—but he had to catch his breath and talk to another human being. He had to tangle himself in the lush world, the world in which he hadn't killed a man in a paisley bathrobe.

"Hey," he said to the attendant who came out to the pump—he couldn't help himself, "I nearly killed a man back there."

The attendant shook his head. "This road's treacherous. All them trees. You come up on a horse and buggy around one of them curves and one of you's a goner for sure."

Carl nodded. It was all right, better, of course, that the man didn't understand. Just so he was able to say it. He wanted to shout it into the dappled light with his head out the window as he flew along the narrow road—nearly killed him! nearly killed him!

Not until he was turning onto Glacier Road did a doubt worm its way behind his ear. Had he been wise and good or only afraid?

Carl knew he was a coward. He kept his terror secret from others, but he couldn't fool himself. Cowardice wasn't the worst thing. It was bad, though, when he didn't stand up for himself, when he'd sluiced the bloody floors for nothing after a day of packing, because Tommy Reinquist told him to and he was scared he'd get fired if he didn't, or when he'd let Mattie's father tell him how to treat a horse. No one was gentler with horses than Carl. He was trying to make it up to them.

He'd been about eight, the day he'd clearly recognized his weakness. He and Hilda, who was only four then, a squat child with cheeks blistered by the January wind, a lazy eye and a running nose, were waiting for her father on the platform outside the feed mill, watching the big boys hoist sacks of oats onto their shoulders and load them onto the wagon. Carl remembered how much he'd admired those boys, and how he'd hoped that he'd be able to carry two sacks at once, one on each shoulder, like Gunther Sweitzer, when he was big. When Hilda whined about the cold, Carl scratched a picture of a fat goose in the snow with a stick to distract her. As he finished, she grabbed the stick away and scribbled the drawing over, tossing snow high into the heavy gray air and chortling. Then, solemnly, she handed the stick back, so he could draw something else.

He was curling white smoke out of a white chimney when he heard the man bellowing and the whip hissing and snapping. The horse that appeared around the corner, pulling a coal wagon, was obviously sick. Its head was low and its feet splayed, and its breathing came in sharp rents between the raw words and the whip.

"I'll show you," the man shouted, standing in front of the wagon seat, "I'll show you!" And then, while the whip coiled black through the air, Carl heard a barking laugh come from the dark opening above the man's red beard.

Carl cringed and stepped back, as Hilda reached her hand into his. The horse, trying to plant its hoof, slipped on a patch of ice and fell to its knees.

"No, you don't." The man leaned back, hauling at the reins, seeming almost to pull the horse back to its feet with brute strength.

But within seconds the horse was down again, one leg bent awkwardly out, and the man dropped the reins and threw all of his energy into the sizzling whip, bringing it down over and over against the horse's back and then reaching forward, hitting its neck, one stroke leaving a line of blood on the ear closest to Carl and Hilda.

"Stop," Carl whispered. In his mind he heard the command as a shout, but from his lips it came only as a thin, watery sound. "Stop it," he said again. "Stop." But he pressed himself tight against the wall of the feed mill, as if he were trying to push himself through it. "Stop," he said, but he only said it to his boots and mouthed it into the wool of Hilda's cap as she stood, huddled against him, her eyes round with surprise.

No one stopped the man. Not Gunther

or the other boys. Not Hilda's father or Mr. Fry who owned the mill. No one stopped him, until Hilda stepped forward.

Looking back at Carl once, as if to be sure she understood exactly what he wanted, she stepped stoutly to the edge of the platform. Then she screeched in a voice that sounded as if she were being turned inside out, "Stop! Stop it! Stop!"

Her cries startled the man. He paused and the whip dropped limp against his hand. They brought Hilda's father and Mr. Fry and the big boys running. They changed everything, so that somehow now Gunther was releasing the horse from the harness, and it was the man who sank to his knees, sobbing, nearly tumbling off the wagon.

"Wife run off yesterday," Mr. Fry said to Hilda's father, and Hilda's father nodded, as if that meant something.

But all right, Carl thought with a serene confidence he'd never before experienced. This time, what did it matter if fear had held him back? He was glad he'd left that man alive. If cowardice had kept him from firing his gun, he was glad he was a coward. In any case, he was finished with the Mathilda who'd tormented him. He'd pursued the trail she'd left to the very end and discovered only a man in his bathrobe, puttering among plants, a man who had nothing to do with him at all. He was in the clear now, free of the mysterious wife he would never know and ready to start fresh with the Mathilda he'd loved settled like a soft blanket at the bottom of his heart.

When, after a nearly sleepless night, Amanda heard no sound from Carl's room that morning, she knew her confession had driven him away. Once she'd wanted him to go, she thought bitterly. Now she couldn't blame him, but it made her sick to think that he'd left because of her, that she disgusted him, and, under the covers, she drew her knees to her aching chest and tucked her face, clotted with tears, against them. *She* wanted to be gone, if, having seen into her soul, he couldn't stand to be around her. Why had she been such a fool as to hope for his forgiveness and expect his help? Things had been fine, just fine, the way they were. If only he hadn't asked her, she thought, thrashing now from side to side in helpless frustration, tangling the sheet and the blanket. If only she hadn't trusted him with the truth. If only they could go back, she would've stuck to her story and she never would've nodded when he pointed to Clement's name.

At last, she forced herself from the bed, washed her face at the washstand and pinned her hair severely. All right, she told herself, pulling the laces of her black shoes tight. All right. But she didn't mean anything by it but a rhythm to take her from one task to the next.

Later that morning, as she did the laundry in the cool cellar, she felt a little better. She thrust the lever of the washer back and forth, mercilessly agitating Carl's dirty shirts in their gray sudsy bath. All right. If he wanted to go, let him. She and Ruth would be just fine alone. Just fine. Better, in fact. But a dart of fear made her lose her grip on the handle for a moment. What would she say? If he didn't come back by supper, how would she explain?

She'd say she didn't know where he went. That was the truth. Anyway, he'd been so strange the last few years, going off on his mysterious errands, emerging from the east woods when they'd thought he'd been in the west field, missing meals and acting excited or moping around so dull and distracted that Ruth should hardly wonder if now he just didn't come back. And Rudy, well, he'd believe whatever Amanda told him.

If he did come back, how would they live? Amanda sagged over the washtub, beaten down by worry. How would he look at her without remembering what she'd done? How would she look at him, knowing that he hadn't forgiven her? Could they stand to hobble on, day after day, appalled by each other?

She realized that he might try to banish her. He might see it as his right, his duty even. After all, could he permit such an influence on his daughter? Of course, she wouldn't go. She had as much right to stay as he did, she told herself, as she squeezed his shirts through the wringer, the farm was half hers. But what if he wanted to take Ruth with him somewhere else?

Let him try, Amanda thought, feeding

another shirt into the wringer's jaws as cold water poured over her reddened hands. Whatever else happened, she would never let Ruth go.

Around ten o'clock, as Amanda was pinning the shirts to the line, a plume of dust floated toward her along the distant road. She fought down alarm, forcing herself to bend and shake and pin, shirttail to shirttail, arms hanging down, no surrender. She was ready, she told herself, snapping a wet shirt hard into the blue sky, ready for whatever he had to say.

He made her wait. He went into the house and came out again, whistling. He went into the barn and came out again, singing. The next time Amanda saw him, she was looking out an upstairs window and he was cresting the hill in the combine. She put a few of Ruth's clothes and an extra dress of her own in her old carpetbag, and tucked in the dollar bills she kept in a coffee can. They'd be ready, if it came to that.

At dinner at noon and at supper at six, he said only the things he might have said two days ago, before she'd ruined it all with her honesty. What had Ruth learned in school, he asked, and what had she sold at the stand, were the late raspberries still coming in, and it'd better not rain tomorrow. Amanda saw him smile at Ruth and at Rudy, but she avoided his gaze herself, keeping her eyes on the plates. But then, after supper, when they were all sitting in the front room—Ruth reading, Amanda mending, Rudy just sitting with his feet up on the hassock for half an hour before shuffling out to his den over the garage— an unusual thing happened.

"Why don't we ever play these?" Carl said, opening the cabinet under the phonograph.

"Ach, they're so old," Amanda protested, not looking up from the sock she was darning, but he paid no attention, and cranked the handle until suddenly "Alexander's Ragtime Band" came bouncing and tumbling into the room.

And then, an even stranger thing, Amanda thought later. Afterward, she could hardly believe it, but it happened just the same.

"Madam, may I have this dance?" He bowed formally and held out his hand.

"Carl . . ." She laughed uncomfortably,

shaking her head. This was not what they did, how they were. What did he mean by it? Was he making fun? But he lifted her hand off the arm of the chair, and she let him pull her to her feet, let him steer her around the furniture, until she realized she was dancing just as much as he.

"Pull that chair back, Ruth," she gasped as she shrank against Carl to escape the smack of the newel post.

When they saw that Rudy and Ruth were trying to polka to ragtime, they switched partners, so Carl could teach Ruth to turkey-trot. "This is the dance your mother and I used to do," he said.

They took turns choosing the records and winding the phonograph, until Rudy collapsed in a chair, fanning his craggy face with a *Ladies' Home Journal*, and Amanda, hearing the kitchen clock strike, remembered that Ruth had school the next day and must drink a glass of milk and go straight to bed.

When the house was quiet, Amanda set out plates and bowls for breakfast the next morning, jigging a little as she moved around the table. In the front room, she found Carl tugging the davenport back into place.

"Here," she said, easily lifting her end and shrugging off the image of her mother frowning at her unladylike strength. Now that the odd dancing was over, she felt even more wary of Carl than before but wrestling the furniture helped. "That was a good idea," she said, almost shyly, testing the waters.

"We should've been doing that all along. Saturday nights, at least. We should've had some kids over for Ruth."

"Maybe so," Amanda said, smoothing the antimacassar on the davenport arm nearest her. She could feel the panic rise even at the suggestion. Didn't Ruth see enough of other children at school?

"I decided something today," Carl said, seating himself in an armchair and scraping his still boyish hair back from his forehead with his fingers.

Now, Amanda thought, still pulling at the white embroidered edge—had it shrunk in the last washing?—he would talk about Clement and Imogene. He would tell her how she'd have to pay.

"I'm going to get a job."

"What?" The antimacassar slid off the arm and fluttered to the floor.

"My cousin Hilda's husband, he's first mate on one of those iron ships. He can get me a good place."

"Oh, a good place. That's good, a good place," she heard herself saying.

"You're right about us needing money," he continued. "I've been distracted and useless for too long here. It's time I got to work."

"You're not useless, Carl." So they'd pretend that she'd admitted nothing, that he was only taking the practical measures she'd been suggesting for a year. He was making this easier than she ever could've hoped. He was letting her run away again, and this time she wouldn't even have to move. But that wasn't, she saw now, what she wanted. She was bone tired of all this running and hiding, of living alone with a monstrous hump of truth strapped to her back. Seeing him sitting there, one hand unconsciously rubbing the hole in his thigh that she knew had never quite closed, she forgot the hysterical regrets of the morning. She wanted now what she'd wanted the night before when he'd stood in the doorway, pointing at the clipping from her scrapbook, and she'd realized that through some silent, miraculous communication of their spirits he'd come to understand her. Again tonight she ached to share with him the events that had pushed both their lives into such lonely paths. She would tell him everything, and then, please God, he would say it was all right; it hadn't been her fault; Mathilda would forgive. She edged toward the abyss. "And that's the only reason you want to go, the money?"

"Why else?"

So he would make her say it first. All right. That was fair. She took a deep breath. She would go on. "I thought," she said, staring bravely straight into his eyes, "what I said, about Clement Owens . . ."

He threw his head back in a sort of half laugh, rose, and went to look out the open window. The weather had changed, Amanda noticed, newly aware of the cool current slipping in over the sill. Summer, worn out, had retreated in a matter of hours, and fall had marched triumphantly down from the north. The air was chilly, and the insects and the frogs, frenzied only the night before, were still.

"It was so long ago," he said to the dispassionate dark blue sky, "and now I can't even remember what she looked like. That's awful, isn't it? I've tried, but I just can't. Not really. Not more than a glint now and then." He turned toward her and said with touching earnestness, "It's hard to know for sure from so far away, but I believe I did love her. And I think she loved me. But you see, I think she must've changed when I went away. I know she must've been lonely and angry with me, too. Yes, I know she was," he insisted when Amanda shook her head. "She told me so, and she had every right to be, the way I joined up without even telling her because I was scared she'd say no. What I think," he continued, and his words slowed as if he were deciphering a puzzle as he spoke, "is that it wasn't really *my* Mathilda who had his baby, but some other woman she became, some other woman I never knew. That's what I think. That's what I've decided," he said, almost defiantly.

Amanda felt as if she'd dropped into a

bottomless pool and was sinking fast. "Carl, no!" she flailed, "Mattie never . . ." But she couldn't grab hold of the right words.

He was sitting beside her then, and he caught the hand she was, without knowing it, beating against the cushion. "Listen, Amanda. Listen to me. I know it was my fault in a way. I didn't have to go so quick like I did. I didn't have to jump at the chance. You were right those times you said I wanted to go. I thought it was the thing a man would do, and I wanted to show her—to show everyone, even my- self—that I was a man. I didn't think about what it would mean, how I would get so far away and not be able to come back." He sighed and looked away. "All I'm saying is that I know what it's like to do something, and then later, the reasons why you did it seem foolish. I know how things can change in ways you never meant. And I'm sure that Mattie would come back, just like I did, if she could, if the baby hadn't killed her. I know she would."

Amanda sat stunned as much by her si- lence as by his misunderstanding. Why wasn't she telling him the truth? His face, closer than she was used to seeing it as he sat there beside her on the davenport, looked different, as if it belonged to a stranger who only resembled him around the eyes.

"I realize what you've done for me and my daughter," he was saying. "I know you gave up your nursing that you worked so hard for. It's not every sister who would do that. And I know it's far more than I can ever hope to repay. But I'm at least going to do my part from now on."

He'd not understood at all, she thought. There'd been no communication of the spirit, no seeing into her soul. And now she was letting him think Mattie . . . oh, poor Mattie. Poor Carl. And along with pity and shame, she felt a trickle of outrage, shameful in itself, that she played only the most peripheral of parts in this version of events. "Carl," she began. My daughter, he'd said, as if Ruth were his alone. Repay, he'd said, as if they were involved in some sort of transaction, as if she'd not lived every minute there with her Ruth for love. How tightly his fingers held the fragile bones of her wrist—should they make her feel safe or terribly afraid? Say it, she told herself, say it. She put her hand on his to make him listen, and her scar smiled up at her. "It wasn't your fault," she made herself say. "It wasn't Mathilda's fault. It was my fault. I let her go."

Of course that hadn't explained anything, Amanda admitted to herself the next week, after Carl had gone to Sheboygan to meet the *Rebecca Rae*. He'd only patted her, uncomprehending, and told her again how grateful he was to her for raising Ruth, and she'd been seized so violently by choking sobs, she'd been unable to go on. So it was worse now than ever before. She'd as good as lied, now, letting him believe the worst about Mattie. Only her vow to reveal the entire truth the very next time the ship docked in Milwaukee comforted her enough so that she could fall asleep at night. Although, with the reassurance of morning, she always recognized that promise as futile.

In the meantime, Carl sent postcards from places like Gary and Duluth that Ruth hoarded in a box that had once held paper collars.

"Where was it the last one was from?" Amanda would ask, deferring to Ruth when people inquired about Carl.

And when she replied Sault Ste. Marie or Green Bay, they snapped their tongues against the roofs of their mouths and shook their heads. "That's a man likes to see the world," they'd say, as if turning circles around the Great Lakes was somehow exotic and suspect. Ruth hardly listened. She'd begun to realize that people always had to say something.

Ruth kept her box of postcards in the house on the island. She liked to look at them there, where she didn't have to share them with Amanda, where the smell of his cigarettes lingered and the crazy patches of light on the floor reminded her of how he'd peeled the boards from the windows. On a map, she located each city from which he'd sent a card and memorized the facades and the vegetation in the picture, believing, although she knew it was unreasonable, that if he didn't return she'd somehow be able to trace him with such crumbs.

Chapter Thirteen

Amanda

People ask about my hand, not just Ruth, but people who have no business wondering. They point; they look aghast. It's amazing what people think they have a right to know.

"What's that?" they say. "Is that a bite? Who bit you?"

My hand could've been bitten at the hospital, back when I was treating those soldiers. You can't imagine how fierce people can be when they're crazy with fear, when they know they're going to die, when they believe you're an angel pushing them toward the grave.

Carl never asked. I think he didn't want

to know what could turn a person into an animal.

———

"Hot enough for you?" Ray asked, passing Ruth one of the drinks he'd carried back to the table.

"Mmm," she agreed. She took a tiny sip of the whiskey sour while he settled into a chair. She nodded and kept her smile fixed. She could think of nothing to say.

"Certainly is hot," she said finally.

He beamed, grateful. "Certainly is!" He stood as Imogene approached the table. "Hot enough for you?"

"Never!" Imogene said, and she grabbed his hand and pulled him toward the dance floor with a shimmy, as a private wave rolled off her fingertips toward Ruth.

Ruth and Imogene had gone dancing every Friday night since the new dance pavilion opened that June of 1937. The pavilion was a platform at the edge of the lake, and when the band was playing, the water carried the music for miles. The summer people, who had cottages or mansions along the lake, depending not so much upon what they could afford but on their idea of what a summer place should be, came to the dances by boat, but Imogene and Ruth, who were "lifers," as Imogene said, came in the Lindgrens' Ford.

"You know you've got a big run up the back of your leg? You better go back in and change," Imogene had said that evening when she picked Ruth up.

But Ruth didn't have another presentable stocking and so the two of them sat there for a minute, examining the run, trying to decide if it was really all that noticeable. Ruth twisted it a bit to get a better look and then—zip—of course, it went all the way up and spread out a bit, too.

She pulled the stockings off—she hated the hot things anyway—and tossed them into the back seat. She rolled the window down as far as it would go and felt the breeze on her skin as they drove.

It *was* hot. Ray was right, if unoriginal. And the velvety, humid air of the dance pavilion was drenched in scent—smoke and cheap fruity perfume, lipstick, shampoo and sweat layered over honeysuckle, grass and gasoline fumes rising from the boats' motors. Ruth's bare legs, which had felt almost racy in the car, now made her self-conscious. When they were crossed, a slick of sweat formed between the top of one thigh and the underside of the other. She tried to keep them beneath the table as much as possible.

These occasions were a trial for her, even though she knew she ought to enjoy them the way everyone else did. The new pavilion was all anyone talked about at Brown's Business College, and though Ruth had dreaded it from the moment she first heard the idea, Imogene made clear she'd have to go.

"Of course you'll go!" Imogene had been taking mental inventory of her dresses, trying to determine whether she needed to petition her parents for something new. "Think of the possibilities, Ruth. Everyone will be there. Bobby Hanser and Harold Koch and all those summer people."

Bobby Hanser and Harold Koch were a couple of the boys Imogene talked to sometimes, when they came into the shop before a day of fishing. But they were definitely not, she explained to Ruth, the fishing type.

"They're sailors," she said proudly, "members of the yacht club. They were talking about racing their A-boats. And they have iceboats, too, I bet."

"What's an A-boat?"

"The big ones, I think. I'm pretty sure." Imogene and Ruth had often admired those grand boats when they flocked on Sunday afternoons. They strung out in the fresh wind to cover almost the whole of the lake, pushing the smaller boats, the fishermen and dinghy sailors, to the edges.

"I'd like to ride on one of those," Ruth often said, and Imogene, who appreciated not only their grace but the gracious leisure they implied, agreed.

From the shore, they gazed through Amanda's binoculars, keeping track of their favorite boats by the numbers on their sails. Imogene liked *V7*, whose deck was sky blue, although she rooted loyally for Bobby's yellow one, as well, but Ruth preferred a sea-foam-green boat.

"That's Arthur Owens," Imogene said, and through the binoculars Ruth could see, when he turned his head, the string that would keep his glasses from falling into the lake.

So that Imogene could get to know Bobby and Harold and their friends better, maybe even go with one of them, maybe even marry one—who knew?—Ruth, every Friday for the last four weeks, had put on her good dress, the one Aunt Mandy had made for her three years ago.

Aunt Mandy disapproved of the dances. "Why do you want to talk to all those strange boys?" she'd asked that evening from the bathroom doorway. "I know your father wouldn't like it."

Ruth had climbed onto the toilet cover to see as much of herself as possible in the mirror over the sink. "All right," she said to Amanda, as she stepped back to the floor with a heavy thump, "I won't talk." She began to arrange her hair, but when the comb caught in a knot and slipped from her fingers, she sighed, exasperated. "I'm only going for Imogene anyway."

"Here. Let me." Amanda picked up the comb and used it deftly to twist Ruth's hair this way and that. She pinned it roughly, not taking care to avoid Ruth's scalp, but the effect was nice. "Such beautiful hair," Amanda said, "just like your mother's. Aren't you glad you listened to me and didn't cut it just because of some silly fashion?"

Aunt Mandy didn't need to worry about strange boys, Ruth thought now, savoring the sweet and sour tingle of her drink. Boys and girls, both, were interested in talking only to Imogene. They pulled her away from Ruth, as soon as the two of them walked in, and hung on her words, the back feet of their chairs poised inches above the wooden floor, as they leaned toward her, offering lighted matches, pink punch, scraps of gossip, whispering "Did ya hear" and "Did ya get a look," glancing furtively over their shoulders at the objects of their stories. Ruth leaned back in her own chair with her sweating glass and her fixed smile and listened as well as she could to the music.

When Bobby Hanser suddenly appeared, Ruth watched Imogene pretend to be surprised, pretend to need coaxing, and finally take his hand and, with practiced skill, lead him to the very center of the floor. Amanda was wrong—her father would like this place, Ruth thought, watching Imogene and Bobby fox-trot and remembering the happy night of the phonograph, although there'd been no more of that in the short weeks when he came home, while the *Rebecca Rae* was docked in Milwaukee or Chicago. If her mother were alive, he'd want to take her dancing. It would be nice, Ruth thought, with a little pain in her throat, if someone wanted to take her like that. But she tossed her head. Who, anyway, did she want as a beau? Certainly none of these. It occurred to her then, as it usually did about this time, that she could make a trip to the ladies' room. No one would notice if she disappeared for a little while.

She made her way between the tables and around the dance floor, dodging elbows, saying "Excuse me" and "Pardon me," and when bodies would not notice and did not budge, turning herself sideways to squeeze between them. A girl pealed sudden laughter into her ear; a man stepped back, grinding his heel into her toe; gauzy dresses swirled; necks were damp with sweat; the music and the voices tangled exuberantly. Ruth pushed open the door marked DOES and slipped inside.

In the cool and nearly quiet room Ruth went directly to the little bench, padded in shiny pink fabric, that was pushed against one wall under the windows, convenient for any female who might feel a bit faint and require a quiet spot to recover. She kicked off her shoes, tucked her feet under her, and pulled a novel from her handbag. She would finish this chapter, no more, and then go back out and keep up appearances.

She'd only read a paragraph when the door burst open, admitting a torrent of noise and two girls Ruth knew by sight as members of Bobby Hanser's set. They gave Ruth barely a glance before one went into a stall and the other leaned over the sink so that her face was only inches from the mirror and pushed her hair off her forehead to get a close look at her skin. She frowned at her reflection.

"She's a forward little thing, isn't she?" the girl in the stall said over the sound of streaming water.

"I don't know, Zita. He asked her to dance is what I saw."

"That's what she wants you to see. I know her type." After a moment she added, "You can smell it on her, didja notice?"

"Smell what?"

"Eau de grub."

"I'll take your word for it," said the other girl. She opened a compact and dusted some powder over her cheeks.

"It's too bad we can't bottle it, sell it to the locals."

"Bobby seems to like it."

The toilet flushed and Zita emerged and joined her friend at the sink. "Oh, you know Bobby and his summer flings. When it's hot, he likes anything in a skirt. He was going on the other day about how cute she was in her little apron, pulling worms out of the dirt by their tails. Isn't that the limit?" As she washed her hands, she leaned toward the mirror and bared her teeth.

"Oh, he's fickle all right. I should know." The other girl crossed her arms.

"Where do I put this?" Zita said, holding up the towel she'd used to dry her hands.

"Give it to her, I guess," her friend said, tilting her head at Ruth as she started out.

Working her way back to her table, Ruth found herself pushed toward the edge of the room until she was almost squashed against the screen that ran all the way around the pavilion to discourage mosquitoes. Below, the waves washed against the pilings, with a rhythm as steady as breathing. She looked out across the dark water and longed for her father to be there, skimming along the slick of moonlight in the rowboat, his arms pulling, his head turning to look over his shoulder to gauge his distance. He wouldn't care about all these other people. He would be coming just for her.

When Ruth turned back she realized with a start that Arthur Owens was looking at her from across the floor. It wasn't nice of him to notice her like that, adrift and obviously alone, obviously uninteresting to everyone else in the room. When had she begun to care about things like that? she asked herself angrily, frowning at Arthur. He was leaning against the railing, talking to the two girls she'd seen in the ladies' room. What had they told him about her? Quickly, she pressed on toward her table.

Imogene and Ray were trying a dance in which he spun her right and then left while she stepped together, stepped together, step, step, stepped together backward. It was something they'd seen Fred Astaire and Ginger Rogers doing, but it turned out to be harder than it looked. Ruth observed that now Imogene had caught Arthur's attention, although he tried to concentrate on his conversation. She saw him laugh and nod, but continue to glance whenever he could in Imogene's direction. Ruth, safe in her seat again, examined him as carefully as she could without being obvious—Imogene would want to know every detail.

One of the women he'd been talking to, the one who'd given Ruth her towel, stepped forward suddenly, grabbing his hand to pull him onto the floor. He was just reaching to set his glass on the rail to follow her when Ray spun Imogene so that she careened full force into his outstretched arm.

Everyone looked dazed for a moment and then there was a flurry of napkins. Imogene and Arthur and Ray were laughing. The woman who had intended to dance looked less pleased. Ruth, who'd been watching all of this as if it were a play, was a little flustered when she realized that Imogene was leading the entire group toward her table.

"This is Bobby," Imogene announced to the table at large. "And this is his cousin, Tom, and Zita and Kitty, and this is Arthur," she said, her hand on his arm. And then, beginning with Ruth, she named everyone at the table. "Now we've all been formally introduced."

Arthur smiled at Ruth and she blushed. Did he know she'd been studying him?

"Would you believe I shot a 76 out there today?" Bobby announced to the table at large as he sat down. Several of the others acted suitably impressed and began to offer their best games for comparison. Ruth was not surprised, however, that Imogene soon dominated the table, although she had never set foot on a golf course. Then Ray danced with Zita and Arthur danced with Imogene.

"Now you'll want to dance with Ruth," Imogene, fanning her face with both hands, announced to Arthur when they returned to the table.

"No, let's go out on the boat," Bobby said.

"One dance," Arthur said, and held his hand out to Ruth.

Ruth would rather not have danced, and

she made a face at Imogene over her shoulder as Arthur led her to the floor. After all, if he'd wanted to dance with her, he would have asked her himself. But Imogene was already telling Tom one of her stories, sweeping her hands through the air so that her bangles jingled, tipping her head so that her rippling curls brushed her shoulders. Ruth gave up and turned to face her partner.

"Hot, isn't it?" she said.

Arthur was easy, relaxed. He held out his hand to her. He smiled. He looked at her through his round glasses as if she were the one he had wanted from the start.

It was only a fox trot, but Ruth couldn't get the hang of the music. She tried to touch him lightly, to rest her hand soft as a moth on his shoulder, but she couldn't quite match his rhythm, and she had to cling to him, heavy and awkward, as he flung her to and fro, her hair loosening alarmingly with every jolt.

But then something happened. Maybe it was only that the heat and the drink overwhelmed her at last. She was still clinging to him, but now she moved with him, flexible, smooth as oil. She let him draw her close until they fitted together. She let him steer her and forgot herself. She spun and threw her head back and watched the ceiling turn; she listened to the music and let her feet jump and slide whenever they pleased. And her smile was not fixed.

When the dance was over and he'd led her back to the table, Ruth looked around in confusion; she couldn't remember which chair had been hers or where she'd left her bag. Bobby rose, pushing his chair back with his knees. "How about that spin in the Chris Craft now? We'll have to keep the speed down in the dark, but it's still a good ride."

They herded down to the pier, jostling and jabbering, uncowed by the Milky Way and the expanse of restless black water. Their voices carried from one end of the lake to the other, as if in a massive theater.

Ruth watched Imogene climb gracefully into the boat and copied as best she could the way Imogene used first Arthur's hand to steady her on the dock and then Bobby's shoulder to keep her footing in the boat. She scowled as she nearly twisted her ankle on the final step, feeling ridiculous in her heels.

"Careful, there," Arthur said.

It never helped, Ruth thought with irritation, to be told to be careful *after* you'd tripped. Her right hand, the one he'd held as he helped her into the boat, was trembling, and she squeezed it in the other.

Almost before they'd found seats, Bobby gunned the engine, and they shot away from the lights of the pavilion. Suddenly he swerved, and Ruth had to grab Tom's arm to keep her seat. He swerved the other way, and she nearly flew into Imogene's lap. Between shrieks of laughter, Kitty and Zita shouted at him to slow down, but he only smiled and swerved again, this time pitching Arthur onto the floor and Imogene on top of him.

Finally Bobby tired of this game and slowed the engine. From a little mahogany cupboard beneath the bow he produced a bottle of whiskey and glasses. Ruth glanced at Imogene, who was smoothing her skirt back over her knees as she leaned calmly against the cushions, and she felt almost sorry for those girls with their smug cracks about the bait shop. There wasn't a whiff of "eau de grub" about Imogene. Obviously this was her natural element. She'd been born to listen to the rich rumble of the engine, to stroke the sleek varnished wood with her polished fingertips, to hold out her shapely hand, adorned with the tasteful, slim ring her parents had given her to mark her high school graduation, for a crystal glass.

"Let's lie down and stare at the stars," Zita announced, sinking to the floor of the boat. She lay on her back with one knee bent, so anyone could see the smooth stretch of her thigh.

Ruth looked away, embarrassed for her.

"C'mon, get up, Zita," Bobby said, offering her his hand, but she batted it away.

"Wait! I can hear the water!" she announced, pressing her ear against the floorboards. She sat up suddenly, grabbed Ruth's hand, and tried to pull her down beside her. "Listen! Turn off the engine, Bobby!"

Bobby did as he was told and, after a moment's struggle to stay in her seat, Ruth gave up and lowered herself to the floor. "Listen!" Zita commanded, and Ruth tensely pressed her ear to the wood. Through the polished floorboards she could hear the water, slapping and sucking, worrying the wooden hull, trying to get in.

Above her, Kitty's voice rang. "Know what I heard about that place?" Her ear still full of the suck and slap, suck and slap, Ruth watched Kitty point over the water. "Some woman drowned her baby on that island during the war. You're supposed to be able to hear it crying late at night. Is that true?" She looked at Imogene, then down at Ruth. "You ever hear it?"

"No!" Ruth sat up abruptly. "Of course not. That's crazy!" But she could hear a baby crying in her mind even now, the thin wail that grew more and more distant but never disappeared. She closed her eyes to shut out the sound, but it persisted and, though her ear was no longer against the floor, she could hear the lake, too, mingled with the crying, and she could feel the water, its wet tongue in her ears, in her eyes, embracing her, pulling her down.

She opened her eyes, but the stars raced toward her and she felt as if she were spinning uncontrollably through space. Her insides rose to her throat in a wave. She scrambled onto the seat and was sick over the side.

Everyone was extremely kind.

"It's the heat," Kitty said. "I feel a little green myself."

"It's because Bobby was bouncing us around," Zita said. "I told you not to drive like that."

"Well, you shouldn't make people lie in the bottom of the boat," Bobby said.

"You're right," Zita said. "I'm sorry, Ruth."

Ruth took the hankie Imogene offered and blew her nose. "I'm all right now. I guess I'm just not used to so much to drink."

"If Bobby didn't serve such cheap stuff," Arthur said, "this kind of thing wouldn't happen. I got sick last week on his gin."

Ruth tried to smile at him, but her lips trembled and her arms were shaking so much she had to cross them over her chest to hold them still.

"You're cold!" Arthur exclaimed. "Hasn't anyone got a jacket?" He went to the bow and returned with a towel left over from that afternoon's swimming. "Come up front with me, why don't you?" he said, gently draping the towel over her shoulders. "The air's fresher away from the motor. You'll let me drive for a while, won't you, Bobby?"

"Sure," Bobby said, settling into a back seat between Zita and Imogene. "Take it around by your place. Let's see if anyone's up."

Arthur started the engine and turned on the running lights with a twist of the silver knob. The inboard began its soothing blub-blub-blub, but Ruth still shivered. In every direction, the water rippled like black crepe. If she dove in here, could she make it to shore?

"So how long have you been coming out here?" she asked to calm herself.

"Oh, years," he said. "The first time was just a few days after the war ended. I must have been about five and my dad brought me out when he was thinking of buying the land. That was when he planned to raise geese on it, you know, for feather beds. He thought they'd like being close to water." Arthur chuckled. "He always has these crazy schemes."

"But then he built a house instead?"

"Well, not instead, exactly. We did have

the geese and after that racing pigeons and then goats, until he converted the shed into a photography studio. He thought he had a quick way to develop film, but it didn't work out. Gave everybody a doppelganger. At the moment, he's revolutionizing the iceboat." He pronounced "revolutionizing" in a mocking tone.

"So you don't think much of his ideas?"

"Oh, no, they're good ideas. He's bursting with good ideas. It's just that bursting makes a mess, and somehow he's never around when it comes time to clean up.

"I've seen you in town before," he went on after a moment or two, "with your mother."

"That's my aunt. My mother died years ago." And then, somehow, she felt like telling him more, maybe because he'd said so much about his father. "She drowned, actually. She fell through the ice."

"Here? On this lake?" Arthur stared at Ruth, remembering the stinging gusts of a long-ago winter day.

"Now over here. Now just from here to there," his father said, positioning five-year-old Arthur. And Arthur stood and stood, inhaling the smell of wet wool as his scarf trapped the clouds of his breath. He was proud to be helping, although his feet were freezing and his fingers numb. He held one end of a piece of string while his father paced deliberately around the property with the other end and stopped now and then to record numbers in his little book. Finally he said, "Enough. You can play now. I'm just going to the car for a minute."

The ice was on the lake, a black sheet of it, lightly sugared with snow, upon which iceboats swooped and darted in the whipping wind, capricious as summer butterflies. Arthur hadn't been able to take his eyes off the frozen lake all the time he was standing, holding his string. It was fascinating. It tempted him to walk on water.

Released from his duties, Arthur stepped onto the lake. His right boot slipped immediately, but he caught his balance and shuffled forward a few steps toward a cluster of fishing shanties hunched against the cold. How deep the ice seemed to go, so deep he couldn't see where the frozen part ended and the water beneath it began. He fell on his knees for a closer look and bent forward, his mittoned hands splayed in front of him, his nose almost touching the lake.

He studied the ice, the bubbles and fissures, the occasional leaf or frond of seaweed suspended in it, the clear patches that seemed to go down and down forever. Where were the fish? He crawled forward on his knees with no notion of where he was going, drawn on by the ice itself.

A rumbling warned him that an iceboat was coming close, and he looked up to see it hurtling toward the shore. Just when he was sure it would crash full speed into the rocks, it spun around, runners scraping, sail luffing, until—fwoom—it caught the air and shot toward the middle of the lake again. As it flew past, two masked faces turned toward Arthur, and a hand in a three-fingered glove rose stiffly in greeting. Arthur waved and chased them for a few yards.

When one of his feet slid, he looked down instinctively, throwing his hands out to break his fall. If the lady had not been entombed in ice, he would have landed in her arms. He saw first the swollen gray hand and then the arm, the purplish fabric in folds, and finally the face. It was turned toward him, the blue eyes staring, the mouth open, screaming without sound, trapped in that bottomless black hole.

He tried to get away, tried to rise and run, but his feet slipped and he fell back in the same spot, as if the hand had grabbed his boot and pulled him down. He managed to slide forward, finally, by staying on his knees and crawling, and in that manner he made his way as fast as he could to the shore.

Once his feet were on solid ground, Arthur began to scream, and he ran up the hill toward the car, screaming every second he wasn't drawing breath. When his father snatched him up, Arthur buried his head in his huge shoulder, trying to blot out the face that was calling him from under the ice.

"What?" his father asked, first alarmed, then soothing, then irritated. "Did you fall? Did you bang your head? Are you hurt? What? What in the hell's the matter with you?"

Arthur pressed his eyes until they ached against his father's collarbone, and finally he managed to point without looking back toward the water. Arthur's father put him down and they walked to the edge of the ice. There Arthur stopped and, when his father took his hand to draw him on, leaned back with all of his weight.

"All right, stay here then," his father said impatiently. "Don't move. I'll be back in a moment."

Arthur watched his father, arms slightly raised, shuffle and slide along the ice, following the trail Arthur's knees had left in the light snow. He saw him stop, reel back, catch himself, and then lower himself slowly to his knees. He saw him brush at the powder with his glove. Then he stood up again and made his way back.

"How did the lady get in the ice?" Arthur asked when his hand was safely within his father's again and they were trudging up the hill toward the car.

"I don't know."

"Shouldn't we get her out?"

"The sheriff will do that, Arthur."

The sheriff came out of his house with a napkin tucked into his trousers. He leaned into the car and winked at Arthur.

"You take the boy home now," he said

as Arthur's father got back in the car. "We know who it is. We'll find her."

So they left the lady in the ice.

"That's it," Arthur said, pulling back on the throttle before a wide lawn, gray under the night sky, that ran steeply up to a white house fronted with looming pillars.

"Lovely," Imogene breathed, pretending, Ruth noticed, that she hadn't often stared from a rowboat at that facade and speculated about the lives inside.

"When are you going to have another party, Arthur?" Zita asked. She stepped onto the seat behind Arthur, as if to get a better look, and rested her hands on his shoulders for balance. "The one you had last year was the best of the season. Don't you remember, Kitty? Swimming in the afternoon and then the dance floor over by the boathouse. And, Tom, remember when Eddie pushed you off the pier?" She laughed somewhat more wildly than the memory warranted. "Oh, Arthur, you have to promise me you'll have another," she said. "You must or the whole summer will be wasted!" She leaned close so that her sculpted hair brushed his cheek. "You promise?"

"Anyone ever tell you there's a depression on?" he said, tipping his head toward hers.

"Well, then we need something to cheer us up!"

"Say, are we gonna sit here all night?" Bobby said. "Let me take the wheel."

And so they rearranged themselves, Bobby and Zita taking the seats up front; Imogene, with a lift of her eyes and a slight shift of her skirt, inviting Arthur into the place that Bobby had given up, and Ruth sliding in next to Ray. Kitty and Tom, who'd begun whispering to each other, stayed together in the back.

"Not so hot out here," Ray said.

"No." She smiled at him. Good old Ray. "It's not bad out here at all."

Bobby pushed the throttle forward suddenly then, and they raced smoothly through the black water, following their own tiny white beam. Greedily, Ruth leaned into the rushing warm air.

Amanda

I was digging a few onions out of the garden, squatting in the dirt somewhat awkwardly because I couldn't bend, when what I assumed was an acorn dropped on my shoulder.

"Hey!" I said, looking into the trees. Another one bounced off my arm. When it rolled into the dirt, I saw it wasn't an acorn but a marble.

"Inside!" Mattie hissed from a window. "Quick!"

"What is it?"

"Shhh. Rudy," she mouthed.

Quickly, I scanned the water. Yes, there he was. His back was to us as he rowed, but only a couple more pulls on the oars and he'd be dragging the boat onto our beach.

The screen door slammed and Mathilda, with Ruth glued to her hip, hurried down to the water. Keeping as low as I could, I scuttled for the back door.

I watched from one of the front windows as they talked, watched Rudy throw Ruth into the air a few times, saw him heft a couple of filled burlap sacks from the boat.

When he started carrying one of them toward the house, I bolted. I ran out the back door again and locked myself in the outhouse.

If, over the last month, I'd forgotten that my situation was a shameful one, I couldn't help but remember it now as I breathed that stink and peered at the back of the house through the moon-shaped cutout in the door.

I didn't come out until I saw Mattie, obviously searching for me. She grabbed my arm and shook me.

"You scared me half to death, Mandy! I was afraid you might have gone in the lake."

That night for the first time in the season the wind shifted to the east and the temperature dropped. I tucked wool blankets around Mattie and Ruth and then spread one on my own bed. It felt heavy after the summer of cotton and sheets. After I got under it, it seemed to pin my arms and legs to the bed and press me into sleep.

———

At Brown's Business College, Ruth and Imogene learned to write shorthand and work the machines. Imogene was good at these things. In two weeks she could type without looking at her fingers. In four weeks she could take a two-page letter from dictation without faltering. And, of course, the accounting was simple from the start. The assignments she turned in were always neat, the white pages clean and unwrinkled, the ink unsmudged.

Ruth, on the other hand, was foundering. Imogene had convinced her that secretarial skills were important, but she missed the job she'd given up at the five-and-dime. She couldn't seem to type two lines before her mind wandered or her fingers disobeyed and punched the wrong keys. It was impossible to remember how many spaces went between the return address and the date, the date and the internal address, the internal address and the greeting. And who cared, who cared, who cared? she thought, tugging at a paper the typewriter refused to release. When she got behind in typing, she kept up with the rhythm of the class by hitting any old keys. While she was supposed to be taking letters about how much Mr. P owed to Mr. Q and in what increments he intended to pay, she sketched tiny figures wearing complicated hats in the margins of her paper. Imogene agreed that some of them turned out rather well.

"Don't worry," she said, leaning over to correct Ruth's shorthand when the Browns were distracted, "you're the creative type."

Imogene had decided that she and Ruth were going to be modern women. When they finished school they would open an advertising agency together in Chicago. She would see to the business side and decide on the angles—she knew what made people want things. Ruth would do the art and write the copy. Imogene was not sure how they would get commissions, but she had vague notions of businessmen in gray suits and horn-rimmed glasses raising their eyebrows in admiration at the originality and style and sheer selling power of their sample ads.

Ruth suspected that Imogene had seen this in a movie. The idea made her anxious, but if Imogene wanted it, she was willing to do her part. She practiced her drawing, experimenting with different techniques she saw in the magazines. She did pen-and-ink renderings of ladies' shoes and watercolors of fruit and charcoal sketches of families frolicking by the seashore under enormous beach umbrellas cut from brightly colored paper. She liked to imagine the apartment they would have together in the city, where friends would stand in the street under their window and whistle for them to open the door. They would shop for groceries on their way home from their office, and they would sing along with the radio while they made chicken cacciatore and salads with tiny mushrooms.

"I'm wrecked, absolutely wrecked!" Imogene announced when class was dismissed for lunch that Monday. "I'll never be able to wear those shoes again." She flexed her pretty ankles before swinging her feet under one of the tables pushed beneath the windows in the typing hall.

"What did you do this weekend?" asked Lillian. She knew what was expected of her. Ruth and Imogene often ate lunch with Lillian and Myrtle, two sisters from Baraboo.

"We went to one of those dances, you know, over at the pavilion."

"Oh, a dance." Myrtle winked in a knowing way that Ruth disliked. Myrtle was older than the rest of them and divorced. She was always hinting at something dirty. "Anyone interesting there?"

"No," Ruth said quickly.

"Yes," Imogene said. "Ruth met someone interesting."

"You don't say. What was he like, Ruth?" Lillian leaned so eagerly over the table that some of the egg salad dropped out of her sandwich.

Ruth was trying to finish her homework for that afternoon, two pages of shorthand she'd neglected over the weekend. "He wasn't anything special, Lillian. He liked the way Genie danced, but who doesn't?"

"When are you going to let me do something with your hair, Ruth?" Myrtle asked, offering cigarettes around before lighting her own. "Men would like the way you danced, too, if you didn't look like an old-fashioned schoolmarm."

"Myrtle can do hair, Ruth," Lillian said. "She does mine, you know, the cut and the wave." She turned to show off the back.

"And the color," Myrtle added. "Under that henna, Lillian's got hair like a mouse."

"It's true. I do."

There was something of the little girl with the black tooth in the way Ruth looked at the sisters then, as if they were the oddities and not she, but now she smiled, as she would never have done before. After all, they were only trying to help.

"My aunt likes it this way," she said. "It doesn't bother me."

The office door at the back of the room opened and young Mr. Brown, the typing teacher, stepped out and strolled slowly through the classroom with his hands in the pockets of his smartly cut trousers. He was known as "young" Mr. Brown to distinguish him from his father, the school's founder, but he was hardly young by Imogene and Ruth's standards. He'd had ambitions once and pursued them to Milwaukee, but had been somehow disappointed. He combed his hair back to show its curl to advantage and kept his nails manicured. While other teachers rolled up their shirtsleeves and smudged chalk on their ties, no one could imagine young Mr. Brown shedding his jacket during the school day. Imogene said that was because he couldn't bear to be separated from the flask in the pocket.

"How're my girls?" he asked, resting one hand on Imogene's shoulder, the other on Ruth's, and leaning between them to put his face next to theirs. He took a paternal stance toward his female students as an excuse to touch them and to stroke their hair. Ruth twitched almost involuntarily like a horse with a fly on its neck. She closed her notebook and studied its cover, waiting for him to move on.

Imogene, though, looked him full in the face and nodded briskly. "Ruth needs to finish her work," she said. "Was there something you wanted?"

Mr. Brown straightened his back. "No, no," he said, "I'm off for my coffee break." He removed his hand from Imogene's shoulder and to compensate gave Ruth's a little squeeze.

Imogene rolled her eyes at his retreating back. "Coffee, I'll bet." She turned her attention back to the table. "I wonder if Arthur Owens will be at the dance this week. Did he say anything about it to you, Ruth?"

"I already told you everything he said to me," Ruth answered without looking up. She slid her notebook in front of Imogene. "Show me how to do 'ough' again. I can never remember."

"You could remember if you tried," Imogene said impatiently but she took the pencil Ruth held out to her.

The woman who stepped into the room just then wore a cinnamon-colored suit and a hat that wasn't the usual cloche, but a new style with a feather, angled to half hide her face. "Would you please tell me where I could find Mr. Brown?"

"Young Mr. Brown or old Mr. Brown?" Lillian piped up.

The woman hesitated. "I don't know. I want to hire a secretary."

"Then you'll want to see old Mr. Brown," Imogene said. She was already on her feet. "I'd be happy to show you to his office."

"Did you see her shoes?" Imogene whispered as she slid back into her seat.

When the woman emerged from the office, she glanced toward the table and raised her hand to Imogene, who waved back.

"What did you say to her?" Ruth asked.

"Oh, I don't know." Imogene shrugged. "Just something about how much I've learned here."

"But you're only in Level Two!" Lillian protested.

"I type faster than most of the people in Level Four. Besides, she wants someone gracious and sensible to answer her telephone and make appointments and keep her schedule in order. I'd be good at that. Wouldn't I, Ruth?"

Gracious and sensible, Ruth thought, those weren't Imogene's words. But they did describe her, part of her anyway.

Mr. Brown came out of his office with a notice and tacked it to the board.

HELP WANTED:

Personal secretary. Typing, filing, some dictation.

Must have good telephone manners.

No experience necessary.

Theresa Owens (Mrs. Clement), W290 N3040 Lakeside Road.

Chapter Fourteen

"Ruth, I've got to get you in that house!" Imogene had stopped to see Ruth and Amanda on her way home from her first day at work at the Owenses'.

"Are you riding your bicycle tonight?" Amanda asked. "It'll be raining in an hour."

"Oh, no, my parents let me take the Ford. I thought it would make a better impression. But let me tell you about this place." She pulled Ruth down beside her at the kitchen table and described the rooms Mrs. Owens had shown her that afternoon, sketching their positions with her finger on the oilcloth, and recalling as well as she could the colors and fabrics and furnishings.

"Two fireplaces, what a waste!" Amanda said. "What's the use of two fireplaces?"

"Well, it's a big room. There's one at either end, you see, so you can use just half the room for an intimate evening or the whole thing for a grand party. And she calls it the living room. Don't you think that's a much better term? So much more . . . I don't know . . . lively than front room. Of course, the whole house is quite rustic compared with their house in town."

"Of course," Amanda said dryly. "Imogene, Ruth tells me you've quit Brown's to do this job. I thought you girls were working toward something better than typing some woman's letters. I thought you were going to be advertisers." She held a plate of coffeecake in front of each of them in turn.

Ruth started to take a piece, but Imogene stopped her with a hand on her wrist. "Wait, Ruth. Try this." From her pocketbook she pulled a smashed triangle of layer cake wrapped in her hankie. "I smuggled it out for you. Isn't it scrumptious? Mocha." She pronounced the word carefully. "The Owenses' cook is from Austria. Did you know Austrians make the best pastry? I'm learning so much from Mrs. Owens. She's the president of all sorts of committees. She's even on the board at that hospital you used to work at, Miss Starkey.

"Ruth, you'll never guess what we had for dinner—lunch, I mean—cucumber sandwiches with the crusts cut off and iced tea with a sprig of mint in it. It tasted so fresh that way. Mrs. Owens says you must grow a patch of mint near your house for iced tea. And you know what she put on the plate—just for decoration, although you could eat them? Wild strawberries— you know those adorable tiny ones? Garnish makes the plate, that's what Mrs. Owens says."

"What's the point of putting something on your plate that you're not going to eat?" Ruth asked.

Amanda breathed deeply to steady her voice. "So where was Mr. Owens while you were touring his house?"

"Oh, he's up in Door County, doing something with ships, I believe. Arthur went with him," Imogene added for Ruth's benefit.

The *Rebecca Rae*, Amanda recalled with relief, was headed for Duluth, nowhere near Door County. "Well, Imogene," she said, "it all sounds very exciting, but hadn't you better be running along?" She forced herself to smile. "We don't want your mother to think we've kidnapped you."

It went on like this, week after week, Imogene modeling a hand-me-down cashmere sweater Mrs. Owens had given her, choosing new stockings to match her employer's shade, and speaking with an inflection she'd never used before. Once, when Ruth wasn't at home, Imogene left a note for her. The message was not written in her usual compact, slanted script; instead the words were up and down, full of curves and loops and fat round letters. The girl is possessed, Amanda thought, holding the page to the light. But she knew that what gnawed at her was only jealousy.

Amanda

The baby was strong now, stronger than I was. It had made me into its creature, with swollen breasts and massive belly, over which the skin stretched slick and tight, like the peel around a currant. It demanded all of my body's attention, all of my food, all of my sleep. It exhausted me.

I heaped quilts and pillows on the davenport in the front room, and it was all I could do to lumber from my bed in the morning to that spot where I spent most of the day, looking through the glass at the undulating lake, a clean blue space between my tangled nest and the brown, yellow and red patchwork of the shore. Swimming was out of the question now. Propped uncomfortably in my cocoon against the cold wall, I could see that the deep blue of the water was unnaturally gorgeous. It was slippery and unstable. It was not to be trusted.

I tried to read an old newspaper, but my mind wouldn't take in the words. I let the pages slide to the floor in a slovenly heap. Without my energy, the whole place was falling apart. The garden had gone to seed.

The squash and potatoes and onions were buried in weeds. The little room where Ruth slept was strewn with sticks, colored leaves, rocks, and even seaweed, as if the outside had moved in. With the advent of cold weather, spiders had crept in, too, and Ruth seemed always to be crouched in some corner poking at a daddy-long-legs with her fingertip.

"Ruth, stop that!" I said, seeing she was at it now. "Here, let's wash your face."

I hefted myself off the davenport and tromped heavily into the kitchen. Ruth pit-ter-pattered behind. I picked up the dish-towel, meaning to wet it at the sink, but it was already damp and crusted with flour in patches. "Oh, Ruth," I sighed, sinking into a chair. "What have we come to?"

"Outside," she said. "Wanna go out-side."

"All right. Let me button your sweater." I kissed her forehead and opened the back door for her. "Be careful. Don't go near the water."

I kept an eye on her from the window and moved desultorily around the kitchen, trying to make sense of the mess we'd let accumulate there.

"Mattie!" I called once, just looking for company. But then I remembered she'd gone to the farm.

I picked up a pile of books and papers she'd let drift into a heap on the counter. Really, reading material did not belong in the kitchen. I carried it into the front room, but all the surfaces there were already covered, so I took my load to Mathilda's room and dumped it on her unmade bed. This way, at least, she would have to take care of it before she went to sleep.

I glanced out the window, then, for Ruth. I didn't see her in the back. I looked out the side window, searching the garden up and down for her red sweater. Nothing. I hurried to the front. There she was, standing on some rocks and leaning over the water.

I opened the door and yelled, "Ruth! Come back here!" But she didn't budge, didn't even seem to hear me. Despite my unwieldy body, I was down at the shore before I was even aware that I'd left the porch. If she'd been falling in, I'd probably have caught her before she hit the water, but she wasn't falling in. She was just stirring the lake, making whirlpools with a long stick.

The rocks were pleasantly warm in the sun, although the air was chilly, and I sat down next to her, every so often wrapping one hand around her leg to steady my nerves. The water rose and fell between the rocks. I couldn't take my eyes off the ebb and flow. Until I noticed the bit of white.

It was stuck between two rocks and had not yet slipped far enough for the water to drag it away. I reached for it, but my fingers wouldn't fit.

"Here, Ruth. Let me borrow your stick a moment."

Wedging the stick between the rocks, I managed to work the white paper out far enough to pinch it up. It was an envelope addressed to Carl. Mathilda must have dropped it when she was getting into the boat.

Of course, I knew what I ought to do, and seven months ago I would have given it, unopened, to Mattie upon her return. But now I was different. Now I was tempted. Now I had to know what Mattie had written about me. Why should I give it back to her? If I hadn't happened to find it, it would have been lost forever. Maybe I was meant to find it, I told myself—that's the way I thought in those months—maybe it was waiting here for me.

In a way, I'd made myself forget about Carl. After all, far away as he was and likely to be killed, he had very little to do with us. What I'd imagined when I thought of Mattie raising my baby was something very much like what we were doing now, except with four instead of three. My baby would be both mine and Mattie's, just as Ruth was now Mattie's and mine. In the family I'd envisioned, there was no place for Carl, for squeaking bedsprings, for private smiles, for suppers with applesauce instead of rhubarb to please a man who had to have everything sweet.

But Mattie, clearly, did not feel as I did. In the letter she told him everything, everything I'd done, everything we'd planned. I was shocked. I saw myself there on the page, the facts of my foolishness and my shame in Mattie's sloppy, black letters. I couldn't stand to look at it. And I couldn't stand for him to see it, Carl with his talk of horses and his smooth dance steps and his birdhouse. I didn't want him to have any part of it.

In the letter, too, I could see that with him she was not herself. That was almost the worst of it. On the pages she'd meant for him, her voice seemed different from the one I knew, not only in the things she'd meant to keep private—that I wouldn't have minded so much—but in her every-day observations as well. I could hardly catch a hint of my Mattie in that letter. And when she and he were together—I could see it clearly now—my Mattie would be gone, and there would be no place for me.

For the moment, though, I could still keep him out of it. And then, well, the longer he was away, the better chance that he'd never come back.

"Ruthie, find me a nice rock, about this big," I said, balling her little hand into a fist.

When she brought me the rock, I crumpled the letter around it and heaved it as far as I could. The water gulped, and it was gone.

"That was a good one," Ruthie said. "Do it again!"

"It's time for your nap."

That night at supper Ruth announced to her mother, "Aunt Mandy threw a letter and it went plop."

"A letter? You mean a rock, don't you, Ruthie?" Mattie said.

Ruth looked at me.

"Yes, Ruthie," I said. "Remember, it was a rock like this." And I wrapped my hand around her fist and squeezed, not too hard, but hard enough to show her that I meant it.

———

Amanda's pulse was racing by 5:30 a.m., and the air, emerging shivery and wet from its bath in the early autumn night, made her hurry still faster. Quickly, she milked the five cows and fed the few other animals she and Ruth still kept. With Carl so often away and Rudy aging and prices the way they were, the fields lay fallow, except for the two she'd rented to Joe Tully. She'd pass him somewhere along the way, if she went up the road toward town, but she wasn't going into town. Instead, she slipped a piece of coffeecake into her pocket and took the path into the woods.

Ever since she'd discovered that Imogene was working for Theresa Owens, Amanda had begun to watch the

Owenses' house as often as she could. Each morning, so far, she'd seen the same thing: Clement in a French-blue robe, presumably terry cloth, angling down the slope of his green lawn toward his charming boathouse, a chalet with gingerbread hanging from the roofline and pink ivy geraniums spilling from the windowboxes. He was handsome still, if anything, more so, at least through the binoculars. His walk was confident but less swaggering; his movements, more tentative than they'd once been, appeared thoughtful.

Languorously, he walked across the sand under the chalet's porch and onto the pier, jouncing a bit to test its firmness, making sure nothing had slipped or warped during the night. Three quarters of the way to the end, he shucked off his robe and let it drop in a heap at his feet. He didn't dive, as Amanda expected, but sat on the edge of the pier, first dangling his feet in the water and then easing his body in, as if lowering himself into a bath. His strokes were sinuous but weary, his arms lifting in slow arcs and then seeming almost to drop into the water again. For twenty yards he pushed forward and then disappeared beneath the water. When he emerged, he was turned to crawl back. He swam this length twice and then stopped, holding onto the edge of the pier. After a minute or two he hauled himself out.

He shrugged back into his robe without drying himself, and she saw him take from the pocket a little box, open it, and transfer something from it to his tongue, before he stretched out flat under the warming sun, his hands crossed on his chest, so that he looked like a man in his coffin.

At nine, Imogene appeared, picking her way down the drive, which was so steep she had to set her feet from toe to heel, and then taking the stairs to the porch with a running step that made her skirt bounce. She lingered a moment at the top, turning to face the lake and standing with one hand on the nearest pillar, as if planting a flag to claim the view for herself. Then she crossed the porch, stood in front of the towering door, and finally disappeared into the great white pillared maw that was the Owenses' house.

But today, after a minute or two, the door reopened, and Imogene was once again on the porch. She trotted back down the stairs and continued down the hill toward the lake. Amanda slid onto the floor of her rowboat, ducking her head below the gunwale, praying she was too far away for Imogene to recognize, but the girl paid no attention to the water or anything on it. Instead, she sat neatly on her heels beside a stand of tiger lilies and began to cut them.

"Doesn't that woman know they won't keep?" Amanda thought indignantly, but the picking of wildflowers disturbed her far less than what happened next.

She'd not even noticed Clement rising, but he was standing now. No, he was already moving, draping the blue robe over his sun-browned skin as he quickly covered the distance to the beach.

"Run, Imogene, run," Amanda found herself whispering from her ridiculous position on the floor of the boat.

He was close to the girl now. Amanda could hear in her mind the voice, smooth as expensive whiskey, and the courtly inflection of his words as he asked if he might carry her flowers. She saw him extend his hand, and then she saw Imogene take it and rise from the arcing green leaves. He invited her to walk, ushering her the way he wished her to go with one hand caressing the air just behind her back. Amanda knew how it was, understood exactly what was happening, even from where she lay with the binoculars pressed so tightly to her eyes that for some seconds she could see only red.

Imogene and Clement climbed the hill, enjoying their time together, laughing, turning to face one another. At the foot of the stairs he laid the flowers in her arms, and they parted, he to go right toward the kitchen, she to go up to the main entrance, but he stopped after taking one step. He turned and followed her with his eyes, watching the way her skirt swung around her knees as she skipped up the stairs.

Meanwhile, Ruth continued to struggle at Brown's.

"Tell us about Imogene, Ruth," Lillian begged. "What did she have for lunch yesterday?"

"I don't see why the great Imogene can never spare a moment to tell us herself," Myrtle complained. "The way Ruth tells it, it'll never be half as interesting."

She was right—Ruth couldn't tell it. She tried to repeat what Imogene had said about the house and Mrs. Owens for them. She described the carpets and the view of the lake, the committees, the pillars, the little sandwiches and even the garnish, but it all came out sounding dull and flat.

Everything felt dull and flat to Ruth. The air had freshened slightly that morning, signaling the end of summer, but to Ruth the coolness was more sad than invigorating. The morning at Brown's, always frustrating, was, without Imogene, also depressing and tedious. She noticed the stains and scuffs on the pale yellow walls and the dead flies heaped on the windowsills.

"Well, the best part," Myrtle said, "is that sometimes she's all alone in that big house with that handsome boy. I know what I'd do."

"Imogene," Ruth said, "is nothing like you, Myrtle."

Imogene was, however, paying even more attention to her appearance than usual, trying all the scents Baecke's stocked and being careful never to wear the same dress twice in one week. Fond as she was of the notion of herself and Ruth running their own advertising agency, now that she was working for Theresa Owens, she was no longer so naive as to think they could pull it off. The step she'd always glossed over in her imagination—arranging the meetings with important men and smart women— was both crucial and impossible. Those sorts of people would never listen to her and Ruth.

She'd met some of them in Mrs. Owens's living room. They thanked her when she handed them her neatly typed minutes. They even asked her opinion once in a while, because they liked her—of course they liked her, everyone did—but she would never be one of them.

Maybe if she were coldly ambitious. Maybe if she were wickedly clever. Maybe if she were a college graduate, she might be able to impress them. But she was none of these things. Imogene was a fair judge of herself. She knew she was rea- sonably bright, unwaveringly loyal and confident. She knew she had persever- ance, good looks and even charm. And she knew that these qualities alone did not

add up to a brilliant career. They would,
however, make for an excellent wife, given
the right husband.

When they'd first met at the dance, Imogene had seen Arthur more as an adjunct
to Bobby Hanser than as a man onto himself. She'd hoped, in fact, that Ruth would
like him when she'd suggested they
dance; maybe then the four of them might
eventually double, since she realized her
acceptance into Bobby's crowd wouldn't
give her much happiness if Ruth wasn't
admitted too. But his solicitousness with
Ruth that night impressed her.

Once she became Theresa's secretary,
he joked with her around the house and often interrupted her work to ask for her help
with projects of his own. He'd constructed
an enormous scale model of the Brooklyn
Bridge in the sunroom, which to her indicated remarkable talent, but pieces always
needed reattaching, and she'd have to
hold two bits together while he applied the
glue. She decided he had a particularly
winning smile, more quirky and open than
Bobby's. Behind his glasses, his eyes, she
determined, were exceptionally soulful.
Obviously he had a promising future and

an excellent family. Soon enough the pleasure of going to work was in the anticipation and thrill of his appearance in the office doorway, and soon after that she stopped driving the Ford when she knew he'd be there, and looked forward all day to the evening, when he would give her a ride home in his Pontiac coupe.

Her plan to become Mrs. Arthur Owens was going very well, but it was difficult to include Ruth, although Imogene tried. "Last night he took me sailing to watch the sunset. It's like you're a gull, Ruth, so quiet and glidey. Next time I'll tell him we have to take you."

"That's all right," Ruth said. She turned on the radio behind the bait shop counter and fiddled with the tuner.

"But I want you to come. I want you to like him."

"I like him."

"We're interested in the same things— travel and music. And he loved *The Awful Truth*—remember how much I liked that movie? He's teaching me some of the newest swing steps, too. Here, I'll show you, so we can all do them next Friday."

Ruth followed Imogene's steps, but she said, "You've never traveled anywhere. You've never even been to Chicago."

"I want to, though, that's the important thing."

Ruth stopped dancing. "We'll go to Chicago," she said pointedly, "when we start our advertising agency." She had to say it. She had to make Imogene admit she was spoiling everything, not just stand aside and let her go, as if there'd never been any promises.

Imogene sighed. "I know. I know I said I'd do that with you."

"You wanted to do it! You made me go to Brown's and now you're not even there anymore!"

"I know. I did." Imogene went behind the counter and hoisted herself onto the stool. She put her head in her hands for a moment and then looked up again at Ruth. "The thing is, now I know that was just a game, just a childish fantasy."

How about sailing to watch the sunset? Ruth thought. That even sounded like a silly nursery rhyme.

"Ruth, no one's going to buy ideas from

us. We'd work and work, if we could even get jobs . . ."

"I'm sure we could get jobs!"

"All right." Imogene raised her hands. "Yes, I guess we could get jobs. Mrs. Owens said she could get something for me in Chicago if I wanted it. Not in advertising, but a job."

Ruth said nothing.

Imogene ran her fingers over the keys of the cash register. "But," she said, "I guess I don't want to go anymore. You have to understand. I can't help how I feel about him. I would understand," she added, "if it were you."

You wouldn't have to understand, Ruth thought, because I'd always put you first. And anyway, it wouldn't be me. But she said, "I know. I do understand."

"But, Ruth," Imogene said, leaning over the counter to take Ruth's hands, "I want us to do things together, all three. You like him, don't you? I know he likes you. Why can't we all three be friends?"

Ruth knew it didn't work that way, and she'd no desire even to see Arthur again after her embarrassing night on the boat, but after all, there was Imogene, looking so hopeful and eager. "We can," she said. "Of course we can, if that's what you want."

Imogene and Arthur began to pick Ruth up at Brown's at the end of the day, and they'd all go over to Frederick's Pharmacy for malts. Arthur lent Ruth books, and they'd talk about them.

"Did you like *The Minister's Charge?*"

"I don't know. I liked it up until the end. Then it was just too awful."

"You didn't think he should have married Statira?"

"No, I think he made a terrible mistake. To be trapped with one woman when he really loves another? It's wrong."

"But isn't he right to take responsibility for leading her on? He certainly behaved as if he meant to marry her, even after he knew he loved Jessie better."

Ruth sighed. "I guess I admire him for it, but it still seems a high price to pay for an innocent mistake. I mean, he thought he loved her. At first."

"A high price? But she isn't so bad, is she?"

"No, of course not, but that's the other problem, what he's doing to her. After all, what makes him think he's so special? He's robbing her of any chance to find someone who really loves her. Does he think no one else will? He loved her once."

"You remind me of Jessie."

"Oh, no." She shook her head and bent over her straw, blushing. "I'm nothing like Jessie."

"Who's Jessie?" Imogene asked, sliding onto her stool. She'd run out to examine a hat in Jackson's next door, while they waited for their malts.

"She's a bohemian," Arthur told her. "An artist. She gives up the hero when she finds out another woman loved him first."

"Does he love her?"

"Certainly. She's exactly what he's been looking for his whole life."

"Then she's a fool," Imogene said. "All's fair in love and war."

"You don't think some things are more important than love?" Ruth asked.

"No. Nothing," Imogene said. She

frowned at her malt. "I probably shouldn't drink this."

"I hope you're not listening to my mother's crazy ideas," Arthur said.

"I was, but if you think I look all right . . ."

" 'All right'? Sure," he said, smiling, "you look all right."

Arthur's car was a two-seater, but they fitted three in easily with Imogene leaning against Arthur's shoulder and Ruth wedged against the door. Amanda, waiting at the kitchen window for Ruth to come home, watched the girl nearly spill onto the drive when the car stopped.

Imogene hung out the window, waving after her. "Eight o'clock tomorrow night!" she called.

Amanda had watched the Owens family closely enough to know the car and to guess who would be driving it. "Are they serious?" she asked later, when she'd poured coffee first in Ruth's cup and then in her own and taken her seat at the table.

It was just the two of them now at supper, as long as Carl was away. Last spring Rudy had decided he was too old to work on the farm, but apparently not too old to marry. They'd had the ceremony in the front room. Amanda had baked the wedding cake, and Ruth had played three songs on the piano, and Rudy had moved into his wife's house in town.

"Are who serious?"

"Imogene and that Owens boy."

"I don't know." Ruth shrugged. She often felt she had to protect Imogene from Amanda's prying questions. Why was it any of her business?

Amanda frowned. "I would hope she'd have better judgment."

"There's nothing wrong with Arthur. He's the nicest boy I've ever met." Ruth was somewhat surprised to realize she believed this. Did he really think she was like Jessie?

Careful, Amanda told herself, it's not worth making a fuss if it turns out to be a schoolgirl fancy. Hadn't Imogene been in love with some other boy just a few weeks ago?

"I just meant, they're only summer people," she said. "I hope she knows there's no sense getting serious over summer people."

Still, she thought, this would bear

watching. She felt as if someone were playing a game with her, making a move and then sitting back with a cruel smile, waiting to see what she would do in response. So far, she hadn't made the right moves. That was obvious. Whatever her intentions, in the clinch, she'd always let her instincts drive her, and her heart, as it turned out, was an idiot, not to be counted on. Here she'd been acting wrong again, even tonight, waiting behind the curtain for Ruth to come home, when it was Imogene she needed to worry about. In fact, raising Ruth was the only thing she'd done right.

Amanda gazed across the kitchen, where Ruth was now pumping water to wash the supper dishes. Probably she'd break one; she often did, hastily rattling the plates together, paying scant attention to the work. Amanda always felt exhilarated near Ruth's wild energy, even though she cringed at the clumsiness that accompanied it. While Ruth knocked things over right and left, Amanda hadn't lost her grip on a single fragile item since she'd dropped her mother's crystal vase the day Mattie and Carl were married. Keeping things whole, she reflected, rubbing the base of her thumb, demanded a great deal of concentration.

After Arthur took Imogene home, he drove aimlessly along the country roads. That summer, the path he'd been following, the route chosen and painstakingly marked by his parents, had forked. His brother could arrange a place for him at the bank or he could start some business of his own—his parents had made clear that their fondest desire was to finance an enterprise conceived and captained by Arthur E. Owens. But a sense that there might also exist some entirely different destination, one that he couldn't yet see but which lay just beyond the obscuring undergrowth of long habit and expectations, troubled him and kept him from moving forward. He had no idea how to hack through that foliage, nor whether whatever he uncovered would please him, but neither did he want to follow blindly the manicured course on which his feet were already set. He was restless; he felt forces massing within him, ready to propel him in whatever direction he chose, but he could not decide. He had given himself the summer to loiter, but now it was fall.

And then there was this girl, Imogene. He felt almost as if he'd conjured her up, the way he'd met her that night and then found her, sparkling and chattering, with her quick smile and easy laugh, at his mother's desk the next week. She clearly admired him, and his mother had indicated she would approve. "Sometimes a blank slate is best," she'd said. "There's something to be said for a girl who's open to influence." Theresa Owens believed it was important to be broad-minded when it came to love.

Imogene was bright and pretty and obviously ambitious. She listened to concerts on the radio to teach herself to identify composers, and she asked his mother a hundred questions about the paintings on their walls. When his mother bought her a ticket to see *A Doll's House* with them in Milwaukee, Imogene found a copy at the library and read it twice, and also *Hedda Gabler* and *The Wild Duck* for good measure. Out of the corner of his eye, as he sat next to her in the theater, he saw her mouthing the lines. He knew it was patronizing of him, but he found her attempts to become cultured endearing. And beyond her looks and her charm, he admired her sense of certainty. She knew where she wanted to go and how to get there. It was tempting to align himself with someone like that, a woman who would take him in hand.

Imogene's friend, however, confused him. Ever since that first night when Ruth had told him about her mother drowning, he'd wanted to say to her, "I found her. She's the lady in the ice." That her mother had called to him through that glassy blackness, that he'd been the one to find her, to discover her blue skin and staring eyes, made him feel close to Ruth, who seemed to hold herself apart. In the drugstore he'd wanted to reach for a string of the hair that was always dripping down along her face, to twine it around his finger. At best, she looked ordinary. Her complexion was not especially clear, her eyes were too wide and her lips too narrow. Still, something reserved, even secretive, in her manner intrigued him. He was sure that she would take him somewhere

he'd never been, somewhere he couldn't
even imagine.

"You drive," Imogene said to Ruth the following evening. "I'm too jumpy. You need
the practice anyway."

Imogene had given Ruth driving lessons
the summer before, but they hadn't taken.
She needed several tries to get the
car moving, and she forgot to look left before she lurched into the road.

"Don't you think he should've picked me
up tonight, Ruth?"

"But didn't he say he'd be driving out
from town? That he'd be late? He wanted
to be sure you were going, didn't he?"

"He was just being polite. Or curious.
Or . . . I don't know, but he should take me
somewhere on a real date, if he means for
this to go on after he moves back to town."

Ruth concentrated on keeping the
wheels on the road.

"Did I tell you he gave me a four-leaf
clover yesterday?"

"No," Ruth said dutifully. She wished
this would be over one way or another,

Imogene and Arthur definitely together or definitely not. She wished she never had to hear another word about him. "I hope you pressed it immediately in a book of poetry," she said.

Imogene buried her face in her hands and laughed. "Yes," she admitted. "I don't know what I'm going to do if he doesn't say something soon. I think I'm in love with him, honest to God."

She sat up straight in the seat then and changed her tone. "What I'm thinking is I should dance first with Bobby. Then maybe with Ray. Make him wait his turn. Let him wonder a little bit. The trouble is he can see me every day of the week, if he wants to. He *does* see me almost every day of the week, so he doesn't realize that if he wants to keep, you know, *seeing* me, one of these days, he's going to have to say something."

Ruth was easing the car into the parking lot at the dance pavilion now. When she turned off the engine, music flooded through the open windows. It was the last dance of the summer. Already the vibrant green had begun to drain from the masses of leaves, and soon the world would draw

itself into its hard shell. Even in a month's
time it would be nearly impossible to remember the smothery, soft lushness of
summer nights. In a month's time Arthur
Owens might be gone.

Imogene slammed the car door. "Now,
Ruth," she said, leaning on her friend to
keep from tipping in her new high-heeled
sandals, as they walked across the gravel,
"if you see we're trying to be alone, you'll
help me out, won't you? Distract Ray. You
know how he loves to talk to you—he
thinks you're a serious person. Or make
him dance with that horrible Zita."

The band had switched from a fast number to something dreamy and the brilliant
pavilion seemed almost to float on the dark
water, if you looked at it from the right angle. Even Ruth sensed its promise as she
filled her lungs with the poignant air of the
coming fall.

"He's still not here, is he?" Imogene whispered to Ruth as Ray escorted her back to
their table.

But just then he was coming toward
them. "Behind you," Ruth whispered, and

Imogene turned and intercepted him. As she led him by the hand smoothly onto the dance floor, he looked over his shoulder once toward Ruth, but she was turned away from him, talking to Ray.

"Not so hot tonight, is it?" Ray said.

"Yes, it's nice." Arthur looked at me, Ruth thought, and felt ashamed.

"I suppose we could dance, if you want to," Ray offered.

"Maybe in a little while." It was ridiculous, despicable, wanting Arthur to look at her. Ruth felt a little sick to her stomach, thinking of it.

"Well, I'm about ready to get myself a drink. Want anything?"

"Yes, please, Ray. Whatever you're having." While she waited for him to return with the drinks, Ruth tried to comfort herself with the knowledge that she was merely being foolish. After all, a glance, a kindness, a dance, an idle compliment— they meant nothing, of course, nothing outside her own silly mind. But wasn't that the horror of it? That there was no true feeling between Arthur and herself, and still she would betray Imogene in her thoughts?

Ruth got up from the table and wandered over to peer through the screen at the winking carnival lights of Nagawaukee Beach across the lake. The waves, distinct in the streak of moonlight and invisible in the darkness on either side, seemed to move much more quickly than they did in the daytime, as if they were part of some frantic river. In their speed, they gave the illusion that the pavilion itself was sliding in the opposite direction, and Ruth had to grab the railing to keep her balance. She looked over her shoulder at the faces tilted back with laughter or forward in concentration.

"C'mon, Ruth," Imogene said, tugging at her arm, "we're going out in the boat again."

It was just as before, Arthur steadying the women in their unsteady shoes one by one as they stepped off the pier and Bobby, standing below, helping them find their footing in the boat. Everyone was talking, laughing, reminding Bobby to bring enough liquor, and ribbing him about the morning's race.

"I was starting to get dizzy watching you reround that mark," Arthur said.

"I had to give you a chance to catch up.

Wasn't I taking my spinnaker down before you'd even finished your reach?"

"But Maynard and Arthur picked the right side of the lake on the last windward leg," Kitty put in. Ruth could tell she'd said it to prove she knew what they were talking about, while Ruth and Imogene did not.

Kitty paused a moment before stepping forward after she took Arthur's hand. "It isn't fair that you're always the last one in," she said.

"I like my job, as long as Bobby doesn't leave without me."

Kitty looked at Arthur significantly. "Shall I save you a seat?"

"Sure." He sounded surprised, Ruth thought, taken aback, but still he said, "Sure."

Kitty nodded. "See you soon, then." And keeping her eyes down as she stepped from the gunwale to the seat, she wiggled the fingers of her free hand in the air.

Imogene, whose turn was next, also looked at Arthur, and Ruth saw her smile, as if the whole outing had not in a matter of seconds been ruined for her. She took his hand lightly, only touching her fingers to his palm, weightless and undemanding.

"Bobby," she said, turning away and planting her delicate shoe, with its high stalk of a heel on the gunwale, "catch me!"

She didn't mean it. She didn't jump into his arms, nothing so reckless as that, but she stepped into the boat too quickly, with too much of her mind focused on acting blithe, instead of on placing her feet. She reached for Bobby's shoulder just as he was putting his hands around her waist, but somehow he lost his balance, and they both tumbled to the floor. Imogene was laughing and groaning at once.

"Genie, are you all right?" Ruth jumped into the boat, and Arthur followed her.

"Yes, fine! No, I don't think so!" She yelped as she tried to put weight on her foot and crumpled onto the seat.

"And she's an actress, too, our little Eau de Grub," Zita whispered to Kitty.

"I'm all right," Imogene insisted, but Arthur said he'd better take her home, and she let herself be helped out of the boat and carried off the pier.

"He's come to visit every day!" Imogene crowed from the chaise in her mother's front room on Sunday. She kept to herself the words and kisses by which he'd made his intentions clear at last.

"So it was worth it?"

"You don't think I did this on purpose, do you?" She leaned forward to rub the swollen ankle she'd propped on a pile of pillows. "Although I was so mad at that Kitty, I wanted to push her in the drink."

"I know, she's hideous. Let's not have anything more to do with those people."

"But they're Arthur's friends. If Arthur and I . . ."

"It's so sweet of you, Ruth dear, to do this for Genie," Mrs. Lindgren said, interrupting her daughter as she came into the room. She stood behind Imogene and smoothed the girl's hair behind her ears.

"Your hands smell!" Imogene protested but she let her head fall against her mother's arm.

"I told her a hundred times," Mrs. Lindgren went on indulgently, "that she'd tip right over in those shoes, but she never listens."

"What am I doing for you, Imogene?"

"Mother, you didn't give me a chance to ask her yet." Imogene turned to Ruth. "The thing is . . . everyone's being unreasonable about my ankle. Dr. Karbler says I can't walk on it, at least for another day, and Mother's scared I'll fall on that hill if I use the crutches. I hate to let Mrs. Owens down. Would you fill in for me tomorrow?"

"But I'm an awful secretary."

"It doesn't matter. She won't rush you, and mostly I do things like answer the telephone and sort the mail. Anyone can do it. It's simple—personal, bills, charity." She mimed putting each in a separate pile. "Pay the bills, keep the accounts, and as far as the charity stuff goes, Mrs. Owens'll look at each piece and tell you what to do."

"Aunt Amanda won't like me missing Brown's. Not after she's paid for it."

"Do you have to tell her? It's only one day, Ruth."

Ruth bit one of her thumbnails. "I suppose for one day it'd be all right. I might as well see if I can do this stuff I'm supposed to have learned. What'll I do until the mail comes?"

"Oh, you'll find something. I'm sure I left some letters from last week on the desk to be typed and sent out. Or you can get Arthur to give you a tour of the house."

"I couldn't do that!"

"I'm only joking. Don't worry, someone'll tell you what to do." Imogene's voice followed Ruth as she left. "Don't forget to wear something nice."

Chapter Fifteen

___

Amanda

In November the baby was so large in front of me, I had to lean back to keep my balance. That must be why I didn't see Joe until he was already on the grass, partway up the path to the house. I was standing at the bottom of the front steps, halfheartedly rolling the acorns off the walk with a broom. There was nowhere to hide, not even a decent shrub to cover me now that the leaves had dropped. My middle stood out starkly behind the narrow broomstick.

I ran. Heavy as I was, running, it seemed, was still what I did best. I ran around the back of the house and pushed Mathilda out the front.

Joe had come with a letter: Carl was on his way home.

In the yard, Mathilda danced. She swooped Ruth off her feet and danced. She twirled and danced. She danced with Joe; she danced with Ruth—Carl was coming home. I sat on Ruth's little bed, trying to keep the panic down. Inside of me, the baby danced, just like Mattie. It kicked up its heels and danced and danced.

Before Joe left, he also told Mathilda a sad story. I could imagine him, holding his cap and bowing his head, pretending he wasn't thinking about what he'd seen inside of me. Poor Mary Louise had had her baby, a girl as still as ice.

———

Amanda steered a straight course through the early morning mist, one hand on the little four-horse Evinrude Joe had given her when he bought a more powerful one for himself. The motor buzzed so loudly she couldn't think, but she had to think. She hadn't decided what she would say or how she would say it, but Arthur had to leave

Imogene alone—that much was obvious—
and Clement, if he had any ideas . . . but
that was unthinkable. Anyway, she told
herself firmly, the time had come to make
clear that this was her place, not his, and
that he had caused enough trouble for one
lifetime.

As she drew close to his boathouse, the
smell nearly beat her back. The weed
barge must have been cutting that morning, and a sea of weeds, studded with
dead fish, clogged the water all along the
shore. She killed the motor before the
stringy fronds could tangle in the propeller
and rowed the little distance to the pier.
She tied her boat, and then on an impulse
got out and sat on the boards where she
had seen him sunbathe. She stretched her
legs out full in front of her and tipped her
chin back to catch the sun. She faced the
middle of the lake, away from the lawn
from which she knew he'd come. If anyone
else found her first, well, let them.

"Motor trouble?" His voice sang over
the weed-choked water, deep and clear as
she remembered it.

She turned to look at him over her
shoulder. Dazzled by the brightness that

had been beating against her eyelids, she
could at first see only light and shadow. He
was just stepping from the grass to the
sand, and he raised his hand to shade his
eyes.

"Need help?"

She didn't answer, could not answer.
Her throat seemed to have swollen shut,
and she trembled. It had been a mistake to
come, a terrible error to think his betrayal
would no longer sear her. Slowly, she
turned to face him, tucking her knees under her chin and wrapping her arms
around them to hold herself together.
When he reached the pier, he was no
longer looking straight into the sun.

"Amy?" He squinted in her direction,
frowning, and then glanced quickly but unmistakably back toward the house, before
hurrying toward her. The boards of the pier
sprang under his weight, so that she rose
and fell with each of his steps.

It seemed natural, his bending to give
her his hand. Her cheek brushed the arm
of his bathrobe as she allowed him to help
her to her feet. She smelled the same old
soap he'd used so many years ago, and
those months with him rushed back upon

her. Yes, for an instant she felt pleasure above all, as his nearness confirmed that a young, hopeful Amanda had once existed and was remembered, and the sweetness of this sensation was only intensified by the bitter realization that she existed no more. This man knew her, *had* known her, she corrected herself, however much he'd abused that knowledge.

He stared and stared at her, shaking his head in surprise. "Amy. Look at you. Just look at you."

And against her will, she exulted in his approval. But she pulled herself back, sorry she'd let him, of all people, catch her up again. "I need to talk to you."

"Of course, of course, Amy. But"—and he glanced, rather furtively, she noticed, to either side along the lakeshore—"not here, I think. Say," he said, brightening, "why don't we take your boat and get away from this stink?"

She hesitated. She wanted to get it over with, but she still hadn't decided exactly what she meant to say. Keep your son away from my friend's daughter? It hardly sounded convincing. "All right," she said. Talking to him would be easier, she told herself, if they weren't standing on his pier in full sight of his wife's windows.

The moment he stepped into her boat, she realized she hated him. He rowed a few strokes to get them clear of the weeds, and she kept on hating him, hated the certainty with which he handled the oars, just as he'd once handled her. She gave the cord on the motor two fierce tugs, and the Evinrude sputtered to life. Slowly, the tiny engine barely creating a ripple behind them, they crept into deeper water.

They didn't try to talk over the engine noise. Finally Clement, who'd been looking over Amanda's shoulder at the receding shoreline, said, "Might as well stop here as anywhere."

Amanda noticed they were too far from shore to be seen, although not if the viewer had a pair of binoculars.

"So, Amy. What is it? Do you need money?"

It was her turn to stare at him. "Money? No, of course not."

"Well, lots of people do these days. It's nothing to be ashamed of. And I'd be happy to see what I could do. I don't know how much exactly, but I'm sure I could loan you something."

"Clement, stop. I don't need money."

"Well, what then?"

She looked away from him over the water. What? What did she want to say? Imogene is our daughter. Was that it? She opened her mouth. "Why don't you go ahead and take your swim?" she said.

"What?"

"I mean I suppose you meant to take a swim this morning. You're dressed for swimming, aren't you? Why don't you go ahead as long as we're out here away from the weeds?"

Obviously puzzled, he said nothing at first, and then began to loosen the knot securing his bathrobe. "Well, all right," he said. "Maybe I will. I like to get in at least a couple of laps every day. Then maybe we can drive around a bit. See that island you were always telling me about."

He remembered the island. Amanda felt disproportionately grateful, and then disgusted with herself for that gratitude. It was funny, she thought, as he took off his robe and climbed onto the seat, how comfortable he acted with her, as if she had no reason to hate him, as if they'd parted on good terms and not very long ago at that, as if none of the terrible things she'd experienced had happened. He dove, shoving the boat several feet away from him as he thrust himself forward. Of course, as far as he knew, nothing much had happened. She'd cried, and they'd broken off, that was all. She realized with a start that he might even think she'd come back to him, that she didn't care anymore that he was married. Or perhaps that was ungenerous, she thought as she watched his slow crawl away from the boat. Perhaps he was only glad to see her again. Perhaps he thought she'd forgiven him.

Ruth reached under the collar of her dress and tugged at the strap that threatened to slip down her arm. It was eight-thirty. She was a full half hour early. Below her, the lake shimmered invitingly. Fishing boats manned by those irregular types who had no morning employment lounged in the pockets along its edges, and far out a man was diving from a little rowboat, his white torso shining in the strong, new sun.

Once she'd begun straying toward the sparkling waves, the slope pulled her down the hill, until she was standing on a concrete sea wall. Two feet below, the lake at its annual low point swelled and receded biliously, raising and lowering its fetid cargo of red and white bobbers, brown paper sandwich wrappers, and stinking dead fish, all caught in a net of weeds. Ruth backed away. She might as well go early to work.

"Coffee?" the maid asked when she'd shown Ruth upstairs to a bright room, in which a roll-top desk stood against one wall.

"Oh, no, thank you." Ruth slipped her hand over a scorched spot she'd just noticed on her skirt.

"Miss Lindgren always has coffee. With cream and three sugars. Like a confection." The woman frowned disapprovingly and with that left the room, shutting the door behind her, and Ruth was left alone to regret declining the coffee.

She fingered the key in the desk. Should she wait or open it? Imogene should've given her more direction. Ruth paced around the room, passing her eyes over engravings and the spines of books without any real awareness of what she was seeing. She didn't want to be caught snooping. She could imagine Mrs. Owens in her wide-shouldered cinnamon suit and feathered hat—although probably she wouldn't be wearing the hat at home—bursting in, wondering why she hadn't gotten started. Hadn't Genie said there was some typing?

Ruth went back to the roll-top, turned the key and slid the top open. Yes, there was a Remington, and a stenographer's notebook open to a page of Imogene's neat shorthand. She slid into the desk chair, separated a clean sheet of paper from the stack and rolled it into the typewriter.

Twenty minutes later she was leaning over the machine, trying to decide whether a mistyped *i* could be adequately covered with an *l,* or whether she ought to start the page over, as her instructors at Brown's

would have insisted. The door opened behind her.

"It doesn't have to be perfect, just legi-
ble," Mrs. Owens said. Mrs. Owens, Ruth
saw, would never burst into a room.
She was stately and poised; in her gray
dress she looked something like a great
blue heron. She glided forward, extending
her hand. "You must be Rose. I'm so grateful to you for filling in for Imogene this
week." Her skin, smooth and cool, made
Ruth conscious of the ink on her own fingers. "Didn't Ellen bring you any coffee?"
And before Ruth could protest, Mrs.
Owens was speaking into a device in the
wall. "Would you bring coffee for two,
please, Ellen? And don't forget the cream
and sugar." She turned back to Ruth and
whispered, "Ellen doesn't approve of
sweets."

For an hour or so Mrs. Owens paced
around the room as she dictated notes for
a speech convincing her circle to donate
funds to establish a summer camp for
poor children. "Help me, Rose. I need to

say something about fresh air, the importance of fresh air and exercise for both
physical and moral growth. How can we
expect these children to develop into up-
standing citizens if we don't expose them
to the healthy innocence of the country-
side? Yes, that's good, Rose, get that
down."

Then, while Ruth transcribed the most
promising lines, Mrs. Owens made telephone calls. "Well," she sighed, setting the
receiver down after the third call, "I guess
that's all I'm going to get done today. I've
got to ooh and ahh over the new pul-
monary wing at St. Joseph's. If you could
just finish up the typing and copy these
into the appointment book, it would be
such a help. If anything conflicts, let me
know." She handed Ruth a few letters.
"Ellen will bring you lunch, of course. Just
call her through the intercom whenever
you want it."

"All right," Ruth said, although she knew
she could never summon Ellen.

"I'll see you tomorrow then? Or Imogene?"

"Imogene, I think."

"Well, Rose," she said, giving Ruth her

cool hand again, "you've been a great help. Thank you." And then she was gone.

Ruth sat down to the typing. The paper she fed into the machine was luxuriously thick and soft, and a rich, creamy color, nothing like the nearly transparent stuff flecked with bits of wood and rag they had to use at Brown's. When she held it to the light, the watermark floated in the center like a secret kiss. Why hadn't she told Mrs. Owens that her name wasn't Rose?

Dear Mrs. Schmidt, I was so plased

Carefully, Ruth rolled the paper out of the typewriter and inserted a new page.

Dear Mrs. Schmidt, I wzs
Dear mrs.
Dre

Ruth yanked the fourth sheet of paper out with a sharp, satisfying zip. Anyone who did that at Brown's had to pay a fine for damage to the machine. Not wanting Mrs. Owens to see how many sheets of expensive letter paper she'd ruined, she folded her false starts and stuffed them into her pocketbook.

She walked once around the room to collect herself and then sat down again. A hairpin poked her scalp. One by one, she drew pins out, searching for the culprit, until her hair hung freely down her back.

Except for the typewriter, everything on the desk was decorated to suggest a whimsical, aquatic theme. She picked up a letter opener with a silver handle scaled like a fish. Beside that crouched a green enamel box shaped like a frog from whose mouth protruded a tongue of stamps. She tore several off, licked them and applied them to envelopes. She would type the addresses later. Then she turned to the appointment book, which was covered in bottle-green leather and had its own little gold pen stuck in a ring on the side. Ruth filled in each obligation from the cards and letters Mrs. Owens had given her. First she wrote in pencil in case she made a mistake, and then she traced over the pencil with the gold pen.

The telephone rang, and she jumped. Was she supposed to answer it? She waited. It rang again, two rings, three, four.

Why wasn't Ellen or someone downstairs picking it up? Finally, on the sixth ring, she lifted the receiver. "Hello?" But no one was there.

Ruth flipped back and forth through the appointment book: Soldiers' Home luncheon, tea for St. Anne's, S. Lemon, Avis home, Garden Club, Library Benefit, Athletic Club, Red Cross, Women's Club, dinner at the Joneses'. She pretended to answer a call. "Yes, this is Mrs. Owens's secretary. . . . Let me see. . . . I can squeeze you in between two-thirty and three o'clock on Wednesday, will that be all right? Thank you. Goodbye." She wished the telephone would ring again.

Ruth closed the appointment book and stuck the pen back into its holder. She got up from the roll-top desk, moved to the table where Mrs. Owens sat, and reached for the fountain pen as if it were her own. She tried her signature on the back of an old envelope—Ruth Sapphira Neumann. Out the window, at the bottom of the hill, the lake like wrinkled tinfoil threw sunbeams in every direction.

Finally she returned to the desk and rolled a fresh sheet of paper into the typewriter. "Dear Mrs. Schmidt," she pecked, keeping to a slow but steady rhythm, "I was so pleased to talk with you last Thursday."

Silently, Arthur opened the door to his mother's study. It had become his habit to surprise Imogene when his mother was out, to sneak as close to her as he could before she detected his presence, or at least before she let on that she noticed him. His first reaction, when he realized it was not Imogene who sat typewriting with her back to the door, was embarrassment at what he'd planned. When he recognized Ruth, his blood jolted. From surprise, he assured himself. That was all that affected him—surprise.

"Hello," he said from the doorway.

As she whirled around, her wrist struck an inkwell, but she caught it deftly before it could fly off the table and disgorge its blue-black innards onto the Persian carpet. She uttered only a startled "Oh," then turned away again in confusion, reaching to set the ink far back on the desk.

"I'm sorry. I didn't mean to startle you." He took two steps into the room. He could think of nothing else to say.

"Genie should be back tomorrow, Wednesday at the latest."

"Is she ill?"

Ruth, struggling to put her loose hair back together, had stuck two pins in her mouth. "They won't let her walk on her ankle," she said as well as she could through closed teeth.

"Her ankle. Of course. Is it better?"

"Not really. That's why they won't let her walk on it."

He was making her nervous. The way he looked at her could almost be described as expectant, as if he thought she might suddenly say or do something amusing. As far as she knew, she'd never done anything to give him that impression.

"That's right, she shouldn't walk on it." He picked up the stamp-box frog and set it down again. "It's very nice of you to fill in."

She shrugged. "Otherwise I'd have to go to Brown's, and I can't stand Brown's."

"Why do you go then?" There it was again, that little smile of anticipation.

"Because Imogene thought I should typewrite, and they promised to teach me. Not that I've learned," she added honestly, "but I don't think that's their fault."

He laughed. "Typewriting's not important."

"Not to you maybe. But to me it is, or at least it should be. Maybe you haven't noticed, but there are precious few jobs out there."

"And this is what you want to be? A typewriter?"

"No," she admitted. "Not really. But what you want doesn't always matter, does it?"

"I guess not." He crossed the room to look out the window toward the lake. "Next week I start work for my brother," he said, drumming his fingers on the table. Then he turned back to her. "Say, we shouldn't be inside today."

"We shouldn't?"

"Summer's almost over, isn't it? We have to take advantage."

Ruth looked doubtfully at the paper in the machine. "You go ahead. I have to finish these letters."

"But I thought you said you couldn't typewrite."

"I told your mother I'd do them."

He picked up the little stack of handwritten letters and counted the pages. "If I do these for you, will you go with me?"

"You can't type!"

"Of course I can." He nudged her out of the chair. Then he rolled up his sleeves and adjusted the chair's position, as if preparing for great labor. "Ah, Mrs. Schmidt," he said, rubbing his hands together as he examined the letter she'd begun. "What shall we say to Mrs. Schmidt?"

He began to type with two fingers in swift, decisive strokes, every half minute or so returning the carriage with a hearty swipe. Ruth, watching the lines emerge from the machine, belatedly remembered to spread her fingers over the scorch in her skirt.

"My father made me learn a few years ago," he said as he started on the next letter. "He said I had to keep up with improvements. I have to say, I'm not sorry now." He looked up at her, quickly, shyly, as the carriage bell dinged.

She watched, fascinated by the certainty of his fingers and lulled by the clack of the keys, until he pulled the last page out. He joggled the finished letters together and tapped their edges on the desk. "Okay, so now can we go?"

In that car with him, without Imogene pressed between them, Ruth leaned tentatively against the back of the seat, aware that there was nothing but space between her thigh and his. She kept her eyes on the sky, a washed-clean, hard blue, and the rough stubble of the recently cut fields. After a while, though, she began to relax. She opened the window as far as it would go and played idly with one hand in the streaming air. The wind teased her hair down again, and she let it snarl, only holding it back with one hand to keep the whipping tendrils from her face.

"Too fast?" he asked, with the same, shy sideways glance he'd given her at the typewriter.

"No. I like it."

They passed fields and farmhouses and barns and little stores with the words *groceries beer bait* and *beer food dry goods* and *cheese chickens beer* painted on their walls.

"Where're we going?" Ruth asked finally.

"I don't know." He shrugged. "How about a picnic? You hungry?"

"Starved."

He pulled over next to one of the all-purpose stores, a place made of whitewashed stone, with two tiny windows. Inside, Arthur started toward an icebox in back, and Ruth followed slowly behind. She liked this store; it was like a cave, pleasantly damp and cool after the dry wind of the road. As she moved along the row of shelves, examining the packages—blackberry, strawberry, raspberry jam, corn flakes, soap flakes, matches—she smelled first mothballs, then vinegar, then cloves, and then cigarettes and rancid sweat.

"Whatcha doin' with him?"

Ruth jumped at the raspy whisper behind her back, knocking a can of tuna to the floor. An old man whose head came only to her shoulder scowled up at her. "Nothing," she said, diving to retrieve the can. She pushed it onto the shelf and backed toward the door. "I'll be outside, Arthur. Okay? I'll wait outside."

What gave that crazy old man the right to talk to her like that? She leaned against the warm whitewashed wall. They were friends on a drive, she should have said. They were taking advantage of the last summer weather. Honestly, she wished Imogene were with them.

Safely back in the car, they pointed out pretty views and charming houses and were pleased to discover that their tastes were just the same. They talked about the people they knew, which reminded them of stories about people they'd known. Arthur told Ruth he'd been thinking he might want to learn to build bridges, and Ruth told Arthur about how Amanda had taught her to throw fits and bark like a dog to keep her out of school. "Let's see," he said, and she demonstrated, and he laughed so hard he swerved the car.

He turned onto a smaller road.

"Do you know where you're going?" she said as the small road became a dirt track.

"My father and I used to stop somewhere around here." He leaned over her to look out the window.

He led her finally to a little river, where he made a nest of rocks for the beer to cool. Then they sat on the grass, and he hacked at the salami with his pocketknife, while she tore the bread.

"Imogene should be back tomorrow," she said, piling haphazard sandwiches on brown paper between them.

"Oh? That's good."

"Yes, her ankle really isn't so bad. I mean, it was bad, but it's better now. Her mother just wanted her to be careful."

"She *should* be careful."

He fetched the beer and watched her throat ripple as she swallowed. The condensation dripped off the bottle onto her skirt.

"I hate to leave the lake next week," he said.

"But you wouldn't like it in the winter. It's bleak and empty as the moon."

"I don't mind that. You can do things outside here, not just scurry from building to building like we do in the city."

"Mostly, we scurry from building to building too," Ruth laughed, "if we're lucky."

"Well, I hope I have a reason to come back for the weekends anyway." He blushed and pulled a few bunches of grass from the ground. They made the light, tearing sound a sheep would make cropping.

.He means Imogene, she thought. He loves Imogene. Did this grieve her because he would have Imogene or because Imogene would have him? Both, she supposed. Both left her alone. But she was Imogene's friend, that was the important thing. And she would be Imogene's friend, with or without her. "Imogene would make a very good wife," she said.

"Yes, I'm sure she would," he said seriously. "A man would be lucky to have her."

Suddenly he tossed the grass he'd collected into the air, so that it fell like confetti onto their heads. "Let's take a walk."

One blade dangled just above her eye. He reached forward to slide it from her hair, and she felt a tiny pang as his finger touched her forehead. Stop that, she thought. You mustn't feel that way again.

Briskly, she stood up and brushed the grass from her dress. "No," she said, "it's getting late. My aunt will worry. You'd better take me home."

Chapter Sixteen

—————

Amanda

I had to admit it was lovely there on the water with the fresh breeze shirring the waves and the sun's warmth soaking under my blouse. The morning had lured three sailboats from their docks, and they zigged and zagged on the dark blue water, their canvas brilliant white triangles against the light blue sky. Clement swam so close that the spray thrown up by his kicking wet my cheeks. Wasn't this enough, more than enough? Our happiness, after all, had once been real, even if he'd lied to spur it on. Why had I, in insisting that I be the most prized, the only beloved, hidden myself away from such delights?

After his second lap, he hung onto the boat, breathing laboriously. Now that his hair was wet and plastered to his skull, I could see how much it had thinned. I wanted to reach over and take his hand. Shhh, I wanted to say, shhh, it's all right. Rest now. Come back in the boat and rest. It made me sad to see him diminished, a man who'd been so vital, but his weakness also made me fond.

Of course, I'd been mistaken about what I'd thought I'd seen a few mornings before. Clement wasn't what he had been. He'd no designs on Imogene. My own suspicious nature had created my fears.

I wanted to tell him about her. I wanted him to know that, in the end, he and I had produced such a one.

"I want to tell you about Imogene," I said. "Imogene Lindgren."

Squinting up at me, he sighed. Yes, I think he sighed. "She's lovely, isn't she?" he said. "In fact . . . if I weren't so old . . ." He looked away from me then, far off toward the other side of the lake, and then he looked back. He may even have winked, although maybe he was only blinking water from his eyes. "But who knows what the young girls like nowadays?" he said. "I might have a chance yet." As he spoke, he turned and pushed off the boat with his feet, so his last words were nearly washed away by the swoosh of the water, but I know I heard them. Otherwise, why would I have felt such a cold horror prickling my skin?

And then I felt the sun burning and raging in my veins. I wanted to ram him with the boat, to drive the propeller over his smug, white back, so that it shredded into ribbons like a worn sheet. I wanted to leap in and hold his head under with my own hands. But I didn't. Of course I didn't. I could never do any of those things.

Instead, I stood up in the boat and shouted for the whole lake to hear: "She's your daughter! Your daughter!"

But he didn't stop. I tugged viciously at the cord, and the motor growled. He must have raised his head at last when the whine reached his ears. Bewildered, he must have watched me go. But I did not look back.

The motor was slow, so damnably slow, it seemed to take hours to crawl away from him across the water, days to reach the shore. Halfway home, I hurled the terry-cloth robe from the boat. It flung its arms into the air, settled on the surface of the lake, and then slowly, as it became water-logged, began to sink.

As I dragged the boat after me onto the muddy shore, I imagined Clement climbing out of the water, calling for a sandwich. He would be ravenous after such a long swim, and my fury would have done no damage to his other appetites either. At least he'd have had to push through those weeds. He was a monster! A monster! His smell lingered on my skin, and I waded into the waves to scrub my hands and to cool my face, which still burned with outrage.

Nagawaukee is not a large lake; anyone can swim its width. How was I to guess he couldn't do what a ten-year-old child can do? I'd forgotten about his weak heart.

Is that true? To be honest, I don't know.

Chapter Seventeen

Amanda

I wasn't ready when the baby was. I wanted to stay forever in limbo, not going forward, not going back, just still. But the baby couldn't be still. We were going on whether I liked it or not.

The pains began at noon on a bright, achingly cold day. Recklessly, I stood at the edge of the island for a last taste of air, daring the world to see. I exulted in the force of the wind, beating and gusting along the new green ice, cold enough to bring tears to my eyes. And then my insides squeezed again.

My water broke around seven. I sterilized the scissors, stifling thoughts of that

absurd vacuum box, and laid them out
with string on a clean towel. I placed my
shoes side by side under the bed in
Mathilda's room, the one we'd decided to
use. I took off my dress and hung it neatly
on the hook behind the door. Mathilda,
poor little thing, flew back and forth from
kitchen to bedroom, sometimes carrying a
glass of water or a blanket, mainly just to
be doing something. But I was calm. I was
ready.

A contraction gripped me, and I made a
sound that must have frightened Ruth.
"Aunt Mandy hurt?"

"Come on, sweetheart," Mathilda said,
holding out her hand to the child. "Let's go
in your room now."

Ruth shook her head.

"Yes, we have to go now. Be good,
Ruthie."

But Ruth lowered herself to a crouch
and, before Mathilda could scoop her up,
scuttled under the bed, drawing the rag
rug in after her as a barricade.

Mathilda reached under and tried to pull
her out, but Ruth clamped onto the leg of
the bed and howled. I had a better idea. I

slipped off the bed and went into the kitchen for a peppermint stick.

"Look, Ruth," I said, holding the striped stick as close to the floor as I could. "Shush now. Aunt Mandy's got candy."

But another contraction made me gasp. The peppermint dropped with a crack as I grabbed hold of Mattie. She helped me back on the bed, and we let Ruth be.

Ruth floating face down, her body spread over the waves like a blue terry-cloth bathrobe. Reach, farther, reach, there—the hair, hold on, pull her up, pull her out. Amanda awoke, her fingers clutching the air, gasping as if she'd been the one trying to breathe under water. Ruth isn't drowned, she told herself firmly. Ruth is fine.

She'd fallen asleep fully clothed, and the hem of her dress was still damp where it had draggled in the water when she heaved the boat out. Her collar had pulled tight around her throat as she slept—per-

haps that accounted for her breathless-
ness—and she loosened the top two buttons.

The day had faded, but it was not yet
dusk. Ruth would be home soon, if she
was not already.

"Ruth?" Amanda stood at the top of the
stairs and called down. There was no answer.

Turning, she faced herself in the landing
mirror, her skin red from the sun, her hair
snarled and matted, her dress wrinkled.
She raised a tentative hand to her cheek.
She'd never had what people called a full
face, but lately her bones had become
more prominent, her cheeks hollow. White
wires threaded through her hair.

What kind of a girl gets so dirty? her
mother's voice said in her mind, but so
clearly that she turned around, half expecting to see her standing there, holding a
washcloth and a brick of her homemade
lavender soap. But that would have been
downstairs near the tub by the stove in the
kitchen. Carl had long since put in the
bathroom upstairs by walling off a corner
of Ruth's room, the room Amanda and
Mathilda had once shared.

She took a fresh dress from the closet and hung it on the bathroom door. While she waited for the tub to fill, she brushed her teeth with a little baking soda, scrubbed the sink and the toilet with cleanser. In her hair, she could still catch the odor of the dead fish and weeds she'd encountered that morning. She'd have to wash it, even though it was probably too late in the day for it to dry properly.

Slowly, she lowered herself into the tub. She hadn't realized how cold and tense she'd been, and the warm water soothed her. She lay back in it, letting her feet and hands float. Lazily, she caressed herself, her stomach and her thighs, the bones and the soft dip at the base of her throat, her breasts. Then she slid deeper, tipping her head back to soak her hair. The water rose gently, like a warm hood over the back of her head, and her hair spread around her neck and over her chest like weeds. The water covered her ears, separating her from the sounds of the air, drawing her down and under.

Amanda sat up suddenly and struggled out of the bath, water streaming from her toes and fingertips onto the mat. Quickly, she dried herself and wrapped her hair in the towel. Then, her skin still damp, she pulled on her clothes. It was really food she needed. How long had it been since she'd eaten? She had to get some supper together. Ruth was always starving after a day wrestling with those typewriters.

The stones in the driveway crunched and pinged as she was peeling the last potato. Amanda slipped to the window and looked out. A man, that Owens boy, Clement and not Clement, was handing Ruth out of the car. Amanda pulled the towel from her hair and tied a scarf around her head. But the car door slammed and then slammed again; the engine noises rose and fell away; and Ruth came into the kitchen alone.

"You were with that Owens boy?" Amanda asked her, as matter-of-factly as she could manage. She lifted the lid from the pot roast, and an exhalation of steam masked her face.

"Arthur? He gave me a ride."

"But not Imogene?"

"No."

So now was it Ruth who had to be

watched? Amanda frowned, studying the young woman's movements, as Ruth began to set the table. "Did you . . ." She stopped herself, not sure how to say it, "drink anything?" she finished delicately.

"Of course not."

Anger, acerbic as bile, rose in Amanda at the thought of the father and son. Why would they not leave her and hers alone? But it was her own fault, she knew. Hiding and pretending, staying and lying, she had, in some sense, kept Clement Owens with her always. One night with him had become a sort of knot around which she'd grown for the last twenty years. Why should she be surprised now if, instead of dissolving, he'd doubled?

But it would be all right, she assured herself. Summer was ending and soon they would go. She only had to wait, holding things in place, a little longer.

Ruth was home safely, and now they would eat a well-balanced meal, Amanda told herself, spooning red cabbage onto Ruth's plate. Everything was all right, then. Everything was as it should be, she thought, surveying the table, except for one detail. "Do you think we should have applesauce, Ruth? There's some in the icebox. Why don't you get it?"

"I don't need applesauce."

"Well, but I think we should have it. It's just in the icebox, in the little green dish."

"I really don't want applesauce tonight."

"But I think we should have it. Otherwise, we don't have any fruit, and fruit is very important. Let's have it on the table, at least, in case we change our minds."

"I want Imogene to be happy," Ruth said, getting up from the table. "I really do."

No, she shouldn't talk about Imogene, not tonight, not when everything had to be kept just so. "We all want Imogene to be happy, of course. Ruth, on the top shelf, behind the milk. You know, I wonder if it'll be too cold. Do you think it is? It shouldn't be so cold that it chills the meat. Maybe we ought to heat it for a minute, so it isn't ice cold."

"But we were going to have our apartment!"

"Apartment? What apartment?" Amanda pushed her chair back slightly. She felt suddenly at a disadvantage with her legs trapped under the table.

"There is no apartment. Not anymore. Genie's going to marry Arthur Owens. He hasn't asked her yet, but he will."

With this jumble of strange syllables, a thickness filled Amanda's ears, followed by a ringing. She drew back from the table, shaking her head. "No," she said firmly, almost brightly. "No, that's impossible."

"Aunt Mandy, what's the matter? Are you sick? Is something wrong?"

Amanda stood up so abruptly that her chair toppled over behind her. "We have to stop them."

"What are you talking about? What's the matter with you?" Ruth had come around the table, and she pressed a palm to her aunt's clammy forehead. "Maybe you should lie down. Do you want to lie down?" she asked, steering Amanda toward the front room. She tried to sound solicitous, but she was afraid. Was this why Amanda had had to go to St. Michael's? "Should I call Dr. Karbler?"

"No! No one else, Ruth. No one else. Only you."

They were standing beside the old davenport now, but when Ruth tried to lower her aunt onto it, Amanda clung and pulled her down too. "Promise you'll help me, Ruth," she whispered. "Promise."

"Of course I'll help you. What is it?"

Amanda continued to whisper, as if in that way the words would not actually be spoken, but somehow pass from her to Ruth in a current of understanding. "Imogene is Clement Owens's daughter."

She's crazy, Ruth thought, involuntarily pulling back from Amanda, as a mixture of fear and disgust, bordering on nausea, rose in her throat. "Stop it," she said. "What's wrong with you? Stop acting like this." She felt an urge to slap her aunt, but Amanda began to cry then, and Ruth rubbed her shoulder instead. "Now, Aunt Mandy, you know that's silly. I don't know who told you that, but you can't credit crazy stories. Mr. Owens and Mrs. Lindgren don't even know each other. And Mrs. Lindgren would never!" A thought occurred to Ruth. "I bet I know who started this. How dare they? That nasty Zita and Kitty. They'll be sorry."

But Amanda had stopped crying. With fingers like claws, she gripped Ruth's shoulders and shook her. "*You* stop it, Ruth! Look at me! Listen to me! This is no one's story but mine. No one knows it but me. Only me. I know he's Imogene's father because I am her mother. She's my baby."

Ruth jerked out of Amanda's grip and turned her face away, covering her ears with her hands. "Stop it! How can you say such a thing?"

If Amanda had suddenly insisted that after all the sky was green and the grass was red, Ruth could not have been more confused, more betrayed. Now, as she turned to stare at Amanda, it was her voice that was reduced to a whisper. "But you said the baby wasn't real."

Ruth

Mama's feet go back and forth, back and forth. Aunt Mandy makes the scary sounds. "Shh, shh," I say, but nobody hears me. I put my head on the now-I-lay-me-down-to-sleep and watch the candy stick. Aunt Mandy's shoes are watching me. I better be good now, good and quiet.

"Shh, shh," I say, but nobody listens to me. Kick, Mama's shoe on the candy stick. It rolls to me and I pick itup, pick the fur off with my fingers. It's still good, I tell myself. That's what Aunt Mandy would say to me. We don't mind a little dirt.

Aunt Mandy makes the scary sounds. "It's all right," Mama says. "Everything'll be all right." But I knew that wasn't true.

I shush and suck, shush and suck. I am good, but still the scary sounds. I wish they'd stop. "Stop," I say, but I only whisper. "I'll be quiet. I'll be good."

My candy's so sharp, it bites my tongue. The blood tastes sweet, so I swallow it down. "Now I lay me down to sleep," I say, but I stay awake.

Mama's on the bed now too. I want to go on the bed, but I'm scared. The noises, stop the noises! And then the noises stop.

"Oh, Mandy," Mama says, "a little girl."

But the little girl is under the bed.

A baby is crying, so I try crying, but it isn't me.

"You have to tell her, Aunt Mandy."

They'd pushed the congealed pot roast and red cabbage, food that looked like a mass of bruises on the plates, into the slop bucket for the dogs and the pigs, and were seated at the kitchen table. Amanda had poured cups of coffee, as if they were settling down to discuss an ordinary problem.

"No." Amanda shook her head. She was stirring sugar into her coffee. "No, we have to think, Ruth. Think." Her spoon went back and forth, clinking on the edges of the cup. "Imogene can never know."

"Think about what? How to dress for the wedding? I'm going to tell her if you won't."

Amanda tried speaking calmly, patiently. She kept her eyes on Ruth's face. Ruth was being unreasonable; she had to be made to see. "You don't want to do that. Think of Mary Louise. It'd kill her, Imogene finding out that way. Imogene finding out at all." She raised her cup to her lips with nearly steady hands and sipped. She felt she'd made a good point, a strong point, one on which she could stand firm. "No, it wouldn't be fair to Mary Louise. After all, she's been a very good mother. You have to agree with me there, don't you, Ruth?"

When Ruth said nothing, Amanda repeated her question. "You agree that Mary Louise has been an excellent mother, don't you?"

"Yes!" Ruth said impatiently. "Yes, of course, but that's got nothing to do with it."

"Oh, Ruth, you're not a mother yet. When you're a mother, you'll understand."

In exasperation, Ruth pushed her cup away so roughly that the coffee slopped onto the table.

"Tch." Amanda clicked her tongue against the roof of her mouth. "You're upset now, Ruth, but try to see it my way." She rose to get the dishrag. "Think of Imogene," she said, mopping the spill. "Think, Ruth, how you feel, knowing this. Just imagine how it would be for her—everything good ruined. Everything she believes in, spoiled for her. You love Imogene. Do you really want to tell her that this is how she came into the world? You have to think of what's right, Ruth."

"Like you did?" The words rang through the kitchen like gunshots.

Amanda had been standing at the sink, holding the rag under the rushing water. Now, suddenly, she bent over, as if tortured by cramp, and slipped down until she was pressing her forehead against the cupboard door beneath the sink. "I can't have her hate me, Ruth," she gasped through her tears. "I can't."

"Shh," Ruth said, crouching beside her, trying to pull her to her feet. "We'll tell Arthur, then, or Mr. Owens. They can find some other reason for breaking it off."

"But she'll find out, Ruth, if they know. She's bound to." Amanda wiped her face with the dishcloth. Breathing in its sour odors, she prepared to use her last resort. "We all make mistakes, you know," she said, rising with her back to Ruth. When she turned around, she squared her shoulders but held tight with one hand to the sink behind her. She made her voice sound hard. "Even you, Ruth, made a mistake."

"What do you mean?" Ruth remembered his fingers on her forehead, and her face burned.

"Your mother was going to raise Imogene for me. You would have been sisters then. You would have liked that, wouldn't you? But when I told you to get off the ice, no." She shook her head. "You wouldn't. You just kept on running. And then . . ." She cast her eyes down for a moment and then raised them again, staring firmly at Ruth. "Your mother died, and I had to let my baby go."

Ruth stepped back, crossing her arms over her chest. But Amanda's words bore into her. "No, I . . ." she began. But her breathing quickened, because she knew she had run. Even now, standing on the soft wood of the kitchen floor, she could feel her feet sliding out from under her, as they scrambled for a purchase on the slick blackness, and remembered that she could not go fast enough, no matter how she tried.

Amanda reached to touch the back of Ruth's neck with her fingertips. Gently, she drew the girl toward her, until she could tuck Ruth's bowed head under her chin. "It's all right," she crooned, swaying slightly back and forth. "You were only a baby. You didn't know any better. But you see"—her voice brightened with pride—"I gave up everything for you. Everything. If I hadn't had to take your mother's place, don't you think I could've gone back to work, or had a family of my own? Instead, I took care of you. Now, Ruth," she sighed, almost happily, "now, don't you think I have the right to ask you to do something for me?"

Moonlight bullied its way into Ruth's room, and she shifted restlessly in its cool glow. She tried to let the idea that she was to blame sink in or, more accurately, that she had unwittingly tugged the first thread, which made her family unravel. Why had she tried to run across that black space? What had she been running from? The kitchen clock seemed to be ticking mercilessly inches from her head. She sat up in bed and threw her pillow against the wall that separated her room from Amanda's. It whacked loudly against the plaster but summoned no answer.

She slid out of bed and dressed, making no effort to keep her movements quiet. On her way out of the house she slipped her father's old jacket off its hook near the door.

The moonshine was nothing like the

light of day, and Ruth had trouble keeping her footing as she made her way down the path through the woods. Step after step, she had the sense of the ground falling away, as when she miscounted stairs in the dark and stepped off the last one unexpectedly. She wasn't sure why she was going to the lake; she only felt compelled to be out of the house in the open air, to shake free of the burden of Amanda's secrets.

Ruth held her face up to meet the night breeze as she worked her way around the rowboat, untying the tarp. Then she slid the boat into the water and began to row.

She'd gone only ten strokes or so when she noticed that her feet were getting wet. She'd forgotten to put the plug in. She leaned into the stern, plunging her fingers into the inch of water that sloshed around the bottom, and easily found the rubber stopper. But something was blocking the hole.

It was a silver box, she found when she plucked it up, the cover decorated in a bold, Art Deco style. Balancing the box on one palm, she released the clasp to reveal tiny pills, like coins in a miniature treasure chest. Ruth floated awhile without rowing, polishing the box with her cuff, as she speculated about who might have left it there. Probably some tramp had used the boat as a bed. They did that once in a while, although they usually left the stench of old sweat and tobacco and an empty bottle behind, not silver boxes.

There was a time, Ruth thought, when she would have half imagined such a charming object to be a gift from her mother, somehow forged at the bottom of the lake and tossed up to land exactly where Ruth would be sure to find it. There was a time when she would have run to present her discovery to Amanda, as she'd given her the arrowheads and the bird's eggs and the fossils she'd come across, and together they'd have built a little cardboard ship for the pirates who'd have stolen the teeny treasure, and perhaps drawn a map and buried the box under the lilac hedge. There was a time when she'd have squirreled it away in the pocket of her dress to share with Imogene, and they would have told each other about the young man, ill with some romantic disease like tuberculosis, cast out by his wealthy

family and condemned to wander the earth
alone, because he'd dared to love the
wrong girl. They would have studied the
faces of the tramps who sometimes sat on
the back steps in the evenings, eating their
suppers, to find and rescue the boy who
had lost his silver box of pills.

All of those times, Ruth knew, as she
sponged the water from the bottom of the
boat, were past. She could barely remember her mother, and Amanda had given her
own daughter away, and Imogene loved a
man she couldn't marry. Was it really all her
fault? She twisted the sponge hard. She'd
been only three, after all. "Why didn't anyone stop me?" she shouted fiercely into
the darkness. Somewhere along the shore,
a dog began to bark.

"Shut up!" a man yelled from the dark
shore.

The dog kept barking, but Ruth didn't
dare make any more noise. She slipped the
box into her pocket and rowed on.

The key to the island house was hooked
on a nail under the low eaves, where she'd
left it the last time she added new postcards from her father to her collection. Still,
she hesitated at the door, and then quietly

walked all the way around the house, peeking between the boards that now only half covered the windows. Only when she'd identified each dark lump as a bed or a dresser or a chair did she unlock the door and go in.

In the bedroom her mother's smell, which she now recognized as lavender, still clung faithfully to the insides of the dresser drawers. She lay on the floor, on the green braided rug, and looked under the bed. It looked too small to be the place where she'd hidden, listening to the baby being born. Listening to Imogene.

Ruth curled on the bare mattress and pulled her father's big jacket tight around her. If she and her mother had fallen through the ice, she thought as she drifted into sleep, and her mother had drowned, but she had not, who had saved her? And why hadn't she saved Mathilda?

Chapter Eighteen

A day and a night had passed since Clement Owens had gone to take his morning swim and hadn't come home again.

"It's that he's gone without his car," Theresa Owens kept saying. "That's what worries me. He wouldn't go anywhere without his car." She repeated this conviction to each of her children several times. She said it to Ellen and to Anna, the cook, and to Augie, who took care of the yard and the cars. "Are you sure there's no car missing?" she asked him, more than once.

The question offended him. She knew as well as he did that the Owenses possessed three cars, all of which were safely in the garage. But he answered patiently each time, "No, Mrs. Owens, there ain't no car missing. Not this time."

She explained her concern to the sheriff, although even without a missing car, Sheriff Kuhtz didn't rule out the possibility that Owens had disappeared intentionally. You saw a fair amount of that when you were the sheriff.

But this fellow hadn't taken a suit of clothes or a pair of shoes out of the closet, at least according to the wife—and you could generally count on the wife to know things like that. It was unusual for a man to go off without his clothes, unless he wanted people to think he was dead. Sheriff Kuhtz had heard of such cases.

On the other hand, it was best, he'd found, to start with the obvious. Although, if Owens had been taken by cramp, it was odd that the bathrobe the maid had sworn he was wearing wasn't on the pier.

On the third day they searched the lake. It was a matter of routine, really; it was difficult to overlook such an obvious culprit when it yawned right in front of them. The family was relieved when nothing turned up, but the sheriff knew bodies were often slow to surface in Nagawaukee Lake. People had been dumping trees and tractors, whole fleets of boats, even houses, down there for decades. A corpse could get hung up in all that junk.

Imogene telephoned Ruth nearly every hour with the latest bulletin. Since no one knew anything, she had few facts to report, but there was still plenty to talk about. The cook had a theory that Mr. Owens had gotten himself mixed up with Chicago gangsters. Mrs. Owens had noticed that his heart pills were missing from the medicine chest. Augie, the driver, suspected a vengeful husband—this last Imogene whispered into the phone.

Of course, she was staying at the house. None of them would have eaten a bite or gotten a wink of sleep if it hadn't been for her. Mrs. Owens had hardly liked her to go home even for her toothbrush and, obviously, Arthur needed her. The sister had come and the older brother. All of them had taken to her right away, and the sister had even invited her to share her bedroom.

"Arthur says he's done this before, gone off for a few days, not come home when they expected him to," Imogene said the day after the search.

"So he'll turn up."

"But Arthur says this is different. Those other times they saw him off. They knew at least he was going somewhere, even if they weren't always sure where and for how long. He waved goodbye—he didn't just disappear into thin air."

After she hung up the telephone, Ruth opened the drawer of her nightstand and looked at the silver box she'd found. Gingerly, she touched one finger to the lid. What did it mean?

Had Clement Owens slept in the boat like a tramp? Or had Amanda taken his pills? But why leave them in the bottom of the boat? Had he been in the boat with her? In the boat and now vanished into thin air. Or into thick water. As Ruth's mother had vanished. As Ruth had almost vanished herself.

"Ruth!" Amanda's voice flew up from the bottom of the stairs. Ruth could imagine her clearly, standing there with one hand firmly grasping the newel post so that her knuckles stood out. "What did Imogene say?"

Ruth opened her mouth. She felt choked and cleared her throat. "Nothing," she called weakly, and tried again. "Nothing new."

Ruth

I didn't know what to think exactly, only that Aunt Mandy had probably been with Arthur's father sometime since I'd last used the boat, which was weeks and weeks ago. Although that was less surprising than it might have been, now that I knew they'd been acquainted with each other. Still, I didn't think anyone else, not even Imogene, should find that out, at least until Mr. Owens turned up with a reasonable explanation for where he'd been. Thinking about it gave me the funny idea Aunt Mandy might be hiding him somewhere on the farm, and I started to look over my shoulder once in a while, when I was in the barn or the root cellar. I was afraid she had secrets she'd not yet told me, and I didn't want to stumble onto them unaware.

Even less did I want to join her in one, so

I assured her that Arthur and Imogene
were in no danger of marrying as long as
Mr. Owens was missing. We could post-
pone her plan.

"I thought you told me Imogene was
staying at the house day and night. Day
and night," she repeated, and I had to admit this was true.

Once Aunt Mandy had decided what
she wanted to do, she wouldn't leave it
alone. That night she came into my bedroom waving the folded pages I'd brought
home from the Owenses' in my pocketbook. She must have fished them out of
the garbage.

"Where did you get these?" she demanded.

"From Mrs. Owens. I made mistakes."

"They're perfect. She'll know the paper,
don't you think?" She held a page to the
light, squinting at the watermark.

I pulled at the sheet, trying to take it
from her. "I know I shouldn't have ruined
so much, but she has a lot. I really don't
think she'll miss it."

"No, I mean Imogene. Imogene'll know
it, won't she?" She ran her fingers lightly,

caressingly over the page. "This is what she uses there every day. My Imogene would remember such high-quality paper."

After I'd gone to bed, she drew a light pencil line to be sure she'd cut perfectly straight and sliced the spoiled ends off with the kitchen shears. The next morning she'd arranged the five sheets in a row beside my plate. "Which one looks best to you, Ruth? Which one is straightest?"

I didn't want to look at them. "I don't know," I said, as sullenly as I dared.

She looked hurt. "I thought you understood, Ruth, that this is for the best. For Imogene. You want to help Imogene, don't you? These little love affairs, they don't mean very much. Believe me." She tried to put her hand on my head, but I ducked. She wasn't thinking about Imogene. She was only thinking of herself. "How about this one?" she asked, pointing to a sheet.

Though I gave her no answer, she pretended I'd agreed. "We'll try this one first then."

"He probably has his own stationery," I said.

She seemed to consider this, then shook her head. "I don't see how you

could get any of that without actually stealing it. Even if you could get into his room,
you don't know where he keeps it."

"I'm not sneaking into his room!"

"Of course not. I wouldn't ask you to do
anything like that." She patted my shoulder. It had been the same, I remembered,
when she was keeping me home from
school. She was always touching me, re-
assuring herself that I was with her, that we
were in this together. I'd liked it then.

When I got home that afternoon, she
pushed a piece of brown paper and a pen
at me. "Ruth, you have to help me with
this." She led me to the kitchen table and
tried to maneuver me into a chair. "I can't
get it to sound right, like he'd say it. You
know him, Ruth. You know what he'd say."

"I'm going to hang up my coat."

"Ruth, please," she said, following me,
holding out her pitiful sheet of paper in
both hands. "Please, Ruth. I can't do this
by myself."

She wouldn't leave me alone. She would
never leave me alone. I snatched the paper
and threw myself into the chair. I made the
chair legs scrape hard against the floor,
scratching the wood. But, as I sat with the

blank page in front of me, Aunt Mandy hovering near my shoulder, nervously rubbing the scar on her thumb, I knew something had shifted between us. Not that she wanted my help—she was always wanting my help, my advice, my opinion. But before this she'd ask me what I thought only to confirm what she'd already decided. When she asked if I liked the striped yellow curtains or the ones with the tiny red wheelbarrows printed on them, she knew which she liked, or which, as she would say, were best. I usually guessed right, and she was pleased. But this was different. This time she really needed my help; this time she really thought I did know best. She really couldn't do this thing without me.

"Sit down," I said, picking up the pen. "I can't think with you hanging over me like that." And then I began to write.

After all, we had to do it.

No, those are her words. We didn't have to do that—there were other courses. But secretly, so secretly I hardly admitted it to myself, I wanted to do this as much as Aunt Mandy did. I even wished our story were true.

Aunt Mandy was pleased with the sixth draft. "This is perfect, Ruth. Perfect. I never would have thought to say it like this."

Dear Ruth,

I come to you in my darkest hour to ask your advice, since I know you love Imogene and would, above all others, know how best to make her happy. Something has happened to me that I can't explain or even understand myself, something I would've given all my future happiness to have avoided. There is no pretty way to put it, so I'll say it out in all its hideousness—I've fallen in love with another. Yes, there it is. Imogene will always be dear to me, but dear as a sister, not as a wife. That is my terrible secret.

I'll keep it secret, Ruth, if you so advise. I know Imogene and I could have a fine life together. I know I could make her comfortable and happy. But wouldn't I be wrong to marry her now, knowing how I feel about someone else? Were I to let her go, wouldn't she soon find someone better who would love her as she deserves? I believe it's true, and yet I can't bear to hurt her. I want to do as she would wish, and I write to you as one who knows her wishes better than anyone. What shall I do?

I thought it was a little formal. Words like "darkest hour" and "hideousness" and "future happiness" sounded unnatural, as if I'd copied them from a book, but Aunt Mandy claimed the letter was exactly the way a man would write, if he were trying to show he was taking a matter seriously.

We had a model for his signature from a book he'd lent me, but we couldn't copy his hand well enough to write the whole thing out. Anyway, Aunt Mandy reasoned, Imogene probably wouldn't think it odd that Arthur would type such a letter. Who knew what form a message like that should take?

I was supposed to type it during the noon break, but when I pulled it out of my satchel the next day, I could hardly stand to look at it. I would have thrown it in the trash, if I hadn't worried that someone like Myrtle or Lillian would pull it out.

"There were too many people around," I

lied when I got home. "I don't see how I'm going to be able to do it."

Aunt Mandy went upstairs and closed her door.

In the morning, though, she was cheerful again. "I just know you'll get a chance to type it today, Ruth," she said. "We have to do this as soon as possible. You never know what might happen."

That day at noon, when Lillian, who'd gone out to the corridor to get her sandwich, came running back in, squealing, "A lady's got kittens out there," I knew who the lady was. One of our barn cats was just weaning her late litter.

I would never have thought that a box of kittens would distract a roomful of business students, but it did. Or at least it kept the girls I usually ate with from wondering why I was pecking away at my machine. Even Myrtle, who came back in when I was in the middle of the second paragraph, had a gray tabby clinging to her shoulder.

"You never said your aunt was so nice, Ruth. She thinks this little sweetie is just perfect for me." She kissed its head, and the kitten, scared to be so high off the ground, cried plaintively. "Baby, what's the trouble?" she cooed, cradling it at her breast. "I'll finish that for you, if you want to go out and say hello. Brown'll never know the difference."

"I'm almost done," I said, as lightly as I could, and waved her away.

I'd typed slowly and made only three mistakes. These I corrected by covering the words with x's. The errors didn't bother me. A letter like that shouldn't be perfect.

That evening I remembered my grandfather's pen with its thick stock, made for a masculine hand, and without prodding I dipped it in black ink and practiced writing Arthur's name over and over until the signature looked identical to the one in my book, until I could sign "Arthur Owens" to that letter as if writing my own name. Aunt Mandy's eyes, across the table, shone in the lamplight. We had done it.

That night we couldn't bear to part, even for sleep. She followed me into my room and watched me undress, and when she'd pulled the covers over my shoulder, she lay on top of them beside me, as she had when I was a child, so that I fell asleep,

pinned tight under the quilt, her head behind mine on the pillow.

When I awoke, I could hear her already
in the kitchen, grinding the coffee. In the
fresh dawn, the letter on my nightstand
looked blatantly false. But I would try it, I
told myself, for Aunt Mandy's sake. If it
didn't work, there was always the truth.

"Yes?" Ellen said, answering the door. "Oh,
it's you." She frowned. "I don't think Mrs.
Owens is doing any work today. Anyway,
Miss Lindgren is here."

"It's Genie, Miss Lindgren, I want to see."

"Miss Lindgren shouldn't be inviting her
friends here, time like this."

"She didn't invite me. I mean, I won't
stay long. I just need to talk to her about
something. It's very important."

"Something about Mr. Owens? You
know something?"

Ruth shook her head, surprised. "No,
nothing like that."

Ellen shut the door without another
word, and Ruth waited uncertainly. She
was about to knock again when Imogene
opened the door.

"Ruth!" Imogene threw her arms around her friend. "How'd you know I wanted you to come? Let's go for a walk," she said, pulling the door closed behind her. "I have to get out of this house.

"I'm worried," she said as they wandered down the slope to the edge of the lake. "I don't know if they'd rather he ran away or was dead."

Drawn by the scudding waves, winking with white-gold sunbursts, they kept walking to the end of the pier. A keen edge to the wind, a hint of the meanness to come, routed the vestiges of summer. If not for the disappearance of Clement Owens, the pier on which they stood would have been dismantled days before, the house in which all of the Owenses now gathered would have emptied.

Ruth was giddy with nervousness. "I've got to show you something," she said finally, drawing the letter from her pocket with shaking fingers. Her heart beat so hard as she passed the paper into Imogene's hand that she thought it might suddenly cause her to leap into the water like a frog.

The wind tugged at the page, but Imogene held it firmly, reading it once and then again. "I don't understand. He sent this to you?"

Ruth nodded.

"When?"

"A day or two ago maybe. I'm not sure. It came in the mail yesterday."

Imogene read the letter again. "I don't understand," she repeated. "How can he love someone else? Who else is there?" She looked at Ruth with eyes so stricken that Ruth's fingers quivered to snatch back the page and expose her lie. She didn't want it to be true anymore. No, she wanted to cry, he loves you, only you.

"It's impossible. He hasn't even seen anyone else. I don't believe it." She held the letter up to read it again.

The paper shivering in Imogene's hand started an answering tremble in Ruth's limbs and jaw. She clenched her teeth and trained her eyes on the white triangle of a sail skimming the waves far out on the water. Under her feet, the boards rose and fell sickeningly. Imogene's hand gripped her arm, and she turned, following her friend's gaze toward the shore. Arthur was coming down the pier toward them.

At first Ruth panicked at the idea of being caught in her lie. Their lie. Aunt Mandy's and hers. She had to hold herself still to keep from yanking her arm from Imogene's grasp and bolting off the pier. Shh, she told herself, shh. She closed her eyes. If they found out, all right. All right. Wasn't that what she'd wanted from the beginning? She'd tried, for Aunt Mandy's sake, but it hadn't worked. Arthur would swear he hadn't written the letter, and Imogene would believe him. They would look at her, mystified. What did she know?

She'd tell them the truth. It would be hard, especially now with Clement Owens missing, to say such things about his father, their father, and Aunt Mandy would be angry. Aunt Mandy, betrayed, would be . . . Ruth couldn't even imagine . . . crazy? Murderous?

Already, Imogene was holding the letter out to him. "Arthur, is this true?"

"Is what true? Is it something about my father? What does it say?"

"Don't pretend with me. You know what it says. Just tell me if it's true."

He tried to take the letter, but she jerked it from his fingers. "Just tell me," she demanded, snapping the words and thrusting her face at him, defiantly. "Do you love someone else?" Her final words dissolved into a sob, and as she pronounced them, she lost her grip on the page, and the wind, seizing its chance, whipped the letter away.

No, Genie, Ruth thought desperately, of course he doesn't. She could almost hear him saying those words, could almost see him pulling Imogene close against his warm body to reassure her.

But he stepped back. "Why are you asking me this now?" His face twisted in anger. "My father may be dead. I can't talk about this now!"

"I don't want to talk about it." Imogene's voice was calm, but she reached behind her, trying to find Ruth's hand. "I only want a simple answer. Yes or no."

Arthur looked down. He looked, Ruth thought, like a shamed little boy. The water, rolling pebbles along the shore, was deafening. Answer, she thought, say no. But the lifeline she was trying silently to throw him fell short.

"I don't know," he whispered.

Imogene gasped and swayed, and Ruth

lifted her arms to catch her, but the weakness lasted only an instant. Surging forward, she shoved at Arthur's chest with both hands. She wasn't very strong—if he'd stood firm, he probably could have kept his balance, but, perhaps from surprise or out of politeness or because he saw a means of escape, he staggered back and fell off the pier with a splash. Imogene ran then, limping on her sore ankle, across the steep lawn and up the drive behind the house, her sleeves and skirt billowing like sails.

Chapter Nineteen

Ruth

Imogene was waiting for me halfway along the dirt lane that snaked up the hill to the main road. She'd gone just far enough to be out of sight of the house, before she veered into the woods and collapsed on the ground, sobbing. I sank down beside her, but I couldn't touch her. Guilt hugged me all around, pinning my arms at my sides. Her misery was my doing, mine and Aunt Mandy's. Like witches, we'd made Arthur love someone else.

"I feel like such a fool," Imogene said finally, lifting her head and wiping her nose.

"You're not a fool." Edging closer toward telling her the truth, I reached to touch her hair. "He loves you," I said. I would have said anything to please her, but I believed this to be true. "He told me so himself that day I was here."

"You saw him that day?" Imogene sniffed, raising herself until she was sitting up, leaning against a tree.

"Yes, we . . ." but I changed my mind and didn't go on. Remembering that afternoon made me squirm. I folded my hands in my lap, trying not to think of how I'd felt when his finger had brushed my forehead. "He said you were something," I said loudly. "He said any man would be lucky to marry you."

"Any man but him, I guess." Imogene was yanking at the feathery stalks of grass around her knees now, tearing them out one by one and flinging them away. "I hate him," she said, tugging at a whole handful of grass. "I hate everything about him." When the grass refused to let go of the earth, she fell forward, burying her face in her knees. "I love him so much! How could he do this to me?" With one fist, she pounded at the ground. "Oh, Ruth," she suddenly gasped, sitting up and pressing her hands against her chest. "You can't imagine how it hurts here. It actually hurts, like something cracked inside."

Why did she suppose I couldn't imagine? I knew what that deep bruise was like. I'd felt it when she so easily rearranged the plans she'd made for us, when I knew she'd never be with me again, never the same way with me.

"Maybe it's because of his father. Do you think? I shouldn't have been so pushy. After all, this must be a horrible time for him, just horrible. He's not really himself."

I looked away from her. The woods were so thick, my gaze could penetrate no farther than a few yards all around, although I knew that in a month or so, when the leaves had fallen, the lake would be visible clear to the other side.

"I know what." I grabbed Imogene's arm. I wanted her to feel I meant it. "Let's go to Chicago."

She drew back, but I didn't let her go.

"You know, how we used to talk about. You can take the job Mrs. Owens said she'd get for you. Maybe she knows one for me too. Anyway, I can find something." I released her then and sat back. I waited.

Imogene put her fingers to her mouth

and tugged at a cuticle with her teeth. "Go to Chicago?"

"Yes. Go to Chicago. Like we said."

"But we don't know anyone in Chicago. Where would we stay?"

"I do. I know someone." Unable to sit still any longer, I got up and began to pace. "Aunt Mandy's friend, Miss Fox. We can stay with her until we find our apartment. She's always saying don't I want to come down for a visit, but Aunt Mandy'll never let me."

"What makes you think she'll let you now?"

"Oh, she won't let me, but I'm going to go anyhow. She's not my boss. She's not even my mother." I felt as though my insides, which had been twisted tight, like the elastic attached to the propeller of a balsa glider, had suddenly been released and were spinning free. Yes, I could go away. There would be places, whole cities, in which Aunt Mandy had no influence, where I wouldn't feel her hands, continually pulling and prodding, combing and smoothing, where I wouldn't need to think about whether Clement Owens would ever resurface or why my mother had drowned. I would be free of her.

"All right," Imogene said slowly. "All right. We'll go."

It had to be quick, I thought, quick. "Let's go right away. Tonight." I thought of Aunt Mandy sitting at the kitchen table with her coffee, like a spider in her web, waiting to wrap her sticky threads around me.

"Tonight? Ruth, I'm going to have to convince my parents. I'm going to have to pack. And talk to Mrs. Owens. I don't know how soon she'll be able to talk to her friends. She has other problems right now, you know. And you have to talk to Miss Fox."

"We'll say we're only going for a short visit. You'll tell your parents you have to get away"—I gestured down the hill—"you know, to forget all this. And maybe it'll just be a few days. Maybe we won't like it. But let's try. Why not try?"

She looked at me, tempted but a little scared, the same way she'd looked when I insisted on giving Bert Weiss my tooth. "All right," she said, "if you find out it's all right with Miss Fox, I'll meet you at the train tonight." She'd risen now, too, and smoothed her hair and her dress. Her face looked fresh, as if her tears had washed it. Her eyes were barely swollen. No one would ever guess that a minute before she'd been lying heartbroken on the ground.

At one point, as we continued up the winding lane, she stopped and looked back. "I had a feeling he was coming up behind us. That he was going to tell me it was all a mistake. A test or something." She looked at me. "Do you think he might realize he loves me after all?"

Actually, I thought he might. I glanced back, too, half expecting to see him breaking through the trees. But I said, "No." I said it firmly. "You don't want him anyway, Imogene. You want to come with me." In my ear my voice sounded just like Aunt Mandy's.

Amanda

I was so tired when Mattie lifted that squirming, flailing, frog-like little being for me to see. Mattie wiped the baby clean and wrapped her in a blanket, then laid her on my chest where she clamped her mouth around my nipple and pulled so that it hurt, as if to remind me that she was real.

"Our baby," Mathilda breathed, stroking her tender head. "Here, let me hold her."

How right they looked together, just like the Madonna and Child. To this day, I can see them, standing over me. "I'm going to be your mama, darling," she whispered. "I love you, my lamb." And she looked at me and smiled.

I closed my eyes. I should have been grateful, indescribably relieved. Instead, I felt bereft. Who was I, if Mathilda was her mama? No, I could not be Aunt Mandy to this one I had fed with my own blood. I could not do it. And, although I can never forgive myself, I hated Mattie then for suggesting it, hated her for being right when I was wrong, for being generous when I was selfish, and most of all for thinking that I would be pleased to see her take my baby from me.

"No," I said, "She's mine. You can't have her." But she couldn't hear me, because I was already asleep.

It was still the middle of the night when I awoke. The wind pushed at the window-panes, but my baby lay sleeping snugly in the drawer we'd prepared for her. I felt drugged. My muscles and my brain longed for rest, but slowly, quietly, I dragged my-self from the bed. "Shh, shh, my baby," I whispered, although she hadn't made a sound. I collected my dress from the door, my shoes from under the bed. Pulling my stockings on was difficult, but I needed to be warm. We were running away, my baby and I.

We would go somewhere warm. Califor-nia, perhaps. And I would change my name. I would say my husband had died in the war. Who would know the difference? Who would care? I didn't need the farm to support me—thanks to my father, I was a nurse.

Mathilda would forgive me. In the end, she would be happier, she and Carl and Ruth, too, without my secret to keep. And someday, maybe not even too long from now, we would come back to visit, maybe even to stay, so Ruth could love her little cousin, just as I loved Mattie. Why hadn't I thought of this from the start?

I wrapped the tiny thing tightly in more blankets, until she looked less like a baby than a bundle. She did not wake, only nestled close, her mouth opening and closing, reaching for my breast in her dreams. I put on my coat, my mittens and my hat, and I put half the money in the house into my pocket. And that was all. What else did we need? I could feed her, after all. I could keep her warm.

The wind, when I opened the door, hit me with a wallop. In the house I'd forgotten how cold it was outside, and my skin shrank from the blast. Still, it was only November, I reminded myself, not the dead of winter. I opened my coat and tucked my bundle against my chest. We would be all right. Besides, it had to be cold for the sake of the ice.

Yes, the ice. I stood at the edge of the lake thinking. All the holes had certainly closed, I had no doubts there. It was the greenness I remembered from the afternoon that worried me. But not too much. No, not very much at all, I have to admit, since I fancied myself so skilled at testing, so good at working my way slowly along, listening for every creak, never shifting my weight too suddenly. I was more worried about slipping with my precious load than about falling through.

I stepped cautiously onto the lake and slid my feet forward, inches at a time. My legs were so sore, I couldn't have gone faster even if it'd been safe, and I nearly turned back, quailing at the distance I had to go to make the train. But I was sure the ice was good. Yes, it would certainly hold us. Gradually but steadily, we moved on, farther and farther out into the lake.

"Wait!"

I could barely hear the tiny voice over the wind.

"Wait for me, Aunt Mandy!"

I turned to see Ruth climbing backward off a rock onto the ice.

"Ruth, stop!" I called.

She turned her face to look at me, but she did not stop.

———

Ruth didn't bother to close the door to her room while she packed. A door had never stopped Amanda from coming in whenever she pleased to straighten the books on their shelves or the items on the top of Ruth's dresser, as she delved for whatever scraps of the day had been left unexamined. A few times, Ruth had tried to compel her aunt to sit still, by leaving nothing out of place, but on those occasions Amanda had rearranged the contents of the dresser drawers.

There was plenty to put to rights now. The room was in complete disarray— blouses slithered from the bed to the floor; hairpins crackled underfoot; books and underwear sprawled together on the chair. But Amanda stood still in the doorway.

"I don't understand. If the letter worked, why does anyone have to go anywhere? Why can't things be the way they were?"

"We're going *because* the letter worked," Ruth said, tossing clothes into Amanda's old carpetbag. "You made me do it, and now Imogene is heartbroken. We made her miserable, you understand?" She held the slip she was packing toward Amanda and shook it for emphasis.

Amanda cringed. "Ruth, that's vulgar. Put your underthings away."

"Miserable, just like I said she'd be."

Ruth threw the slip into the carpetbag. "She thinks Arthur doesn't love her, never loved her. She thinks she was a fool to believe he did."

"But she'll get over it. After a little while, she'll be glad. We saved her, Ruth." Amanda was rubbing her fingers over the base of her thumb. It made Ruth want to scream.

"Well, she doesn't know that, does she?" she sneered instead.

"But you know it, Ruth. You know it had to be done."

Did she? Why had she written that letter? Because Amanda had insisted? Or because she'd seen a chance for herself? But Ruth was sure that if Amanda hadn't dragged her into her scheme she'd never have been so selfish. "It doesn't matter," she said. "She wants to go away now, and I'm going with her."

"Ruthie, I know what." Amanda stepped into the room and began to fold a blouse as she talked, laying it out on the rumpled bed, squaring the shoulders precisely, smoothing the fabric with her fingers. "Why don't we all three go out to the island for a few weeks? It's not very cold yet, and it'll be so pretty with the leaves turning. You don't remember living there, Ruth, but it's very relaxing. Very refreshing. And when we come back, the Owenses will be gone." She gave the perfectly folded blouse a little pat.

Ruth stopped packing. "They won't be gone until they find Mr. Owens."

Amanda stood silent for a moment, her hands still at her sides. "Clement was a good swimmer," she said finally. "I don't think he could have drowned."

"I hear my mother was a good swimmer too."

"Ruth, what do you mean?"

Ruth had hit her mark; she could tell by Amanda's face and the fear, real fear, in her aunt's voice, and it scared her, so that she closed the carpetbag, not caring whether she had everything, only wanting to run. "Nothing, nothing. Just let me go."

Amanda stepped into the doorway. "You can't, Ruth. I can't let you go."

"Why not? You let my mother go, didn't you? You rescued me, but you let her go. Well, now you can let me go too. What's one more?" She snatched her arm from Amanda's grip and clattered down the stairs.

"Ruth, stop! Come back!" Amanda stood at the top of the stairs. She pushed one foot over the edge. It wouldn't be so hard to let herself go, to step for an instant on air and then crash down and down. Not so hard at all.

Amanda lifted her hand from the railing. I'll fall, Ruth. I'll fall if you don't come back, she thought. And, as the door slammed, she lost her balance.

Ruth

The walk to the train was harder than I'd thought. The carpetbag flopped and banged awkwardly against my legs, and I'd packed so many books that I had to stop every ten steps or so to shift the load from one hand to the other. At the end of the drive and then again at the first turn in the road, I thought I heard Aunt Mandy's voice sifting through the trees, and I looked back toward the house and held my breath, so I could listen. It was nothing, though, but a voice in my head. I pushed it out with my own voice. Keep going, I told myself, just keep going. You'll miss the train.

Stumbling a little, my heavy bag pulling me forward, I struggled down the hill, past the Jungbluths' pasture, where three Guernseys raised their heads to watch as I went by. Then I trudged up the slope of Glacier Road, sweating under the winter coat I'd had to wear for lack of a better way of carrying it. At the top, I passed the icehouse, which would be nearly empty now, ready for its winter crop. I'd expected on this march to sense my bond with Aunt Mandy stretching until it snapped, but I could feel nothing but exhaustion and frantic haste as I hurried along the final mile into Nagawaukee.

I thought the Lindgrens might overtake me now in their car, Mrs. Lindgren making a nervous inventory of the contents of Imogene's luggage, Mr. Lindgren tooting the horn before he pulled over to pick me up. But the road was empty, the houses I passed quiet. Inside them, I knew, people were settling down to their familiar suppers.

Finally, with aching arms and sweating back, I lugged my bag up the worn wooden steps of the platform. I looked up and down to find the little human knot that would be Imogene and her parents, but the platform was empty. My jaw hurt from clenching it all those miles. I thought, I've missed the train, and I was at once desperate and relieved.

"Ruth!"

I turned from the tracks to see Imogene hurrying toward me.

"Where's your suitcase?" I asked.

"In the car." Slightly out of breath, Imogene bent and lifted my bag.

"Your parents are letting us take the car?"

"Not my parents' car. Maynard Owens is driving us down. You know, Arthur's brother. I told you about him." Imogene straightened, setting my bag back on the platform. "Arthur told him what happened," she explained, "and he came over. To see if I was all right. If he could do anything for me. He says they all miss me and even if Arthur's a fool, he isn't."

"What do you mean? Are you in love with *him* now?"

"Oh, Ruth." Imogene clicked her tongue. "Nothing like that. I mean, he's very sweet, but I couldn't . . . not now, not after what happened. Not so soon, anyway. I mean, I feel awful, Ruth. He broke my heart. It's going to take a long time to heal."

But it would heal, I saw that. In fact, it had healed already. Maybe Aunt Mandy was right about these things not meaning very much. I didn't blame Imogene. It wasn't as if Arthur had been in her heart her whole life, the way Aunt Mandy had been in mine.

Aunt Mandy, whom I'd left behind. I felt around inside myself for the gaping hole, the way I'd once poked my tongue into the space my tooth had left. But there was no space, no agonizing well of despair. All was solid.

Imogene put her hand on mine. "Stop that, Ruth."

"Stop what?"

"You're doing what your aunt does, rubbing that ugly scar."

I dropped my hands to my sides, but I knew why I couldn't find a rip, although I thought I'd torn free. The simple truth was, she'd wormed her way in so deep, I'd never get her out. If I changed my name and went to the ends of the earth and never came back, still she wouldn't let go. She was stuck like a burr in my hair. No, it was deeper than that—she was inside me like a bone or an organ. She'd seeped into my blood with the air I sucked into my lungs.

"I'm so glad we're going, Ruth. You were so right. It's exactly the thing to do." Imogene took my arm, partly to start me walking, for I seemed to be rooted where I stood, and partly so that she could lean close to confide, "I wish we'd done it months ago!"

"So do I," I said, but still I couldn't move.

"Ruth? Maynard's waiting." She hoisted my bag now and didn't complain of the weight. "He's got to drive both ways tonight."

"Yes," I said. She started down the platform ahead of me, a little nervous, eager to be off. It may have been the way she swung her arms or the impatient look she gave me when she turned and saw that I

still wasn't following, I'm not sure, but I
suddenly felt as if I'd been staring for years
at the silhouettes of two faces and finally
saw the vase in the white space between
them. She'd been Aunt Mandy's baby. I
couldn't believe I hadn't guessed it on my
own long before. And then, as quickly as
I'd caught the glimpse of Aunt Mandy in
her, I lost it.

Aunt Mandy was selfish, but what she
wanted for herself was me. Imogene, too,
maybe, but mostly me. She'd given Imogene up, but she wouldn't let go of me.
How could I leave someone who loved me
that much?

"Imogene," I said, and she turned back.
"I can't go. I'm sorry."

I thought she might be angry. After all,
I'd talked her into this, but she only sighed
and studied my face for a long moment.
She must have decided this was different
from my refusal to swim at the island or to
go to the dance or to play secretary for her
at the Owenses', because she didn't try to
persuade me. "Are you sure?"

I nodded.

She came back and stood before me.

"Do you think . . ." she began and stopped. "Don't be angry, but would you mind if I went without you?"

"You want to go without me?"

"No," she said, "I don't want to go without you, but if you won't go . . . well, you're the one who made me see it was a good idea. It is a good idea."

Numbly, I reached into my pocket and held out to her the scrap of paper on which I'd written Eliza Fox's address.

"You don't think Miss Fox would mind?"

I shook my head.

"I would wait, in case you change your mind, but the people Mrs. Owens called expect me on Monday. You said to hurry."

"It's my fault," I said. "You go ahead."

"I'll look out for a place for both of us, just in case."

"Yes, just in case."

At the end of the platform she stopped, opened her purse, and began feeling around inside it.

"Did you forget something?" I called, and I felt a little flutter inside me that must have been hope that she, too, had decided to stay.

"Here," she said, running back. "Keep

this for me." And she pressed into my hand the blue marble.

I went to the end of the platform and watched her get into the car. She waved until I couldn't see her anymore, and I kept waving even after that, squeezing the marble in my other hand. She's only going to Chicago, I told myself. You could be there in two hours. But I knew it didn't work that way. When people left, in my experience, they stayed gone. Except for Aunt Mandy. She'd come back to me, just as I was going back to her now.

Chapter Twenty

Ruth

Imogene is coming this summer. She's bringing her husband—Jack, she says his name is—and her baby daughter, Louisa. Named for her grandmother, Aunt Mandy said, and winked at me, yes, winked. Often now, I see how she must have been, before my mother's drowning made her hold herself tightly for fear of losing herself in guilt and grief.

She was lying in a faint at the bottom of the stairs, her arm and collarbone and three ribs broken, the night Imogene went to Chicago.

"I knew you'd come back," she whispered when the doctor and I lifted her onto the davenport. "I knew someday you'd come back to me."

"I've only been gone three hours," I said, but she didn't seem to hear.

I nursed her. She had to tell me what to do, but she said I did it well. I have very gentle hands, she said. I read to her, and I prepared her favorite dishes. I even tried something new—chicken cacciatore which we agreed turned out very well. "Your mother used to make something like this," she said.

I knew she meant it as an invitation, but I was afraid to begin. "When I was running on the ice," I ventured, and stopped.

"Yes?" she said, encouraging me.

"When I was running on the ice," I said again, "what was I running from?"

"Running from?" She smiled, flexing her fingers the way the doctor had prescribed. "You weren't running from anything, Ruth. You were running to me."

As soon as I could leave her alone in the house, I motored to the middle of the lake and dropped the silver box in. The next morning, a man on the double-decker excursion boat spotted Mr. Owens's body washing against the concrete base of the Stoltzes' boathouse. It was supposed to be the last tour of the season, but the sensation kept the boat running for three weeks into October.

I gave up typing. It turns out I'm a farmer after all. I've always been good with the animals, and I've discovered that I can drive a tractor a lot better than I can work office machines. With Mr. Tully's help, we broke even last year, and now that I've talked my father into quitting the Rebecca Rae, we can build the herd, and I'll bet we turn a good profit. It's a sad fact that the war over in Europe has been a big help to us financially.

I like the farm. It's a world unto itself, a steady universe where the animals go in, go out, eat, sleep, and eat again. I like knowing that the black fields will blush green, and then the corn leaves will saw against one another and the tomatoes swell until they split their skins, and that then the ground will sleep under its cold, white sheets. On a farm, the earth has secrets, and the weather has passions, but people don't matter so much.

Arthur Owens has asked me twice to marry him, but although each time my heart begged me to agree, I've said no. I couldn't move away, you see, and I'm not sure that he'd like to stay, what with the bridges that'll need building all over the country—all over the world, he says—once he finishes school. Still, on Sundays he comes out from town. He helps with the work, and then we walk in the woods or go for a drive. In the winter, if there isn't too much snow, he takes me out on his ice-boat. Snug against each other, we rattle along, our legs turning to stone in the wooden shell, while the stinging wind brings tears to our eyes, and chips of ice pepper our faces. "Faster," I cry, "faster," and he flattens the sail, until one blade hikes into the air, so that, were the ice to open beneath us, we would simply fly over the crack.

Imogene wants to stay on the island when she comes. She thinks her husband will like it. I didn't like it, the idea of Jack on our island, but Aunt Mandy said, "You'll have to get used to that," and I knew she was right.

We waited through the early spring,

while the ice, whining and sighing, gave up its bed, until the bright morning when the lake was alive and dancing again, as if it had never been still. April 13, 1941. That's a good place to finish. In our coats and gloves and galoshes, we dragged the boat to the water and headed toward the island, to see what had to be done to ready it for Imogene.

Released from their ice prison, the waves tossed themselves against the hull with ecstatic abandon, pitching up a fine spray that shimmered in the fledgling spring sunlight. I dipped my fingers in, and instantly my hand ached with cold. That must have been what it felt like, the night I drowned.

Amanda

Ruth wasn't even wearing a coat, just her nightgown and slippers. Her little teeth were chattering. I could see her shivering as far away as I was.

"Get back in the house, Ruth!"

But she wouldn't listen. She slid forward, oh, so carefully, onto the ice, holding her little arms out for balance, that peppermint stick still clutched in her hand.

"I said, get back!"

That time she caught the anger in my voice. She stopped but did not go back. She stopped and began to cry. And then it was almost as if my baby had heard her, because she began to cry too.

"Don't cry," I said to both of them. "Be quiet. You have to be quiet now. Don't cry." I was nearly crying myself. It was so cold, and I was so tired.

Far behind Ruth, a triangle of light appeared at the front of the house as the door opened.

"Wait, Aunt Mandy, wait. Please. Wait for me," Ruth called, and she began to run as well as she could across the slippery ice.

My heart was broken, but, knowing Mathilda would hear her now and come after us all, I turned my face toward the dark shore and went on. I moved as fast as I dared, sliding and slipping, trying to keep my feet under me, desperate not to be caught, desperate not to fall. The baby cried more insistently with every step.

"Ruth, come back!" Mathilda called. "Mandy, bring her back!" I seemed to hear her footsteps pounding on the ice. "Amanda, come back! Come back!" All around the lake, anyone with an open window could have heard her. But I turned my ears to the wind and my eyes to the night. I would not come back. This baby was mine.

Mattie snatched Ruth up into her arms.

"Take Ruth home, Mattie! Get off the ice!"

But Mathilda wouldn't listen. We were far out on the lake now, and she kept on sliding toward me, clutching Ruth to her chest.

"Go back, Mattie!" My words were desperate now. I knew, even before the ice complained, that the two of them were too heavy for it to bear.

And then the ice creaked. Scared, I stopped and stood still. Mattie heard it too.

"Put Ruthie down!" I shouted, but the wind blew my words away.

Mattie's voice, on the other hand, sailed

right to me, as if she were screaming in my ear. "Mandy, please come back, come back to me!"

I was frightened, then, with the ice creaking under me, too frightened to go on. I decided to go back.

The moment I started, it happened, as it has happened every night since, whenever I close my eyes. The ice cracked and stopped my heart. Mathilda, with Ruth in her arms, lurched left and sank to her waist, then to her shoulders, and then they were gone, both of them, gone.

I ran then. It's hard to run on the ice, harder still with a newborn in your arms. I heard splashing. I heard her calling me, "Mandy, help! Help me, Mandy!"

But my feet would not go fast enough. I slipped. I fell to my knees. I seemed to be getting no closer. I left my baby on the ice and tried again and again, throwing myself forward, screaming Mattie's name.

By the time I reached the hole, Mathilda had already pushed Ruth back onto the ice, but she had disappeared. I lay on my stomach and reached into blackness. The water was so cold. I reached and reached, until my hands were numb, but I could catch nothing.

And then, though I could barely feel it, my fingers tangled in Mattie's hair. I pulled, gently, so as not to lose my grip, but swiftly as I dared.

With a gasp, she broke the surface.

"Mattie!"

I pulled her sodden arms around my neck. For an instant, she hung there, safe in my arms.

But the ice refused to hold us. A piece cracked off under my shoulder and my head splashed into the black water. Down Mattie went again, but I held on, the collar of her nightgown bunched in my fist. Now that I had her, I could never let her go, not even if she dragged me down after her.

And she was dragging me down after her. The ice beneath my other shoulder gave way. I tried to work myself backward, to shimmy my hips, to dig my toes and my knees into the ice. I was so strong, and she was so tiny, I couldn't believe that I would not pull us both to safety. And then the ice beneath my chest gave way.

If Mathilda had not surfaced again, if she'd not thrust her frozen, drowning body back once more toward the sweet air, we would all of us be dead, Ruth and Imogene, frozen on the ice, Mattie and I beneath it. But she did come back. She opened her mouth for breath, and then she closed her teeth on my hand and bit with all her might.

I would've held on. I would not have let go. I didn't even feel the hurt. But my fingers opened. They just opened. And Mattie slipped through.

I reached and reached again. "Mattie!" I screamed, pushing my head under that black freezing water. But she wasn't there. I reached. I called. But she wouldn't come back.

Finally I saw Ruth, a still, little shadow on the dark ice. So much time had passed. I forced my breath between her frozen lips. I pressed my numb and bloody fingers to her neck to find her pulse. But I was much too late. She was gone too.

I picked her up and carried her to where I'd left the baby, wrapped both of them in my sweater and coat and carried them in one bundle together as fast as I could across the ice.

And here is the miracle. With that warm

little body pressed next to her, Ruth thawed. She came back to life. When I reached the shore I heard her cough.

I knew Mary Louise would be a good mother, so I gave the baby to her. Her arms went out for that child, as though she'd been waiting for it, as though it was meant to be. I hadn't thought what I would say.

"It was terrible," I managed at last. And out of my mouth came something like the story Mattie had made up about the farm girl. "The baby's name is Imogene," I said. "Please take her."

Why is Ruth in her nightgown? I thought they'd ask. Where is Mathilda? Where is Mattie? I wanted to scream it myself. But Imogene had all their attention.

Soon Ruth and I would steal away, but for now I held her close in the Lindgrens' spare bed to warm her. I felt her pulse grow strong, as I pressed her as tight as I dared against my skin.

I will have you, I thought. I will keep you. We will begin again.

PORTER COUNTY PUBLIC LIBRARY SYSTEM